The key Le
Meribel. A No
involvement ed.
"From now to
concentrate on work alone." She pushed the
heavy blue door.

"Hiya, flower! Surprise, surprise!" came a chorus
of cheerful voices. Jennifer and Caroline, who'd been
waiting to welcome Laura to her new home, were
hovering in the tiled hallway with big smiles on their
faces. "But you're so early! The champers isn't even
cold yet."

"Hey, how lovely!' exclaimed Laura, delighted. "I
wasn't expecting you till much later. How come
you're not at work still?"

"I managed to scarper off early," explained
Caroline, her dark eyes dancing. "But Jennifer's lost
her job. The revolting old Russki sacked her
yesterday!"

"Good riddance, I say. Sod the horrible old goat!"
giggled Jennifer, tossing her blonde mane. "Welcome
to your new abode, Miss Forsythe, with your live-in
bodyguards! 'Fraid it isn't terribly tidy," she continued apologetically, "but we've nowhere near
sorted ourselves out yet. Caro's got the smaller
bedroom and you're sharing the big one with me."

Christine Vincent was one of the first British women stockbrokers on the New York Stock Exchange. She lives with her husband and three children in Hampshire. This is her first novel.

Monte-Carlo Girls

Christine Vincent

CORONET BOOKS
Hodder and Stoughton

First published in Great Britain in 1994
by Hodder and Stoughton
A division of Hodder Headline PLC

A Coronet paperback

10 9 8 7 6 5 4 3 2 1

A CIP catalogue record for this title is available from
the British Library.

ISBN 0 450 59649 4

Typeset by Keyboard Services, Luton

Printed and bound in Great Britain by
Cox and Wyman Ltd, Reading

HODDER AND STOUGHTON LTD
A Division of Hodder Headline PLC
338 Euston Road
London NW1 3BH

To Wil and my three boys

Prologue

Dawn – Tuesday, 9 September 1969 – The South of France

Eventually, she wiped the tears from her eyes, and as she wrenched her key into the ignition, the engine roared into life. The open-topped car hurtled through the deserted streets, the screech of its tyres reverberating hollowly against the tall, flaking buildings, echoing the pain in her heart. Soon she reached the switchback mountain road, the highest Corniche, with its hairpin bends and dizzying drops into infinity and death.

The cool air felt like balm as it whipped pale blonde tendrils of hair from her face, and she pressed down harder on the accelerator. Blinded by tears, oblivious to danger, she put her foot flat down. The speed excited her. Now she was invincible, in control of her destiny. Nothing mattered any more. Faster she drove, and faster, into the ghostly grey fingers of dawn: until, at last, she was lighter than air.

She didn't hear the crunch of metal, the sickening thump and crash of the tree exploding into a million shards; she just soared peacefully like a spectral bird on silent wings – on and on, above it all, into ever-darkening, ever-quietening blackness.

Chapter 1

Monte-Carlo, May 1969

Laura's heart sank as Pierre emerged from behind his car, a
hulking black Simca that reflected the blackness of his mood.
Instead of going back to her flat, he drove her up a lonely
mountain road where he parked on a rocky outcrop, ostensibly
to look at the view in the moonlight. He reached for a Gauloise.
The match rasped aggressively, the flame briefly lighting his
aquiline nose and dark, hooded eyes. Looking across, he saw
her fine-boned face with its neat, straight nose and enormous,
slanting blue eyes, now cold, with no love in them any more.
Laura felt a sense of foreboding as she caught his familiar
brooding expression.

"*Et moi, hein?*" he nagged. "What about me? All you care
about is your frivolous English friends and those endless
parties. There's no place any more for the man who truly loves
you in all this selfishness! No place for your Pierre, *hein?* All
you can think of is painting your face and wearing your tarty
cocktail dresses!"

He grabbed angrily at the thin diamanté strap of her dress
which snapped, causing the silky blue material to slither down,
exposing one breast. She quickly tried to cover herself. "No!"
Pierre whispered, and stopped her, holding a fist to her face.
Laura flinched and tried to escape from the car.

"If you move, you'll be sorry," he threatened, his
expression menacing.

Unclenching his fist he began to caress her breast very

gently with the tip of his finger, watching with fascination as the nipple hardened at his touch. But Laura sat rigid, stonily looking straight ahead, her cupid's-bow lips compressed into a tight line. Pierre's face darkened at her lack of response. He seized a hank of her long pale hair and forced her to look at him.

"That pretty face . . . those pretty breasts," he murmured quietly. "If you don't do what I want I could make you truly sorry."

He lit another Gauloise and took a long puff, holding it vulgarly between finger and thumb like a labourer, exposing his teeth and hissing as he exhaled slowly and blew the smoke into her face.

"See this?" Pierre whispered thickly, holding its red-hot glowing end close to Laura's breast, then drawing the cigarette slowly up her neck to her pale cheek. "How would you like me to rearrange your complexion, *hein*? Burn you so no one else would ever want you . . ." He tightened his grip on her hair, and yanked her face to his, so that she could feel his hot nicotine breath. *"Hein? How would you like that?"*

Laura couldn't believe this was really happening to her. There was nothing for it now but to grit her teeth and conciliate; humour him as usual. She would rather have slapped him; throttled him for his bullying ways, but he was too strong for her and his anger too dangerous.

"Pierre," she said quietly, "please let's go home, and I'll make us some coffee. Let's just talk things over. Please?"

She found a safety-pin in her evening bag and mended the strap of her dress while Pierre finished his smoke and watched her with cold hostility. Then he casually flicked the Gauloise out of the window, and drove back down the winding mountain road to her flat. Later, in his desire for Laura's body he forgot his anger, and she put her resentment on hold for the sake of peace.

Now it was two o'clock in the morning. Laura was fraught with tension. Her long, flaxen hair spilled over the pillow, framing a delicate heart-shaped face, and her large blue eyes were clouded with misery. She wished sleep would come and soothe her frayed nerves. But there was little chance of that. Pierre's anger was too palpable and frightening.

He was sleeping quietly. She looked at him dispassionately. His brow was furrowed, and his long black lashes threw shadows on to his cheeks. Pierre's lips, almost colourless in the moonlight, were pulled down into a scowl across his tightly clenched jaw. His strong, broad shoulders and deep chest looked hard and unyielding. One arm was thrown proprietorially over her breasts, the other buried in the pillow behind his head. His whole demeanour revealed a long fermenting anger. How could he sleep so soundly with such rage inside him?

Laura gently prised her lover's arm off her and slid away. She would have liked to get out of this stifling bed, go out on to the small balcony and see the bright, peaceful moon reflected on the water. But she was fearful of waking Pierre.

Instead, she lay quietly staring at nothing in particular at the very edge of the bed, so that she wouldn't have to touch any part of him. Tonight was like so many other nights. A violent row, culminating in passionate sex that at least stopped the fighting, but was now more an expression of anger than anything remotely resembling love.

Earlier that evening Laura had gone to a British Consular reception, after which she'd hoped to slip away to spend the night with friends. But, as usual, Pierre had tracked her down.

Who would have thought that all the sweetness, all the wonderful times she had shared with Pierre could have crumbled to nothing but this bitterness and regret? Nothing would ever bring back their happier days. Wide-awake, with no hope of sleeping now, Laura's mind drifted back in time.

Two years ago, aged eighteen, on a brilliant, sunny April morning, full of optimistic aspirations, she had stepped off the night train in Monte-Carlo. And all because of her father's intransigence! During her schooldays in Devon Laura had always dreamed of following her brothers to university. But her father, a country GP, though a kindly, well-meaning man, had been firmly against the idea. He didn't want any daughter of his turning into a blue stocking! Her mother wondered if this were any reflection on herself, a vague academic who wrote research papers that no one read, and tried to intervene on Laura's behalf. But to no avail. Laura and her younger sister could be secretaries, Dr Forsythe suggested, and Mrs Forsythe had capitulated and immersed herself in another dull tome. Laura was bitterly disappointed, but obediently enrolled at secretarial college after leaving school.

After that she took the first job offered to her, as a means of saving money to go abroad. She stuck it out for a year, and then at the tender age of eighteen, she left home. If she wasn't allowed to read Modern Languages at university, she'd learn them from the horse's mouth. Her parents, who approved of independence, did not try to stop her. Originally her itinerary had been Italy, France and Spain. But, somehow, Laura had landed up in Monte-Carlo with a one-way ticket, a hundred pounds in her pocket, and a taste for adventure. Monaco seemed a good compromise, being near the Franco-Italian border; not to mention its glamorous reputation.

Her search for work in the first few days proved ineffectual. Food and board were expensive even in the run-down hotel she had chosen. So she asked for a chambermaiding post to tide her over, which meant she had no overheads, and some pocket-money to swell the coffers. But the work was slave labour. From six in the morning until eight at night, with a stocky Calabrese peasant woman, Laura toiled at cleaning lavatories, turning mattresses, making beds, polishing baths, vacuuming floors, dusting, scrubbing, and carrying huge bales of laundry down to the bowels of the hotel. Unremitting misery. And all the time she wrote cheerful, newsy letters to her family. She was too proud and independent to let them know of her privations. Where was the romance and adventure, she asked herself miserably? The last straw came when Laura was woken at dawn for yet another day's grind and found to her horror that she was still in her dirty working clothes. She had collapsed on to her bed the night before, through sheer exhaustion, without eating or washing.

Enough was enough. How could she possibly land a decent job when she had no free hours to search for one? So she told the hotel proprietor a white lie whilst crossing her fingers behind her back. She said she was ill and had to return home immediately, packed her meagre bags and found an even tattier hotel in Beausoleil, a small French town just behind Monaco. She asked for their smallest room and negotiated a discount for a month's payment in advance and no maid service. This was her last-ditch attempt to find a worthwhile job. And in the meantime she resolved to discover the more glamorous side of the Riviera, even on a pittance. In between job hunting she would explore the whole of Monte-Carlo on foot, visit the Casino, lie on the beach, and return home with a tan, at least, if all else failed!

There was an extra spring to her step the next morning, as she walked down the elegant boulevard des Moulins and approached the Casino gardens. The flowers, the immaculate grass, the stately palms seemed brighter, the sky more blue, the fountains more musical than before. The Casino resembled a large, creamy wedding-cake, with its ornate, stucco front and delicate finials. "Heavenly!" said Laura out loud. Monte-Carlo was paradise, and she vowed to make every effort to stay.

Purposefully, she made her way to the post office where she studied the telephone directory and made a note of all the local American- and English-sounding companies. She planned to visit them in turn to ask for work. Nothing ventured, nothing gained.

Her first port of call was disappointing. Looking down her pince-nez with obvious disdain at Laura's long blonde hair and short skirt, the elderly English receptionist at Chambers & Co, Solicitors, told her that they had a full complement of staff. Undaunted, Laura headed for Kulikis Shipping & Oil next. The lobby of La Rivera was cavernous and dark. Tentatively, she knocked on the heavy mahogany door with its smart, brass nameplate. Her heart was hammering. "Steady, Laura," she murmured. "Nothing ventured..."

Suddenly the door swung open and she was temporarily blinded by the bright interior. She stood framed in the doorway blinking uncertainly for a few moments.

"Yes?" came a peremptory bark.

Laura shaded her eyes to focus on the owner of the voice. "Well?"

She took a deep breath and announced her purpose.

The tall, elderly man distractedly ran his fingers through his thinning hair. "Look, I'm up to my ears," he said dismissively. "My secretary's ill and the place is a shambles..."

"Perhaps I can help?" she interrupted daringly. "I'm a trained secretary."

"Oh dear," he muttered. "I just don't know..."

"Let me give it a try."

The man looked uncertain. So Laura took the bull by the horns and stepped past him into the room.

"Good heavens," she uttered. The office was a nightmare: the desks were littered with papers, there were newspapers on the floor, there was a telex rattling away in the background, and reams and reams of paper spilled out of an excitedly chattering Reuters' ticker, which had jammed and was overprinting a thick black mess. No wonder the poor man was in such a state.

"You can't work like this!" Laura exclaimed sympathetically. "Here, let me sort out your machine."

With one bound, she lifted the heavy perspex lid, switched the ticker off, and tore off the jammed paper. Then she raised the bail bar and extracted the inky, pulpy mess which was tangled in the carriage. She wound on fresh paper, and, switching the machine back on, smiled winningly at the amazed businessman. He had grey hair and a salt and pepper moustache. His eyes were a very pale blue, crinkled round the edges, and turned down like a mournful bloodhound's, belying an optimistic and cheerful nature. He had a strong jaw, and jutting, crooked lower teeth, not quite disguised by the overhanging moustache. In his early sixties, he had an upright, military bearing and was an absolute caricature of the distinguished English gentleman. Laura immediately warmed to him.

"Well!" he exclaimed. "Well, well! How does a delicate young thing like you know about complicated machines like that? I just don't know what to say. Except of course, thank you. Without my share prices and stock-market reports I'd have been paralysed today. But let me introduce myself, young lady. Patrick Fitzgerald, investment director of Kulikis Shipping & Oil. And who might you be? A lady mechanic?"

Laura looked back at Fitzgerald, amused. She and her brothers had always fiddled with machines brought back with triumph from jumble sales. Broken typewriters, duff sewing machines. Nothing fazed them.

"Laura Forsythe," she replied. "And I'm sorry I can't shake your hand, because mine are black! So glad to have been of help. Would you like me to stay on, even if it's just to sort out your machines and make your coffees?"

So started Laura's career in investment management, inauspiciously at first, as an office junior, with inky hands. But within a few months she had taken over from the elderly, neurotic senior secretary, who left in a huff. Since then Laura's rise from the ranks had been exceptional, and she was now indispensable to Fitzgerald.

I've come a long way since then, thought Laura, and added ruefully, careerwise, anyway. She glanced at Pierre, who was now snoring lightly. She wished she could say the same about her love life. It had gone from bad to worse over the last few months.

"Oh, Pierre," she sighed to herself. "What happened to us? Who'd have thought it could come to this?"

She tucked her elbows behind her head, remembering better days.

The day she met Pierre Lejeune was etched as firmly in her memory as it if had been yesterday. It was in the boulevard des Moulins, during her lunch-hour, shortly after starting her job at Kulikis. She was admiring the beautiful clothes and jewellery on display, and dreaming of the day she'd be rich enough to indulge herself. Not looking where she was going, she suddenly jumped as she collided with a tall stranger. While apologising profusely she found herself looking up at the most handsome man she'd ever seen. A shade over six feet tall, he was broad-shouldered, and resplendent in a black and gold uniform with a white peaked hat. He had a full, smiling mouth, beautiful melting brown eyes, and a way of looking at Laura that made her heart skip a beat. Nobody had ever given her such blatantly appraising glances before. At home she had always been part of her brothers' gang, and treated as such. She stood rooted to the spot, spellbound by the Frenchman's glamorous charm. Eventually she realised she was making a fool of herself and made to move on.

"*Alors, mademoiselle,*" he said reluctantly, when she thanked him and turned to go. "*Je vous souhaite une bonne journée.*" And he smiled winningly, saluting smartly, his white gloved hand contrasting sharply with the dark, tanned features. Laura smiled back, impressed by his politeness and formal manner. She wondered if all Frenchmen were as courteous and attractive as this police officer. She sensed that he was watching her as she walked away, but resisted the temptation to look back. Somehow, she knew she would see him again.

And she did. She often went windowshopping in the boulevard des Moulins in her lunch-hour, and the handsome Frenchman, who by now had introduced himself as Pierre Lejeune, strolled beside her for longer distances each day. At last, after a week of polite conversations, he plucked up courage to ask her for a date. Why not? thought Laura. The police in Monaco were known to be an elite force, held in high esteem by everyone. And besides, he was gorgeous.

She would always remember the wonderful times that followed. Touched by her innocence, Pierre unfolded the mystery and wonders of physical love, with infinite patience and tenderness. There were magical days and nights of endless passion. The sweet, pure days of first love, with walks along the sea shore, soft words mingling with the quiet whisper of the surf, romantic dusks together with the fresh smell of pines wafting in the air, and endless, enchanted nights wrapped in each other's arms. *Les nuits blanches*, Pierre had laughingly called them. White nights and golden dawns! Laura didn't seem to need sleep in those days. Her romance with Pierre kept her on a buoyant cloud all day long. Life was happy and simple.

She had adored the strength and power of him. They made love wherever and whenever, even on the beach one sultry night, with the waves lapping around them. He'd been describing the *feux follets* on warm nights, when you could run your hands through the water, creating a veil of phosphorescence in the sea. Laura suggested impulsively that they go to Cap d'Ail right then and see for themselves, and they'd jumped in the car, rushed to the beach, kicked off their shoes and swished their hands around in the shallows. She'd been so enchanted by the effect of the swirling glow at the water's edge that she threw off all her clothes and went deeper into the waves, whirling her arms round and round in the water, shrieking like a child with the sheer excitement of it all.

11

'Come on in, *cheri*! See the glow! It's absolutely magical and the water's like velvet. It's so warm!"

Pierre was carried away by Laura's enthusiasm, and her nakedness, and joined her, splashing around and willingly indulging in childish horseplay.

"*Je t'aime!*" he'd suddenly cried. "*Je t'aime comme un fou!*"

He swept her up, lifted her high out of the water, gazing at his playful nymph with adoration, then gently lowered her down against his body, until her face was just above his. He kissed her with a tenderness that consumed them both, and folded her long, slender legs around his waist, and entered her, standing chest-high in the sea, lifting her effortlessly up and down, up and down on his hardness, with the languor that her weightlessness in the water allowed. Then walking back into the shallows, supporting her fragile weight in his strong arms, her own wrapped tightly around his neck, he gently lowered her down, and continued making love to her on the wet sand, the tiny ripples of waves sucking and soughing around them . . .

Laura sighed. It was such a beautiful memory. A tear ran unchecked down her cheek. And now everything was spoiled. There was no going back, because he'd violated their love, time and time again, crushing out her affection. Now there was nothing left but bitterness, rancour and profound regret.

The first signs that all was not perfect in Laura's life emerged when she got to know Jennifer Morgan and Caroline Browning, two wildly social and very amusing English girls. She first met Caroline at Chambers, the solicitors. Fitzgerald had sent her there for advice about a permanent work permit. She was dreading it. After all, a year ago she had been dispatched with a flea in her ear by Miss Pince-nez. But luckily there was no sign of her when Laura poked her nose round the door. The friendly, dark-haired girl at the desk explained with refreshing irreverence that the old biddy had retired. She was very helpful and could foresee no problem in Laura's applying for a permanent work permit. After a while, they introduced themselves and started chatting on a more personal level. Caroline had come out to Chambers on a sabbatical, as part of her training for a law degree. She was registered as a student, though earning money, and had already stayed in Monte-Carlo far longer than planned.

"Who can blame you?" laughed Laura. "It's wonderful out here!"

"I can't believe you've been here a year!" Caroline exclaimed. "How come we've never met?"

Laura smiled. "Oh, work and my French boyfriend, Pierre, seem to fill my time. I've never met anyone except his friends and family . . ." and her voice tailed off.

Caroline thought she detected a slight wistfulness in Laura's words. "Well then, how about a complete change to your routine? Come and meet Jennifer, my adorably nutty flatmate. She's a scream! Why don't you come round for a drink after work? Do say you'll come! It would be such fun! Say seven thirty?"

Laura was sorely tempted, but backtracked. "Oh, I'd love to," she faltered, "but I'm supposed to be meeting Pierre later."

"Let him wait! Surely you're allowed five minutes to yourself occasionally? Go on. Be daring. Leave him a note."

Laura was persuaded, and from then on, the first doubts appeared about her seemingly idyllic relationship with Pierre. The more time she spent with Jennifer and Caroline, the more her time with Pierre seemed dull and monotonous. She saw another life beckoning. Her new friends were in their early twenties, just a little older, and had lived and worked in Monte-Carlo for much longer. Glamorous and worldly-wise, they represented all the sophistication Laura yearned for. Through them, she met other ex-patriates – attractive, amusing people with money and influence – who introduced her to a world of cocktail parties, black-tie dinners in smart places, beach parties, barbecues, speedboats and water ski-ing. It was so much fun! Never a dull moment; be it giggly evenings over a bottle of wine in the Café de Paris or wonderful, unforgettable concerts up at the Palace. She'd even seen Nureyev and Fonteyn dancing in the courtyard there, in the presence of Prince Rainier and the beautiful Princess Grace. Now she was really living!

Pierre just didn't fit in any more. He felt threatened, and hovered around like a black shadow; a glowering, unwelcome presence, embarrassing her in front of her friends. Laura began to be irritated by Pierre's jealousy and his reluctance to take part in her new life. She hadn't come to the Riviera to tuck herself away and stagnate, for heaven's sake! Where was Pierre's sense of fun, his spirit of adventure, his zest for life? Laura realised they were growing apart. Although it was inevitable, she couldn't stop feeling sad and guilty about it.

Nothing she did was ever right. Pierre even resented the extra time she put in at work. He said ambition was unfeminine, her desire to build a career, unnatural. Soon their differences of opinion turned into heated arguments; their arguments into passionate rows which then erupted into violence, because Laura was clever with words and could always out-argue him. Eventually Laura recognised it was over for her; that she didn't love Pierre any more. But out of a misguided sense of kindness, she couldn't bring herself to hurt him by making the final break, and the affair had continued for several months out of habit and convenience. It had always been so much easier to let him into her bed than to fight him off. To let things drag on and hope that his obsession with her would lessen and he'd finally let her go.

And though she detested him most of the time now, she still hadn't gone off him sexually. He still had a strong hold over her. Perhaps because he was her first and only lover, which bound her to him in body though not in soul. He still had the power, even now, to make her cry out with pleasure because he knew her body so well. She still responded to his touch instinctively, but there was no affection. And afterwards there was nothing. Just darkness and cold indifference.

Right now, all Laura could do was lie quietly, longing for dawn, counting the long hours till morning. At least this would really be the last night, she thought with weary relief, glancing at the dark and sullen face on the pillow beside her. Enough was enough. Tomorrow she was going to leave him. It had been planned in secret with her friends over a month ago. But at the moment she was too tired and battle-scarred to feel any sense of triumph.

Chapter 2

Laura's bags and boxes were piled up in the vast echoing entrance hall of the Grand Palais de France, ready for her imminent departure. It was four o'clock in the afternoon. Exhausted from a long day of packing and tidying, Laura made one last circuit round the flat, now empty and anonymous-looking. Everything was tidy and in order. No one would guess how many dramas and wretched scenes this innocuous little studio had witnessed.

Wanting to forget, Laura stepped out on to the little balcony for one last look at the view, and a reminder of the happier days. The sea stretched into blue nothingness, so pale in the reflected sun that it merged with the sky and made the few boats look as if they were suspended in mid-air. She would miss the view, but that was all she'd miss. She sighed. It was time to move on.

She approached the concierge's desk with trepidation, and handed him her keys. He looked taken aback.

"*Alors, vous partez déjà, mademoiselle?*" he said, his thin weasel face twitching. "*Aujourd'hui-même? Eh bien*, I thought you were leaving next month. You seem in a sudden hurry, *hein?*"

God, but the concierge was nosey!

"Yes," she replied irritably. "I *am* leaving today, but the landlord has a month's rent in lieu of notice, and you'll find the place immaculate, so what's the problem?"

"*Alors, mademoiselle!*" he continued petulantly, waving his hands around. "You could have given me prior warning, *hein?*

Just to leave like this, and not tell me. It is not polite!"

"I don't see what difference it makes when I choose to go, if the rent's paid up anyway!" There was more than an edge of irritation to Laura's voice now. Really! The man was being insufferable, especially as she was in such a hurry to leave.

The beady eyes hardened. "Well, then, it is customary to leave a forwarding address in case of difficulties. *Ça, au moins, hein, mademoiselle?*"

"I'm sorry, no," Laura replied quickly. "I have my reasons for not wanting to do that. Now, if you don't mind I've got things to do."

The concierge became distinctly truculent. No matter. All she cared about was getting away from Pierre. The last thing she wanted was for him to know where she was going! Realising he wouldn't help her with her luggage, she hefted all her bags and effects on to the pavement by herself in stages, whilst the man looked on, staring at her legs as she walked to and fro in front of the desk. This irritated her even more, but at least his bad manners released her from the obligation to tip him, which really would have added insult to injury.

Her baggage made an unimpressive clutter on the pavement outside. She hailed a taxi and the helpful driver quickly stuffed her effects on to the back seat and into the boot.

"Allez, mademoiselle," he said with a friendly smile. *"C'est tout? Eh bien. On y va alors!"* He walked to the passenger side, and opened the door for her with an exaggerated flourish. Laura knew perfectly well that long legs and blonde hair had quite a lot to do with his pleasant attitude. She looked round nervously. No Pierre. The coast was still clear. It seemed too good to be true!

"Le Meribel, s'il vous plaît," she asked, as she climbed into the front seat of the hired car. She massaged a complaining muscle in her right shoulder and watched with no regrets as the Grand Palais in the *vieux quartier* of Beausoleil slid from view.

* * *

A quarter of an hour later, Laura's taxi drew up outside the Meribel, in a fashionable area near the centre of Monte-Carlo. This was a grand old-fashioned apartment block, of eight floors, with an imposing frontage of heavy cream columns supporting an ornate pediment. The Meribel was set in an avenue of old and substantial villas built in the rococo style, whose faded yellow elegance could be glimpsed behind lines of fresh green robinia trees.

Laura hadn't gone far to avoid Pierre, but she hoped he'd be less inclined to cause a disturbance in Monaco. Surely he would not be so foolish as to risk his livelihood by molesting her on his own patch? None the less, she still felt she'd be safer in this small principality where the streets were constantly patrolled, than in the unsalubrious streets of Beausoleil. Monte-Carlo was heavily dependent upon respectability, and everything was geared to making the rich and famous feel secure enough to squander their fortunes there.

The driver willingly helped Laura with her boxes and bags – loading them into the lift, and out on to the sixth floor.

"*Alors, un petit café, mademoiselle?*" he tried, as he looked into her eyes flirtatiously. "*Et . . . je vous aide à démenager?*"

Laura demurred politely. She could manage by herself now. She gave the young man her best smile and a tip to match, and practically had to push him back into the lift to get rid of him.

The key scrunched in the lock of No. 613, Le Meribel. Another place, another chapter. "No involvements for quite some time," she vowed. "From now on, I want a peaceful life and to concentrate on work alone." She pushed open the heavy blue door.

"Hiya, flower! Surprise, surprise!" came a chorus of cheerful voices. Jennifer and Caroline, who'd been waiting to welcome Laura to her new home, were hovering in the tiled hallway with big smiles on their faces. "But you're so early! The champers isn't even cold yet."

19

"Hey, how lovely!" exclaimed Laura, delighted. "I wasn't expecting you till much later. How come you're not at work still?"

"I managed to scarper off early," explained Caroline, her dark eyes dancing. "But Jennifer's lost her job. The revolting old Russki sacked her yesterday!"

"Good riddance, I say. Sod the horrible old goat!" giggled Jennifer, tossing her blonde mane. "Welcome to your new abode, Miss Forsythe, with your live-in bodyguards! 'Fraid it isn't terribly tidy," she continued apologetically, "but we've nowhere near sorted ourselves out yet. Caro's got the smaller bedroom and you're sharing the big one with me."

"You're not hiding that bloody frog Lejeune in one of your cases, are you?" teased Caroline.

"God, I should hope not!" giggled Laura. "All the trouble we've gone to, hatching this plot and finding a new flat together in order to be rid of him."

"We've managed to sneak your car into the underground car park and Caroline's sorted out the rent and everything, but we're going to have to put your name on the lease because we haven't got proper work permits like you," explained Jennifer, before smiling wryly, "we're just casual workers!"

Caroline laughed. "Shirkers, you mean." Then added mock-accusingly, "At least, Jennifer is! She came out here three years ago, with some deb's delight on her arm, then summarily ditched him: invited herself to spend a couple of weeks with muggins, and has been sponging off me ever since. Give or take the odd job that lasts about two minutes, she's a permanent beach bum! At least *I've* got the genuine excuse of being a law student!"

Jennifer started to protest, then gave up and stuck her tongue out at Caroline. She turned to Laura, changing the subject. "Cup of tea, sweetheart?"

Laura nodded, smiling. Caroline's brown eyes twinkled, and she threw her tanned arms in the air expansively. "When the champagne's cold, and you're all unpacked, we'll drink to your new life in tax-free and sin-free Monaco! Come on, Jen, give Laura a hand with her things. I'll brew up and be with you in a tick."

Caroline bustled off into the kitchen and Laura had a quick look round before unpacking. The sitting-room was quite large, and comfortably furnished with a sofa and armchairs, a sideboard and small round dining-table, and multi-hued scatter rugs on the blue mosaic floor. Through the sliding glass doors, which ran the whole width of the room was a deep balcony, shaded by blue sun-blinds with fringes. The view from the balcony was the cream 'C' wing opposite of the large, horseshoe-shaped block and the exotic gardens below, with palms, agaves and brilliant-hued flowers and lawns. In the middle was a tall, ornate fountain, whose gentle hiss and splash of water could be heard even on the sixth floor.

Back through the hallway was an adequate kitchen in pale cream, with a table to seat four in the middle. There were three plain eye-level cupboards, a worktop next to a large gas cooker, and a very large fridge. The sink was an old white china one, with a ridged wooden draining-board under the window. Caroline's bedroom was quite small, but had enough room for a wardrobe, basin and chest of drawers as well as a small divan bed with a side-table.

The room that Laura and Jennifer were to share was large, with a built-in wardrobe all along the back of it. There were two large windows, and a bed on either side of the room with bedside tables, and in the middle a chest of drawers with a mirror behind, and a vase of artificial roses on a white crocheted runner. This main bedroom led into a small bathroom, quite modern by French standards. There was even a separate shower.

They had done well. Laura's whole impression of No. 613 Le Meribel was one of space and light, and in spite of the clutter, Laura was sure she'd be happy living there with her new flatmates. She felt very optimistic about this new beginning. Pierre Lejeune was in the past now.

Jennifer and Laura set to work in the shared bedroom, cramming Laura's clothes and possessions into what little space there was left in Jennifer's bulging cupboards.

"Crikey, talk about fitting a quart into a pint pot!" exclaimed Laura with disbelief. "I've never seen so much stuff. What on earth do you do with all those clothes and shoes? It's like a bazaar in here."

"Yeah," laughed Jennifer, as she fought to wedge in another dress. "Why do you think Caroline opted for the smaller room? She knows my untidy habits of old. But, honestly, I'll try to improve; I really will!"

All thoughts of a peaceful and tidy existence evaporated in the days to come as three busy lives collided in the process of day-to-day living. Laura, already dismayed that her clothes seemed to have been squashed into oblivion by Jennifer's horde of dresses, wondered why the floor and sometimes even her own bed were carpeted with more of Jennifer's effects. The bathroom, too, was always an indescribable mess of spilt toothpaste and mascara round the basin, talc on the floor, flimsy panties and bras drying over the showerhead and discarded tea mugs round the bath.

"Well, I suppose anything's better than life with Pierre," Laura grinned ruefully, "and at least Caroline is tidyish."

"I'll clear up when I get back," promised Jennifer, but as she was ever the social butterfly and never returned till the early hours, things appeared to have started as they would continue.

"A messy flat, though, is infinitely preferable to a messy life," Laura reasoned, and learned to weave her way through the chaos as she got herself ready for work.

Patrick Fitzgerald was investment manager of the vast fortunes of Taki Kulikis, president of Kulikis Shipping & Oil.

Taki was one of the richest men in Monaco after Onassis, who had virtually owned the place, but was now gradually decamping to his Greek islands. Indeed, one very rarely even saw the yacht *Christina* moored in the harbour of Monaco these days.

Laura had steadily become indispensable to Fitzgerald over the past year. From humble beginnings she had catapulted like a meteorite to responsibilities far beyond her years. Her only training had been as a shorthand typist, but as she was a fast worker she quickly disposed of the mundane secretarial tasks. This gave her the opportunity to become more involved in the investment portfolios, growth charts and day-to-day movements of the stock-market, which fascinated her. It was exciting!

Laura had a quick brain, an aptitude for figures, and a photographic memory. It allowed her to memorise important telephone numbers and instantly recognise stock and share symbols that rattled out continually on the Reuters' ticker in the office. She could shout out the relevant company names at Fitzgerald's sudden demand much more quickly than he could look them up. He found himself instinctively deferring to her when he was on the line to his brokers, and often remarked that he would be lost without her.

"You have a brain like a computer!" he'd joke, and look at her quizzically. Privately he marvelled at the razor-sharp person hiding under those drop-dead good looks. However much work he threw at Laura, his charts would be up to date and various other important tasks accomplished on her own initiative. Eventually, realising that her efficiency allowed him to leave her alone in the office for longer and longer periods, Fitzgerald took the opportunity to travel and build up more interesting and diversified investments in new growth companies.

Even though she was only twenty, Laura had begun to understand the logistics of 'empire building'. Thus, whilst she was building up her own power base in the office, she was enabling Fitzgerald to extend his horizons, too. Very convenient for both of them.

Laura now felt she needed a secretary of her own, to type correspondence, answer phone calls, keep the files and run errands. She no longer had the time as she was taking on so much. She seemed to be working longer and longer hours. These days she had to come in to the office before eight in the morning and quite often she'd still be there until eight at night!

The ticker was chuntering away rhythmically in the middle of the large, airy office, sending out reams of paper from the roll in its rounded metal casing. She walked over to the machine and waited until the last bulletin had ended. Deftly she tore off the previous night's output, and sighed. As usual there were at least ten yards of information to be edited and collated! As she always liked to ensure that Fitzgerald had the closing prices to hand the minute he came through the door, she quickly took the scissors and set to. She wondered whether Fitzgerald would be amenable to lashing out on an extra salary for a junior, especially for this type of task. Surely he'd see reason? After all, he was always pleased with her and so visibly appreciative of her skills. Not to mention that there had been two of them when she first joined! Laura decided to tackle her boss about it as soon as possible.

"Good morning, Mr Fitzgerald," Laura sang out from behind her desk as he strode in, whistling cheerfully, the *Wall Street Journal* tucked under his arm.

Fitzgerald smiled broadly at his protégé. There she was, immaculate as ever in her pretty blouse and tailored skirt, hair swept up into an elegant topknot.

"The coffee's freshly brewed," she told him, "your performance charts are done, and yesterday's closing prices are on your desk with the portfolios."

"You know, Laura, you're a saint! What would I do without you, eh?"

He looked approvingly at her and at his tidy desk. The girl was a miracle. She made his working day run like clockwork. Fitzgerald chuckled and shook his head wonderingly as he sat down and admired her neat columns of transactions and the growth charts in front of him. Her assiduous work had saved him many tedious hours of phone calls to brokers. What a lucky man he was!

He picked up the *Wall Street Journal* to read the stock-market summary, then looked across at Laura over his half-glasses. "By the way," he said, "How about lunch some time soon? You've been working so hard lately. I think you deserve to be spoiled a little."

Laura smiled disarmingly at her boss. "That would be lovely, thanks." This boded well for her: a few glasses of wine, Fitzgerald in a mellow, receptive mood; couldn't be better.

'How about really soon?" Fitzgerald continued, removing his glasses and looking at her more intently. "I think I shouldn't have neglected you for so long. You're more decorative than Kulikis and his cronies, and much more deserving. They don't know how much they should be indebted to you! Could you look in my diary and see when I'm free?"

Laura picked up the book, and was pleased to see an ideal gap in his engagements.

"Today, as it happens," she informed him.

He smiled, his pale blue eyes crinkling paternally at her, and nodded, "OK. Can you book the Brazil, then?"

"With pleasure, Mr Fitzgerald," she said, picking up the telephone.

"Strike while the iron's hot," she thought optimistically, and immersed herself in the morning minutiae of the Kulikis empire.

Chapter 3

Jennifer blinked as a ray of sun streaked across her pillow,
yawned and reached for a cigarette. Her head throbbed as she
bent to find her lighter at the side of the bed. Groaning, she laid
her head back on to the pillow very gently. She hooked a long
tanned leg out of the sheets to push away the clothes lying in a
tangled heap on the floor where she'd thrown them at three in
the morning. Her toe found the cold metal of the Dunhill, and
she wriggled down the bed to retrieve it without bending
forward.

Lighting the cigarette, she reflected on the events of the
previous few days. She had been sacked from her job at the
Exclusivités de France for being late yet again. So what? She
could do better than work for a lecherous white Russian in a
dreary boutique at Monte-Carlo Beach. She was ready for the
big time! This was to be her third summer in the South of
France and if she didn't make it now, she never would. At first
it had seemed so glamorous to land a job in one of the world's
renowned playgrounds for the rich. Anyway, she reasoned
moodily, when she'd originally met the old fool at the Hôtel de
Paris, he'd offered her a modelling job! But Exclusivités was
never a contender for fame and fortune.

What a let-down! The reality had been very different; a
mere shop assistant in an unflattering black uniform with a
white collar that made her look like a governess! And no
interesting millionaires had flocked into the shop – only their
endlessly bitching wives who looked askance at Jennifer and
fingered the clothes disdainfully. As for the Russian! He was

greasy, he smelt, and his pudgy hands were of the wandering variety. The interior of the shop was as dark as a grave and just as chilly. The clothes were as expensive as they were unfashionable. Yes, she was definitely better off out of there.

The problem was, she was stone broke. Not only broke, but in arrears with the rent, too. Laura and Caroline were generous and understanding, but probably not to the extent of subsidising her profligate lifestyle for ever. What next, she wondered, inhaling the calming menthol cigarette appreciatively.

She squinted at her Patek Philippe; it was eleven thirty. A dull chord jangled in her subconscious. Hell, wasn't she supposed to be meeting someone at midday? She sat up with a start and winced as the pain jarred in her head. "Oh God, who invented booze?" she groaned, as she tried to recollect the events of the night before. If only she could remember!

She stumbled out of bed and into the bathroom, where she stubbed out her cigarette in the basin. A cold shower would freshen up and focus her thoughts. The water felt like cold pins piercing her as it hissed and ran in rivulets down her slender body. She held her face up to the spray, hoping it would smooth out the excesses of yet another late night. "Come on, Jennifer babe, think! And think fast!"

Suddenly it came to her. The millionaire Thingamybob Thingamyjig. God, what was his name? Julius Thingamy. Julius, Julius. Oh crap! Why won't my brain function? Wait! – Crap rings a bell. Yes! Krep. Julius Krep. That's who it was. She towelled herself dry in a fury of haste, glancing in the mirror: dark rings under her eyes, sopping wet hair.

The harassed girl rummaged around the poky bathroom looking for make-up to repair the damage, and her eyes lit on Laura's cosmetic tray. Foundation, shadow, mascara, a stick of Erace – all neatly arranged in compartments. Wonderful! She immediately set to work on her ravaged face. Out went the rings, on went the shadow; deft strokes of black mascara on the long lashes framing her grey eyes. Already the face looked more awake. With a surprisingly steady hand she traced the outline of her full mouth using a lip brush and filled in the rest with a lighter shade of pink to accentuate her slight pout. She finished with a dusting of blusher and looked at her reflection with approval.

She ran a brush through her long, wavy titian-blonde hair hoping that it would be at least half-dry by the time she had run to her rendezvous with Krep. She threw on a turquoise sundress that stopped six inches above the knees, bootlace straps revealing just enough cleavage to excite the imagination, and grabbed her bag. Damn it! Where was she supposed to be? Ten to twelve already. Think, girl, think!

The Brazil. That was it. The Brazil! Julius Krep, midday at the Brazil.

"Oh, hell and damnation!" swore Jennifer. Her key had once again gone missing. At last, she found it, under her bed. Then the lift took for ever to arrive. She hoped Laura wouldn't mind that she'd borrowed her make-up and ten francs from the kitty again. She must get her act together one of these days, or Laura and Caroline really would throw her out. There was a limit to their tolerance, after all!

She set off at a running pace, keeping to the sunny side of the winding streets leading to the main boulevard, allowing the sun to dry her hair. As she sped through the old town she relished the cool feel of the heavy lion's mane flopping damply on to her bare shoulders. Running at midday was hot work, especially on a hangover! The sun had leached practically all the blue out of the sky, and the flaking yellow buildings baked in the reflected heat.

She turned into the narrow avenue de la Costa with its variety of tiny bijou shops and a patisserie on the corner, wafting out its sweet, familiar smell of croissants and freshly baked bread. Her high-heeled sandals clicked smartly on the stone paving as she ran on between the tall, uneven buildings looming above, with their faded green shutters and wrought-iron balustrading. At last she reached the broader boulevard des Moulins. Here were the most elegant shops of all; mainly couture, jewellery and fine arts. To her right were the formal gardens with their gaudy, jewel-bright flower-beds and emerald-green lawns, fronting the famous Casino.

Jennifer checked her watch again. Just past twelve. Nearly there now. If only she could remember what this meeting with Krep was about, apart from the fact that he was a millionaire and she, of course, desperately needed money! As the Brazil came into view, she slowed down to a leisurely pace, tossing her golden hair casually, ascertaining that it was passably dry.

Julius Krep looked approvingly at the beautiful young woman striding gracefully into the restaurant. His dark eyes glinted and his pencil-thin moustache twitched in anticipation of the mouthwatering meal he hoped to make of her later. He had offered her a job on his yacht the other night, an enormous three-masted schooner moored in Monte-Carlo harbour – as a 'hostess'. For himself initially, of course, but for influential friends, too, if the occasion arose, and they needed sweetening. He wondered how broke her kind of broke was: whether she was desperate enough to consider anything ... really anything ... to get herself out of hock!

Jennifer's large grey eyes took in Krep's moon face and slicked-back hair. God, but she must have been really tanked up the other night even to consider a rendezvous with him, rich or not! He was the absolute epitome of the spiv. That little moustache really took the cake! As for the white seersucker jacket bursting at the buttons to let his podgy little body escape ... She suppressed a hysterical urge to scream with laughter, and instead gave him her version of the flashing smile that betrays nothing.

"Hello, gel! Take a pew!" the millionaire urged, without getting to his feet.

"Thanks," murmured Jennifer, noting the lapse in manners.

"Like a nice glass of champagne, sweetie?" he asked in a silky voice.

"Why not?"

He stretched back and clicked his fingers at the waiter who had acquired the discreet habit of ignoring Krep's vulgarity in return for the large tips he left.

"Glass of champagne for my beautiful companion, there's a good lad!" said Krep.

The dark-haired waiter swung the champagne out of its silver cooler with a flourish, and poured, finding it easy to put on a show for Krep's delectable date.

Jennifer smiled, *"Merci bien."* Privately she wondered why the rich man had to be so unappealing and vulgar, whilst the waiter, earning a pittance, had to be so desirable. "Sod's law!" she muttered under her breath, taking in his long lashes and lithe frame with approval.

"What was that, sweetie?" asked Krep, his eyes narrowing attentively.

"Nothing," lied Jennifer, darting him a look of pure innocence. "I so enjoyed the other night at the Black Jack." It was all coming back to her now in dribs and drabs.

"So did I. So did I. I love being seen in the company of a gorgeous girl. Does wonders for my reputation!" He smirked at her, pleased with himself, and picked up his glass.

"At what cost to mine?" she wondered.

The millionaire took a sip of champagne, and took a long, hard look at her as he put down the glass. His short, stubby fingers toyed with the stem suggestively, and his navy-blue eyes glazed over with lust. His lips parted, like two fat pink slugs, garnished with a fleck of saliva. God, but he was repulsive! He had at least three chins, and a sweaty, pallid face that looked as if it had never seen fresh air. The nerve of him to assume his money could buy her body!

"Shall we order?" she chirped brightly, hoping to interrupt his train of thought.

"OK, duckie, anything your little heart desires!" he crooned, then turned away to summon the ever-obliging waiter.

But his attention was suddenly diverted as he noticed a tall, distinguished man and a breathtaking young woman, hair swept up into a chignon, entering the restaurant together.

"Well," he breathed. "Two beautiful blondies in one lunch-hour. I'm quite overcome!"

Jennifer turned. Oh hell! It was Laura with her boss. Slightly disconcerted at being caught in such unsalubrious company, Jennifer nevertheless smiled brightly and waved.

"You know that gorgeous number, sweetie?" Krep asked, swivelling round in his chair again to take a better look, and showing off his paunch.

"Of course. That's Laura, my flatmate, with her boss, Fitzgerald. She's a PA who helps look after the Kulikis fortune."

"Wow! Brains as well as looks, eh?" The paunch went into overdrive. His jacket was an erupting Vesuvius whose buttons must have been sewn on with steel cable.

"I'm not exactly underendowed with brains myself, you know!" retorted Jennifer hotly.

"Underendowed you're certainly not," murmured Krep silkily, turning his attention back to her again and eyeing the tanned swell of her breasts rising from the flimsy shift. He put out a pudgy hand to push a strand of hair from her cheek, and lowered his gaze and thoughts. His eyes glittered as he imagined her titian-gold hair spread all over his black satin pillows, and himself sliding in and out of that firm golden body. He groaned inadvertently, and salivated as he mentally tasted and probed at her musky sweetness with his tongue.

"Collar and cuffs match, do they, love?" he murmured huskily, and overcome with the heat of lust, he mopped his face with a silk hankie.

But Jennifer ignored the innuendo and took a large swig of

champagne. She put her chin on her hands, and leaned on her elbows, giving him the benefit of a one-thousand-yard stare. Krep studied her generous mouth, the little curved nose with a scattering of freckles, and her wide-apart grey eyes, framed with the longest lashes he'd ever seen. She was slightly flushed with anger, which made her even more appealing. God, but the girl was a great looker! And she had spirit, too. A cut above the rest, he decided. He must get her on to his yacht soon. Maybe he could throw a big party for her; invite some big names. That would impress her!

Laura turned and smiled quizzically at Jennifer, amazed at her unsavoury companion. He had lechery written all over his face. She decided against introducing Fitzgerald to them, much to Jennifer's relief.

"Mr Krep," said Jennifer, interrupting his thoughts. "Weren't we about to order?"

"Oh, yes, girlie. Forgive me. My mind was on other things." And he grinned at her lasciviously, putting a damp hand on the back of hers. "Anything you like, eh? How would you like a dozen oysters to start with? You know what they're good for!" His voice was thick and silky, and his eyes glassier than ever.

Yuk! she thought, and made another grab for her glass, to rid herself of his fat hand.

"There's no 'r' in the month. They'll be past their best, thank you," she answered crisply, trying to keep the contempt from her voice.

"I stand corrected!" grinned Krep, unabashed. "How about smoked salmon then, beautiful lady?"

"All right. Then for the main course I'll have a steak tartare and mixed salad, please."

"Nice to meet a girl who knows her mind. I'll have the same starter and then the veal, I think."

Krep summoned the waiter, who was now hovering close by, and ordered the meal in appalling French. Jennifer stifled a giggle. The waiter grinned patiently and answered him in fluent English. Meanwhile he treated Jennifer to a dose of his grecian profile, dark sloe eyes and sweeping lashes. Golly, but he was sexy! What a shame he had nothing to offer except his body.

Jennifer forced herself to think about practicalities. First things first. She was in debt. She needed a job, not seductive eyes! With a mammoth effort, and a megawatt smile, she turned her full attention and devastating charm on to Julius Krep.

Laura arrived home from work in high spirits. The lunch had gone very well, and Fitzgerald had been very amenable to the idea of getting her an assistant. This would allow him to delegate even more responsibilities to her, he explained. She knew this would free him to further his ambitions by extending the portfolios, which already earned him a hefty percentage. The more money he made for the Kulikis empire, he'd added, twinkling, the happier they were, and the more willing to grant his requests.

"Absolutely no problem, my dear," he had beamed, "and as you're smart enough to have your very own secretary now, it's about time you called me Fitz. 'Mr Fitzgerald' is absolutely out now."

He continued to beam supremely for the rest of the lunch, having offered the delighted girl an enormous pay rise commensurate with her status as his second-in-command.

Laura went into the kitchen to get a bottle of Coke, humming happily to herself. But she stopped short and eyed the sinkful of washing-up with distaste. On the table were two glasses powdered with the remains of Alka-Seltzer; Jennifer's no doubt. In the bathroom she found a cigarette stub staining the basin brown and her own make-up scattered all around the edge.

"Jennifer!" screamed Laura. "You're the absolute end.

Come here and clear up this mess. Who said you could borrow my make-up?"

"I'm sorry, Laura. I was in a desperate hurry. I'll tidy everything now. Ooh, my head!" she wailed, glancing into the mirror. "God, I've seen better things crawl out of mouldy cheese!"

"I'll say! You do look a sight. What on earth were you doing with that fat creep at lunch-time? I didn't dare introduce you to my boss."

"Oh Jeez, don't remind me. I know Krep's foul, but he's offered me some work on his yacht; you know, that lovely three-masted job in the harbour . . ."

But Caroline interrupted the conversation, suddenly appearing in the doorway and grinning sardonically. "Don't tell me. A hostess. I've heard it all before. You know what you're supposed to do? It's horizontal shift work."

"Shaftwork you mean!" giggled Laura, perching on the edge of the bath. "And with the likes of her revolting lunch-time companion, she'd need chloroform to numb her brain insensible first."

"Better by far to give it to Krep and immobilise him!" sniggered Jennifer, making her way back to her unmade bed, where she collapsed in a tired heap. "I should have guessed his intentions'd be purely dishonourable," she continued, gazing ruefully into space, "but I've gone and accepted his invitation anyway to the big party he's holding on Friday."

Caroline and Laura followed her, raising their eyes to the ceiling.

"So what the hell?" continued Jennifer defiantly. "Nothing ventured, nothing gained. There's film producers and everyone going to be there. I'll just keep an open mind and see if there's anyone influential I can chat up. Don't want to miss my first really big opportunity to mix with the jet set now, do I?" She reached for a pack, lit a cigarette, and drew on it reflectively.

"Hey, but what's Jean-Claude going to think of being stood up on a Friday night?" Caroline asked, plonking herself down beside her and fiddling with Jennifer's Dunhill.

"Oh, him. Jean-bloody-Claude," she retorted, irritably brandishing her cigarette. "I've ditched him. He wants to get married, and I'm not nearly ready for that yet. Besides, he's getting more and more tightfisted and dreadfully suburban these days. In fact, he's so utterly boring, I'd rather play with myself than go to bed with him." Jennifer frowned and scratched her head distractedly. "At least, I think I've ditched him. Bit like Pierre, really. Too thick to get the message."

"Well, I have to hand it to you little heart-breakers," remarked Caroline, stroking the gold lighter with admiration. "Your men certainly don't want to let go. What the hell do you do to make them so tenacious?"

Jennifer looked at Laura for inspiration; then just shrugged her shoulders disparagingly. "Dunno, really. Do you, Laura?"

"Do I what?" she asked vaguely, standing in the middle of the untidy room.

"Do you know what we do to hang on to our men?"

"Hmm," she pondered, folding her arms. "I guess maybe it's because we don't."

"That's a cryptic answer if ever there was one. Thanks, girls, for nothing!" muttered Caroline moodily, shaking her dark brown curls.

"How did your lunch go with the boss, Laura?" asked Jennifer, taking a languid puff of her cigarette.

"Pretty good. Got myself a secretary and promotion. Hard work occasionally pays off." She smiled triumphantly, her eyes sparkling.

"Smug cow!" sang Jennifer and Caroline. "It's all right for some!"

"Right, that's enough from you two." Laura laughed. Walking over to the bed she shook the prone figure, commanding, "Jennifer, get up! You promised to clear the mess you left in the bathroom. Let's get this place ship-shape. I'll cook dinner when I've cleared the kitchen. I'll wager that's your washing-up in the sink, too, you lazy old trout!"

Jennifer grinned and slowly made her way to the bathroom. "You're not in your office now, bossy-boots. This is home, sweet home."

"Get on with it, Jen, and stop complaining! I'll sort out the sitting-room, and we'll eat out on the balcony," Caroline said as she headed for the hallway. "It'll be fun to spend the evening chez-nous instead of painting the town red. Let's open some wine and celebrate Laura's promotion and Jennifer's elevation to the jet set!"

Later that evening, the lone man watched, as the three English girls, two blonde, one brunette, talked and giggled on their balcony, from his vantage point – dead opposite in Block C, across the gardens – with the aid of powerful binoculars. He had rigged up a hammock, as if he intended to spend an enormous amount of time out there. Just watching and waiting.

He pushed on the railings to let the hammock swing very gently whilst he reflected on his luck. This was very handy for him. He had all the time in the world to watch his prey: to watch and wait. *Mon Dieu*, What a lucky break! And they were delicious . . . all of them. So vulnerable . . . So near . . .

"*Alors, mes jolis poulets. Oui,*" he murmured in a hoarse and sibilant whisper.

His narrowed eyes were black with thwarted desire, as he reached down for a glass of cold beer, and gulped it down. Slowly he removed the froth from his upper lip with his tongue, exposing cruel teeth, and a mouth drawn back in an animal snarl of contempt. Then, his expression changing to a satisfied smirk, he settled back into his hammock and raised the binoculars to his eyes again.

Chapter 4

As the week progressed, Laura and Caroline immersed themselves in work, whilst the jobless Jennifer did her best to eke out the precious few francs she had left. At least she had no need to spend any money on food, because she was never short of invitations to drinks and dinner parties, where she sometimes pocketed the odd cigarette for her handbag when no one was looking. She spent endless lazy days on the beach, topping up her tan and finding out on the grapevine where the action was. Keeping socially active was a good ruse for avoiding the stultifying Jean-Claude. He detested frivolity.

When all's said and done, she reflected, they really had nothing in common. The relationship had lasted a year – on and off; the offs being longer than the ons. Jean-Claude was twenty-six years old and good-looking. He was hard-working and would be successful one day, but he was dull and had no sense fun. What was the point of having a handsome escort if she never went anywhere exciting? Jennifer craved affluence and creature comforts. She'd been brought up in the lap of luxury. Chauffeur-driven to school, holidays in Barbados, a villa in St Jean Cap Ferrat, a stately pile in Ireland, shopping sprees in Harrods. Then her whole life collapsed when her father lost his money in a property venture. It was a major tragedy for the whole family.

All she wanted was what had been hers by right. She'd been brought up to expect the best. She'd always had a generous allowance. Life had been too easy and it had stifled any work ethic in her. Though she was ambitious and capable she couldn't tolerate the hard grind, the slow climb to fame and fortune. Being poor felt unnatural, and she was still finding it hard to adjust. Perhaps Krep would open a few doors for her, provide the first rung of the ladder to success. He'd be bound to have rich and influential friends.

Certainly poor old Jean-Claude would never be her gateway to paradise. All he could talk about was his accountancy studies and marriage. Heaven help her! She was still only twenty-two. The thought of being Mr and Mrs Pen-Pusher with 2.3 children in a dreary little French suburb appalled her. Well, one of these days she'd have to be decisive and make a break. Maybe she'd do something about it soon; but not right now. Jean-Claude would do for the present.

At last, on Friday came the big day. Krep's showbiz party! "Quick, Laura, Caroline!" panicked Jennifer, "What can I wear? What about my hair? Oh hell! I do so hate being broke."

Caroline, all dressed up for the evening, looked up from painting her nails bright red to match her silk blouse. "Oh God," she sighed, "just listen to her! You're a knockout however you are, and well you know it! As for what to wear, well, you have more clothes than both of us put together. What's the fuss for that lecherous old creep anyway? All he'll want to do is take off whatever you've got on, so what difference does it make?"

"Yuk and double yuk, he's bad enough with his clothes on!" Jennifer's face convulsed, and her flatmates giggled at her expression. "The thought of him without really makes me gag!"

"Well, for heaven's sake stay sober enough to know what you're doing. You could get sold into white slavery if you don't keep your wits about you. Krep's no more than a very rich pimp, remember, with his wretched hostesses and slobby entourage, and it's only his tons of loot that make him even remotely acceptable."

"It's all very well, Laura, to be scathing about his money,

but I'm flat broke and I wouldn't mind just a tiny fraction of his millions. It's what I'm expected to do for it that worries me. All the same, I'll go along for the pickings. This could be my big break at last! Who knows, I may be discovered as a major talent in films: Sam Spiegel is going to be there, you know!"

Caroline inspected her nails to see if they were dry. "Frightfully impressive," she drawled wearily. "Tell me the old, old story!" She picked up her evening bag very carefully, holding it with the tips of her fingers. "Well, we're off now. Can't wait to hear about it in the morning!"

Laura and Caroline set off for an evening with friends, whilst Jennifer finished getting ready. She chose a white *crêpe-de-Chine* dress – an Ossie Clark – with criss-cross straps across a very plunging back. Sexy but not over the top. She wore a triple-row pearl choker her father had given her for her seventeenth birthday, and matching pearl studs in her ears. Every inch a film star – but with class! "Eat your heart out, Bardot!" she mouthed at her reflection. Pleased with herself, she set out for the short and pretty downhill walk to the port.

About halfway there, she passed the Hôtel de Paris and glanced up at the wide carpeted steps where all the rich people lingered, showing off their finery. That'll be me up there, one of these days, Jennifer vowed. There were crowds filing into the Casino, too; bent on making – and usually losing – a fortune. She continued on past the majestic rounded wing of the hotel that faced the sea. Right at the top were the panoramic windows of the exclusive Grill, which enjoyed one of the best views in the world. Further round the bend, she gazed longingly into Hermès, as she always did. To her left was the Piscine des Terasses, for the *crème de la crème* who could afford to stay at Monte-Carlo's most exclusive hotel. It was not long before the harbour came into view with its impressive backdrop: the towering Rocher de Monaco, on which perched the pink, floodlit palace of the ruling Grimaldi family.

All the way down the hill, which curved naturally down to

and around the harbour basin, old fashioned globe lanterns adorned either side, looking like a double string of twinkling fairy-lights. The larger yachts were all lit up, and the ones entertaining, dressed over-all. It was easy to spot the *Xerina* with her three giant masts looming up into the velvety night sky. Her streamlined white hull was illuminated by downlights, which threw soft reflections into the still water. Her gold-painted bowsprit reared gracefully from the bow, small lights picking out her silhouette. Krep's yacht was truly magnificent, the most beautiful Jennifer had ever seen, and reminded her of the ones in fairytale books of her childhood. Her dignity and grace seemed somewhat at odds with Krep's obese vulgarity.

The *Xerina* was moored stern-to on the nearside of the harbour. A gangway with steps led from the pontoon up to the aft deck, which was festooned with coloured lights, and thronging with glamorous people in black tie and glittering dresses. Jennifer boarded the fabulous yacht, and was soon accosted by a smart waiter offering champagne cocktails. "*Merci,*" she said as casually as she could, and took the cool, frosted flute with a practised nonchalance.

"*Pas de quoi, mademoiselle, je vous en prie!*" bowed the waiter.

"Well, here goes!" she breathed as she mingled amongst the guests. "Wonder where the old fart's hiding? I'll avoid him as long as possible and circulate."

Jennifer had always been blessed with an easy manner and had the knack of engaging total strangers in conversation without seeming pushy. That she was also an opportunist would never have occurred to anyone but the most jaundiced cynic! She had a natural charm and a ready wit, but she was also a good listener. Added to that she had the wonderful knack of making every man feel powerful and irresistible by simply ensuring she'd be below his eye level during conversation, so that she could gaze up into his face with an expression of wrapt earnestness through her long black lashes. It worked every time. Men were for ever telling her that she was intelligent and understanding (instead of just highly desirable, which was actually nearer the truth).

She looked around her for a familiar face. Good! There was her gay friend Terry Martin. He was always ready with snippets of world-weary gossip. She waved at him brightly, and he was soon by her side. He was wearing a white crushed velvet smoking-jacket, and matching flared trousers with gold braid down the leg. His shirt was a purple waterfall of frills, topped with a fluorescent pink bow tie. Terry was medium height, early fifties, in good shape but for a very slight pot-belly, and heavily tanned. His hair was a wispy mouse, and slicked back with Panthène from his rather fleshy face. Apart from when he smiled, which was often, his pronounced lower lip jutted in a pout, which gave him a petulant expression completely at variance with his sunny nature. Jennifer adored him.

"Jenni, hi! Great to see you!" he drawled, drawing heavily on a Sobranie in a long, ebony cigarette-holder. "I'm just back from California. Just sold another bit of real estate to cover my next year of high living!"

"Never done a day's work in your life have you, Terry?" Jennifer chided.

"Ooh, talk about the pot calling the kettle black, darling. Anyway, what have you been doing lately to earn your keep? Not that you need to really, with what you've got! You're *sitting* on a gold mine, duckie, if only you knew it; just lie back and count the cash! God, it's so easy for you gorgeous girls. If I was straight I'd pay to have you, any time."

Coming from anyone other but Terry, Jennifer might have been insulted, but somehow he could carry off the most outrageous remarks with panache.

"Really, Terry, you're incorrigible!" she giggled. "I'm not a tart. I wouldn't dream of doing it for money!"

43

"You might say so, sweetie-pie," replied Terry with a theatrical sweep of the Sobranie, "but women prostitute themselves for less, dearie. Prostitute themselves for a couple of kids and security. It happens all over the world, even in dullest suburbia ... God, who needs that?" His smooth, round face was a picture of outraged despair and his eyebrows shot up like inverted commas.

"Don't be so sour and cynical, Terry," she said, laughing at his dramatic expression. "That's called marriage, and it's what most women eventually aspire to. A man, a family and a home. It's a romantic ideal, and it works pretty well most of the time."

"All right, duckie, let's just call it a *legalised* form of prostitution, then. Depends what you're doing it for." His brown eyes twinkled as he tilted his glass towards her in the form of a toast.

"There's more to life than sex and money!" she giggled, clinking hers to his. Then, her eyes sweeping round the aft deck, she whispered urgently, "Tell me, who's here of any note? You're the walking-talking *Who's Who!*"

"Pretty much everyone – film producers, starlets – all of them boringly hetero," he answered, stifling a yawn. "Come on, I'll introduce you to some of the rich and famous! Want to try your luck as a film star? There's old fatty Spiegel with his entourage."

So saying, Terry drew her into Spiegel's group. The party was in full swing now. Waiters with trays of canapés and champagne glided round as if they were on wheels. The soft night air was full of laughter and animated voices. The atmosphere of heady glamour was enhanced by the setting and the subdued lighting as diamonds sparkled on ears, necks and wrists: blonde, coiffed heads shone, and perfect teeth glowed in deeply tanned faces. The champagne continued to flow, and Jennifer drank freely, loving every second of it and forgetting her earlier promises not to get carried away. Spiegel, the very epitome of the successful film tycoon right down to the fat cigar and sycophantic starlet, was attractive and entertaining company. He exuded power and glamour, which fascinated her. This was really living! What a party!

Jennifer was already very light-headed when Krep appeared out of the blue, and seizing her by the arm, exclaimed, "Sam, you've pinched my favourite lady."

Bloody hell, thought Jennifer. He would have to turn up and spoil my fun! She gave him a thin smile and a vague 'hello'. Sam smiled expansively, and turned back to his circle of friends.

Julius was dressed conservatively in an expensive black dinner-jacket, plain white pin-tucked shirt and neat, black bow tie. But he was bursting out of the cummerbund, and resembled a piebald barrage-balloon. He looked her up and down appraisingly. "Wow, what a dress! Come with me, you gorgeous thing. Let's grab something to eat." Then he turned to Sam and his friends and grinned, "Have fun on me, boys and girls. That's what parties are for!"

Despite her feeble protestations, Krep bore her away. For a small man, he was very powerful, and he firmly propelled her through the party crowds. She felt it would be unseemly to resist, and anyway, what could happen to her with all these people around? "Come on, precious," he cajoled, "I want you all to myself."

Without letting go of her arm, he whispered something to a convenient waiter, and led her down below to the most beautiful saloon, with chandeliers and *objets d'art*, silk cushions, priceless rugs, and all manner of the most unseamanlike accoutrements she'd ever seen.

"Heavens," she exclaimed, "does this boat ever see the ocean wave?"

"Not often, my sweetheart. But we go out when the sea's flat calm for short trips every now and then, just to keep the engines from seizing, and to air the sails. She's moored here for most of the year. But in the autumn, she follows the warmer weather, and my skipper takes her to the West Indies.

Don't often get time to get out there, though. I just send friends there for various business deals and the like." He motioned her on to a large white sofa, and placed a full glass in her hand.

"Talking about business deals..." Jennifer interrupted, sinking into the plump, silk cushions.

Julius waved his short arms impatiently. "Yes, lovely, I was coming to that. He sat down next to her, and leaning forward and inclining his head towards her, asked, "How would you like to work for me, then? As a sort of personal assistant. I need a quality girl like you to help me conduct my business affairs. Classy bird like you gives me credibility, see?" His moustache rode up at the edges as he smiled at her persuasively.

The waiter came in with a tray of smoked salmon, salads, finely sliced ham with melon, and canapés of caviar, which he quietly laid on the low table, facing the silk sofa on which Krep and Jennifer were sitting. A silver cooler stood close by with the ever-present champagne.

"That's OK. We'll help ourselves." Impatiently Krep waved the young man away, and gestured to Jennifer. "Go on, ducks. Dig in!"

Jennifer was quite ready to eat, and set to with relish, recklessly washing the delicacies down with yet more champagne.

"Good appetite you got there, girl," Krep remarked.

He watched her, fascinated by her almost childlike enthusiasm, and riveted by her looks. Krep had met many beautiful women in his life, but there was something about Jennifer that simply took his breath away. That hair! Clouds of burnished gold! Those beautiful grey eyes that looked straight up into his so sincerely, and gave him their full and earnest attention. He loved the way she hung on to his every word. And he could watch her mouth for ever. The way her lips moved when she talked. He loved her voice, too: classy, yes, but not over-much – just husky and well modulated.

Everything about her sent sweet chords soaring into all his senses. Yes, this girl was a real stunner. She made him weak at the knees. Yet she had a very vulnerable quality about her, a sort of innocence, despite her confident and polished air, that made him all at sixes and sevens. It was ridiculous, but he felt completely lost. She was not in the usual mould at all.

All that being said, he knew he just had to have her. With a helpless and sinking feeling as he felt his baser instincts take over, he launched himself back into his usual line of banter. Force of habit. But so, what the hell, damn it! . . . He was out of control. Come what may, he had to have her! Maybe she'd go along with it. Maybe he'd get lucky. After all, nothing ventured, nothing gained.

"Now," he crooned, "let's stay on the business tack while we eat. What do you think then, Jen? Would you like to work for Julius Krep Enterprises?"

"Well . . ." she said dubiously, shaking back her hair. The movement made her head swim. With a mammoth effort she continued. "Forgive me if this seems dense, but I'm not sure what my duties would be."

Julius edged closer to her, and looked into her eyes compellingly. His eyes were the colour of dark slate, with green flecks around the pupils. Jennifer noted with surprise that they were attractive and expressive. But every now and then there were four of them. God, she thought, I wish I weren't so drunk!

"Sweetie," he continued quietly, "all I need is a girl to keep my businessmen occupied and happy. Good conversation. That sort of thing. You know . . ." He twirled a hand in the air like a conductor leading his orchestra. "Pour the drinks. Look pretty. I'll give you a dress allowance. You can buy whatever you like. Spend what you like, I'm not fussed." He topped her up with champagne, then put his hand on her knee.

Her voice came out rather slurred. "Occupied and happy . . ." she giggled, and studied her glass. "Doing what?"

She took a good slug of champagne, and flopped back into the cushions, not bothering to move his hand. Her head was floating in the clouds somewhere. He seemed to be offering a good deal here.

"Oh, just looking beautiful, like I said before. Improving the scenery a bit." Julius grinned roguishly. Jennifer smiled back at him, noticing through a blur that his teeth were very white. Money for jam, a job like that!

"Fancy an intercourse ciggy?" he joked, reaching beside him and opening a gold cigarette case. Jennifer was too drunk to wince at the cliché.

"Thanks," she said, and lit up. The cigarette had an unusually sweet taste and smell, but she leaned back, drawing heavily on it, relishing the waves of relaxation wafting through her, enjoying the sensation. Life was good, everything seemed tremendous just now. Krep's voice was soothing. His hand was caressing her hair. Suddenly she didn't mind. God, wasn't life just the greatest? Everything was so wonderful. Just wonderful.

"Come with me, sweetness. I've got something for you." His voice caressed her.

Jennifer rose and followed him without a murmur. In fact she couldn't even feel her feet. She was walking on air, as if suspended. What a lovely dream! Obediently, she had taken Krep's hand, and here she was now, in his magnificent stateroom. In the middle of this opulence was a gigantic circular bed with black satin sheets and pillows.

Black satin? Black satin? God, but how appallingly, wonderfully ghastly! She kicked off her shoes and threw herself backwards, giggling, on to the dark, downy softness of the pillows to see what pure hedonism felt like; slithering on the slippery satin, gradually becoming enveloped, imprisoned by glorious, blissful, vulgar luxury. Oh, but she must close her eyes, and sleep and dream for ever!

Krep stood, silently peeling off his clothes, transfixed by the sight of the beautiful acquiescent blonde in her white dress, a vision on black satin, bombed out of her mind, and past caring. He knelt on the bed, naked, and gently pulled the dress down her body, revealing round, firm breasts. He sucked the pink nipples in turn, slid off her brief lace panties, and drew his mouth down her belly to the golden vee of her mound, then to the dark-pink lips, which he flicked and probed insistently with his tongue.

Jennifer gave in to the glorious feeling engulfing her and began to moan and move with a rhythm of her own. She grabbed his head and locked him further to her, thrusting her pelvis more urgently. Her moans grew louder, until she could bear no more and the force of her climax threw her head and shoulders up in a spasm. Then as the agonisingly delicious waves ebbed away, she woke up with a start, opened her eyes and shuddered involuntarily as she saw Krep's glittering eyes, his pomaded hair, his slack lips and chin dripping with her juices, between her widespread legs.

As if completely mesmerised, she stayed rooted as the little man knelt up, whispering, "Now, my lovely, it's my turn!"

Her eyes took in a heavy pot belly, great rolls of flabby white flesh, below which just protruded a purple stubby object, advancing inexorably towards her face. Hell's teeth!!!

Suddenly her stomach lurched into her throat. "Excuse me, I'm going to be sick!" she groaned, hands clapped over her mouth.

With one bound she was off the bed, grabbing her dress, throwing it over her head, and was out of the stateroom, whilst Krep still knelt, paralysed with rage and frustration, looking for all the world like a giant white slug, marooned in the middle of his vast, black satin bed.

Chapter 5

Jennifer could not remember getting off the yacht, or how she got home. But the next morning she had a dreadful head on her, and no shoes with the dress that lay crumpled on the floor. The thought of her escapade with Krep brought bile into her mouth, and she couldn't get the image of his bulging, naked body out of her mind.

That was some cigarette, she recalled. What an idiot she'd been not to cotton on at the time that it was marijuana. That, on top of the champagne she'd swigged, was her undoing. Thank God she'd managed to escape: unfortunately, though, not before she had succumbed partially to Krep's advances. She shuddered at the thought of him greedily sucking her. God, she must have been high! She shook her head to rid herself of the memory. Ah well, so much for getting a job! What now? And so wondering, fell asleep again.

Laura and Caroline, meanwhile, were in the kitchen making breakfast. As Caroline put the old chrome coffee-pot on to the table, Laura heaped several warm croissants on to a large plate. They were both in tee-shirts and shorts, ready for a day at the beach. Laura wore her waist-length hair in a thick plait, and Caroline's curls were caught up in a high pony-tail.

"Vote I take Jennifer a cup of coffee to get the rundown on last night," said Laura, taking a small saucepan of boiling milk off the burner, and pouring it into a jug.

"You'll be lucky if she's awake yet," answered Caroline, filling two mugs with coffee on the worktop beside the cooker.

"Let's finish breakfast and then we'll both take some in for her."

The girls sat down at the kitchen table, dissecting the events of their own evening, which had been spent at an auberge up in the mountains which specialised in spit-roasted lamb. It had been a fun crowd, French and English mixed. Paying no heed to English good manners, the girls dipped their croissants into the milky, aromatic coffee, *à la française*. A very civilised way to start the day!

"I wonder why Jennifer wasn't back as late as she usually is? You'd have thought that sort of scene would be just up her street," remarked Laura, looking at her buttery fingers. She reached for another croissant, and covered it in apricot jam.

"Well, eat up and save her at least one croissant. Let's have the post mortem!" laughed her flatmate, and got up to fetch another mug for Jennifer.

The girls came in silently and put a mug of steaming coffee by the bedside of the prone figure swathed in rumpled sheets. Eliciting no response, they waved a warm croissant under her nose.

Jennifer moaned. "Jesus, leave me alone. I'm in a bad way."

"Not likely," grinned Caroline, shaking her shoulder. "We're here to get the rundown on last night. What happened? Come on, spill the beans!"

"Sit up, Jennifer, don't be a spoil-sport. Tell us all!" cajoled Laura.

This was too much, thought Jennifer. She was really suffering, and all her friends wanted to do was make a joke of it! Talk about adding insult to injury!

"Oh, you heartless bitches!" she groaned, with her eyes shut. "Come to gloat, have you? Jeeez, it was awful. I can't tell you, it's all too bloody revolting."

"Wow, that bad, eh?" they teased.

"Yes, and worse." Her eyes opened slowly, and she took in two grinning faces. They could at least show some sympathy, she thought, clutching her shrieking head. Still, they had brought her breakfast in bed. Maybe they did have a shred of compassion lurking somewhere in their hearts.

Jennifer struggled up on one elbow, grabbed the mug and gulped back her coffee. "Ah . . . that's a bit better. Hand me the croissant. I might get quite human in a minute!"

Laura thoughtfully plumped up the pillows behind Jennifer, who settled back in comfort, coffee in one hand, croissant in the other. The girls then sat on the floor cross-legged, with upturned, expectant faces. Between mouthfuls, a mournful Jennifer then gave them a full account of the evening and its squalid outcome, sparing no detail. Laura and Caro were riveted to the end. That was some party!

"Honestly, what arrogance!" exclaimed Laura, "A blowjob in return for a party invitation! Anyway, he's so repulsive. I ask you!" She got up and sat by Jennifer, taking her hand. "Well, chicken," she murmured kindly, "it rather looks as if you drew a blank last night in your quest for stardom."

"Yeah, looks like it, doesn't it?" replied Jennifer ruefully, reaching for her cigarettes. The pack was empty. "Unless you count my starring role in a porno movie, with Krep's fat mug in my pussy . . . Mademoiselle la Morgan of the matching collar and cuffs, as he so crudely put it. Hell, it's so bloody galling!"

Well, at least he knows you're a genuine blonde now!" grinned Caroline.

"Shut up!" Jennifer snapped, somewhat miffed at such cavalier cynicism, but then started to laugh.

"Honestly, Caroline, isn't that rather beside the point . . ." began Laura indignantly. Then catching her friends' expressions, she fell back on the bed, giggling helplessly, clutching her knees with mirth.

"God, Jen," Laura spluttered, "you're such a clot, and you do ask for trouble sometimes! Ah well, better luck next time, maybe. Come on then, finish your coffee, and we'll bring you another. Then let's all scoot off to the beach. A good dose of swimming and sun will help clear the cobwebs away!"

Laura was right. As it was only May the beach wasn't crowded. The French like the sea to be warm before they'll swim. The English, more stoic and used to the chilly waters surrounding Great Britain, think the Mediterranean in May no hardship at all. The yellow sand stretched in an endless curve, interrupted only by an occasional sprinkling of beach umbrellas and coloured towels. There was nobody in the azure-blue water. For a public beach, it was pretty good, and always clean. Way up at the top of the beach was a rough and ready snack-bar, selling beer, Coke and *croque-monsieurs*. As the girls had already eaten breakfast, they were not likely to use it until much later, maybe for a long, cooling drink.

They laid out their raffia mats, and put up a large, multi-coloured umbrella. They were wearing their bikinis underneath their clothes, so it was just a question of peeling off tee-shirts and shorts. Then liberal helpings of sun-oil were smoothed on to already-tanned bodies.

"Oh boy, what bliss!" sighed Laura, flopping on to her mat. "What is it about good sun that's so relaxing?"

"The warmth seeping into your skin . . . so soothing. Acres of sun-warmed, naked flesh! Mmmmm. Just the smell of Ambre Solaire is enough to evoke all kinds of sensuous memories!" murmured Caroline, stroking oil on to her thighs. Little gold hairs glinted in the sun against her tan.

"Get you!" scoffed Laura.

"Could do with a bit of male talent, though," Jennifer said, scanning the sands over her prone elbows. Then her head flopped down again.

"You'd have thought her tussle with Krep would be enough to put her off men for at least five minutes, wouldn't you?" laughed Caroline, screwing the top on to her Ambre Solaire. She tucked it into her beach-bag and reached for her paperback and sun-glasses.

"Oh, come on!" retorted Jennifer, "Be fair. Krep's not a man. He's a huge creepy slug with a moustache. Anyway, let's not mention him unless you want me to throw up. Talking of men, though, how've you managed to hide from Pierre so successfully, Laura?"

"I might say the same to you of Jean-Claude," murmured Laura, raising her head and squinting across at her. "Fingers crossed, that's all I can say. Let's hope they've both got the message at last. Now, I'm going to take forty winks, and invent a gorgeous man for my dreams. For the moment I really don't want the real thing."

So saying, Laura dropped her flaxen head on to her arms, and closed her eyes. Blissful though the penetrating rays of sun felt on her back and in spite of the idyllic setting, she was unable to relax and switch off completely.

At the pit of her stomach came an empty feeling she couldn't really fathom. She was beginning to miss, really miss, the presence of a man in her life, but was unwilling to admit it. Images of Pierre kept flitting into her mind. Surely she couldn't be missing him; not with the memory of the constant haranguing and sleepless nights still so strongly etched on her brain? And yet . . .

No it wouldn't do to hanker after lost love. Her career had to be her focal point and *raison d'être* now. Things were going so well without him dragging her down. She smacked her small fist into the sand to emphasise her determination, and blinked as some grains flew up and peppered her in the face. "Oh, shit!" she hissed, as she brushed herself off. "Shit to the world."

"Laura!" chided Jennifer, sitting up, and picking up her straw hat. The sun was too hot on the back of her neck, and she still had a headache from last night. "It's not often we hear you swear! You're obviously learning bad habits from the disgraceful company you keep."

"*Touché*, dear heart," came the murmured, sarcastic

reply. "Now let me sleep, and dream of uninhabited desert islands."

Whilst Laura concentrated on thoughts of celibacy and Caroline dug her nose into a book, adjusting the beach umbrella to shade her, Jennifer just mooched; arms wrapped around her legs, knees drawn up under her chin, hat tilted over her nose, as she stared dreamily at the sea. Jennifer was one of those fortunate and rare people who could empty her mind at will when it suited her and just float in a contented void.

The girls left the beach at around four thirty, glowing with well-being from sun and sea. They sauntered back to the Meribel via the boulevard des Moulins, window-shopping and avidly admiring the tempting and expensive array of jewellery and couture – unfortunately way beyond their means.

'One of these days..." murmured Jennifer, gazing into Cartier longingly.

"Huh! Just flutter your eyelashes and whistle, and Krep will buy you anything!" said Caroline.

"Ah, yes, if only it were not his whistle I'd have to blow: again and again!" she tittered, wrinkling her nose with distaste.

Laura grinned, "Everything has its price, and you know what they always say: there's no such thing as a free lunch!"

Back at No. 613 the girls hung their bikinis out to dry, showered, fell over each other in the small bathroom, and tripped over the profusion of shoes and clothes Jennifer had pulled out with her usual indecision at what to wear. She was standing naked and dripping in the middle of the bedroom floor mulling over the problem when Caroline came through.

"Hmmm. Nice pair of titties," she said, tweaking a breast as she pushed past.

"Hey, hands off, you lezzie moo. You've seen it all before!" giggled Jennifer, unabashed by the familiarity. "Now... Shall I wear pink, or blue?"

The phone rang amidst all the chaos and Caroline snatched up the receiver. "*Oui!*" she shouted. Her eyebrows went up in mock despair, as she listened to what sounded like a tirade of abuse. "*D'accord, monsieur. D'accord. Oui, maintenant. Je le ferai toute-de-suite,*" and she flung down the receiver.

"Bikinis on the balcony. The concierge says no laundry on balconies – terms of the lease! I ask you!" She disappeared to the sitting-room and made her way to the balcony in her bra and pants, slid open the french doors and removed the offending articles.

But, just as she was turning away, a flash of light caught her eye from the balcony opposite. Suddenly feeling vulnerable in her state of undress, she quickly dashed inside. Normally she would have investigated further, but even from behind the comparative privacy of the tinted glass doors, she still felt exposed. Somehow, she had the prickling, uncomfortable feeling that someone had been watching her.

Caroline returned to the bathroom with the swimwear. She had a worried frown on her face.

"What's up?" asked Laura, taking the bikinis and hanging them over the shower-rail. "You look a bit pale."

"Well, forgive me if this seems dramatic or bizarre, but just now when I was out on the balcony, I got a strong creepy feeling someone was spying on me through binoculars."

Laura's eyes widened. "What? A peeping Tom, you mean? Good heavens, how weird. Are you sure?"

"Well, yes... Almost. I guess not one hundred per cent sure, but I sort of sensed that someone was watching us. I saw something flash like light catching on glass." Caroline scratched her head in puzzlement. "It wasn't a very nice feeling."

"Let's hope it's nothing more sinister than some drip looking for thrills. We'd better not walk around in the buff near the windows, hey?" suggested Laura sagely. She leaned towards the mirror, and carefully applied her mascara, with the tip of her tongue between her teeth.

"Perhaps you're right." Caroline looked thoughtful. "Maybe it's just a one-off and nothing to worry about. Now, about this evening's arrangements, are we booked for the Poisson d'Or at Menton with the usual noisy crowd for tonight?"

"Yep," said Laura, replacing the black wand and taking out a lipstick. "Should be the usual bag of laughs. We're going on to that night-club on the headland afterwards. You know, the one on the beach, with the fishing nets and the lobster-pot lights."

"Great. Another late night, then! I'd better get my skates on and tart myself up." Caroline headed off to her bedroom, smacking Jennifer's bare bottom as she passed through again. "Come on, Lady Godiva. Clothes on. We're off in five minutes."

"Whaat?" shrieked Jennifer, who had made no progress at all. "But I'm nowhere near ready!"

"Tough!"

The door bell rang as Caroline crossed the hallway to her own room. She opened the door a fraction. "Jean-Claude!" she exclaimed. "What are you doing here?"

"I've come to see Jennifer, of course. Well, aren't you going to let me in?"

"I can't! I'm not dressed."

"Et alors? Qu'est-ce que ça peut me faire?" he retorted with a grin on his face.

"You might not mind, but I do. So wait a minute while I throw on a dress. Hey, wait!"

But Jean-Claude was already inside the hallway and making his way to the bedroom door. He opened it with a flourish, gazing with hunger at the still-naked Jennifer standing in the middle of the room. His sudden appearance in a smart blazer and slacks took her totally by surprise, and she remained speechless with dismay. Jean-Claude was not a welcome sight. She'd been looking forward to a relaxed evening with her friends. Now here he was, all dressed up and deciding otherwise!

"Well, I'm glad to see you're prepared for me!" he grinned, and strode towards her, urgently unzipping his fly and pushing himself up inside her before she could resist. Reacting too late, she angrily tried to push him off, but he clamped his hands hard to her buttocks, rooting her to the spot. She realised that the more she wriggled, the more the pompous Frenchman would think she was enjoying it. Damn him. She punched his shoulder ineffectually, but he just laughed in her face. It seemed she couldn't win.

"You shit," she hissed quietly. "Get off me! Laura's just through there in the bathroom."

"*Et alors?* This won't take more than a minute. My need for you is too great."

Squeezing her slender flanks, he thrust against her with long hard strokes as they stood locked together, and then groaned seconds later as he spurted hot and copiously inside her. As she felt him grow weak, she angrily unclenched his hands from her behind, clawing him with her long, painted nails.

"You shit! You conniving, rotten bastard!" she shouted as he pulled out of her. "The last of the great French red-hot lovers. Fuck you!"

"I just did," he grinned, zipping his trousers.

"Call that fucking? Big deal! Much ado about ten seconds of nothing!"

"I'll make it up to you later, *ma belle*," he answered. With a rueful grin on his face, he studied the backs of his hands, which were well-lacerated. Bloody well serve the arrogant bastard right, thought Jennifer.

Then his voice took on a crooning tone. "*Ma petite Anglaise*, I can never resist you. Come back to me. Stay with Jean-Claude. I need you. I want you back," he wheedled, pressing his handsome face close to hers and twining his fingers in her hair. Jennifer studied him thoughtfully. He did have his good points. He certainly scored high in the looks department. His smile, when he remembered to, was devastating. He was just over six feet tall, broad-shouldered and had golden-brown eyes and tumbling chestnut curls. It was a pity they didn't get on. Still, his good looks and lithe, tanned body were infinitely preferable to slug-like Krep's.

"You'll do for the moment," she said coolly, pushing him out of the room. "Now let me freshen up and get dressed."

From the bathroom Laura called, "Hey, what's going on? You and Jean-Claude a numero again?"

As if to confirm her surmisal, Jennifer appeared in the doorway, dishevelled, naked, and somewhat flushed. "I suppose you could say that," she admitted, slightly abashed. "Anyway, he's much better looking than Krep, and it'll be a convenient excuse for the moment to keep the little lecher at bay."

"Well, do hurry up, or we'll be late," Laura said, spraying herself liberally with Ma Griffe. She was wearing tight, black crèpe trousers and a silver halter-neck top, showing off a hint of cleavage and smooth, tanned shoulders. "I presume lover-boy has invited himself along for tonight, has he?"

"Yeah," Jennifer said, a laconic smile on her face, "It'd be a bit much to slope off now leaving his passion to cool, when he's still burning with ardour for me! Anyway, I have some unfinished business for later."

"Nympho!" laughed Laura. "I'll get him a drink while we wait for you then. Hurry now, won't you?"

Jennifer had a quick wash, ran a brush through her hair and drenched herself with Laura's scent. Then she picked up the first dress she could find amongst the many she'd thrown on the bed earlier, a baby-pink mini, and flung it over her head.

Meanwhile Laura made her way to the balcony where a smiling Jean-Claude was drinking wine with Caroline.

"Oh, I see you've already got a drink!" she remarked sociably. "Oh Lord, there goes the doorbell again!" Laura walked quickly to the door, her high heels clicking on the tiled floor.

"*Bonsoir, mademoiselle. Des fleurs pour vous. Voulez vous signer, s'il vous plaît?*"

She signed the delivery note and, puzzled, pulled the card out of the small envelope in the bouquet, which was of pink orchids and bud roses:

"Jennifer, just a small token of my continuing esteem for you. No hard feelings. Love, J.K."

"Well, well!" she exclaimed, going through to the bedroom where she found Jennifer dressed and ready at last.

"These are for you." Laura said, handing over the magnificent blooms and the card.

Jennifer, eyes wide with curiosity, took the flowers, and after admiring them, read the card. She was amazed that Krep was still pursuing her after she had snubbed him so patently.

"Golly," she remarked. "A persistent man. He's obviously really got the hots if he's not even annoyed that I threw up all over his carpet and ran out on him last night!"

Laura smiled and winked at her. "Play your cards right and you'll be the next Mrs Krep."

"Not likely!" she retorted, wrinkling her nose. "I don't fancy him one bit, rich or not! Anyhow, I'll bet you anything he's firmly married to a nice Jewish momma back home in London. His sort always are. It's tough luck that millionaires are always so bloody unattractive, too."

Jean-Claude suddenly appeared in the doorway. His mouth was smiling, but his eyes were hard beads of suspicion. "*Alors, qu'est-ce qui se passe?*" he demanded. "*Ah, des fleurs!* For my beautiful and faithful little fiancée. Who are they from, my fickle *allumeuse?*"

Oh God! Here he was again, with his accusatory manner. The bouquet really was none of his business. Why couldn't he just leave well alone? Jennifer glared at him coldly, resenting his possessive manner.

"Mind your own beeswax, you nosey parker. Just concentrate on being nice to me this evening, and count yourself lucky I'm still speaking to you."

Jean-Claude had parked his grey Peugeot saloon right by the entrance of the Meribel, and made towards it, but Jennifer exclaimed, "Oh, let's not take your boring old car, Jean-Claude! Laura, can't we take the Spitfire on a lovely evening like this?"

"Only if you let me drive!" said the chauvinistic Frenchman, not relishing the idea of being passenger to any female, however attractive! Laura was happy to comply. The concierge looked on disapprovingly as the three girls and one male squashed into the open red sports car. They were all giggling and shouting as Jean-Claude revved off into a loud racing start for extra effect.

Jennifer looked at his handsome profile, the hazel curls whipping around his temples in the breeze, and felt a rare glow of desire for him. "I quite like you when you're fun, J-C," she remarked. "Why can't you be like this more often?"

"Because most of the time you're such a bitch," he retorted sulkily.

"Well, let's try to enjoy ourselves this evening? OK?"

Jean-Claude smiled at her beautiful face. She was irresistible; he just wished she would be more compliant. Why couldn't she be like the French girls, who were brought up to do as they were told? *Mon Dieu*, but Jennifer was wayward; for ever distracting him from his accountancy studies. Always pushing him away, and then enticing him back with her looks and sexy body!

"*Oui, mademoiselle*," he sighed, "I'll do my best to please you, difficult as you are."

The dinner at the Poisson d'Or was fun, and very noisy. The restaurant was on the main promenade at Menton, opposite the beach. It was brightly lit, with long, crowded tables

62

crammed close together all the length of its glassed-in front. It was all the waiters could do to squeeze in between everyone for the orders, but they were used to the struggle and enjoyed the good-natured heckling of their clientèle. The Poisson d'Or was very popular with the young, because it was not expensive and wild behaviour was not frowned upon. In fact, the waiters rather encouraged the raucous atmosphere by shouting at all and sundry and singing very loudly. It was not at all the place to choose for a romantic tête-à-tête, but for a young and extrovert group who wanted fun and laughter, it was the ideal venue.

Jennifer had far too much to drink, and ended up dancing down the long table with a rose between her teeth. Jean-Claude had tried to remonstrate with her, but in the end gave way with a gallic shrug, reasoning that one day she'd realise the error of her ways and grow up. He'd forgotten it was her very wildness that had attracted and excited him in the first place, and continued to drive him mad with desire. The trouble was, he could never contain himself with her in bed, and always came far too soon. Such bliss, so cruelly and prematurely ended!

He watched her as she writhed gracefully and sensuously down the table, barefoot in her short, clinging dress, her golden hair rising up in a cloud, framing the doll-like face and pouting mouth – seemingly oblivious to the sensation she was causing in the restaurant. The waiters looked on, entranced, shouting encouragement whilst flitting about with enormous platters of sea-food held aloft. The stocky, white-haired patron didn't object. The unscheduled cabaret was pleasing to the eye, so it was good for the *ambiance*.

The patron then flourished a large bottle of good Cognac at the group, smiling, "*Alors, à votre santé!*"

Caroline pulled him into a chair and he poured them all small measures of brandy on-the-house, whilst she and Laura charmed him, and he tried to look up Jennifer's dress.

"Her knickers are pink to match her mini," explained Caroline helpfully, reading his mind. The patron laughed wickedly, shaking his head, "Ah, you English, *alors hein?*"

The light mood of bonhomie continued as the contingent of friends poured out of their cars and into the Al Fresco. The night-club was aptly named, as a large part of it was open to the sky. The added effect of fishing nets and lobster-pot lights slung high across the dance floor from corner poles, gave it an atmosphere of intimacy. It was already very crowded. The group managed to get an obliging waiter to push a few free tables together for the dozen or so of them, and take their order speedily and good-naturedly.

"Hey, Caro, look, there's Terry with some friends. Hey, Terry!" Jennifer waved, and Terry responded with a delighted smile. But Jean-Claude curtly pushed her hand down.

"No! Don't make a spectacle of yourself. It's bad form to wave and shout at men." Jean-Claude glared at her petulantly.

"Oh, you spoil-sport," she flung back angrily. "What a dull old fart you are! We're here to have fun, aren't we?"

Terry was already making his way over, bringing two male companions, both flaxen-haired and deeply tanned. The men were unbelievably good-looking, conservatively dressed in light shirts and dark slacks, and towered over Terry in his orange shirt and puce flares. The taller of the two was classically handsome, with a full mouth, and straight thick hair that flopped forward on to his face. His eyes, of the palest blue, were enormous and very soulful. The other one had the same shade of flaxen hair but wavy, and curling in wings over his ears.

"Hi, there, lovers!" Terry drawled, waving the ubiquitous cigarette-holder. "We've got buckets of champagne we'd love to share with you. And we've got no one to dance with. Can't dance with my buddies here, now can I? We'd get thrown out!" He giggled conspiratorially.

"Push your table over and join us, do! And bring the champers; I'm sure we can force ourselves to help you drink it," urged Caroline.

Jean-Claude glowered as Terry made his way back to supervise the table-moving operation. Actually, all he did was wave his cigarette-holder around ineffectually, while his companions pushed the table across and ferried over the champagne.

"You English are like sheep," Jean-Claude grumbled, "always crowding together, always acting the fool and drinking too much."

"Oh, do shut up, J-C. You're being a bore. Anyway, idiot, Terry's American, and he's also a *pédé*, and so are his friends probably, so you needn't be jealous if we dance with them, which I intend to do, as you always refuse."

Jean-Claude threw his hands in the air. *"Mon Dieu!* And now I have to be seen in public, consorting with *pédérastes en plus, hein?"*

Jennifer didn't bother to dignify the complaint with a reply, but got up to offer Terry a dance.

"Darling, but of course! On condition my friends can dance with Laura and Caroline."

"Delighted!" the two girls chorused.

Caroline nabbed the taller man, and the other one took Laura's hand. The three couples made their way to the floor, leaving the sullen Frenchman glowering into his drink, to the strains of the Beatles' 'I Wanna Hold Your Hand'.

"What a fabulous dancer you are!" Laura exclaimed after a few minutes, when the music quietened down into 'Let's Go to San Francisco'.

"You're pretty fabulous yourself, darling."

The voice was very upper-crust English. The eyes were an unusual turquoise, very striking in the deeply tanned face, and his nose was aristocratic, with a high, pronounced bridge to it. He had a devastating smile and a strong chin with a cleft in it.

What a shame he's camp, she reflected.

"What's your name?" he continued, "Mine's Quintin Farmiloe, by the way, and Terry's friend's called Tab. Very peculiar names these Americans have. Apparently he's in films."

"Looks just like the famous Tab Hunter to me. Probably is him, knowing Terry. Most of his chums are in showbiz."

Quintin smiled artlessly. "How come you know Terry? Are you an actress? You've certainly got all the attributes." He pulled her closer to him, and putting his face next to hers, whispered, "And you still haven't told me your name."

"No," Laura laughed. "I'm not an actress. Not at all! I'm a PA to the investment manager of a shipping and oil company in Monaco. You know, big portfolios of stocks and shares. And my name's Laura Forsythe. As for Terry, everyone knows him. He's always throwing parties and inviting the world!"

"That sounds a very high-powered job for a gorgeous little thing like you!" The turquoise eyes danced as he lowered his voice seductively. "Would you like to invest in me, sweetheart? I'm opening a night-club in Monte-Carlo soon."

Laura was surprised at Quintin's flirtatious manner and didn't know what to make of him. "Not quite our scene, I'm afraid," she said, drawing away from him and studying his face intently. "We're more into huge blocks of companies, and dollar bonds worth millions."

Quintin laughed and his face lit up mischievously. God, but he was magnificent when he smiled.

"It wasn't finance I was after," he grinned, "I've got all the money I need for this venture." Then he eyed her up and down with a warm and sleepy expression, taking in the glistening, honeyed shoulders and the hint of cleavage revealed by her brief, halter top. "And the only asset stripping I'm into is that of the female form. Now, yours is quite something!"

"But I thought . . ." said Laura, flustered and quite taken aback.

"Reckoned I was queer, did you?" Quintin shot back quickly. "To tell you the truth, I probably would be if the world weren't so full of irresistible women! I just like sex – lots and lots of it, as long as it's with someone gorgeous who's as greedy and agile as me!"

Farmiloe grinned lasciviously, running his eyes down her body again. God, but this little blonde was too much! Rather in the mould of Princess Grace, really: stunning in the classical sense. What beautiful bonework she had; high cheekbones, and a short, rather imperious nose over a pretty mouth, with a well-defined Cupid's bow. And those eyes! A clear blue with such an intense and intelligent expression. All those attributes, together with a simply glorious body! Suddenly he felt a tremendous urge to touch her all over, to run his fingers through that silky, flaxen sheet of hair and mess it up; to dive headlong into that irresistible pool of perfection and make great waves and ripples! He had to make a conscious effort to stop his body responding to his imagination, but was unable to hide the expression on his face.

Now she was looking back at him, shaking her head slowly, obviously recognising his train of thought. She smiled, "Wonderful setting this, isn't it?" by way of changing the subject.

Quintin took a deep breath to recover his composure. "Ah, but you wait till you see my night-club! It'll be *the* place to hang out. I'll invite you to the opening night, shall I? There's nothing like beautiful birds for pulling in the punters. Pity you're already spoken for, or I'd offer you a job as manageress right now!"

Imagine what a draw she'd be, a girl like Laura. He'd have punters flocking in by the hundreds! What a shame she seemed the studious sort. Never mind, Monte-Carlo was doubtless full of beautiful girls like her, he thought, casting his eyes around. What a change from the over-made-up London dollybirds, with their sticklike bodies, white lips and painted lashes. He'd had his fill of them. London bored him. He suddenly needed to get out. He was in a rut and he had to escape the ratrace whilst he was still young enough to take the plunge. He was not quite thirty yet. A good time for change. He craved sun, sea and total glamour. He'd heard from the grapevine that Club X in Monte-Carlo had closed down, and had flown out in great excitement on the spur of the moment. He made an offer, put his London club on the market, sold it immediately, and now, *voilà*, here he was.

"Not me, thanks," he heard Laura say. "I have ambitious long-term plans. But I know exactly who would be interested! The one who's dancing with Terry. My flatmate, Jennifer. She's out of work, and loves the night life!"

His eyes focused on Terry's dance partner. Yes! Now she was really something, too, and how she could dance!

"Wow!" he whistled. "What a delicious dolly! What a mover! She's stunning, too. Funny, you're both very alike, and yet somehow different."

Jennifer and Terry, who were about the same height, were performing a mock-solemn balletic *pas de deux* on the dance floor, without turning a hair.

"I know. People always say that," Laura replied smiling at their antics. "Some even think we're sisters. But when you get to know us properly, we're not the same at all. It's just that we've both got long blonde hair, and blue eyes. Except hers are more grey really, and my hair's slightly lighter, and dead straight."

"Two stunning blondes. A recipe for disaster – and loads of fun, too. I'll bet you lead everyone a merry dance."

Quintin squeezed her hand and his eyes crinkled teasingly at the corners. Laura was so earnest: so innocent. He'd really enjoy leading her astray, and she'd probably thank him for it one day! After all, what good was a career to a woman, compared to having fun whilst she was still young and beautiful?

"Jennifer, yes. Me, no," she replied breathlessly. "I'm too busy concentrating on my work. No time for men."

"I can't believe that! What a waste!" he retorted, deciding to tease her. "What about each other, then? Ever shared a bed with her? Have you any idea what a turn-on that can be?"

Laura's bright blue eyes widened with surprise. Quintin's voice rose with excitement at the thought of the two girls making love, their long blonde hair in disarray, their willowy tanned bodies intertwined . . .

"Quintin!" exclaimed Laura in disapproval at his outrageous suggestion. "What a disgrace you are! I'm shocked."

Her face was a picture. She was so easy to wind up. "You're really frightfully English, aren't you?" he went on, baiting her. "Oooh, how I'd love to see you all flushed and dishevelled with sex, begging for more, instead of the cool ice-maiden you pretend to be."

"Enough, you naughty boy!" Laura admonished, blushing. Then, recovering her composure, she became businesslike. "Look, do you want me to introduce you to Jennifer? I can arrange for you two to meet at a more appropriate time, if you like. Not right now. She's dancing and unlikely to be in a business frame of mind. In any case, she's got a sulky and jealous boyfriend with his beady eye on her at the moment. Let's go back to our table and you can give me your number. I'll get her to call you if you're serious."

OK, Quintin reflected, he might have got nowhere with Laura, but it was an evening well-spent if Jennifer agreed to be manageress at his new club. She was just the ticket. His disco in London was renowned for its success. It was always packed. He'd sold it for a bomb to a colleague. All he needed was the same formula transported to the Riviera, and he was set for another killing! Quickly, he wrote his number on the back of an Al Fresco card, and handed it to Laura, smiling warmly into her eyes.

"You're absolutely divine," he said, "but I really must be off.

I'm a bit jet-lagged, so I think I ought to scoot and catch up on my beauty sleep. Thanks for dancing with me, and promise me we'll do it again at my own place, OK?"

Quintin kissed her on both cheeks, and squeezed her tiny waist. Then he waved goodbye to Terry and Tab, blew a kiss to the others and left.

Laura watched him go, smiling at the memory of his outrageous remarks as she toyed with her glass. He was undeniably attractive. Disconcertingly so. She could feel her vows of celibacy waning by the second. But no, she reasoned. Any woman getting involved with him would be courting disaster. Quintin was the archetypal lovable rogue.

Laura glanced round and decided it would be diplomatic to humour Jean-Claude, so she negotiated her way down the row of chairs, sliding into the one next to him. "*Alors, Jean-Claude. Tu ne danses pas?*"

"*Mais si!*" he replied enthusiastically, and to her surprise, hoisted her to her feet and led her to the floor. The music had slowed to a romantic ballad, and he folded both arms around the small of her back, pulling her very close. "*Ça t'ennuit pas de danser le slow avec moi?*"

"No," she replied in English. "I don't mind dancing the *slow* with you." It felt strange and yet familiar to be in a Frenchman's arms again. There was a faint smell of Gauloises about him, redolent of Pierre. She shivered.

"Do you think Jennifer will get annoyed?" he asked hopefully, breaking the mood.

As if Jennifer would care! Poor deluded Jean-Claude! He was in a bad way with his infatuation.

"Jean-Claude!" Laura laughed, "Knowing Jennifer, she probably won't even notice!"

He lapsed into moody silence, and put his cheek on Laura's hair, enjoying the silky feel and fresh smell of it and the warmth of her against him. This little girl would be a lot less trouble than Jennifer, he thought. She was the serious type. Not a flirt like his wayward fiancée. But it was Jennifer's body he wanted in his arms. He sighed. Life was never easy.

The couple continued to dance for a while without speaking, each wrapped in their own thoughts. Then suddenly when Terry and Jennifer passed close by, Jean-Claude rather ungraciously lunged away from Laura and seized his reluctant girlfriend. It didn't bother Laura half as much as Jennifer, who now looked very truculent.

"Come on then, darling!" Terry laughed, taking Laura's hand and whirling her round. "Let's leave the love birds to it while we whoop it up!"

Everyone loved Terry for his generosity and disarming friendliness. He drew hordes of attractive people round him, and threw his money around with reckless abandon. Unfortunately, he had never learned to recognise the hangers-on and freeloaders who shamelessly took advantage of him. His real friends loved him for himself, his sincerity and sheer exuberance.

"Are you having a lovely time, dear heart?" Terry asked Laura, smiling into her eyes. "You look simply glorious. Honestly. I wish I could wear a frock. I'd really go to town!" He brushed at his eyelashes with the back of his finger, and fluttered them dramatically. "I'd drip with diamonds, and teeter on glorious Italian stilettos, and spend my life in the beauty parlour getting beautiful men to massage me and do my hair. What a life!"

"Terry, darling, you're such a card!" she laughed. "What's wrong with women? Have you ever tried one?"

"Dearest lover, there's *nothing* wrong with women. They're fucking gorgeous. It's just that I want to *be* one, not *have* one. Don't get me wrong. I love women. I adore them, love their company, adore to go shopping with them. Tell you what, I'll buy you a frock tomorrow if you want; shall we do that?"

"Clot! Tomorrow's Sunday!"

71

"Whoops!" he said, flicking his hand downwards, limp-wristed. "And so it is. Let's take a rain check. Oooh, how I love this song. It's so-o-o- sexy." Terry shut his eyes and pouted his lips, making Laura giggle. "Oooh," his voice went falsetto, "smooch with me, dear heart. Let me put my cheek next to yours and make Tab jealous!"

Laura laughed again, and gave Terry a resounding kiss on his cheek. "Come on, Terry, I need a rest, and I'm thirsty. Let's go and attack the champagne."

They manoeuvred their way back through the dancers to their table, where Terry continued to amuse everyone around him. Laura sat back in the shadows watching the dance floor, envious of the thronging couples swaying languorously and lovingly to the music – and found herself missing Pierre.

She knew it was silly, but she couldn't help it. Sometimes all the good memories came flooding back and filled her with nostalgic regret. How she wished things could have worked out, that he could have lived up to her romantic ideal. If only he had been less possessive, less disapproving: made an effort to understand and admire her ambition. Pierre had none at all. He was perfectly content to be a policeman for the rest of his life; pounding the same pavements, in the same town, with the same colleagues. He neither wanted, nor sought promotion.

The frustration he doubtless felt at her being more successful, more intelligent, and far better educated than he was must have filled him with helpless rage. Hence the violence, the only way Pierre knew to assert his power – through superior physical strength. Laura had to admit she had not been perfect either, but Pierre had been so wrong to put all the blame at her door.

She sighed. It was hopeless, really, to have let it all drag on for so long. The only part of the relationship that had been good was the physical side. That part of their life had been wonderful. She missed it so much. Suddenly the vivid memory of his body on hers overwhelmed her. Low down inside her came a warm rush of feeling and a dull, sweet ache of longing.

Laura shivered involuntarily and told herself not to be silly. It wasn't Pierre himself she missed as much as the actual physical presence of a man, of affection, tenderness and romance. Pierre was in the past now, and belonged there for good.

Chapter 6

It was three o'clock in the morning by the time Jean-Claude and the three girls got back to the Meribel. The key scrunching in the lock of No. 613 seemed incredibly loud in the silent and dark building, causing explosions of drunken giggles and exaggerated shushings, as they all tip-toed into the flat. Caroline stumbled and dropped the keys on to the tiled floor in the hallway with a dreadful metallic crash, and was rewarded by shrieks of laughter.

"*Oo, là là. Ces sales étrangers!*" wailed up a voice from the flat below.

"Ssshh. That silly old biddy from downstairs has woken up," giggled Jennifer. "God! I wish she'd wear earplugs or something. These bloody mosaic floors! Every sound carries."

"All right, then, let's take our shoes off at least, so we don't wake the whole world!" said Laura sensibly.

Still giggling, but quietly, they all slipped their shoes off and left them lying on the hall floor.

"Anyone for coffee?" asked Laura.

Jean-Claude looked impatiently at Jennifer, lust written all over his face. "Not for me, *merci*," he said pointedly.

He was in a hurry to get her into bed, but as he'd been annoying her all evening, she purposely ignored him and brushed past him into the kitchen, where Caroline was putting the kettle on.

Jean-Claude followed her, remonstrating quietly, but she replied airily, "I'm not turfing Laura out of her bed just to accommodate you. Anyway, you're pissed, you silly sod."

Not only pissed, but a dead bore. Jean-Claude glared, his gold eyes like torches, and then lapsed into a sulk.

"Listen, dafthead," said Caroline kindly, misreading the situation, "you and Jean-Claude can have my room. I'll bunk up with Laura."

Oh, Caroline! Why did she have to be so bloody good-natured? Jennifer could hardly wriggle out of her well-meant offer without seeming ungracious! Now she was stuck with Jean-Claude all night, and probably for the rest of the weekend too. Damn and blast!

"Right, coffees all round?" Jennifer said brightly, hiding her irritation. She noticed that Jean-Claude had lost his glower now. In fact, he was looking distinctly smug.

"OK, then. I'll have a quick one!" he said amiably.

"Isn't that the usual story?" Jennifer smiled through gritted teeth. The girls fought to keep straight faces, but the subtlety was lost on the Frenchman.

Jean-Claude gulped back his coffee. His hand crept up Jennifer's thigh, but she pushed it away irritably. He could bloody well wait. It was amazing how long she could make a coffee last, when she wanted to. Then she deliberately embroiled herself in a long conversation with Laura and Caroline on English politics. With any luck he might fall asleep at the table!

Some hope!

"*Alors – tu viens, cherie?*" he murmured eventually, when he saw she had at last drained her mug, and the conversation was flagging. He got up rather too hurriedly, and made his way to Caroline's bedroom.

"Nighty night, *mes amies!*" sighed Jennifer to her flatmates, her eyes raised to heaven in mock martyrdom, adding *sotto voce*, "I'm off like a lamb to the slaughter!"

Laura laughed. "Huh! I seem to recall that earlier on you were boasting about unfinished business!"

"Well, a lady can change her mind, can't she? After all, it's a woman's prerogative, and all that jazz." And with that, she left the room.

It was ironic that Jennifer, who was in a bad mood and feeling no desire, was treated for once to a long and tender bout of love-making. This was doubtless because Jean-Claude's earlier emission had taken the edge off his usual urgency, and drink had slowed his reflexes. She was all confused again about her feelings. When he was like this, she still fancied him, and enjoyed his body. If only he weren't so cloying and possessive the rest of the time! He stifled her with his narrow outlook, his insistence on marriage. She couldn't envisage spending the rest of her days with an accountant and his boring family.

Jennifer wanted too much, too quickly. A life of glamour and wild parties. Wealth and luxury. Yet her restless search for adventure had only yesterday led her into the revolting scenario on Krep's yacht. She shuddered at the memory of his whale-like body. A high price to pay to satisfy her ambitions. What a contrast between the latter and the handsome young Frenchman now cradling her tenderly in the small bed! But fancying Jean-Claude occasionally was no compensation for her boredom with him the rest of the time! She really ought to ditch him, and move on to greener pastures

But, in her usual fashion when everything got too complicated, Jennifer emptied her mind and drifted off to sleep like a contented cat, so putting off any decisions until the morning . . . or maybe next week.

Jean-Claude, meanwhile remained wakeful till nearly dawn, his head full of plans for their future, his heart full of ambitious dreams. From time to time he looked down at Jennifer's sleeping and peaceful face, all wilfulness gone. He wished that she could always be this vulnerable and childlike, and he the masterful husband he truly believed he could be.

Nobody got up until mid-morning on Sunday, except Jean-Claude, who had to get back home for an outing with his parents to see cousins at St Paul de Vence. Jennifer was relieved to see him go. She had been dreading the possibility of lunch with his colourless parents, making stilted conversation. They were not keen on the idea of *une anglaise* as a prospective daughter-in-law, and would have thrown up their hands in horror if they actually knew what a wild number she was! She tittered to herself as she mentally pictured what the looks on their faces would have been if they'd seen her dancing on the table last night. What a hoot!

Jennifer lay back with her elbows behind her head, reliving the events of the previous evening. She was still giggling as Caroline entered the room.

"Well, what are you grinning at? Can I have my bed back now, please?"

"*May I!* Please, Caroline, get your grammar right."

"Well, of all the ungrateful b..." Caroline began, but Jennifer smartly threw her pillow at Caroline.

Couldn't a girl come into her own bedroom without being attacked? Jennifer was a cheeky swine. Caroline hefted the pillow back, laughing.

Jennifer pulled a face. "Don't be cruel to girls with hangovers!"

"You started it!" retorted Caroline, hands on hips. "Get out of my bed, right now!"

Jennifer's bottom lip came out in a mock pout. "You really ought to be feeling sorry for me. Not only did Jean-Claude keep proposing this morning, but he was really randy last night, just as I wasn't in the mood!"

"That makes a change. You're usually like a cat on heat."

"Shut up, you old cow!"

"Charming! Well, when's the wedding then?" asked Caroline teasingly, sitting down on the bed. That was one sure way to wind Jennifer up.

"Never. I'm right off the idea. Imagine – he suggested moving in with his parents while he finishes his accountancy course." Jennifer punched the pillow in disgust. "Lord, what a nightmare – what a recipe for immediate divorce! His mother can't stand me, and his boring old fart of a father keeps looking at my tits."

"I think I get the picture! It's not my idea of a way to start married life."

Jennifer pulled a face. "Hand me my ciggies, Caro. And how about that lovely coffee I can smell brewing? I need sympathy."

Jennifer was pushing her luck now. Caroline held up an admonishing finger. "Sympathy you can have. A servant I draw the line at. Get your own ciggies and get your bum out of my bed." Then she wrinkled her nose and stuck out her tongue. "You can change the sheets whilst you're at it too, seeing what you were up to last night!"

Jennifer groaned and made heavy weather of fishing for her clothes from the floor. She found her cigarettes and lighter and lit up. Throwing her dress over her shoulder with an exaggerated flourish, and wearing it like a stole, she strutted out of the room, naked – delicately holding her shoes aloft by their straps in one hand, cigarette in the other.

"Hey! Remember the peeping Tom. You're going to make his day!" called Caroline.

"Oh, sod the Bin Rat!"

"Bin Rat?" asked Caroline, puzzled.

"The rat with the bins. Geddit, slowcoach?"

"Oh, very clever! I didn't know a dummy like you was capable of such wit," Caroline teased. "And you forgot your knickers and the sheets, you lazy moo."

But Jennifer, framed in the doorway, stuck out her bottom, wiggled it, tossed her head, and made off towards the kitchen. Lucky old her, to have a bum she could wiggle with no wobble. Sick-making! Caroline grinned fondly. Jennifer always succeeded in getting a laugh, in spite of being a pain.

"Hey!" Caroline shouted at her retreating backview. "Do

me a favour. Don't forget those sheets, huh? And while you're at it, take your dress and shoes back to your room. Otherwise they'll be in the kitchen for a week."

"Nag, nag, nag. I might as well be with J-C!" grumbled Jennifer, but complied good-naturedly.

A few minutes later, Jennifer came back into the kitchen wearing an embroidered silk kimono. The coffee had finished percolating, and Caroline was heating milk on the stove.

"Mmmmm – what a wonderful smell," said Jennifer. "Where's the bacon and eggs?"

Caroline shook a fist at her. "If I had something to hand, I'd throw it at you."

"Where's Laura?" asked Jennifer, plonking herself down at the formica table.

Caroline picked up the coffee-pot and turned towards the table. "Washing her hair."

"I didn't hear the shower."

"Well, maybe she's sitting on the loo now! How should I know?" She poured hot milk into three mugs.

"Throw me some coffee then, Caro," Jennifer entreated. "It smells too good to resist a second longer."

Caroline bowed and scraped like a servant, crossing her eyes comically *"Voilà, mamzelle!* And *voulez-vous un* peeled grape with it?"

"Who's demanding a peeled grape, then?" asked Laura, drifting in with her waist-length hair soaking wet. "Not our Lady Muck, the randy rose dancer?" She smiled a thanks at Caroline, picking up her coffee from the worktop.

"What's this then? A get-Jennifer day? Are you two sulking because you had a loverless night?"

Laura giggled wickedly, and drew up a chair. "Not everyone has sex at the top of their menu like you, Miss Morgan. 'Our hungry Miss Morgan must have an organ.' Sounds like a good lyric for a song, doesn't it!"

"Oh, do shut up," pouted Jennifer. "What a beast you are,

Miss Goody-goody Forsythe. Just because you've forsworn males for all of five minutes!"

"Now then, will a delicious *pain au chocolat* each stop us all sparring?" Caroline waved a fat brown-paper bag under their noses, and greedy hands snatched at the contents. "What shall we do on this auspicious Sunday?" she asked.

"Why auspicious?" they demanded, sinking their teeth into the buttery, melting pastry.

"Because Jennifer is reconciled with her lover, and Laura has lasted at least two whole weeks without Pierre."

Laura laughed, but Jennifer protested, "Hey, wait a minute: one night in bed with me again doesn't give Jean-Claude a claim to the rest of my life." Her slanting grey eyes were full of righteous indignation. "Anyway," she added petulantly, "it's a convenient excuse to keep Kreppy away if I can dangle a dark and handsome lover in front of him."

"Actually, talking about two whole weeks," said Laura pensively, "I'm amazed that Pierre *is* keeping such a low profile. Perhaps he's finally seen the light."

"God!" Jennifer added, "I wish Jean-Claude would get the hint, too. We need a total change of men. Rich . . . handsome . . . famous . . . sexy, and that's just for starters."

Caroline helped herself to more coffee, and slid the pot towards her friends, saying, "Well, then, let's go for a change of scene. I vote we all get out of here today. We'll go to St Tropez. I know it's more than a couple of hours by car, but the beaches are more fun, and then we can end up doing the rounds of the harbour cafés. Plus most of the shops are open there on Sundays, unlike here."

"That's a fabulous idea, but I'm still broke," said Jennifer ruefully, topping up her mug. "I haven't a bean! And I feel really embarrassed, sponging off you two all the time!"

Jennifer's money problems were really beginning to bite. It was awful being dependent on everyone's generosity!

"Oh, come on. I think we can stand you a sandwich and a few

drinks today!" replied Laura generously. "It's a brilliant idea to visit St Trop. It gets too claustrophobic here sometimes, and M-C's a bore on Sundays. And that reminds me, I think I got you a really good job last night, with that blond fellow Quintin I was dancing with."

Jennifer began to perk up. The prospect of a handsome boss was appealing.

"He's opening a night-club and wants a dishy manageress. I've got his phone number. Remind me to remind you tonight to give him a ring."

"Hey!" exclaimed Jennifer, clapping her hands delightedly. "Brilliant. Fabulous. That's just up my street! What's he like, though?"

"Oh! Lecherous, over-sexed, and an opportunist of the first order I'd say."

"Ah," Jennifer sighed mistily. "A man after my own heart."

Many things happened in the week that followed. Laura's career continued progressing since her assistant, Mary, had arrived. Flowers kept arriving for Jennifer from Julius Krep. Jean-Claude kept turning up uninvited, and Laura's and Caroline's capacity for subterfuge was tested to the limit by the varied excuses they were expected to furnish in order to explain Jennifer's absence (usually while she was hiding in the loo)!

Jennifer duly applied over the phone for the plum job of managing Quintin Farmiloe's new discothêque night-club, called Le Disco. Quintin asked her for an interview the next day.

The new club was right in the heart of Monte-Carlo; just a stone's throw from the Café de Paris and the Casino. It was tucked between two popular restaurants. A very favourable spot for drawing in prospects. Tentatively, Jennifer walked through the entrance door. It was like walking into the black hole of Calcutta after the glare of the sun. Inside, the club's decor was all black: carpet, walls, ceiling – with lacquered tables and squashy banquettes, over which were cleverly-lit black and white posters of scantily dressed models reclining languidly.

Jennifer blinked, trying to focus through the gloom. When her prospective employer came into view, she studied him. She'd already admired him from a distance at the Al Fresco, but close to he was even better. Definitely the dangerous type. She didn't realise up till now that a blond man could smoulder, but Farmiloe did! A trendy dresser, too. He was wearing one of those Deborah and Clare shirts; fawn, with red owls printed all over it, and the collar had rounded ends. Most of the buttons were undone, showing a tanned chest and a chunky gold ankh. His cream trousers were very tight. But then, he had the physique for it. He extended a warm welcome to Jennifer. He had a wonderful smile and a natural charm. What a contrast to dour old Jean-Claude in his dark and conservative clothes!

Within minutes he was enthusing about his club. "The dance floor will be illuminated from underneath, and there will be strobe lights for the fast music and soft, coloured lights for the slow numbers. We have the very best turntables and sound – from Juliana's – and sexy disc-jockettes. Monaco's never seen anything like it!" Quintin's eyes glowed with pride and enthusiasm as he hopped around the floor, gesticulating wildly to demonstrate all the facilities on offer.

"Not a very original name though, Le Disco," sniffed Jennifer, then added teasingly. "Why don't you call it something controversial, like Le Soixante-neuf?"

Quintin laughed. "That would not please certain quarters, and well you know it! I'd probably get thrown out before I even started! Anyway," he continued, "I called it Le Disco on purpose so that everyone would know it was a young and trendy *boite-de-nuit* without having to advertise the fact. Even the most old-fashioned diehards should know that a disco's all fast dancing and disco-dollies playing the very latest music. It's the trendy, groovy young I'm after, not the dowagers at the Summer Sporting and afficionados of Aimé Barelli's foxtrots!"

"Trendy . . . groovy . . ." laughed Jennifer. "What sort of a word's *groovy* for heaven's sake! Not much fits that description round here!" She pulled a wry face.

"Oh great!" sighed Quintin. "I see I'm really going to have my work cut out if a glam and fab number like you doesn't even know what groovy is!"

Jennifer laughed, and leaned back against a table in her short yellow dress, deliberately showing off her slim, tanned legs. Quintin's turquoise eyes swept downwards and his nostrils flared seductively. She smiled inwardly: men were so easy to provoke!

"Come, now, you exaggerate," she retorted mildly. "Monte-Carlo's very parochial, you know. Time's stood still here for decades. England might not be that far away geographically, but in terms of trends and attitudes, especially London, for instance, it's light years ahead!"

"What made you come here, to Monaco then, if it's so old-fashioned?"

He ushered Jennifer to sit more comfortably on a banquette, and handed her a glass of Coke. He pulled up a chair and sat facing her, crossing his long legs and leaning on one elbow in a very relaxed manner. As interviews go, it was a very informal affair. Quintin was very easy to talk to. Jennifer felt herself warming to him, but not only for his devastating good looks. He was very friendly and natural, too, and had a tremendous sense of humour.

"Monaco and I go a long way back," she explained. "When I was little, our family had a lovely villa with a pool, nearby on Cap Ferrat. We used to spend all our holidays here, so I knew the area well. That was in the good old days when money was no problem. Then Daddy made a speculative property deal in '65, and lost practically all his loot, and I was packed off to secretarial college so's I could earn a living! Anyway, I didn't fancy being a secretary in London, so I left Queen's and did a bit of modelling. Then an ancient aunt left me a small inheritance, and I came out here on impulse three years ago with a boyfriend. Then I sort of stayed on with Caroline, whom I knew from schooldays. Unfortunately, it didn't take long for my money to run out. Anyway, I've been managing to keep my head above water, doing this and that. I don't regret leaving the college, though, because I'm not at all cut out for office work."

Quintin was a sympathetic listener. "No," he agreed, "I can't imagine you doing the filing or sitting at a desk! How old are you now, then?"

Jennifer made a small moue of surprise. He was very direct. But then, this was an interview. In that context it was a perfectly acceptable question.

"A gentleman should never ask," she smiled, toying with her glass, "but seeing I'm not old enough to have to lie about it yet, I'm twenty-two, if you must know!"

He grinned at Jennifer. "Old enough to be responsible, then."

Jumping to his feet and pacing about, he continued as if he were talking to himself, "The sooner you can start the job the better! There's plenty of things to get on with whilst all the refurbishing's being done. Your short stint of secretarial training will be jolly useful. There are workmen to organise, bills to be settled. Also I need mailing lists for the opening night and cards sending out. You must know who's who around here. Do you want to get stuck into that?"

Great! Had she clinched it? It certainly looked like it. This could be her lucky day.

"When?" asked Jennifer, trying to contain her delight.

"Yesterday!" grinned Quintin.

"So the job's definitely mine then, is it?" she asked, hardly daring to believe her luck.

Quintin nodded. "Definitely!" he laughed, proferring his hand to shake on the deal. He looked as pleased as Jennifer felt.

"Right-on then, Groovy!" she quipped with a flashing smile. "I'm learning fast, eh?"

Laura did not leave work until nearly eight o'clock. She would just have enough time to catch the delicatessen before it closed. She fancied their spit-roasted chicken and Waldorf salad. She'd get enough for Jennifer and Caroline, too. She set off down the boulevard de Suisse, through the old Roman archway and passed the yellowing post-office building before turning sharp right towards the square of the Hermitage Hotel. The friendly patron served her, carefully wrapping the food and placing it in a brown-paper carrier bag. The delicious smell and sight of the food made Laura's mouth water, and she suddenly realised how tired and hungry she was. She was looking forward to a quiet evening reading with her feet up.

As she made her way up towards the boulevard Princesse Charlotte, she was suddenly conscious of footsteps behind her. She quickened her pace, feeling uneasy. But whoever was following stuck to her route doggedly. Her heart beat faster and her mouth went dry. She was just about to break into a run, when she heard her name being called. The voice was familiar. Laura froze with a sinking heart, realising her worst fears. It was Pierre. He caught up with her and took her arm. She stiffened.

"What do you want?" she asked defensively.

"Oh, that's not very nice, Laura," he remonstrated. "After all our time together, at least you could have explained to me why you just disappeared into thin air. I was devastated." Pierre's eyes were dark and haunted, as he studied her face, hungry and desperate for a remnant of tenderness, of recognition of his pain.

"I'm sorry," said Laura curtly. "It seemed to be for the best. I just couldn't take any more." The last thing she needed was a scene with Pierre. Her nerves had been in shreds, and she had felt guilt and remorse for so long before leaving him, that somehow she had none left when she actually took the plunge.

Pierre looked very handsome and appealing, but Laura felt no regret. However, the pain in his eyes was so searing that Laura had to look away. She didn't want to be confronted by the consequences of her actions.

"Pierre, please," she implored, "please leave me alone. You know it's for the best. Everything was so bad between us. It was unbearable."

"Not for me!" he pleaded. "Not for me, Laura. I love you. I want you back. I can't bear life without you. Please, let's give it one more try."

The look of pain and tenderness on his face came close to melting Laura's kind heart. She hated to see him suffer like this. But she was resolute. It would never work again. Her love for him was dead, and had been for a long time.

"No, Pierre," she said quietly. "I'm truly sorry, but no."

And she started to walk away. He was still in uniform, thank God. She was relieved because she knew that even Pierre would never be foolish enough to make a scene whilst on duty.

"Laura!" he called quietly, in a faltering voice, as she walked on. But, as she had guessed, he didn't follow her. Next time, perhaps she would not be so lucky. She had obviously been optimistic in assuming that Pierre had given up on her. Laura sighed as she approached the Meribel. He'd be bound to know where she lived. Monaco was such a small place, and the police kept tabs on all foreign visitors. She was glad to reach the sanctuary of No. 613, and even more pleased to find Caroline there. Laura was not in a mood to be alone now. Kicking off her high heels, she padded to the kitchen with the food, and her flatmate in tow.

Then Caroline dropped a bombshell. But at least it took Laura's mind off Pierre. Caroline had to return to England immediately because her brother had decided to leave the family law firm, and she was needed to fill the breach.

"I had hoped to spend the rest of the year here," she said ruefully, "but such are the commitments of family life and business!"

Laura was crestfallen.

"Don't look so concerned, Laura," Caroline reassured her. "It's always been on the cards that I'd join them at some stage. So now I've got to leave the sunshine for the smoke!"

"We're going to miss you so much! It won't be the same without you," Laura said sadly. "On a practical note, though, I'm glad Jennifer's found herself a job, or I really would have been in the schtuck!"

Caroline smiled, and the dark eyes twinkled in her round face. "Are you sure it really is a job he's offering, and not something else? Quintin looks a total roué to me!"

"He is a devil!" Laura admitted. "But the club's real enough, and he's already given her masses to do. And a reasonable salary. She's really thrilled. Looks as if she's landed on her feet at last."

"Good. It's about time she had a decent job." Then Caroline looked preoccupied for a moment. "Talking of salaries and practicalities, I'll let you have a month's rent money in lieu of notice. That'll give you plenty of time to find a replacement for me."

"No!" Laura exclaimed. "That's far too much. Honestly, we'll be OK. Especially now that Jennifer's sorted herself out."

But Caroline was insistent. Laura had no choice but to accept her generous offer.

"Is Jennifer down at the club now?" Caroline asked.

"Yes. Working on a guest list for the opening night. Should be fun. Shame you're going to miss it."

Caroline nodded ruefully, then brightened as she suggested, "Let's go down to the Café de P after our chicken salad."

So much for my quiet evening, thought Laura. But Caroline deserved a memorable send-off.

"Yes, absolutely," Laura enthused, "and Jennifer can join us later; Quintin, too, and we'll have a thoroughly rowdy evening, drinking to your future!"

Chapter 7

However regretful Laura was at losing such a good flatmate and confidante, she was extremely glad to seize the opportunity of moving bag-and-baggage out of Jennifer's clutter, and taking over Caroline's old room for herself.

"It's an ill wind," she mused.

"Jennifer," Laura told her later, "no hard feelings, eh? You know I love you very much, but am I ever glad to be out of your mess and muddle. Peace at last!"

Jennifer grinned good-naturedly. Then a shadow of guilt crossed her face. "But what about rent and everything, Laura? I still owe you money, and didn't even stump up for the deposit!"

"Oh, come on. After all you and Caro did for me during the Pierre saga, what's a few hundred francs here and there! We can keep the old wolf from the door. I earn good money and certainly don't resent having subsidised you a bit."

What on earth did money matter compared to peace of mind? Laura would never forget Jennifer and Caroline's help. She had lost count of the number of times she'd sought refuge with them late at night in their little studio to escape from Pierre's rages. Theirs had been an ever-open door of kindness.

"But," Laura paused, and her china-blue eyes flashed fiercely, "don't you dare borrow my make-up ever again, or I'll send you a bill!"

"God!" said Jennifer, clapping her hand to her heart

dramatically. "You idiot. You had me really worried for a minute."

They laughed and looked at each other fondly.

Laura took Jennifer's hand and shook it mock-solemnly. "Our debts to each other are herewith expunged! You can start with a clean slate now you're earning again."

Jennifer squeezed her hand gratefully. "I promise I'll do my best to make ends meet." Her eyebrows drew together dubiously. "But can we afford the flat, just the two of us?"

Laura pondered. "Obviously Caroline's share is going to have to be made up between us two, but I don't mind personally, because it's less of a crowd, just two in the flat. It really hinges on you, Jennifer, whether you can afford the extra, knowing your habit of living beyond your means."

Jennifer was hopeless with money. But perhaps now she had a proper job with a regular pay-cheque things would change for the better. Laura felt she deserved the chance to prove herself.

"Ah," she sighed ruefully. "Champagne tastes on a beer income. I know. My fault for having had such a privileged childhood. I don't think I'll ever learn how to be frugal now. The habits are ingrained."

Laura smiled tolerantly. "Look," she said, "let's play it by ear, and see how we go. No panic for now because we still have Caroline's contribution in the kitty."

It seemed strange at first without Caroline, but Laura relished the peace in the evenings now that Jennifer was working permanently at the disco. Fitz kept her very busy. Her office hours were spilling more and more into her leisure time. Laura did not resent this as there was nobody else making demands on her. She needed some time to herself, though, to unwind the tangles of the last few months. Apart from that one short encounter in the street, Pierre had once again receded into the distant past, like a bad dream whose horrors had faded; no longer causing that sudden rush of fear or panic, no longer distracting her from her ambition. Laura still felt she had missed out by not going to university: it must eventually hold her back that she had no degree. But there must be some way to gain qualifications whilst still remaining in her job. What about some form of diploma? She decided to do some research on her own. There had to be a way to move ahead.

Jennifer was enjoying her new job. Being paid to socialise was a dream come true. She was rushed off her feet every evening, greeting guests and friends, organising tables, recognising the notables from the also-rans and seating them accordingly. The club had taken off immediately. Quintin's strategy had been effective, but Jennifer also had to take much of the credit for the club's instant success. She knew all the right people. Together they made a good team.

Quintin agreed. He would have greatly enjoyed some teamwork with her in bed, too. His eyes gleamed as they followed her retreating backview. Beneath a silver sequinned top her skin-tight blue satin trousers clung to a delicious little bum. It was high and firm and a fitting crown to her endless legs. He loved the way it moved when she walked. He had done well, landing her. Mainly thanks to Laura. Jennifer's looks and popularity pulled in the punters. And she was an excellent worker, too. But though Quintin lusted after her, sometimes achingly, he decided to leave well alone. His practical side told him that the continuing efficiency of his manageress was paramount to the success of his new business. Any distractions where Jennifer was concerned would be foolish and inappropriate ... for the moment, anyway.

Now that exquisite and reserved Laura, he thought. She was something else. She was free, and a challenge for the taking...

Quintin had a small business proposition to put to Laura, and took his chance one Friday evening when she'd been persuaded by Jennifer to come down to the club for a special party. Laura was all dressed-up, having come straight from a reception at the Metropole, in a short black dress with dainty sequinned straps, whose glitter, also outlining the plunging 'V' of her bodice, automatically led the eye to a tanned, firm cleavage.

"Obviously bra-less," noted Quintin, sidling up quietly, lasciviously eyeing her assets as she sat on a high stool at the bar.

"Quintin . . . Up here!" ordered Laura, pointing to her face. "I'm a firm believer in eye-contact."

"Firm, yes. I agree." he continued, and swept his eyes off her breasts up to her face, where he met her amused blue gaze, quite awe-inspiring in its intensity. Laura did not waver.

"Well," she asked, "and what is this little business proposition?"

Farmiloe led Laura away from the blasting speakers, to a newly designed quieter area of the club for the more discerning clientèle, who preferred to sit and watch the dancing and only hear the music in the background, allowing them to talk over their drinks.

"It's my girls, Laura," he started, "my disco-dollies. They need somewhere to stay, and I understand you have a spare bed now at your place, in Jennifer's room."

"Oh, I don't know Quintin." Laura sounded uncertain. "I'm not that keen to have strangers parked around the flat."

"Well," he replied, "they wouldn't be strangers, would they? I mean, they'd be workmates of Jennifer's."

Quintin could see he had his work cut out here. Laura was no pushover. It would be a shame if she turned his proposal down. It would be very convenient to have his staff lodged under the same roof.

"And how many are we talking about?" she continued. "A whole retinue of them? One at a time? No, I really don't fancy the idea at all. I'm sorry."

"Please, Laura. You've no idea how much it would help me out. I'm in a bit of a quandary, actually."

Quintin gave her an appealing smile, but Laura did not react. She was still frowning and looking very negative.

"I really think it would be impossible," she continued, shaking her head. "You see, the concierge is already funny about having Jennifer around. When I signed the rental agreement I had to agree not to sublet; so strictly speaking I'm breaking the law. I got round it by fibbing that Jennifer and Caroline were personal friends staying over for a while. I'm already pushing my luck without taking in genuine lodgers. I would imagine that what you're asking is for your dollies to pay me rent, yes?"

"Well, yes," he admitted, "but we could easily get around that. I'll just dock it off their pay at source and hand the cash straight to you. No questions asked. Can't you just do it for a month while I think up other arrangements?"

It was more strategic to put this over as a temporary move. Often a pro-tem measure became a permanent one. Quintin was not one to give up easily.

"Where have they been staying up to now?" Laura's eyes danced mischievously, as if she full well knew the answer.

Quintin grinned. She was quick. Or was she hedging? Trying to side track him?

He put a finger to his lips. "That's a trade secret. But, you know, business and pleasure don't mix. And I always succumb to temptation when I have dollies around my flat, and that mucks up our working relationship. Things get complicated."

Quintin put his hand on hers and summoned up his best 'little boy' expression. Eyes wide, mouth forward and turned up at the corners, head to one side. It generally worked wonders with truculent females; though this one was sharp, rather than truculent.

"Come on, Laura, be a love," he pleaded, huskily, appealingly. "It's just to tide me over while I organise an

95

alternative. Please? . . . Pretty please?"

Laura stared back, amused, but unmoved.

Time to change tack, he decided. "Anyhow," he added craftily, "I was under the impression that you and Jennifer both needed the money."

"Not me, Quint. I don't have a money problem."

Laura discreetly extricated her hand, and dazzled him with one of her rare, full smiles. She had a pretty mouth and beautiful teeth, but what struck him especially was the brightness of her eyes when she smiled, a brightness which lit up her face and everything around her.

"Personally," she continued, "I can afford having the rent split two ways, but I'm not so sure about Jen."

His eyes flashed as he jumped in for the kill. "Exactly! You've just hit the nail on the head. Jennifer already owes me this week's pay, so there'll be nothing left for the rent anyway! You know how generous and vague she is. She's always ordering champagne for her friends 'on the house' and I'm afraid I have to deduct it from her wages. After all, business is business, and this is nobody's free party."

"Oh dear," Laura sighed. "Typical of our kind-hearted friend. So, she'll be in the red again by next week, will she?"

Quintin nodded ruefully. Inwardly he was pleased. It was in the bag now.

"Oh hell, Quintin, you are the end!" she continued irritably. "It's a real cleft-stick situation. I really don't want to do this, but I suppose in the circumstances I don't have much choice. I can't carry Jennifer for ever."

Laura furrowed her brow and pondered a bit. She had painted herself into a corner. But Quintin was right. Laura would be continually out of pocket as things stood. Jennifer was, and always would be unrealistic about money. She would make a beneficial deal with him.

"Tell you what, Quint," she said. "Pay me two-thirds of my rental, plus an agreed sum to cover laundry and sundries, and you're on. I'll work out a reasonable figure. That'll cover Jennifer and one lodger. It saves me the bother of having to chase round for their share. How soon do we have to take this wretched girl on?"

"As soon as you can, really. She arrives the day after tomorrow."

"Oh, blast. I hope she's bearable. Caroline's a hard act to follow."

"She should be. A friend of mine recommended her. An ex-deb and all that. She'll be fine, you'll see."

Laura raised her eyes to the ceiling. "An ex-deb, eh? I suppose we'll just have to take your word for it."

"Thanks, Laura," Quintin said gratefully. "You're a tough chick, but a good one. How about a bottle of Krug to celebrate?"

"Well, why not?" she laughed. "It's a charming way to settle a deal."

Although the champagne mellowed and relaxed Laura during the course of the evening, Quintin could see that his customary charm was not having its usual effect. Every so often, a shadow crossed her face and the intense blue eyes became wary. There was a long story behind this, he decided. One day he might succeed in getting those defences down. But the evening had not been wasted.

"At least I've made a useful deal with her," he reasoned, "and you can't win 'em all!"

On Saturday evening, knowing full well that Jennifer would be there, Julius Krep strolled into Le Disco, dressed in dark, shiny suit and loud tie, with an entourage of friends. Blimey, thought Jennifer. Where does he get his ghastly clothes?

Smiling politely, ever professional, Jennifer showed him to the best table. Narrowing his eyes, Julius studied her, trying to weigh up the *status quo*. So far she'd ignored his flowers, his renewed invitations for drinks on the yacht, or anywhere else for that matter. He obviously needed to change tack. Put different pressures on her. Be more persuasive, use harder tactics.

But now here she was – a captive of her job. No escaping him this evening! Her long red dress was gorgeous. It clung to her every curve, was slashed either side from breast to thigh and laced together with thin straps; showing lean, gleaming flesh between the tiny criss-crosses. He had a sudden fantasy of pulling hard at the laces so they'd unravel, making the dress slither down her naked body. And what a body hers was, he remembered. Beads of sweat were forming, and he pulled out his hankie.

"Now see here, boys and girls," Krep announced importantly, mopping his face, "here is the woman of my dreams. I send her flowers every day, invite her to all the nicest places a girl could imagine, throw a party for her, and what happens? She cold-shoulders me quite heartlessly. Jennifer, my beauty, Julius Krep is at your feet – he's beside himself with raging desire and hunger. What must he do to earn your attention – even the slightest acknowledgment from your cold heart?"

He flourished his hankie ostentatiously, and bowed to her. Jennifer laughed. Thank God the girl had a sense of humour. He was not averse to playing the clown, if that's what appealed to her.

"Julius, from you that is quite a speech," she said. "Where did you learn it? Have you been reading Shakespeare?"

"You see how she treats me, eh?" Julius waved a hand in her direction, playing to his audience with a rueful expression on his face. His friends settled themselves round the table, casting her the odd lustful glance. They were obviously impressed. "You'd think I was an ignorant barrow-boy, the way she carries on!"

But Jennifer wasn't playing. She assumed a business-like, almost prim manner. "Mr Krep," she said coolly, "I expect your friends are all thirsty, and dying for our best champagne.

Shall I ask the waiter to bring you a magnum of Krug?"

"Yes, please, girlie. Whatever the best brew, we'll 'av the shampoo!" Krep chuckled at his wit, and his friends obligingly joined in. "Now come and join us, will you? I want to feeeel you near me!" He was still standing next to her, and made a grab for her hand.

"Julius, I'm working!" Jennifer said quietly, backing away. "You must know I'm busy, especially on a Saturday night."

Julius studied her through half-closed eyes. All right, little birdie, he thought. Back away from me if you like. But you're trapped. I'm here for the evening, and I'll get you in the end!

She took a deep breath and controlled her anger. "Look, why don't you sit down and make yourself comfortable," she said politely, "I must see about your magnum, and I'll be back shortly."

"Make it quick, love," he wheedled. "I'll pine away without you!"

He flopped down heavily into the banquette like a walrus.

She could feel his eyes boring into her, watching her every move. Jennifer felt uncomfortable. There was something sinister about his interest in her. God! imagined Jennifer, what if Krep, or one of his henchman were the watcher with the binoculars? Their Bin Rat! Anything was possible. She shivered. Perhaps she was being melodramatic. But Krep's relentless pursuit of her made her feel hemmed in and vulnerable.

She hastened away, looking for Quintin, who got a waiter to look after Krep and his party immediately. But he insisted she accept the invitation to join Krep's table.

Her face fell. "Oh, Quintin, please," she groaned. "He's such a lecher. He's all over me. Give me a break!" she pleaded. The thought of spending the entire evening fending off Krep was more than she could bear!

But Quintin was unmoved. "Jennifer – I'm sorry. It's part of the job. Krep is loaded, and I mean loaded. He's just the sort who can make or break a concern like this. You can handle his type – in any case, you're going to have to learn to manage this kind of situation with aplomb. That's what you're here for. Go to it, there's a good girl."

Her heart sank. How humiliating to endure Krep's company after what he'd done to her on the yacht. The memory still rankled. It made her skin crawl to think of that tub of lard clambering all over her.

"You're a beast and a bully!" she hissed, stamping her foot in rage. God, Quintin could be a pig sometimes!

Farmiloe laughed unsympathetically, "Well, tough titty! He who pays the piper calls . . ."

But Jennifer was already crossing the floor. Quintin *was* beastly. But he was right. She had a job to do, and if it entailed putting up with Krep and his braying gangster friends this evening, then so be it!

"Hiya, beautiful," Krep grinned up at her lecherously. "Take a pew, right here." He patted his knee invitingly.

Jennifer ignored the request, drew up a chair and sat opposite him, just out of reach. Undeterred, he leaned forward and seized her wrist, smacking it with an exaggerated kiss, and handed her a glass of champagne.

"Thanks," she said, coolly, adding under her breath, "I'm going to need more than one of these!"

But it wasn't so bad, after all. Krep's friends were not the crooked bunch she had assumed them to be. They were actually very amusing. A mixture of ages. Just businessmen in dark suits: away from their wives and out to enjoy themselves. It was all good harmless fun. She put up with the odd ribald comment, and teased them back. As Quintin had said; the kind of situation she could handle with aplomb. Here she was, enjoying the undivided attention of half a dozen men, all flirting with her and making her feel like a princess. And being paid for it to boot! Perhaps even the ghastly Krep was bearable! She could think of worse ways to spend an evening. As the waiters kept the drink flowing, Jennifer was getting very light-headed.

So much that she suddenly found herself accepting Krep's request to dance, without turning a hair. She was surprised to find what an accomplished dancer he was, amazingly light on his feet, and agile for one so overweight.

"Well, at last I've got my arms around you," he murmured seductively.

Her proximity was overpowering. Why did she have to wear a dress like that? Didn't she have enough sex-appeal already to slay an army, without bringing bondage to mind? Honestly, those thin little straps criss-crossing her bare skin . . . It was too much! Images of her subjugation at his hands overwhelmed him as he imagined himself in complete control of that glorious body. He recalled the vision of Jennifer sprawled in naked abandon over the black satin. Suddenly, he was too hot. He broke into a sweat and felt himself stir. God almighty! That sort of thing only happened to eighteen-year-olds. Control yourself, man! He fumbled for his hankie again. Then he shut his eyes, counted to ten, and forced himself to remember the worst business deal he'd ever made. The hideous thought of losing good money washed over him like a cold shower. It had the right effect. His recovery was instantaneous.

Krep dabbed at the beads on his nose, distancing himself slightly from Jennifer.

"What a tiny little thing you are!" Krep said in a calm voice. Having regained his sang-froid he trusted himself to give her another appraising glance.

Jennifer looked down at his glistening moon face. In her high heels she was at least five feet ten. "Nonsense," she teased. "I'm taller than you are!"

"Duckie, nearly everyone *is*," he grinned, his navy-blue eyes dancing. "I meant slim, not tiny in height. What are you anyway, love?"

"Five seven according to my passport," she stated, tossing her thick blonde mane down her back.

"Well," he replied importantly, drawing himself up as much as possible, "I'm five feet six and a half. And don't forget the half inch. Every little bit counts!" And he winked at her, twinkling conspiratorially.

Jennifer laughed in spite of herself. He was irrepressible. He had a natural flair for comedy that caught her off guard. "You're a horror, Julius, but really quite funny sometimes. You've got rather an appealing smile."

"Hooray!" Julius chuckled. "Strike a light. The girl gave me a compliment. Wait, I think I feel faint!" He grabbed her hands, shut his eyes, and swayed comically on his feet.

Jennifer giggled. Krep opened one eye.

"Don't get carried away, Julius," she teased, "one something-or-other doth not a thingummy make, or whatever the saying is."

"One swallow doth not a summer make," Julius replied, surprising her. Then he looked into her eyes lasciviously. "Although there's a particular brand of swallow that could my evening make!"

She affected a stern expression. He was a cheeky beggar. He shouldn't push his luck. "Now then," she admonished, "don't be filthy!"

"Sorry," he said, trying to look contrite, and not succeeding. "I promise to behave."

"You'd better!" she threatened, but there was a smile hovering round her lips.

Julius decided to take advantage of their truce. She was in good-humour now. If he played his cards right, he was still in with a chance. Jennifer was a challenge he was determined to conquer.

He smiled warmly. "Now, beautiful," he said in his most velvety, persuasive voice, "how about a trip to San Remo in the Riva tomorrow? Would you fancy that if the sea's calm? It doesn't take long in a speedboat. We can be there in time for lunch."

102

Jennifer looked at him suspiciously. What was his game, she wondered? But Krep grinned back at her disarmingly, raising his eyebrows in supplication. The expression was appealing and made her laugh again.

"Hey, luvvie" he cajoled, "what d'you say? A spot of Italian food; a look at Italian fashions. The shops there are fabulous."

She relented, and thought, why not? There'd be no harm in it. It would be fun to take a trip into Italy. A change of routine. After all, there was really nothing to do in Monaco on a quiet Sunday except go to the beach again.

"Well," she said slowly, "as long as you're on the level and don't slip me any Mickey Finns or reefers, you're on. Behave yourself, and I'll make a deal with you. If you let me bring Laura, the answer's yes."

"Anything you say, darlin'," Julius replied, staggered. "D'you think she'll want to come?"

"If she does, then OK, it's San Remo tomorrow! Why the hell not?"

The hammock swayed slightly as its occupant reached for his binoculars. He licked his lips. She was on her own. Easy meat. It was becoming easier to follow their movements now. There seemed to be a pattern even to *their* disreputable lives. They had no discretion, these girls. No shame. Flaunting their bodies all the time.

"*Ah, mon joli poulet,*" he murmured darkly. "One of these days you'll pay in full. Just you wait."

He took a swig of beer and wiped his lips with the back of his hand. The thought of the blonde with no clothes on made him feel violent and excited. He'd take one more good, lingering look, and then go to his bedroom to work off his excitement in front of the mirror.

"Not long now," he vowed. "Not long now, pretty baby."

She'd have to be dealt with, eventually. The sooner the better . . .

* * *

Laura had been reading for over half an hour, relaxing in a chaise-longue on the balcony. But she was so tired that the pages became blurred. She threw the paperback down beside her, closed her eyes tightly, and then tried to focus into the distance to clear the blur. Suddenly her eyes took in a quick movement across the garden. What was it? A flash of light, a reflection? Alarmed, her heart thumping, she jumped to her feet, leaned against the balcony railing and thoroughly scoured the block opposite and the gardens below. It was difficult to pierce the gloom of the fading light. So, try as she might, she really could see nothing suspicious. Apart from the gentle splashing of the fountain below there was no sound or movement; nobody about and nothing untoward in the shadowy garden. Hers was the only balcony that was occupied at the moment. She reassured herself that the half-light was obviously playing tricks on her eyes, and that she shouldn't be so silly. There was no sign of Caroline's watcher with the binoculars. It was just her imagination.

"Come now, Laura," she told herself crossly, "you're getting paranoid!"

She sat down again and reclined back, watching the night fall, lights flicking on in the horseshoe-shaped block, savouring the sweet scent of the flowers drifting up from the exotic garden below. She wondered whether many single, eligible young women like herself would actually be relishing the peace of being unattached, not desperate for a date on a Saturday night! "Peace, sweet peace!" she murmured to herself.

Not for long. Suddenly the phone rang, intruding shrilly and insistently into the silent night. Reluctantly Laura got up and went indoors.

"*Oui?*" she answered. "*J'écoute.*"

"Laura? *C'est toi?*" whispered the familiar voice.

"Pierre," she answered warily, her heart sinking. "What do you want?"

"You know what I want," he replied truculently.

"Please. Haven't we gone through all this enough times? It's over between us. You know it is."

"I just want to talk to you."

"No. There's nothing to say."

"Just let me see you for five minutes. I beg you."

"No, Pierre."

"Why not?" he demanded accusingly. "Why can't you see me? Is there someone else with you?" His voice rose in anguish. "I can't stand the thought of you with somebody else. It kills me."

"Pierre," replied Laura softly, "I swear to you there's nobody else. The only thing that takes up all my time now is work. There's no room in my life for anything but work. And that's the way it's going to be for a long time. Don't torment yourself with thoughts of other men. Up to now there's only ever been you. Please accept that, and let's try to be friends. I don't want you to hate me or feel bitter."

There was silence at the other end.

"Pierre, are you there?"

There was still no answer. But after a few seconds, Laura thought she heard a muffled sob, and then the phone went dead.

Jennifer was surprised to find Laura still up when she returned from the disco in the early hours.

"Hiya!" she called out cheerfully. "Did you have a good evening? You've had a late night for once! Hey, guess who was at the disco this evening? Bloody Julius Krep!"

Laura smiled weakly. She looked pale and strained.

"Hey, sweetie," Jennifer's voice was concerned. "What's up with you? You don't look too good."

"Oh, nothing really," Laura replied unconvincingly.

"Nothing, my foot!" retorted Jennifer. "Come on. What's up? Tell Auntie Jennifer."

Laura sighed heavily. "It's Pierre. He telephoned, and made me feel all guilty again. It just upset me, that's all. I wish he'd leave me alone."

"Did he turn nasty?"

"No. Not at all. It's sort of worse really, when he acts the broken-hearted lover. I feel such a heel."

Jennifer bridled. "God, Laura! Don't be so silly. Have you forgotten the times we gave you tea and sympathy when that bastard had turned you into a quivering heap? He's a vicious bully. He practically wrecked your life, destroyed your self-confidence with his violence and nastiness. How can you forget all of that so soon? Come on, chicken. Do be sensible! Don't let him get to you. You've got to tough it out. You've already got this far. Try to get him out of your mind for good."

Laura sighed again. Her eyes were dark hollows, and her face looked pinched. She needs a break, thought Jennifer. She needs some fun. All she ever does is work and worry. It was no way to live. Then she remembered Krep's offer. It would do Laura the world of good to get out of the flat and out of the principality tomorrow. A sea trip and change of surroundings would help take her mind off this unhappy evening.

"Hey, that reminds me," she said determinedly. "Talking about taking your mind off things, Kreppy's invited us out on the Riva tomorrow morning. He's going to take us to San Remo for lunch."

Laura's face clouded over, and she shook her head. "No, Jen," she said adamantly. "I couldn't! I'm going to feel like death tomorrow. I'll look like a wraith, and how am I going to recover in time for a hard week's work on Monday?"

"Don't be silly, Laura. You don't think you can sit around here alone all day tomorrow, do you? You simply can't risk it with the mood Pierre's in. Remember it's Sunday, and he won't be at work. He'll have the whole day to brood, probably get himself into a rage, and then who knows what he'll do?"

God forbid! It was unlike her to feel so helpless. Laura

fought to stop tears welling up. She must get a grip on herself. Jennifer was right; she had to stick to her guns, or Pierre would take control of her life again.

"Everything will be OK," said Jennifer with conviction. "One way or the other, we're going to sort this out, you'll see."

Laura nodded, her lips a firm line of determination. Then anger flooded over her, galvanising hidden reserves. She clenched her fists and her eyes blazed. Damn it. Sod Pierre. Why let him ruin her life? After all, it was just a phone call, nothing more. So what? She must get on with her life. Be positive and plan ahead. Starting with tomorrow. Jennifer's earlier suggestion of a day out was a good one, she decided.

"What was it you said about a trip to San Remo tomorrow?" she asked innocently; but there was a vestige of a smile on her face, a look of challenge in her eyes.

Jennifer laughed triumphantly and gave her a hug. "That's the spirit!" she said approvingly.

"OK, then," Laura determined bravely. "San Remo it is. I'll be chaperone and tell Kreppy to behave himself!"

Chapter 8

The trip on the Riva turned out to be great fun. The girls could not help exchanging smiles when Julius turned up at the flat to pick them up in the inevitable white ducks, brass-buttoned blazer and navy-blue peaked cap proclaiming 'Captain' in gold braiding.

One of the most likeable things about Julius, and somewhat of a redeeming feature, was that he didn't take offence at being considered a bit of a joke. On the contrary, he seemed to relish it. It was almost as if he knew he was a 'wide boy' and larger-than-life character. He obviously enjoyed cocking a snook at the world and didn't give a damn what anyone thought of him.

"Like the gear then, girls?" he beamed unabashed. "Now, you'll have to get yourselves some warm sweaters and windproof jackets. There's going to be a fair bit of breeze on the water, the speeds we'll be running at! Hope you're good swimmers!"

"Thanks a lot, Kreppy," said Jennifer. "You planning to throw us overboard?"

He laughed. "Depends, duckie. Ask no questions tell no lies, I always say."

The speedboat was beautiful. It was a classic in varnished wood, the real McCoy, a dream vessel. And to own a Riva as a mere *tender* was a piece of one-upmanship way beyond anyone's wildest dreams! There was obviously more to him than met the eye.

Jennifer was slowly beginning to warm to Krep, although she didn't altogether trust him, as she hadn't yet forgiven him for pulling a fast one on her at the party. Drowning a girl in champagne, feeding her a joint and then pushing home the advantage was not a gentlemanly thing to do in anyone's book.

Nimbly the girls leapt on to the Riva as if to the manner born, whilst Julius untied the mooring warp. They helped push it away from the pontoon and brought in the fenders as Julius started the engine. Expertly he steered the vessel past the other yachts and out of the harbour mouth, into the open sea. It was flat calm, and the water a lovely misty blue towards Menton, and beyond that, Italy. As the boat picked up speed there was a pleasant cooling breeze on their faces. The seats were leather, and very comfortable. This was fun.

Jennifer studied his profile as Julius stood at the helm of his boat, totally engrossed. There was something old-fashioned about his looks, something of the matinée idol of yesteryear. Maybe it was the moustache and slicked back hair. But also there was something in his bearing, small as he was, that lent a kind of stature, even a dignity to him. Perhaps it was just that success and money lent him this aura, or perhaps he already had a self-assurance that was inborn.

When he wasn't all dissipated with drink and lechery, he was oddly appealing and had great charm. His prominent teeth gave him a dashing smile and a strong mouth and chin in repose, and he really did have quite a nice profile, if it hadn't been for his paunch.

"What are you staring at, duckie?" asked Julius, disturbing her reverie.

"Your funny face," Jennifer answered quickly, rather abashed that he'd caught her looking at him.

He flashed her a jaunty smile. "Used to be quite handsome in my younger days. Quite a lad!"

"You still could be, if you lost some weight."

"Do you mind?" he grinned, patting his paunch affectionately. "It cost me a lot of money to grow this."

"You should spend the same to lose it, then. You never

110

know, you could get lucky if you shed that beer-gut."

"Strike a light, precious, I'd spend a million just to get you back in my bed!" Julius sighed ruefully.

Jennifer laughed. "Well, are we going to die of thirst on this bloody boat?"

"That's right, love, change the subject. Typical, eh? The bubbly's to starboard under the seat. Here, next to me. Careful as you uncork it. Could be a bit lively the way we're bouncing along."

It was not an easy task pouring champagne on a Riva skimming the waves at thirty knots, under the bright Mediterranean sun, "But I could probably get used to this!" she thought glibly.

Meanwhile, Laura had positioned herself aft. She knelt on the seat, facing the other way, elbows on the squashy leather seat-back, watching Monte-Carlo receding. The formidable Rocher de Monaco jutted proudly to the sky, forming a protective phalanx to the harbour's left. Behind the harbour and to the right, matchbox-size apartment blocks were flung haphazardly against a girdle of towering, navy-blue mountains. Monaco was beautiful. Listening to the crisp swish of the wake, feeling the wind in her hair, and taking in the beauty around her, she felt serene, calm. Last night seemed unimportant now. Receding like the harbour into a distant haze.

"Laura, love, would you like a glass of bubbly?" asked Julius turning back to address her profile. But she didn't hear him. She was in a world of her own.

Then in an aside to Jennifer he whispered, "Hey, is your little friend always this pale and quiet?"

"No, not at all. But she's had an overdose of boyfriend trouble, and she works too hard. You're not seeing her at her best today."

Julius chuckled and his eyes flashed wickedly. "Gawd help the poor sod who does, then! Talk about irresistible!"

"Aaargh, do shut up!" complained Jennifer. "There's nothing more boring than having to listen to compliments from a man about another woman, even if she is your best friend."

"Ooh, luvvy, does Julius detect a slight note of jealousy there, eh?"

"Hah! Don't flatter yourself, mister. And point your nose at the coast to your left, or we might land up in Africa!"

Krep laughed. "If you weren't so pretty, young lady, I'd throw you overboard for your lip!"

Julius smiled to himself. The easy repartee between them was a good sign. He could feel the ice beginning to melt where Jennifer was concerned. God but she was desirable! He couldn't recall ever being so infatuated before. What was it about this particular woman that excited him so much? After all, a man in his position could always have women by the dozen.

Could it be that he was bored by the whole charade; bored by the sameness of it all? Had he become cynical at the realisation it was only his money that talked – was a strong aphrodisiac generally where women were concerned? But Jennifer, now . . . she was a different story. She didn't seem fazed by his money at all. She wasn't so easy to impress. She was far too classy to be swayed by the trappings of wealth!

What a challenge she was! But apart from being hopelessly inflamed by her looks, he really *liked* her. He enjoyed her company, her bright and earnest expression, her gutsy zest for life. He didn't think he could ever get enough of her. He knew he had his work cut out, but he was always turned on by a challenge in business, so why not for a woman? He was ruthless when it came to pushing through a deal. He would use the same relentlessness to win her over.

Yes, he determined, clenching his fist, she's going to be mine. However long it takes, I will succeed! In the meantime, he would charm her pretty friend. He needed all the allies he could get in his quest for the golden girl of his dreams.

Taking pity on the wan-looking Laura, Julius took her hand, and smiling kindly, coaxed, "Come on, Laura, duck. How about a spin at the wheel, eh?"

She demurred, shaking her head.

Undeterred, he said, "Come and sit here, by me. I'll show you how, and we'll go slow at first. I promise I'll take the wheel from you before we get inshore. Go on, precious. I tell you, there's nothing to it!"

Laura felt it would be rude to refuse. Julius was playing the perfect host. Besides, she'd promised herself she was going to make the most of the day. No brooding over the phone call. No introspection. Gingerly she took the white leather-trimmed wheel. Julius had throttled right down.

"See, duckie? There's nothing to it." His large bulk pressed so close to her was disconcerting, but the tone of his voice was gentle. She didn't feel threatened or defensive. He was babying her. It was comforting. Julius seemed a much kinder man than Laura had imagined. Maybe she and Jennifer had judged him too harshly.

Away from the lee of the shore, there was a slight swell. The boat wallowed and swished gently in the water with the sudden lack of acceleration. Then Julius slowly pushed up the throttles and the engines hummed with a low-throated roar. The bows lifted and the boat cut through the waves cleanly and steadily. The wake started to rise and churn behind them. It was exhilarating to be in control of such a powerful machine.

"This is fun!" smiled Laura, gripping the wheel more confidently as she felt the breeze lift her hair.

Julius sat next to her, idly admiring her profile and the white blonde tendrils of hair glinting in the sun against the honey gold of her tan. It was very satisfying to be in the company of two such young and glamorous blondes. He looked round to see what Jennifer was doing and saw that she was preparing to sunbathe on the large curved leather sunbed, astern. She peeled off her sweatshirt, revealing a minimal bikini in the palest teal, held together with three strategically placed white plastic rings. Very precarious. Very sexy. Julius tore his eyes away. It was too much!

Jennifer smiled to herself, and stretched out contentedly on the soft white upholstery. She closed her eyes, lulled by the powerful throb of the twin engines and the hiss of the wake, as the Riva sped through the water. She could just overhear the murmurings of Julius laying on the charm with Laura and was rather touched by his chivalry. He obviously had a good heart. Tentatively, she began to warm to him.

The rest of the day flew past in a blur of shops, sightseeing and a very pleasant lunch in a glassed-in promontory overlooking sea and rocks. Laura had lost her wan expression as the excitement of the boat trip and unfamiliarity of Italy took her mind off the drama of the night before. Julius was attentive and amusing company. Both girls were impressed by his generosity and kindness. He could bring a lot of fun and glamour into their lives. A summer of boat trips, parties, jet-set people and film stars lay ahead, if they could keep him charmed and at arm's length. What a prospect! Perhaps the rumours of orgies, wild women and unsavoury gangsters on his yacht were exaggerated by those jealous of his success and money. Had they been hasty in pre-judging him? Only time would tell.

Laura and Jennifer would never forget the day Nova was introduced to the household. She was a tall, heavily made-up redhead. She was not far off six feet, with too obviously-dyed untidy hair and untidy habits. She reeked of cigarettes, and her fingers were stained yellow from nicotine. Her eyes had a vacant stare about them, and her expression was sullen. Both girls were dismayed. Surely there was no way this creature would fit into their cosy and happy set-up. Gamely they attempted polite conversation and tried to help her settle in. But their attempts were coldly rebuffed. At first, the girls attributed her rudeness to reserve or shyness, but after a while they gave up making excuses for her and put her down as a thoroughly bad lot.

After a few days the relationship was reduced to polite hostility. It was best to ignore Nova, but it was difficult to ignore her untidy ways. Laura thanked her lucky stars she didn't have to share a room with her. It was fortunate that Jennifer was so vague and untidy herself, and less likely to mind the mess. But Laura was still obliged to pass through the shared room at least two or three times a day, to get to the bathroom, so it was impossible to turn a blind eye to the chaos.

"Oh Lord, Jennifer," she complained. "I'm not happy about this, but I suppose the extra rent money will be welcome. Do you think she's as bad as she looks?"

"I'll say. She smokes like a chimney and leaves her butts everywhere, doesn't seem too fussy about her personal hygiene, and as for that bloody panda eye make-up! She could trip over her false eyelashes! And eeugh!" Jennifer screwed up her face. "Those enormous knockers wobbling around like white blancmange. As for her fat arse . . . like two tom cats fighting under a blanket! She's a revolting sight in the buff. I've never seen a thicker, blacker twat! She could hide a battalion in there. It's shaggier than that dreadful red haystack on top of her head!"

"God, don't! I think I'm going to be sick. All I can say, is thank heaven I'm up and out of the house before the creature emerges from her pit! But Jennifer, if you weren't so damn profligate, we could still be living a peaceful life, just the two of us."

Jennifer stuck out her tongue. "When does a leopard ever change its spots, huh?"

Laura's blue eyes were teasing. "You never know, if this girl's as bad as she looks, you could be forced to change the habits of a lifetime."

Jennifer grinned back at her wryly. "Well, you know what

they say: it's an ill wind – but old habits do die hard!"

"Just as well you're both flighty night-birds and I'm not," Laura said, "so she'll be out of my way most of the time! For heaven's sake keep an eye on her; I don't trust her. Perhaps you should have a word with Quintin. I don't think I can stand her much longer. And how on earth am I supposed to explain her away to the concierge? She could do with a bath in disinfectant!"

Jennifer, who could generally persuade the most taciturn to talk, found Nova completely uncommunicative. All she could gather from her was that Nova had found the deb scene in London "not at all groovy man. Not my trip," that she had met Farmiloe a couple of months back at Tramp, through a friend who recommended her, and he'd offered her a job in his disco in Monte-Carlo.

"Seemed a groovy idea, man, so here I am."

She addressed everyone as 'man', regardless of sex, and steadfastly avoided eye contact. Her vocabulary seemed very lacking: a paradox, given the obviously expensive private education her parents must have lavished on her. Somehow, it seemed to Laura and Jennifer that everything became soured by Nova's arrival. She took the shine off their happy and idyllic summer. It would seem in retrospect that everything started to go wrong from that moment on. The time would come when both girls would rue Nova's unwelcome intrusion into their lives.

Jennifer was having a restless night. She'd had a bad quarrel with Jean-Claude, who was being insufferable as usual. He criticised her job, saying it was unsuitable for a young lady, and that his parents would never approve. The nerve of him! She had finally lost patience, and had told him for the umpteenth time that their affair was over. But this time she really meant it. He had no right to rule her life. Anyway, she was enjoying the summer too much to care whether or not the disco was a serious career move. It was irrelevant, and nothing to do with that pompous idiot. Shortly afterwards, while she was still fuming, Julius had walked into the club and asked her to come to Sardinia with him on his yacht. God! That was the last straw. Men thought the whole world revolved around them and their desires. Just whistle and girls would drop everything and come running at their slightest whim! At present Jennifer wished a great crater would open up and swallow both Jean-Claude and Julius. The foul Nova, too, for that matter.

Jennifer tossed and turned, but sleep seemed to evade her. Everything was so confusing, she wished she could blank all her thoughts out. She looked at her watch. Nearly three in the morning.

"God, I wish I had a sleeping pill!" she exclaimed. Throwing back the crumpled sheets, she went into the bathroom to see if Nova had any, rummaging through her bag of assorted junk.

"Jeez, what a mess! Let's see, KY Jelly, pessaries, diaphragm – ooh, yuk, it's still gungey. God, you'd think the dirty, lazy old cow could at least rinse the thing after using it. Ugh! Codeine, eyelash glue . . . Ah, a pillbox! What the hell's this strange powder in it? Talc?"

She snapped the little silver box shut, perplexed. "Crikey, what's this odd ball of stuff? Plasticine?" She squeezed it. No, not plasticine. Too sort of sticky and sweet-smelling. Bit like dark honey gone hard. Weird! A book of matches from New York . . . A broken mascara, leaking eyeliner, a cracked mirror, a biro with the inside missing. Stacks of pills: all shapes sizes and colours.

At last, success – a grimy 5mg Mogadon, rattling around at the bottom of the most bizarre collection of stuff ever seen! Jennifer broke the large white tablet into pieces, gulped it down with half a glass of water, and headed back to bed. Fairly soon, she was feeling grateful for the relaxing waves that were overtaking her, allowing her to drift into oblivion, a temporary respite from the thoughts that were plaguing her.

Later that night Jennifer had the most peculiar sensation of watching Nova performing an erotic and strange ballet with two naked men. At one point, Nova was kneeling on the floor facing one man, who was standing with a long object in his hand, slowly pushing it into her mouth, and the other was kneeling close behind her, sinuously writhing against her whilst grasping her hair with both hands.

It was so dark with the shutters closed that it was hard to distinguish reality from dream, or one body from the other, and sometimes they all appeared as one heaving mass in the theatre of her mind. Then the three stood up and the men stood aside, stroking themselves as the statuesque female danced, caressing her full breasts and writhing solo for a while, until the naked bodies all merged again. The girl stood in between them while the men slowly pushed their loins back and forth into her, in uniform rhythm. No one seemed to utter a sound, and Jennifer felt strangely lulled by the silent, dark, gently swaying masquerade enfolding in front of her. Then darker waves engulfed her completely, and the dream slowly faded into total blackness.

Next morning, Jennifer rose later than usual, and being unused to sleeping pills, still felt quite comatose. She stumbled into the kitchen to make herself a coffee, and found Nova sitting naked at the table, with the previous night's eye make-up smudged all down her face. She looked a complete wreck. She did not acknowledge Jennifer, but just sat there, smoking and staring blankly into space through a haze of cigarette smoke.

"You'll catch fire one of these days!" Jennifer said irritably, fanning away the smoke, visibly annoyed at Nova's presence. Normally she did not emerge from her bed until well after midday.

"Mmmm," was all Nova could manage.

"Conversational, aren't we?"

As Jennifer heated the milk for her coffee, she remembered

the peculiar dream sequence. Unless it was reality blurred by Mogadon . . . Turning round, she took in the enormous breasts staring at her, their weight sagging on the table against which their owner slumped, spiky hair even more matted than usual above the ravaged face.

God, no, she thought. Who could possibly want that disgusting creature! Could she ever be the object of any man's lust, let alone two!

She poured the boiling milk on to the coffee granules, enjoying the aroma. As she took up the cup and saucer to take her brew as far away from the repulsive Nova as possible, the girl got up and left the kitchen. Jennifer eyed the retreating redhead with distaste, noting a stream of colourless liquid tracing a path down an inner thigh.

"Yuk, how revolting!" she thought. "Thank heaven I'm not hung-over, or I'd throw up on the spot. I think I deserve a cigarette now, broke or not."

She lit up, drawing long and appreciatively on her precious last one, in between sips of hot milky coffee. The sight of Nova and the thought of her nocturnal antics had completely taken away her appetite. She decided to go to the beach without breakfast and to skip lunch because she couldn't afford it anyway. It was time, too, that she and Laura had a serious talk about Nova. There was no way they could put up with her any longer. She was a revolting slut and unliveable with. Of course, Jennifer conceded that she herself was no angel. Carefree, maybe. A flirt, yes, but never sordid. Never vulgar. Compared to Nova, she was whiter than white, and the sweet Laura was a saint! There were limits, and Nova exceeded all of them.

Laura had felt much better since her day out on the boat with Krep. She needed to, because in the days that followed, Fitz kept her tightly shackled to the grindstone with work piled upon work. As the shares turned over within the portfolios grew in volume, Laura was permanently on the telephone to brokers and Swiss bankers; passing on orders, entering executions, cancellations, changing limits and advising Fitz of large share-price fluctuations where relevant. So many brokers were touting for chunks of the rapidly growing business that Fitz was being entertained practically every lunch hour. This meant that Laura's own long midday break was generally spent at her desk tying up loose ends, instead of on the beach or at the Metropole pool. It seemed to her that these days her responsibilities were similar to those of a junior fund manager, but her status was only that of PA. Maybe it was time she tackled Fitz on the subject of gaining further advancement. Surely Fitz would know of courses that were available? But would he feel threatened by an over-ambitious assistant? She must tread carefully. Still, she would never know unless she tried. "Remember, nothing ventured..." she murmured to herself.

The opportunity came sooner than she expected.

"You know what, Laura," Fitz said later that day, "I think you ought to see these brokers instead of me sometimes. It's a good way of gaining experience. Why should I be entertained all the time whilst you're stuck in the office doing all the donkey-work? Anyway, all these business lunches are not good for *la ligne*!" He looked down ruefully, patting his middle.

Laura paused for a moment of thought, scissors poised as she prepared to cut out the latest share prices for him. This was an ideal opportunity for her to push ahead with her plan.

"I wonder? I know I'd appreciate the extra responsibility," she said carefully. "But you see, Fitz, instincts are all very well, but I know I'd be happier if I had a really firm grounding in the business. I'd hate to be taken for a 'dumb blonde' when the conversation gets too technical. It's almost a language in itself – the terminology and *brokerese*! However, I've been wondering for some time if there were any courses in investment analysis or brokerage I could study after hours."

She handed him the prices. He took them, but didn't look at

them. Instead he stared at her, his pale blue eyes thoughtful, his brows raised in surprise.

"A girl . . . studying stockbroking and investment analysis? To tell you the truth, it's not something I'd *ever* have thought of!"

Laura smiled patiently. "Oh? Why ever not? Here you are, offering to let me do business with your brokers, and I've got no formal qualifications. Well, not on paper anyway!"

For a moment he looked taken aback. "Well, come to think of it, I suppose you're right; qualifications are important in this field. He rustled his papers, preoccupied for a few moments. Then he looked at Laura intently. "Let me think about it for a while, will you?"

For the rest of the afternoon Fitz disappeared into his office, and Laura wondered if she had pushed too hard. Maybe she'd offended him by showing too much ambition. After a while she became depressed. No man seemed ready yet, especially in the world of high finance, to accept a woman into their ranks. Perhaps all her hopes had been in vain. If she couldn't win over the charming and affable Fitz, what hope would she have in a harsher, city environment?

She could hear Fitz's muffled voice through the closed door. He very rarely shut it. Perhaps he was really miffed. Mentally kicking herself for her impetuous suggestions, Laura threw herself into double-checking the orders and executions book. Then she did the performance charts. Concentrating on figures helped clear her mind of imponderables and ugly thoughts.

Finally Fitz's door burst open, and he marched towards her smiling. "Laura!" he shouted. "I've come to a decision. There's no reason why you shouldn't do a diploma course in broking to start off with. The New York Institute of Finance runs a very comprehensive one."

He smiled at her bemused expression and drummed his fingers on her desk reflectively, patted a stack of portfolios meaningfully and then added, "The more I think about it, the more I'm sure it would be a damn good thing for both of us if you were properly qualified. So I've done some scouting around on your behalf. And as it will benefit them in the end, the firm can pay the tuition. But do you think you'd have the time or the application to stick to it? It's pretty dry stuff and a lot of hard work for a young thing like you."

Laura's face lit up with delight. It seemed all her worries had been for nothing. "Yes, definitely, Fitz," she replied earnestly, thrilled that Fitz had been so accommodating. A diploma from the New York Institute of Finance was a tremendous start on the ladder to success. "For such a good career move," she went on enthusiastically, "I would always *make* the time. I'm not afraid of hard work. There's plenty of opportunity in the evenings. With Jennifer working at the club, I have a lot of time to myself."

"Well, Laura, if you're sure you can handle it, then OK. Get to it!" Fitz picked up a performance chart and waved it at her absentmindedly. "Wilder at Howson May will have the details. I'll get back to him straight away. When you've got all the relevant forms, I'll sign your enrolment. Then we'll send off the cheque, and you're away. I expect you'll probably know more than I do when you've completed the course!"

John Wilder at Howson May International was more than happy to oblige Fitzgerald, his biggest client, in getting Laura's course sorted out. Within minutes, he telephoned to say he'd just telexed the New York Institute of Finance. They would be sending enrolment forms within days, he promised.

Laura's eyes sparkled as she laughed excitedly. This was too good to be true. "Thanks, Fitz. Wonderful! I can't wait!"

Chapter 9

That same morning, back at the flat, Jennifer was delighted to find that Nova wasn't there. Her bed had not been slept in. She'd obviously found yet another willing male, or males. God, but men weren't very discriminating when it came to easily available sex! Jennifer was still amazed at Nova's talent for picking up partners. She really was *so* repulsive!

Good. There was no sign of the Biⁿ Rat in his hammock, either. Now she could relax and sun herself on the balcony. She made herself a milky coffee and plumped up the cushions on the lounger. With a contented sigh she flopped down. Life was good. Down below the fountain hissed and bubbled happily. There was a datura in bloom, its huge, tubular waxy flowers like suspended handkerchiefs, and geraniums growing up the trunks of the palms twined as high as the second floor, making colour splashes of bright pink and red everywhere. The gardens were beautiful. She took a sip of coffee. Later she would buy a paper and maybe go down to the beach to work on her tan.

Then the door bell rang. "I'll bet that silly bitch has forgotten her key again," thought Jennifer mutinously. But it wasn't the dreaded Nova. Of all people, it was Jean-Claude! What on earth did he want?

"*Alors, toi,*" he announced importantly, striding in as if he owned the place. "I've decided to take you to my cousins' place at Vence."

Jennifer was dumbfounded. The last time they'd met, she

had told him it was all over between them. And now here he was, carrying on as if they were still a going concern. So typical of him. Did he never listen? Jean-Claude was casually dressed, in jeans and a blue tee-shirt. This was not at all his usual attire. Jennifer had to admit that he did look very dishy.

She had already been to his cousins' villa near St Paul de Vence. It was beautiful – set high up, surrounded by woodland – and it had a lovely secluded terrace with a swimming-pool. The views from the villa were absolutely stunning. Jennifer had often wished it were Jean-Claude who was rich, and not his relations. She would have been far less inclined to take his proposal of marriage so lightly if it had been underlined with seriously luxurious trappings like this villa. It so reminded her of her idyllic childhood holidays at St Jean Cap Ferrat.

"Don't be silly, Jean-Claude. I can't get time off to go away with you. I have a job, as you well know, even though you don't approve." Jennifer folded her arms obstinately. "Quintin would never allow me to swan off just as the club's getting off the ground."

Jean-Claude's amber eyes flashed with irritation. "Oh, you and your stupid night-club. *C'est pas du tout sérieux, hein!*"

His pompousness was infuriating. Jennifer bridled and shot him a warning look. "It's my job and I earn good money. Don't knock it. The answer's no."

Jean-Claude realised he was walking on thin ice, and his tone of voice changed. "I'm sorry," he said, "I didn't mean it. Two days, *cherie:* it's all I'm asking. *Sois raisonnable!*" he cajoled, fixing her with his golden stare, and stroking her shoulder gently with the tip of his finger. "I've managed to earn a break because I'm ahead in my studies. Two days are all I ask. Two days of lying by the pool, eating ourselves silly, and making love. *Alors, mon ange, fais-moi plaisir!*" he wheedled, smiling disarmingly.

He took her in his arms and nuzzled her ear. He ran his fingers gently down her back, pulled her tightly to him and kissed her mouth softly. His lips were warm and parted. Jennifer's resolve began to melt. With the sudden flood of desire for him she could feel her nipples tingling as they rapidly hardened against his chest.

"I haven't seen you for ages," he murmured, covering her face and neck with small kisses. His thumbs insistently caressed the erect nipples with small circular movements. Jennifer squirmed with pleasure. "Come on, sweetheart," he breathed huskily, "give Farmiloe a ring. Surely he can spare you a couple of evenings, especially at the beginning of the week?" He pouted his lower lip and looked longingly into her eyes. The chestnut curls tumbled appealingly over his forehead.

On second thoughts, she had to admit that a couple of days at the villa lounging by the pool, and good food and drink – were beginning to appeal. Especially as the wetness between her legs reminded her that she was feeling very horny, and Jean-Claude was eminently desirable at the moment.

"OK, then," she said, pulling away from him. "I'll see what I can do. When are you planning to go?"

Jean-Claude's face brightened. "I want to go now. The villa's free because they've all gone off to Deauville for a couple of days. The maid'll still be there for meals and everything, so there's nothing to do but be lazy and have a good time. Anyhow, it suits my aunt for me to stay while they're gone so I can keep an eye on the place."

Jennifer was sorely tempted. She needed a break from Monaco. Too many late nights. And perhaps – she glanced at Jean-Claude surreptitiously from under her lashes – a couple of days away with him might help her decide whether the relationship was worth salvaging. But what about Quintin? He relied on her for the smooth running of the club. Was he likely to grant her time off?

She looked dubious. "Do they know you're planning to bring the dreadful *Anglaise*?"

Jean-Claude laughed sardonically. "*Mais non. Bien sûr que non!*"

"Why? Would they disapprove?"

"They'd disapprove if I brought any female on her own, let alone you!"

"Thanks a rock, chum. What if the maid told on you?"

The amber eyes danced mischievously. "Aha! But I have her firmly in my pocket!"

Jennifer looked daggers at him. "Bet you've had her in *more* than your pocket, you swine."

He was not about to rise to the bait. "*Ça c'est mon affaire. Ça ne te regarde pas*," Jean-Claude replied with a grin.

He pulled her into his arms again and Jennifer's senses responded afresh to the familiar smell of Gitanes and Monsieur de Givenchy. So what the hell? She'd give it a try. Krep was beginning to crowd her with his constant flowers and invitations. She needed to get away for a bit to collect her thoughts and sort out her muddled life. After all, the worst Quintin could do was to say no. She picked up the receiver and dialled his number.

It proved a rather easier job than Jennifer imagined to persuade Farmiloe to let her have a couple of days off. This was undoubtedly because he had a new disco-dolly, the ghastly Nova, to distract him.

"But of course, darling," replied the velvety voice. "I don't mind if you have a little break. You've been a godsend to me! But you must be back by Wednesday, because we've got an important party then."

"You're an angel, Quint. Thanks!"

"I'll kill you if you're not back for the party, though!" he threatened. "Have a good time sweetie-pie, and behave yourself if you can until Wednesday!"

As if . . . Jennifer laughed as she put the phone down. She

turned round to Jean-Claude, and gave him the thumbs-up.

"OK, J-C. I'll chuck a few things in a bag, and then we're off."

Jennifer rummaged around getting a few things together, but on Jean-Claude's insistence didn't take much. He told her all they needed were swimwear and casual clothes. Besides, he was in a hurry to leave. So she just packed a couple of bikinis, tee-shirts and shorts and a cotton shift, and then threw in her sponge-bag on top.

He chivvied her on, and took her tote bag impatiently. But, just as he was pushing her out of the door, he suddenly stopped and asked, "What about Laura? Shouldn't you leave her a note or something?"

"You're right. Maybe I should phone her at work."

"No, she'll probably be busy," he said bossily. "Don't bother her there. Go and get some paper and leave a note on the kitchen table. She'll be bound to see it when she gets in."

Jennifer hurried off to get pen and paper from the sitting-room at his bidding, where she wrote a hasty few words to leave for Laura in the kitchen. But when she got back to the hallway, she was surprised to see Jean-Claude emerging furtively from her bedroom, still clutching her bag. What had he been up to, nosing around in there?

"What were you doing in my room?" she asked, puzzled and frowning at him. She could not fathom his strange, guilty expression.

"Oh, I just had to go to the bathroom quickly," he answered uneasily. Jean-Claude cleared his throat and his eyes slid away from her gaze uncomfortably. He fiddled with the straps of her tote bag, and his voice sounded tight and artificially cheerful. "*Alors, on y va, hein?*"

Laura looked up and smiled as John Wilder came into the office, just before lunch. He was a tall, gangly American in his mid-thirties. He had an open, smiling face, and thinning, sandy hair.

"Hi, Laura. Still as beautiful as ever, I see!" he said. "Guess what I've got for you."

"I wonder?" she answered, smiling hugely.

Wilder flourished an envelope in front of her, and laid it down reverently,

The New York Institute of Finance, it said. Her enrolment papers!

"Hooray!" she cried. "Thank you, you wonderful man!"

Impatiently she slit open the envelope and extracted the form. Wilder looked at her questioningly, as she scanned its contents. He waited till she looked up.

"Are you going to take the Stock Exchange exam and join our side of the fence, then?" he asked, curious.

The Stock Exchange exam? Laura suddenly sat up. What an interesting notion. It had never crossed her mind to think that far ahead, to be that ambitious!

"No," she replied slowly. "That's not actually what I planned. Just the diploma, to help me in my dealings with people like you." Then she added jokingly, "So I'll know you're not spinning me a line!"

"Is that so?" he smiled. "Didn't you know that we were all already petrified of you, with that gorgeous English voice of yours? It sure makes me feel like a hick every time I listen to you!"

Laura laughed and said teasingly, "Once I'm well into my studies, you'll really have to watch your p's and q's then, won't you? Just think, you might even be obliged to take me out to lunch!"

"Yes, please, ma'am!" Wilder chuckled, as he made his way out of the office.

Laura felt she was really coming to grips with her career now. But the broker had just sown an interesting seed of thought. It hadn't struck her until Wilder mentioned it, that this diploma would broaden her horizons in more directions than one. It would help her existing job on the investment side, obviously; but also it could lead to her qualifying as a broker on the opposite side of the fence.

If she really took the plunge and went all out for the New York Stock Exchange and Securities Dealers exams on top of the diploma, she would probably be among the first, and certainly the youngest British female with that particular qualification in Europe. What a coup! It would be a crowning achievement, and something to be very proud of.

How exciting to be in the forefront! Women weren't even allowed on the Stock Exchange floor as yet back in the UK, so Laura would be a very rare commodity in a hitherto all-male preserve! Her eyes sparkled at the challenge. This could be more than just a dream. It was all within her grasp if she really pushed the boat out.

Just think! There were big commissions to be earned in stockbroking, especially if one landed a big fish like Fitz, or say someone like Krep. The possibilities to be exploited by this extra qualification were all too exciting for words.

Laura was firmer still now in her resolve to tackle her studies with the New York Institute of Finance, however boring and tedious, with relish – given the possible future opening up in front of her. And it was there for the taking. John Wilder had already suggested it, so it had to be feasible!

Laura arrived at the Meribel after work bubbling over with excitement. Happily brandishing her New York Institute enrolment papers, she was longing to tell Jennifer about her latest plans. But there was no sign of her. She went into the kitchen for a cool drink and picked up Jennifer's note. Her face fell as she read the hastily scrawled message. Her euphoria evaporated as she realised she'd be alone with Nova in the flat for two whole nights. The prospect was unappealing. Such was Laura's distaste for Nova's company, that she would sooner let her have the free run of the flat every evening until the creature went out to the disco at nine, than spend any time alone with her. Laura decided to eat at the Café de Paris, and to complete her enrolment form over dinner and a half-bottle of champagne, in the open air. It would have been so much more fun to share her good news with Jennifer. But now all that would have to wait.

Nova mooched around the flat sighing. She was bored. It was her night off and there was nothing to do. Normally she'd have gone down to the port to pick up a crew member for the night, but she was sick of Greeks and Lebanese; and the Swedes were lousy in bed. No. She'd give it a miss for once. Perhaps she'd find some talent in the Café de Paris. Only thing was, money was short. Her last fix had not been cheap, what with the train fare to Nice and the taxi ride to the Arab quarter. God, what a hell hole that was!

The only consolation was that her two stuck-up flatmates were out, thank God. The last thing she needed was another lecture from that sanctimonious Laura on her untidy ways. So what if she chose to throw her clothes and towels on the floor? It was nobody's business but her own. And Jennifer was away for a couple of days, too. Good. Now she'd have Quintin all to herself at work. Of course, there was no way the randy bastard would dream of taking Nova out on her night off. He just used her and dumped her when he felt like it. Not like the precious Jennifer, or Laura. She was sick of the way he sucked up to those two. They could do no wrong in his eyes. Stupid bitches, the pair of them. They'd get their come-uppance one of these days. If Nova herself didn't see to it, someone else would! She grinned nastily at the thought.

She prowled around the kitchen, opening cupboard doors, looking for a drink. No luck. The stingey cows had hidden the booze. She found a Coke in the fridge, and swigged it straight from the bottle. Looking out of the kitchen window, she noticed a hammock swinging on the balcony opposite. Christ, the man had binoculars, too! Pervy bugger . . . She'd give him something to look at all right. Lifting up her tee-shirt with her free hand, she sniggered, "Get a load of these, you poor, frustrated sod!" and waggled her enormous breasts at him. Then she stuck up two fingers and wondered idly whether to show him the lot; drive him nuts! No, she had better things to do than please some pathetic pervert.

The door-bell rang. "I'll bet it's more flowers for that vain bitch from that common little millionaire!" she thought jealously. Perhaps she wouldn't bother to answer the door. It rang again, followed by a loud knock.

"Shit!" she exclaimed, and padded to the door.

Things were looking up. Framed in the doorway was a real looker. He was tall, and very handsome in a sullen kind of way. At the sight of Nova he started. She was wearing nothing but a fluorescent green tee-shirt, which barely covered her bottom.

"Where's Laura?" he asked arrogantly, eyeing her protruding nipples, as they were impossible to ignore.

"Why should I know? I'm not her keeper," she said rudely. It irritated her that the man was obviously Laura's rejected lover. Not half-bad though, she thought, flicking her tongue slowly over her fleshy red lips and pouting.

"I need to speak to her urgently," he said, more courteously this time, and making an attempt to smile.

That's more like it, thought Nova. "You could always come in and wait for her." She fluttered her heavy false lashes at him coquettishly.

Pierre Lejeune looked at her, unmoved. Things were going really downhill if this was the kind of company Laura was keeping now! He would never have allowed her to have friends like this one! It was obvious Laura needed him more than ever these days.

"Oh? Are you expecting her back soon, then?"

"She's usually back from work by now. She'll probably be here any minute," Nova lied, fairly sure that Laura would be eating out. She usually avoided Nova like the plague if she could.

"In that case, I'll come in for a little while, and wait."

Pierre followed Nova into the sitting-room, and sat down in the middle of the sofa, his large hands resting awkwardly on his knees.

"By the way, my name's Nova. Would you like a coffee?"

"No, thanks."

"Can I offer you anything else?" Nova asked, putting her hands on her hips flirtatiously, and sticking out her breasts. The movement made her luminous tee-shirt ride even further up her large thighs.

Pierre was fascinated by her blatant attempts to be seductive. This over-made-up trollop was handing him sex on a plate. He stared at her nipples again. Perhaps he should take up the offer. She was quite likely the sort that liked it rough. The thought of punishing Nova brutally for the loss of Laura was pleasing, and he felt his body responding. The girl came sidling towards him and squeezed herself against him. In an instant Pierre's thoughts died, and he went cold. *Mon Dieu*, but the woman stank! Didn't she ever wash herself? Disgusted, Pierre leapt to his feet and crossed the room to escape her.

"Pretty flowers," he commented breathlessly, gesturing wildly at Krep's latest love-token, an ostentatious arrangement of orchids and white lilies on the table. Anything to deflect that disgusting creature's attention off him.

"Yes, aren't they?" sneered Nova, her eyes black with hatred, furious at the Frenchman's rejection of her. Now was her chance to get even. "They're Laura's, from one of her many beaux."

"You're lying," snapped Pierre. "Laura has nothing but her work to occupy her. She's not a slut like you."

Nova bridled. The bastard! How dare he insult her like this? "Go on then," she taunted, "read the card."

Pierre picked up the small card tucked into the bouquet. "To my blonde angel . . . with love always . . . Julius," it said. His mouth dropped open. Then he looked at Nova with contempt. No! The bitch must be lying.

"How do I know they're not for Jennifer?" he asked. "She's a blonde, too."

"Jennifer's gone away with her fiancé, Jean-Claude, to Vence. So there!" Nova jeered. "Your saintly little Laura's got herself a sugar-daddy to sleep with, amongst all the others."

Pierre balled his hands into fists, seething with jealous rage. It couldn't be true. No, it just couldn't be! Not his beloved Laura. He walked stiffly to the sliding doors, and, wrenching them aside, went out on to the balcony. His heart was hammering in his ears, and his mouth went dry at the thought of Laura in another's arms. He stood there for a while, breathing deeply, to allow his anger to dissipate. The redhead was jealous, he decided. She was the slut, not Laura. After a while, he felt a little calmer, but he was still uneasy. Gazing into the middle distance, he was suddenly distracted as a flash caught his eye. *Mon Dieu*, but someone was spying on No. 613 with binoculars! Now why would that be? What could be going on? As Pierre tried to focus his mind, the watcher, obviously worried that he'd been spotted, climbed out of his hammock, turned on his heel, and fled.

Aha! thought Lejeune. There's a familiar sight. I recognise that creep. It's none other than that rich weirdo, Ratti. Bent as a nine-franc note!

Lejeune had pulled in Louis Ratti many times for soliciting and molesting young girls and boys. But all his life, Ratti had been able to buy himself out of trouble. Though the black sheep, he came nevertheless from a rich and very influential Monégasque family. Now this could be very useful. He owed Lejeune. He would use Ratti to keep an eye on Laura. To find out if what the redhead said was true. One way or the other, he had to know.

* * *

Jean-Claude was in a very romantic mood. It struck Jennifer
that he was going all out to woo her back. She was enjoying
the attention, especially in this wonderful setting. Beside
the swimming-pool was a huge stone terrace, sun-warmed
and surrounded by a pergola clothed in vines and scented
roses. There was a long table with a slate top, still infused
with the warmth of the sun, laid for two, with finger bowls
and flowers. The maid had prepared asparagus spears with
vinaigrette, then *blanquette de veau* and salad to follow.
Now they were alone. Jean-Claude opened a bottle of
champagne with a resounding 'pop' and let it foam into two
very tall flutes.

Heavens! thought Jennifer in amazement, wonders will
never cease! Normally he would be far too stingey to lash out
on champagne! It must be from his uncle's cellar, she decided
ungraciously. She giggled to herself. Oh, well, who cared
whose champagne it was? Jean-Claude was looking especially
fancyable. Perhaps she should appreciate him more. Perhaps
he was destined for success in the long run: maybe he'd have a
set-up like this one day. It would be worth waiting for. Jennifer
breathed in deeply and shut her eyes. The night air was
redolent with the perfume of pines and scented roses. What a
wonderful evening. What a dream.

She was going to have a ball tonight. She was in a heady
mood, mellow and sexy. Jean-Claude looked good in blue, his
dark curls cascading over his temples. She felt a sudden urge
to sit on his lap and wrap herself round him. Kicking off her
shoes, she picked up her glass, and crossed over to him. She
half-drained her glass, set it down, snaked a long, lean leg over
his, and sat astride him.

"*Alors, poupée!*" he murmured, lowering his thick lashes
over his amber eyes, "what are you wearing under that little
dress?"

"Nothing," Jennifer whispered. "My bikini was wet, so I

took it off earlier." She pulled up his tee-shirt, drew up her knees, and caressed his ribs slowly, with the inside of her thighs. "Mmmmm, I like the feel of your bare skin against my legs. It's sexy."

"What about the *hors d'oeuvres?*" he whispered.

"Who needs asparagus? I have plenty of delicious things you could nibble."

He grinned at her wickedly, then kissed her long and deep. His hands found her breasts and gently squeezed them. He pulled up her dress to her waist, and ran his hands over her smooth, silky buttocks. Then, wrapping her legs around his waist, and bracing her weight with his strong thighs, he stood up. Roughly pushing away the settings, he laid her down on the table.

"Eat," he ordered, leaning over her and dangling an asparagus spear over her mouth. Jennifer giggled, raising her head and reaching for it with her lips. He laughed and drew it away. "No. Shut your eyes first. That way it'll taste better."

She complied. He was right. She nibbled at the long, delicious spear as he slowly pushed it into her mouth. The oily dressing brought out the delicate flavour of the smooth, slippery asparagus, and made her mouth water for another.

"More," she sighed.

"Open your mouth," he commanded. Gently he dribbled in some champagne.

"Mmmmm. Lovely. More please."

"Wait." She could hear him breathing deeply and fumbling around above her.

"Come on!" she coaxed.

"It's coming," he murmured. "Keep your eyes shut then. Now taste this."

Jennifer started. Her mouth was suddenly very full: of a texture and taste that was completely different. She grinned inwardly, and slowly, wickedly, sank her teeth into the meaty mouthful. Jean-Claude flinched, and pulled away in haste.

"*La vache!*" he cried. "You were supposed to suck, not bite!"

"Darling, but you forgot the vinaigrette," she crooned, opening one eye.

"That wasn't asparagus," he retorted, his face flushed and his eyes dilated.

"Oh?" she giggled, feigning surprise. "You could have fooled me!"

"Bitch!" he said, and gave her a playful slap.

Jennifer smiled, hooked her long legs over his shoulders, and pulled him closer to her. Jean-Claude, seizing her slender flanks, thrust himself deep inside her, scattering china and cutlery, which clattered on to the tiles and smashed into little pieces.

"Damn!" he groaned, as his senses overwhelmed him, and he came almost instantly. "You beautiful, beautiful bitch."

Chapter 10

When Jennifer returned on Wednesday, Laura could tell immediately that the interlude with Jean-Claude had not been a success.

"Oh dear!" Laura said sympathetically, as she caught Jennifer's expression. She decided to leave her own good news until later. "Do you want to tell me all?" Laura led her into the kitchen, where she had made a pot of tea.

"Oh Christ!" Jennifer sighed, flopping down at the table. "I've made up my mind to boot J-C out. I'm sick of him and his bloody PE."

"What d'you mean, PE?"

"Premature ejaculation, of course. What else? And he'd never dream of making up for it in other ways. The hallmark of the truly selfish and thoughtless lover. He thinks he's God's gift, but in reality he's an utter bore! All he wants to do is get married and turn me into a little housewife. It's absolutely the last thing I want. So there's not much point in staying together, is there?"

"Not really," agreed Laura. "But what's new, Jen? You've been saying this since the beginning. You've never really got on, have you?" She filled a couple of mugs and brought the steaming brew to the table. She sat opposite Jennifer, looking at her intently and leaning on her elbows. She was still in her office clothes, but had pulled the restraining pins out of her hair. The white-blonde mass looked incongruous spilling wildly all over her navy suit.

"No. You're right," continued Jennifer. "God, he gets on my

nerves. Always pretending to be so saintly. No bloody coincidence he's got the same initials as Jesus Christ! I ask you, all he can talk about is his career, and the map he's drawn of my future is anathema to me. We have absolutely nothing in common at all. I've been so bored these last two days. The only way to shut him up was to get randy, and even that was no good. In fact he's hopeless. And then I couldn't find my bloody pills, so I just had to hope for the best. I'm sure I packed them though, because they're always in my sponge bag."

A look of concern crossed Laura's face. "Oh lord! I hope you were careful, or he was."

"Oh, J-C said he'd take care of that side of things, and not to worry," Jennifer said vaguely, propping up her chin on two fists.

"Well, what's next then?"

"I don't know. All I know is that I want more in life than being the little woman in the background. I haven't the patience, and besides, I'm far too spoiled and selfish. I'd like someone who's already achieved his ambitions, when *I'm* ready, and not before." She punched the table to add meaning to her words, and sat back, waiting for Laura's opinion.

"Then for heaven's sake finish with Jean-Claude right now!" Laura advised. "Don't do what I did and hang around for kindness' sake, because it turns out just the opposite. Look at the mess I was in because I was too silly to take the bull by the horns! Jean-Claude's not going to like it any less later than now, so make a clean break and be blunt about it."

"Do as I say, and not as I do, eh?" answered Jennifer thoughtfully.

"Yes, that's exactly it."

"All right, then. I think I'll get absolutely ratted tonight at work, so I can muster the courage. God, I really need a drink. Maybe I should get myself laid by Quintin to cheer me up! Now he's always good for a laugh."

"Oh, Jennifer!" Laura exclaimed irritably. "What purpose would that serve? You've enough on your plate already. You know he's an absolute shit where women are concerned. He's an utter user and a bastard."

Jennifer looked dreamy. "But rather dishy with it. I'll bet he's really something in bed."

Laura folded her arms disapprovingly. "Well, rather you than me. You're a glutton for punishment!"

"Actually," Jennifer continued with enthusiasm, "on the subject of bed, but in another context, you'll never guess what happened the other night, before I went away."

Surely not more drama? This was turning out to be one hell of a summer. Did she really want to hear this, she thought wearily? But curiosity overcame her and Laura put down her cup. "No, but I'll bet you're about to tell me. Fire away, then!" She put her elbows on the table, all ears.

"Nova was having it off with two guys at the same time." Jennifer put her feet up on her chair, and hugged her knees.

Laura was aghast. "Never! Where?"

"Here in the flat, you daft thing. In my bedroom. I saw the whole thing! At first I didn't know if I was awake or dreaming because I was all groggy on Mogadon. Anyway, I know now I didn't imagine it. So there she was, kneeling on the floor being humped by one man whilst sucking the other for starters. Then she sort of danced around a bit, and rounded off by rogering them both together, standing up, as a grand finale."

Laura's blue eyes registered total incredulity. "Whaat? I mean how ... God, I don't believe my ears. How could she have *two* up her at the same time?"

"Oh Laura, do use your loaf!" Jennifer giggled wickedly. "Anyway, I told you before she could accommodate a battalion up there, didn't I?"

"Oh, thank you very much!" said Laura, her mouth turning down in disgust. "Spare me the grisly details. But if I'd been you I'd have been livid. It's already bad enough her bringing one guy back. But two, and in the same room with you! Honestly! What a slut!"

"Laura dearest, if only you could see your face! It's a picture of outraged moral indignation. Well, I'm off to Bedfordshire. I wonder what the floor show will be tonight?"

As Jennifer turned to leave the kitchen, Laura added, "I still don't believe you. I'll bet you're just having me on, but let me tell you, just in case you're not ribbing me, if she ever tries anything remotely like that within sight of me – Quintin or no Quintin – she'll be out on her ear in a flash."

"Hah! Quintin would probably ask to be invited along. Just his cup of tea, troilism, in any combination – though maybe even *he'd* draw the line at a ravaged floozy like Nova."

Laura yawned dismissively. "I still think you're just winding me up."

"Whatever you say, dear heart! Good night, and sweet erotic dreams to you, too!"

The next week was uneventful for Laura, but Jennifer was as good as her word. She told Jean-Claude flatly that the relationship was over, that she didn't want to marry him – now, or ever. He accepted the situation with a kind of arrogant dignity.

"We'll see," he said. "We'll see about that. But I bet you'll change your mind quite soon." Then he looked at her with a cold and knowing expression, before turning on his heel and bidding her a disdainful '*adieu*'.

"Just like him! Typical!" she fumed. "And what was that look for? Some sort of a threat? Arrogant, pompous twerp!"

Jennifer hadn't enjoyed telling him the unpalatable truth; but was relieved now that it was all over, as if a huge weight had been lifted off her shoulders. *Au revoir*, Jean-bloody Claude. Good riddance, and hello freedom! she said to herself, ever the optimist.

As the weeks progressed, Laura became immersed in her

study course, which had arrived at the office in a large envelope emblazoned, New York Institute of Finance. Please open immediately. The course was well organised. The first two lessons arrived together, so that when she returned lesson one for correction she could embark on the second one, with the third tutorial on its way to her, and so on.

"Only eighteen stages in all, and then the final examination. I must be mad," she sighed, daunted, as she engrossed herself in 'History and Function of the New York Stock Exchange'.

"Ooh, yuk! How absolutely ghastly and boring for you!" Jennifer commiserated, discovering Laura late one night with all her course papers spread out on the kitchen table. She was chewing on a biro and practically tearing her hair out.

"Fitz was right, Jennifer," Laura groaned. "This is really dry stuff. Unbelievably tedious. But I've stuck my neck out, so I've got to put my money where my mouth *was*!"

"I'd make you a coffee, but I think a double brandy would be more the ticket!"

Laura sighed again. She'd as good as finished her lesson. It only needed retyping, and she could do that at the office.

"Let's get out!" she said decisively. "I know it's past midnight, but I need some fresh air. My brains are all scrambled."

Jennifer nodded. "Brilliant idea. I could do with a change of scene, too, after the smoky, noisy club. Let's go."

Laura glanced at Jennifer discreetly. It was unlike her to complain about smoky night-clubs. She looked pale and peaky, even under her tan. Too many late nights, she decided. Burning the candle at both ends as usual.

The lift graunched to a halt at their floor. Laura wrenched the black wrought-iron gates to one side and the girls stepped into the lift, which then slowly and painfully made its way down to the ground floor.

Laura pulled at her hair distractedly and made a wry face at
Jennifer. "Oh lord," she sighed, "what have I done? Me and
my big ambition. Well, I'm committed now, so I'll just have to
get on with it."

Jennifer's expression was sympathetic but preoccupied.
The lift stopped with a sudden jerk at the ground floor.

"Bloody thing!" grumbled Jennifer, tugging at the black
gates. "It was probably made in the Iron Age."

"Like the plumbing!" added Laura, sardonically. "On that
note, where's the dreaded Nova?"

Their footsteps echoed eerily on the pale blue marble floor
of the deserted lobby as they made their way out of the
Meribel.

"Why on that note?" Jennifer asked.

"Plumbing the depths, I suppose!" snorted Laura.

The still night air was cool and overladen with the scent of
orange blossom. They turned right, down the tree-lined
avenue.

Jennifer grinned wryly. "The old cow's as pissed as a rat and
said she was going to the Tip Top for a spag bol. She won't be
back till dawn, thank God. I've told her to come in quietly, and
that I'll throttle her if she wakes me!"

"How are things going with you two?" The girls linked arms.

"Nova's weird," said Jennifer. "She's so vacant – sort of
spaced out half the time. I've never seen her eat here, at the
flat. She just smokes incessantly, and makes coffee when she
can be bothered. I think she's too lazy to cook."

"Too thick, you mean. One way or the other, we've got to
get rid of her. Keep a close eye on her, will you, Jen?"

Jennifer nodded. "Oh, I am. Don't you worry. I loathe
the bitch. I'm looking for any excuse to get Quint to sack
her."

"Good," said Laura. "Let's have a quick coffee at the Roxy,
and then bed!"

Jennifer, who generally slept like a log, was unusually

restive that night. She could not push out of her mind that she was well overdue, and her breasts were very tender. She was increasingly puzzled that her pills, which were always in her sponge-bag, had not been there at Vence. They had mysteriously turned up at the bottom of her untidy wardrobe on her return. The more she thought about it, the more it didn't make any sense.

As soon as she'd found them, she had taken three pills at once to make up for the nights she'd missed. "Rather like shutting the stable door after the horse has bolted," she'd remarked, nonchalantly knocking them back with a glass of Coke, and hoping for the best. That was over two weeks ago now.

She tried to dismiss her forebodings by shrugging them off in her customary fashion. But this time the spectre of unwanted pregnancy kept creeping back, like a tenacious virus. Worrying was a totally new and unwelcome experience for her. She recalled an earlier conversation with Laura, in her bedroom.

"Apropos," she'd asked, "have you heard from J-C?"

"No, thank God. But my period's overdue, and I'm never late – ever. It's getting very worrying. And I can't understand why my pills were missing at Vence. Even though I'm disorganised about everything else, I always keep the pill in my sponge-bag, so that I remember to take it first thing in the morning."

"You don't think Jean-Claude might have sabotaged the things, do you?"

Jennifer winced. Laura had just voiced her inner fears. She'd been hiding from the awful truth. Trying to tuck it away, ostrich-like. Putting her head in the sand in the belief that nothing so dreadful could possibly happen to her.

"What? Hidden them on purpose, to trap me into pregnancy, you mean? Would a man ever be that devious? I know women do that kind of thing but it's not usually a man's

style. Although I wouldn't put anything past Jean-Claude."
Jennifer clapped her hand to her mouth at the mere thought of
it. "Dear God, no. It's unthinkable! How absolutely bloody
awful if he got me pregnant. What on earth would I do?
Abortion's still illegal here. Everything to do with sex seems to
be illegal and yet it's supposed to be the land of the Latin
lovers. *L'amour, toujours l'amour!* What hypocrisy. Talk
about double standards!" Her face crumpled and her grey eyes
were shadowed with worry.

Jennifer swallowed hard as the sour taste of bile filled her
mouth. Please, let it not be! Perhaps tomorrow everything
would be OK. Maybe her cycle had gone haywire. It
sometimes happened that way, didn't it?

June blazed on. President de Gaulle was turfed out and
replaced by the universally disliked Pompidou. Rows blazed on
between the girls and Nova, whose slatternly ways were
intolerable.

The Monaco Grand Prix came and went, causing noise and
disruption. At night, hordes of braying Brits decades older
spilled untidily out of noisy bars and milled about the streets,
easily recognisable by their untrendy clothes and their pink and
perspiring faces. Too much sun and local draught lager,
Jennifer thought scathingly. At times like this it was
embarrassing to be British. Only they would have the gall to
wear those ghastly Sta-prest trousers and white poplin shirts
with sleeves rolled unfashionably above the elbow!

"Seen one Grand Prix, you've seen 'em all . . ."
Impatiently Jennifer followed the temporary, tortuous and
lengthy diversions through the town. Crossing dizzyingly high
bridges, pushing past shuffling cattle-like crowds, hemmed in
by blank hoardings which obscured the circuit from all but
paying customers, she grew daily more irritable and tired. It
took ten times longer to get anywhere. Shopping was a pain,
going to the beach was a pain, in fact everything was a pain!

It was impossible to sleep beyond dawn, as from first light racing-cars were revved up and engines were tested for hour upon hour; an ear-splitting, screaming roar reverberating round the mountains and buildings. Nerve-shattering. A sickly haze of high octane fuel lingered in the hot, June air. The flat smelt of sump-oil and axle grease as Nova doubtless blew and laid the polyglot team mechanics from end to end when her flatmates' backs were turned.

"Perhaps one of them will do us a favour and stick a spanner up her works," muttered Laura, "or maybe a club hammer and a jack, and leave them there."

"Would the old cow feel the difference?" rejoined Jennifer. And afterwards, when the principality returned to normal, peace still didn't reign.

The last straw came when Jennifer was woken up at four in the morning by another of Nova's bizarre floor shows, this time with three men. Enraged at being disturbed, and sickened by Nova's blatant indiscretion, Jennifer snatched up her bedding in order to use the sitting-room. On her way out of the bedroom, one of the men had grabbed her and murmured, "Hey, darling blondie, how about joining us, literally?"

"Go to hell, you revolting pig!" she shouted, and wrenched herself away in disgust. Life was bad enough already without being pawed by a sick-making degenerate.

Next morning, Jennifer remonstrated vehemently with Nova. But she sullenly denied all.

"You must have been dreaming, man," she droned in her usual monotone.

"I can assure you I didn't dream being grabbed by one of your perverts last night," Jennifer snapped. "God, but you're disgusting! Why can't you sod off and be revolting elsewhere?"

Nova said nothing, but lit a cigarette, blowing smoke into Jennifer's face by way of a reply. Jennifer was hit by a wave of nausea. Infuriated, she snatched the cigarette from the redhead, and stamped on it. Then she left the kitchen in disgust, resolving to use the sofa every night now. It was the last straw, on top of everything else. Jennifer could no longer hide from the truth. She'd woken up feeling sick every morning for the last few days. Come what may, Nova had to go. She was evil. Jennifer couldn't stand having the bitch around a moment longer.

She decided to take her problem to Quintin at his flat. At first he laughed when Jennifer catalogued Nova's misdemeanours. "Hmm. Sounds rather fun. Why didn't you join in, darling?"

"Oh, do shut up, Quintin, you perv!" she complained, and then went on to mention Nova's other strange habits: the permanently dilated eyes, the vacant expression, the sticky ball in her sponge-bag, every kind of pill, and the strange white powder.

Suddenly Quintin's face blanched. "What? What's that you say? I don't believe it! They'll close me down. I can't have this. They'll close us down!" His voice trembled.

"What is it then, Quint?" Jennifer asked, alarmed at his change of tone, "Drugs? Coke? Is that what all that weird stuff was?"

"Ssshh, you silly girl. Keep your voice down! Walls have ears. We've got to get rid of her. Not a word to anyone, do you hear?" he hissed.

Quintin was horror-struck. His handsome face had paled and his tan was a peculiar shade of grey. The turquoise eyes darkened with panic. His hands nervously flicked at the flaxen waves over his ears.

Orgies he could handle. Yes, great. But drugs? Drugs, no. Not the really heavy stuff. Especially in a place like Monaco! It was a well-known fact that Princess Grace had an absolute horror of them and that any sniff of suspicion spelt doom for anyone involved. Those suspected were immediately ejected from Monaco, with no form of redress. The expulsion was carried out under a cloak of utmost secrecy – the press were never informed, and nothing was ever mentioned again. But somehow it was arranged that suspects would never again be allowed south of Toulon. Banned from the Côte d'Azur for ever more!

Monaco, whose whole industry and lifeblood was that of tourism, stood to live or die on its reputation. One never saw vagrants, drunks or undesirables of any sort – nor even *femmes de nuit* there. Monte-Carlo had to be squeaky clean. The last thing it could afford was a drugs scandal, and of this the Palace was well aware.

Quintin quaked at the very thought of his club being embroiled in a drug raid. Horror! Loss of licence, loss of goodwill, loss of everything. And all the money he'd invested too! He'd be kicked out of the Riviera, bags and baggage, his whole life in ruins, his business wrecked for ever.

"Leave her to me, Jennie, darling," he said. His voice was tight with worry, his eyes darting from side to side in agitation, "but not *one* word. Promise?"

"Anything you say, boss. Anything to get rid of the slut. She's loathesome and probably spreading clap all over the place, too. I'm spraying disinfectant all over the flat."

Farmiloe placed his hands protectively over his trousers, and rolled his eyes heavenwards.

"From clap and pestilence, good Lord, deliver me!" he prayed aloud.

"Oh, Quintin, you didn't! You didn't! Not with Nova? Good God, how *could* you?"

"Well, she's a broad-minded bird, a groovy chick and she played any game, any which way. She was a real sport." Then he suddenly turned from his reverie, eyes widening with alarm, "You don't really think she's got clap do you?"

"But of course, and probably crabs, too; she's always scratching herself, and never washes. And all the men she's had, dozens and dozens! She had some revolting-looking pessaries in the bag as well. I can guess where she shoves those." Jennifer was by now enjoying Farmiloe's obvious discomfiture as she piled on the agony.

"Great Scott!" he cried. "I'm off to the medic right now. From clap, pestilence, crabs and pessaries, good Lord, deliver us all!"

Quintin shot off, his handsome features still grey and tremulous with fear and panic. Jennifer breathed a sigh of relief, licked her finger, and chalked an imaginary figure '1' in the air. "Operation Slut Sabotage. Success."

She walked back to the Meribel for a celebratory coffee. One major problem solved. But it wasn't long before other demons came to bring her back down to earth again. Her bra was much too tight, and cut into her breasts, which were swollen and painful. Without a doubt she was pregnant. At least six weeks now.

Jennifer was devastated. "It's me who needs the medic," she sighed in anguish, "not Quintin, the silly fool. God, what on earth am I going to do?"

Nova was seething with rage and bitterness. She'd just got the sack, and been told to catch the next plane home. Just like that: with no redress. What a bastard Quintin was. And she'd been looking forward to a long, hot, lazy summer of fun and sex. What was she to do now? Her father wouldn't stump up any more money. He'd stopped her allowance, to get her to clean up her act. There was nothing for her to do in London, and most of her friends had turned their backs on her. Now Quintin had discarded her, too, like an old rag. Those two bitches had cost her her job. It was all their fault. How else would Farmiloe have found out about her little habits? God, how she hated those two arrogant snobs! That snotty Laura and her stupid diploma, and Jennifer, who fancied herself no end. They'd treated her like dirt under their feet from the very outset. This time they'd pushed her too far. She'd show them both!

She stormed around the flat, breasts heaving and wobbling with anger, throwing bits and pieces into her battered leather case. She went into the bathroom and picked up her sponge-bag. The zip was broken and a small white plastic package fell out. Hell! There was no way she was taking that through Customs. Farmiloe wouldn't vouch for her if she were caught. He'd just tell them she'd been sacked, and deny all knowledge of anything else. She'd be in really big trouble then, and this time it could even mean prison. Still, the stuff was too good to waste. Maybe she'd have a quick snort now for consolation.

Then, suddenly she had a better idea. Oh, yes, she sniggered to herself. Brilliant! How about planting it: hiding the packet in the cistern? She could tape it to the inside of the lid. Then after she'd been back in London a while, she'd phone the police anonymously to tip them off about it. Perhaps wait a couple of months, so no one could suspect it was her. Fab notion! She'd have the last laugh all right. Groovy, man. The cops would be round in a flash and the two cows would be chucked out in utter disgrace.

"Well now, you two bitches..." Nova sneered, her large red mouth curling with contempt. "You haven't heard the last of Nova. Not by a long chalk..."

Laura and Jennifer had a small celebration the day Nova was sacked. What a relief it was, to have the flat all to themselves.

"Just like the good old days, hey?" Laura said happily. "Just the two of us. No Pierre, no Jean-Claude, and no ghastly Nova. What bliss!"

Not quite, thought Jennifer, because Jean-Claude had left his unwelcome legacy inside her. But she made a brave attempt to smile, and lifted her glass in celebration.

"To the two of us!" she said cheerfully. There was still a chance things would go right. She had to believe that, and not wallow in self-pity. Somehow, there had to be a way out. Jean-Claude was not going to defeat her!

Ratti sighed and trained his zoom lens on to his quarry. It was always difficult to see which one was which. The redheaded slut had gone. He'd seen her packing her things. What a disgusting tart she was! She had always been instantly recognisable, but now she was out of reach. Too late to deal with her now. Pity. She deserved it more than most: she was the worst he'd ever seen. Still, he had his new toy to console him. He should get some really good shots with the Nikon. And so he should, it had cost a packet. When he blew up the pictures he could study them in detail. Then he would know which girl to sort out first. Shameless bitches.

Ratti jumped as the door bell rang. Blast. Who could that be? His ex-wife asking for money, no doubt. Or his mother, carping on about his failure as a son. Castrating bitches, all of them.

Cursing under his breath, he swung the door open. It was Lejeune, his old adversary. What in hell could he want? Ratti felt instantly guilty. Surely Lejeune wasn't on to him again? Was it a crime to take pictures? Ratti started to babble incoherently, and his pale blue eyes filled with tears, which ran down his long, white nose, much to Lejeune's irritation.

"Oh, do shut up, Ratti," he interrupted impatiently. I haven't come to arrest you this time. But I want you to do something for me. I know you've been watching flat 613."

"*Et alors?* They're only English whores, so what do you care?" whined Ratti defensively, wiping his nose with the back of his hand. "I haven't done anything wrong."

"No," Lejeune snapped. Perhaps that slut Nova was right. Now Ratti would provide the answer. "But if you don't do as I say, I could make life very difficult for you."

Ratti was all ears. He didn't want any trouble. He agreed instantly to keep an eye on the blondes, and to report any visits and all movements back to Lejeune. This was good. Not only did this give him free licence to carry on his crusade, but it would keep him in good standing with the police for a while.

What a coup! What a stroke of luck! Now he had the law on his side, too.

"Watch the birdie, girls," he sniggered later, as he settled back into his hammock. "You've really got it coming to you now!"

Chapter 11

"Look, that silly ass is in his hammock again," said Jennifer, as she drained the last of the bottle into Laura's glass. She couldn't face any more wine.

"Oh, let's ignore him. He's a pathetic joke. If all he can do is look at us, he must have a pretty dull life!" retorted Laura.

"True," agreed Jennifer. "Actually, I was feeling a bit queasy. Must be too much wine. Would you like to go out for a small breather in a while? I fancy a bit of sea air."

It was well past midnight when the girls walked through the deserted lobby of the Meribel, the lift gate crashing hollowly shut behind them. Somehow, it always made them jump, more especially at night. The air outside was still, and warmed by reflected sun of the buildings and pavements. The avenue was deserted, give or take a couple of thin cats who emerged from the ornate iron balustrading to wind themselves around the girls' legs. They stopped for a while to pet them.

"Shall we take the short cut?" asked Jennifer.

"Should we? It's a bit spooky at this time of night, but it would save us ten minutes."

The pair made their way to the main boulevard, chatting amiably about their past week, and admiring the boutiques which were still lit up. At last, they reached an old stone archway, leading to some ancient steps descending to the shore road. Hundreds of them, or so it seemed, winding down in stages and changing direction with the rocky hillside. It was much quicker than taking the well-known routes. Their footsteps rang hollowly on the walled-in stone steps, as the girls slowly descended in the pitch dark. They stopped for a moment to get their bearings.

"God! Talk about the black hole of Calcutta!" Laura giggled nervously.

"Perhaps this wasn't such a good idea after all," Jennifer rejoined.

Suddenly Laura jumped, as she thought she heard a footfall higher up the stairs.

"Sssh!" she whispered, aware of a prickling feeling at the nape of her neck. Were they being followed? God forbid. All kinds of sinister possibilities crossed her mind.

Jennifer's whispered voice was tense. "What?" Her nails dug into Laura's arm.

The two girls stood completely still in the gloom of the old stairway listening intently. But they could hear no sound at all, except for their own fast breathing, and the insistent chirruping of crickets. They waited a few moments longer, until they were reassured no one else was around. There was a rank smell of urine emanating from the stone wall enclosing them. God, thought Laura, Frenchmen were disgusting! Relieving themselves anywhere the mood takes them.

"Let's get away from here," Laura said quickly. She extricated her arm and rubbed at the nail marks. "It's nothing. Just my imagination playing tricks on me."

"Hardly surprising, in the circs," Jennifer commented, as they continued down the last flight.

But Laura did not wish to dwell on vague fears and probabilities, and quickly changed the subject. "What were we talking about before I got paranoid?"

"My money situation," Jennifer replied gloomily. "It's not brilliant. By the time Quint's deducted the rental and the other bits I owe him from my pay, I have about twenty-five francs left over for the week. Just about enough to keep me in ciggies!"

"Poor old you. Can't you ask him for a rise?"

"What? The only rise he's interested in is of the male anatomical variety!" Jennifer grinned sardonically. "Well, I don't know. I suppose when things are really under way, he might consider paying me more. He does seem to appreciate my efforts, but I wish I wasn't so broke."

At last, they reached the wide shore road. The girls crossed to the other side, where two acres of land had been reclaimed from the sea in a rectangular peninsula, now overgrown with scrub, and tatty, coarse tufts of grass. Eventually, a skyscraper hotel was to be built on it with pools, and boutiques and cafés. Thousands of tons of sand would be imported to make a beach, and mature palms and plane trees craned in, and planted as if they'd been established for decades. Now, it was still peaceful and deserted, hundreds of yards of no-man's-land, surrounded on three sides by whispering, lapping waves.

"You're a clot where money's concerned," Laura said as they walked along the nearest water edge. "Perhaps when your debts to Quintin are settled, things won't seem so bad."

"No, I suppose you're right. But what I really need is a millionaire to bail me out." More than ever, now, Jennifer thought dully.

A faint whisper of breeze ruffled the girls' hair and clothes. Laura could see the lights of the harbour half a mile away. She fancied she could make out the three tall masts of the *Xerina*. "What about Julius Krep?" she asked. "He's filthy rich, good fun, and pretty generous by all accounts."

"Julius? You know I don't fancy him." Jennifer pulled a face. "He reminds me of the little Michelin X man. I do admit he's a bit nicer than I originally thought. In fact, he's really good company; quite a devil, though. I'll bet you he's the kinky sort!"

"I should have thought you'd take that in your stride, young lady. Par for the course – the way you talk."

Jennifer winked. "You know me, all bark and no bite. I'm quite chaste at heart."

Laura laughed. "What a load of bull! Really, Jennifer, who

are you kidding?" She stretched her weary limbs, yawning in the fresh sea air.

By now they'd reached the far end of the peninsula. Ahead of them the sea stretched endlessly and darkly to the horizon. There was no moon. The girls stood motionless, enjoying the faint breeze on their faces, lulled by the gently swishing wavelets beside them.

Laura yawned again. "Well, I guess we'd better head back. I must keep my grey matter in peak condition, ready for all the knowledge I've got to stuff inside."

"I really admire you," Jennifer said enviously as they turned back. "I wish I had your ambition and self-discipline. You'll go places on your own merit. Whereas little old me, I just want to find someone to buy me a ticket for the free ride there!"

Jennifer looked forlorn and childish as she paused for a moment to look towards the harbour. Laura smiled affectionately at the beautiful profile silhouetted against the faint lights in the distance.

"Trouble is," Laura said wisely, "either way, there's no such thing as a free lunch, as the old saying goes."

"Nope. You're right . . . as always," Jennifer smiled. Then she stiffened suddenly. "What was that?"

Laura jumped in alarm. Her eyes widened, and she clutched at Jennifer's arm. Maybe she hadn't imagined those footsteps earlier. Maybe they'd been followed all the way from the Meribel! But who could it be? Would she and Jennifer have the strength to fight off an assailant?

"What is it?" she breathed, her throat constricting with dread.

"I don't know," Jennifer whispered, her words tumbling out in panic. "But I swear . . . I mean, I thought I saw someone darting around . . . Over there, behind the scrub, towards the road."

Laura's pulse quickened and her stomach knotted. The two girls stayed still, clutching each other for comfort. They scanned the scrubby, arid terrain thoroughly but could see nothing moving in the gloom.

Eventually, Jennifer laughed nervously. "Come on," she said, "it's nothing. I must have imagined it. The light's very poor. Paranoia's obviously catching! We're a couple of nervous wrecks and we'd better get some sleep to calm ourselves down!"

Next morning Laura was in a rush. She had overslept, as she and Jennifer had stayed up very late, celebrating Nova's departure. It had been a good evening, apart from their slight scare. But now she was late for work. As she got to the door, she found a white envelope on the floor. Impatiently she picked it up and slit it.

"Whore," the note read, "I know what you're doing, and who with."

It was type-written, badly, with several errors and crossings out. Laura was aghast. Which of them was the object of the poison-pen note? And who could the sender be? The envelope was blank. No clues there. Nova? It was possible, but surely she'd left the country, though one couldn't be certain of that. Pierre? Unlikely. He'd stayed away since their last meeting. Perhaps it was Jean-Claude. All three of them had reason to be bitter. Or could it be someone else? Maybe it was their peeping Tom. Perhaps last night wasn't imagination at all. It was an awful thought. Laura shivered at the possibility.

"Damn!" she exclaimed, scrunching up the note and ditching it. She'd say nothing to Jennifer for the moment. She had enough on her plate already. And now, she must go. She was ten minutes late for the office, and there was stacks to do. She had a very busy day ahead of her, as usual.

This was not turning out to be a good day for Jennifer. She was very depressed because time was marching on, and her problems wouldn't go away. Then the wretched telephone rang three times, and each time the caller hung up without speaking. It was infuriating as well as worrying.

"Oh, hell and damnation!" she cursed. All she wanted to do was crawl back to her bed for the rest of the day and forget about everything. But it was already midday, the flat was stuffy, and now her bed looked rumpled and uninviting.

"No," she decided, "the beach and a change of scene are what I need." She went into the kitchen to make herself a coffee. The telephone rang yet again. This was the last straw! Jennifer snatched it up, boiling over, and shouted, "If you don't clear off, I'll call the police, you pervert!"

But another voice intervened. "Hey, darlin', I'm not much cop at French, what you're saying doesn't sound too friendly!"

"Oh, Lord, Julius. I'm sorry. I thought it was someone else!" Jennifer ran her hands through the golden tangles of her hair.

"You having trouble, love?"

"Well, no. Not directly. But some idiot keeps ringing and then hanging up. It was getting on my nerves."

"Maybe a spot of lunch at the Café de Paris would help take your mind off things."

"Very sweet of you, but I think I need a swim more."

"Oh, come on, gorgeous. I'll treat you to those palm hearts you like, or smoked salmon, or both. Whatever your little heart desires. And a good glass of bubbly'll cheer you up no end! Then you can have your swim. I've got a cabana at Monte-Carlo Beach. I'll run you there in the Rolls. You won't need to bring towels, everything's there – all the mod cons. You can spend all afternoon soaking up the sun. You can enjoy the luxury all by your lovely self, because I've got deals to make later."

It was too tempting to refuse, and she'd enjoy Julius' chirpy company. Besides, she needed cheering up.

"OK, I'm persuaded. But you're not to get lecherous!"

"Scout's honour, beautiful. I'll pick you up in ten minutes."

"No. Actually I'd enjoy the walk. I'll see you at the Café, OK?"

Monte-Carlo Beach, no less! Well, she'd enjoy seeing it from the millionaires' side at last. She might even stroll past the Russian's ghastly boutique in her bikini – swanning around with the rich and famous just to rile him! She couldn't wait to tell Laura later. Jennifer put on her briefest bikini, slipping a short cotton sun-dress over it. Then she slung her small canvas tote bag over her shoulder, and made her way out of the Meribel, her cares temporarily 'on hold'.

Julius and Jennifer had lunch on the terrace outside the Café de Paris, overlooking the Casino and its gardens. It was pleasant sitting at the small round tables in the sun, waiters rushing around cheerfully, their trays held high. Today there was even a string quartet, adding to the cosmopolitan atmosphere. The Café de P as the girls affectionately called it, was a favourite meeting-place of the young and fashionable. One could always be sure of seeing a familiar face or group there at any time of the day or night; guaranteed entertainment and company for those in search of it.

Jennifer ate very lightly – *coeurs de palmiers* and smoked salmon as Krep had predicted, but he tucked into three courses with great gusto.

"I usually eat at the Hôtel de Paris, but it's a bit stuffy for a young thing like you, eh?" Julius said.

As he carefully wiped his moustache with a napkin, his dark slate eyes studied hers, which were masked by huge blue sunglasses, covering half her face. Noticing his amusement at the exaggerated frames, she stared back defensively. They were the latest in Op Art fashion.

"I expect so," she replied. "I can't say I've ever eaten there, actually. It's usually the Roxy, the Tip Top or here. Only lately I've been too broke even to contemplate eating out!"

Julius looked dismayed. "Duckie, why didn't you say? I thought your job at the club was well paid?"

"Oh it is, really. I can't complain. It's just that I've never acquired a good sense of economics, unfortunately."

"My sweet girl, I don't like to think of you without enough money to eat out and have fun." His voice was kindly, concerned. "Let me help you! I'll write you a cheque to tide you over." Julius reached into his inner pocket for a pen and his cheque-book. His jacket gaped open, exposing acres of bulging belly.

Jennifer immediately regretted having let slip her precarious financial state to Julius. It simply wouldn't do to be beholden to him in any way, because it would make it doubly difficult to justify holding him at arm's length. Out of the frying-pan into the fire she'd go. No thanks! Having just succeeded in getting rid of the oppressive Jean-Claude, the last thing she needed was to lose her newly-found independence. Jennifer didn't want to be at the beck and call of another demanding male, even if he were a millionaire.

"No," she replied insistently. Then she smiled, remembering her manners. "Thank you. It's really nice of you, but I couldn't possibly let you do that just because I'm too feckless to make ends meet. Things are sorting themselves out slowly. Honestly."

Looking very dubious, Julius tucked his cheque-book away, and patted his pocket absently.

"Thanks for a lovely lunch, Julius," she said when they'd finished. "How about *Le Beach* now?"

Julius smiled broadly. Jennifer liked his face when he smiled. The prominent teeth made him look vulnerable and boyish, disguising the rogue and opportunist underneath.

"OK, precious," he said with apparent sincerity. "but if there's anything I can ever do to help, you let me know, eh?"

"Scout's honour!" she quipped, borrowing his line. "*Allez, on y va!*"

Julius dropped her off at the beach, telling her the chauffeur would come back to pick her up later.

"Well, duckie," he said regretfully, "got to leave you now because I've a lot of work on!" Then he smiled, "Have a lovely time, and order what you like. OK? 'Bye, lovely!" He blew her a kiss and got back into the car.

"What a life!" thought Jennifer as she waved him goodbye. "A Rolls to drop me off at Monte-Carlo Beach Club, and then it comes back to take me home!"

The attendant at the entrance kiosk grinned knowingly and gave her the pass to Krep's cabana. Jennifer slowly walked into the Beach Club beside a line of shady, scented eucalyptus. To the left of the shaded path, several orderly rows of green and white striped cabanas stretched in a curve that followed the contours of the sheltered bay. Krep's tent, actually more like a mini-marquee, and obviously one of the most expensive, was in the front row of the elite, lining the water's edge.

Julius was right. Everything was there. Even a vase of flowers on the table in the shade inside. At the back was a partitioned-off changing area, complete with full-length mirror. She slipped off her dress and shoulder bag, hanging them on the pegs provided. There were piles of neatly folded, crested beach towels placed on top of the compartment for shoes. The rest of the cabana was taken up with chaises-longues and a low table, for those who wanted shade and privacy, or even a sleep.

On the table next to the flowers Jennifer was intrigued to discover a small exquisitely-wrapped parcel with her name on it. She took it out to the sun terrace. Here several luxuriously padded chaise-longues invited total relaxation, more crested beach towels thoughtfully draped there for the purpose. Carefully she unwrapped the gift. It was the most beautiful Emilio Pucci bikini, in shocking pink, turquoise and green, and must have cost a fortune.

"Wowee!" she whistled. "What a fabulous thing! Far too good to swim in!"

There was a message on the attached label: "I guessed your size because I am an expert judge of beautiful bodies! J.K."

"Cheeky sod! And how did he know he'd succeed in getting me here anyway? Talk about counting his chickens!" Jennifer exclaimed, but smiled because she was quite stunned and won over. Just what she would have bought herself if she'd had the money. What an enigma he was. Scored ten out of ten for good taste in presents, but a resounding nil when it came to his own clothes! Not that it helped any to be so rotund. No suit, even from Gieves & Hawkes, could look good on a frame like his.

After sunbathing for a while, Jennifer took a cool dip. Afterwards as she dried herself, she decided to try on the lovely Pucci number and take a stroll around the entire complex. Julius was right about her size. The brief, beautifully-cut bikini fitted like a glove, and complimented her body to perfection. The vibrant colours suited her, too, enhancing her golden tan and hair. She admired her reflection in the mirror, pleased with life, her cares forgotten at being so thoroughly spoiled in such paradise.

Dressed in the very latest fashion, she felt more than at home with the stars and millionaires' wives lolling around in their droves. Jennifer sauntered slowly along the water's edge, with the lithe grace that years of ballet had bestowed on her, eyeing the occupants of the other cabanas discreetly. Whilst heads automatically turned at the sight of her because she had a glorious head of titian hair and an enviable figure, she was only one of many more. Monte-Carlo Beach was full of glamorous women, all with perfect hair and bodies.

But the men! Now that was a different story. Some of them looked as if they would sink with the weight of their huge, dark, leathery pot-bellies and the heavy solid-gold jewellery they wore. Many of them were playing backgammon in the shade of their tents. They obviously did not come to the beach to swim, but just to eat, drink and stare at the girls, in between bouts of board and card games. Nobody smiled, and there was no animated conversation or activity at all, apart from the occasional lifted glass, tinkle of ice and the odd idle glance at the young girls who strolled around showing off their sex-appeal.

Seems as if being filthy-rich gets rather boring by the looks of this lot, she observed. Still, I suppose there's not much else to do when you're a millionaire except to hang round where all the other ones are! Same time, same place, same faces every day. Well, it's all new to me, and this is great! I'm probably the only one who's enjoying myself here!

Jennifer followed the path that led to the Olympic-size swimming-pool, fringed by enormous palm trees, around which lounged the younger element. There were even a few children frolicking in the water. Behind the pool was the nightmare boutique she knew so well, but she did not go in. Further along was a restaurant, still packed with people enjoying an extended lunch. She walked past a soaring fountain under whose roaring watery curtain youngsters splashed and played with complete abandon. They were as yet untainted by the boredom afflicting their elders.

"I wonder how long it would take me to get fed up with being rich? Probably never! Right now Miss Morgan is mighty pissed off with being poor. I could get used to this routine all right – no problem. Julius, play your cards right, and you never know . . ."

On the other hand, though, could she ever pretend to love a man she really didn't fancy, even if he offered her the world? If she were constantly surrounded by beautiful things, enveloped in luxury, cocooned in silk sheets, rich beyond her dreams . . . would an overweight, slightly vulgar and comical millionaire suddenly turn into a highly desirable Adonis? Well . . . it was questionable. Maybe if she just shut her eyes, lay back, enjoyed the silken luxury and thought of Paul Newman, reality would vanish and she could acquire a dream lifestyle at the flick of fantasy.

After all, millions of other women all over the world just shut their eyes and lay back every night. They had to, for varying reasons; some enforced by tradition, for instance; like the arranged marriage – to a total stranger! Others, because it was simply the done thing, in exchange for mundane considerations like security, a nest to feather, companionship. She thought back to her conversation with Terry: "Women prostitute themselves for less, dearie ... a couple of kids and security ..." Words of well-worn cynicism from the mouth of a well-worn and cynical queen!

Then why couldn't she have it all? Why did she need the thrill of the ultimate love-affair? Hell, it was all there for the taking if she could just set her sights a little lower than perfection. All she had to do was give Julius the green light. He was hooked – there were no two ways about it!

Did there always have to be an ultimate price to pay for the privilege of wealth? Jennifer shuddered slightly as she remembered the rolls of white flesh. Ah, yes ... Laura was so right. There is no such thing as a free lunch!

"Oh God!" she groaned.

Why did she seem to be at a crossroads in her life? Nothing appeared simple any more. Why was she so confused? Could it be extra hormones surging around and stirring things up? But no. Please, she absolutely did *not* want to think of that dismal problem! Yet it was always there these days, perched on her shoulder like an oppressive cloud.

The voice came as a welcome distraction from her unwelcome thoughts.

"Mademoiselle Morgan? Monsieur Krep asked me to look after you. Would you like to order a drink, or something to eat?" asked a smiling man in a smart white jacket and black trousers.

Golly, but these waiters were well-trained. How did he

know her from Adam, or rather Eve? Jennifer was dying to ask him, but restrained herself. Obviously these guys were well-versed in the art of making the top people feel like . . . well . . . top people. It was part of his job. But she still felt incredibly flattered and pampered.

"Ah, merci. Just a Diabolo Menthe, *s'il vous plaît."*

"Je vous l'apporte à la tente, mademoiselle?"

Yes, why not? She could go back to the cabana and take some more sun, have her cold mint drink and then maybe stroll round to the far end of the beach later.

This is really cool, she thought, as the brooding storm clouds of worry rolled away under the temporary panacea of luxury living. I could spend the rest of my summers like this – no problem!

Chapter 12

That evening when Laura came in from work, Jennifer was full of the joys of her day. She waxed lyrical about Monte-Carlo Beach, the bikini and the lavish cabana. She described the pool, the restaurant, and her walk to the very end of the beach – the best spot of all – the Vigie.

"Honestly, Laura, you should see it! The Vigie's on an idyllic promontory you reach by a winding path through this lovely wood of fragrant pines and gigantic magnolias. It's so beautiful it's unbelievable. There's this raft you swim to, tethered about a hundred yards out, and you can sunbathe in perfect peace and all you hear is the ripple of the water around you as the raft bobs around. Sheer bliss! And to think that you're in one of the most enviable spots in the world! It's just packed with the most beautiful people! The whole place is utterly divine. Will you come with me one day? We're both invited to go there any time. Julius said!"

Jennifer sat on the bed enthusing, her eyes sparkling, as Laura changed, carefully hanging her pink linen suit in the wardrobe.

"Sounds great," murmured Laura dreamily, standing barefoot in her lace underwear, "if only I didn't have so much work on. Whenever would I find the time to lounge around in such glorious idleness? Anyway, I thought you said Julius was repulsive, and nothing would induce you to get involved with him?"

"Hey, hang on! Maybe repulsive is a little bit strong. Anyway, who said anything about involvement? Since when has an invitation to the beach meant sex?"

"Any invitation from a male means sex, doesn't it?" She took off her bra to inspect her suntan in the mirror. It was progressing well. Her breasts looked very white against the honey-gold of her body.

"That's a bit cynical coming from you, Laura! Or is our little romantic growing up at last?" Laura's reflection smiled back at her from the wardrobe mirror. "Actually, on that subject, past romance that is, I still haven't heard a word from J-C. That's a relief, to say the least! Unless he's the anonymous caller."

Laura raised her brows in surprise. "What caller?" she asked, reaching for a pale blue tee-shirt.

"Oh, nothing really. But someone rang three times this morning, and then just put the phone down without speaking. It could be anyone."

Laura was alarmed, but decided to say nothing about the anonymous note. No reason to make mountains out of molehills.

"Perhaps it was just a wrong number," she said reassuringly. "By the way, how are things with you? Are you still overdue?"

"Well, to tell you the truth, yes," Jennifer said, trying to keep her voice light. "But I'm sure it's nothing to worry about. Just a blip in my cycle. Anyway, I'm in no panic. Let's change the subject, eh?"

Laura looked at Jennifer with concern. If Jennifer was trying to hide from the truth she was making a poor job of it. She tried to reassure herself that Jennifer would be all right. Laura didn't want to dwell on the possibility of pregnancy, but was very worried. What a mess it would be. This was one scrape Jennifer wouldn't be able to fly out of with her usual ease. No money, no prospects and apparently no question of resolving it with a convenient and early marriage.

A few days later, Laura and Jennifer had more problems to

contend with. Nova had left a parting gift. Her legacy was crabs!

Privately Jennifer was sickened, but tried to make light of it for Laura's sake. Everyone and everything seemed to be conspiring against them both. Laura was worried that her ambitions were beyond her, and Jennifer had the spectre of pregnancy to contend with. It was sheer hell! Jennifer felt close to collapsing in tears.

But she took a deep breath and forced a casual front. "Serves me right for kidding Quintin about it and laying on the agony," she commented wryly. "Though God knows how it spread to us. Nova must have used our sheets, or borrowed our underclothes. And I thought it could only be transmitted person to person. Eeeuk!"

Poor Laura was absolutely mortified. "We can't go to the doctor with crabs! What on earth would he think?"

"Don't worry, I'll sort something out straight away." Jennifer reassured her.

Damn Quintin! He was really going to get it in the neck this time. It was all his fault, foisting that foul creature on them. Now everyone was paying for her slovenly habits. Jennifer marched off to his flat in a towering rage, and thundered on his door.

"Golly, Jen! You look cross. What on earth's the matter?" Quintin asked in alarm as Jennifer marched in, pushing him aside, and slammed the door shut with her foot.

Her eyes blazed. "Cross is the understatement of the year! Bloody hell, Quint, I've got good reason to be. That slut Nova's spread crabs all over the flat. And it's all your fault."

"Hey, wait a minute!" he blustered. "How can it be my fault if you got them from her?" Then his eyes narrowed lecherously. "Anyhow," he added slyly, "I wouldn't have thought she'd be your type, and certainly not Laura's."

"Oh, don't be so foul!" Jennifer bit back. His feeble attempt at humour really took the cake in the circumstances. How could he joke at a time like this?

Quintin grinned wickedly, and she continued crossly, "Damn you. It's no laughing matter. The bloody creature must have borrowed our clothes or slept in our beds." Then she snapped, "Please will you stop laughing! You'll probably notice them yourself soon and die scratching!"

Quintin went pale. The grin faded instantly. "Oh Christ, that's all I need as well as clap."

"You don't mean . . . ?"

He nodded ruefully. "Yes. I'm on antibiotics for ten days."

Now it was Jennifer's turn to grin nastily. "Serves you right! I've got no sympathy for you at all." She stuck her chin out determinedly and fixed him with fierce grey eyes. "What are you going to do about us and our infestation? I don't see why we should suffer the ignominy of going to the doctor about it." She grabbed his shoulder and shook it angrily. "Honestly, Quint, you are the limit!"

It made a change to see the normally chipper Quintin look so hang-dog. Shamefaced, he promised to sort out the problem. An hour or so later, he arrived on their doorstep with the remedy. Laura was too mortified to ask him in for coffee. Anyway, neither girl was in a sociable mood – given the circumstances.

Laura and Jennifer each took an age in the bath, soaping and re-soaping themselves with the special shampoo, and afterwards massaging in the lotion, which smelt awful. Thank heaven it was the weekend now, so Laura did not have to go the office smelling like a chemistry experiment.

Fortunately, the treatment was effective, and the girls had immediate relief from the unbearable itching. All the sheets and covers had been whipped off the beds and sent to the laundry. As an extra measure, they bought an insecticidal fumigant. Then they shut all the windows, opened all interconnecting doors, and went out in the car for a few hours whilst the smoke wafted through the whole flat, decimating any surviving creature. It seemed to the girls that the fumigation was symbolic. Perhaps now the whole spectre of Nova and the blight she had put on their summer would be eradicated.

Laura and Jennifer drove up to La Turbie. The red Spitfire hugged the spectacular twisting road as it crawled up the mountain-side, where the breezes were already cooler, and the views over the hazy, sprawling bay below were magnificent.

Laura parked the open-topped car and took a deep breath. She leaned back with her arms behind her head, looking up at the clear blue sky. The sensation of eternity put everything into perspective, and made all problems seem smaller. There were no dark corners for strangers to lurk in up here. No nasty surprises. Everything was peaceful, bright, beautiful.

She sat in silence for a few minutes, admiring the sweeping vista below them. The famous Casino, with its pale green cupola, ornate turrets and finials clothing it like filigree icing on a cake, and further in the distance, to the right, Prince Rainier's pink palace on the towering rock, were both outlined in miniature against a sparkling blue sea. This had to be one of the most breathtaking views in the world.

After a while, Laura turned to Jennifer, who looked very pale. She was fiddling with her hands and completely oblivious to the lovely surroundings. Concerned, Laura said, "You don't look well, Jen. What is it? Not the worst news?" Then she noticed tears glinting in Jennifer's eyes. "Hey, it really is bad by the looks of you. Tell me about it."

"It's worse than the worst," Jennifer sniffed. "I'm well and truly up the spout. At least nine weeks. That's two periods I've missed now, so there's no question I'm pregnant." Her eyes were black hollows of despair.

Laura was horrified. Although forewarned, she'd been

171

dreading this, but Jennifer hadn't mentioned her worries lately. Laura had hoped her problems had been resolved. Now she felt guilty that she'd perhaps been too busy and preoccupied with her own work and studies for Jennifer to confide in her.

"Oh God," she cried. "I'm so sorry. What are you going to do? What about Jean-Claude? After all, it's his fault, his responsibility!" Laura felt her anger rising. What bastards men were. It was sickening to witness the havoc they could wreak on women's lives.

"Of course it is; but can't you see? That's what he wants. To play the noble daddy, the loving spouse." Jennifer ran a hand through her pale hair distractedly, while a tear ran unchecked down her cheek. "He's trapped me, or tried to, but I'm not going to let him win. He played a really dirty hand."

Finding a Kleenex and handing it to Jennifer, Laura asked gently, "Abortion's still illegal here. What other choices are there except to marry him and have the baby?"

"No. Absolutely no," Jennifer said emphatically. "I never want to see him again, especially now." She hated Jean-Claude with a vengeance. What he'd done was unspeakable. Angrily, she dabbed at her eyes and then blew her nose loudly.

"Could you go back to England? I'd lend you the fare. Would your parents help you?"

"Oh God, Laura, I'm twenty-two! I can't land my problems on my parents' doorstep now. I'm supposed to be grown-up. Anyway, my father's got his own problems. It's all my mother can do to handle those! No. There's got to be another solution. Let me work it out in my own time."

Laura shook her head sadly. Jennifer looked worn out with worry. "It'll be too late soon, Jen. I wish I could think of something, but I'm not nearly as worldly as you."

"I do appreciate your concern," Jennifer squeezed Laura's hand, "and I know you'd help if you could, but this is something I've got to work out myself. I'll sort it out, just you see!"

Jennifer made a courageous attempt to smile, but drew little comfort from her bravado. Her eyes were dull and despairing. What a disaster! She was really in it up to the neck this time! She simply had to think fast and pull out all the stops, or the whole of her life would be blighted.

There was a strange smell of disinfectant mixed with smoke pervading the flat when the girls got back.

"It should fade soon," said Laura reassuringly, "probably by bed time."

"Golly, I hope so. The smell reminds me of school loos and hospitals!" Jennifer remarked, wrinkling her pert nose.

After a light dinner, she went off to work at the disco, and Laura plunged back in to her studies, taking her papers out on the balcony. She was well into 'The Securities Exchange Act of 1934' when she distinctly saw the binoculars focused on her from the balcony opposite. Really! This was too much. Especially on top of the nasty note and suspicious phone calls.

Alarmed, she collected up her folder and went inside to call the concierge. He tried to make light of her suspicions, but she insisted he come up so that she could point out the relevant flat. Then he could tell her who its occupants were. Reluctantly, the concierge complied, but when he arrived, he immediately started arguing with her.

He waved his arms around saying, "But mademoiselle, he's only looking at pretty girls, *hein?* It's not against the law, you know. Anyway, I feel I cannot divulge the names of tenants just to anyone."

Laura was livid. How dare the little man be so pompous? Wasn't she a tenant, too? And who was he to call her 'just anyone'? Didn't she pay rent and have every right to privacy like the others? Or was there one set of rules for Laura, and another for the rest of the tenants? Why should the girls put up with being spied on every day? As if they didn't already have enough to contend with: poison-pen writers and silent breathers, and everything else! She stood her ground adamantly; arms folded obstinately, and told the warden she'd involve the police if he didn't deliver.

"*D'accord, si vous insistez,*" the concierge grumbled, "*Le monsieur en face s'appelle Ratti. Monsieur Louis Ratti.*"

Laura was still up when Jennifer came back. There had been no further sign of the mysterious watcher with the binoculars, so Laura had immersed herself in her books again. As an extra precaution, she had double-locked the doors, and not ventured out on to the balcony again. She had also closed the shutters outside the french doors for the first time ever, it would seem. It needed tremendous force to pull them across. The well-rusted hinges had squealed their protest vehemently, and the shutters were full of dead insects and cobwebs.

"Hey, what goes on?" Jennifer demanded as she came into the sitting-room wearing an incredibly short crocheted lace dress, "An orgy? Why are the shutters to the balcony shut? God, how claustrophobic!" She fanned her face dramatically with her hand.

Laura smiled with relief at Jennifer's dramatic entrance. She'd had a distinctly uncomfortable evening hiding behind the shutters. It annoyed her that the watcher, who up till now had seemed a bit of a joke, was adding to her feeling of insecurity. Thank heaven she had company. Now she felt less afraid. She told Jennifer about the peeping Tom, and wondered if the name Ratti meant anything to her.

"Ratti? Is that the name of our dear Bin Rat? Very apt I must say." Jennifer looked puzzled. "Not a name that rings any bells with me. Probably likes the look of us when we flash our tits around!" she replied airily, flopping into an armchair.

Good old Jennifer. She always saw the lighter side of everything. The eternal optimist. Maybe she was right.

"Hmm. That's more or less what the concierge said, too, though not in those exact words!"

"You can bet your guns it's what he meant, though, the lecherous little git! Oh well," she went on, "I expect the Bin Rat will leave us alone, now he knows he's been spotted."

Laura collected up her papers into a folder and put them away. We should be so lucky, she thought. She was distinctly uneasy about the latest events. And now, their mystery spy had been revealed as a complete stranger, whose name meant nothing to either of them. What could it all mean? Why was everything piling up to disrupt their lives?

Chapter 13

The girls soon found themselves well into July, and with a new flatmate, Henrietta. Another rich ex-deb, but infinitely more respectable than Nova. She was rake thin, with prominent cheek bones, white skin, and long, straight black hair she could almost sit on.

"Interesting," observed Laura, discussing her with Jennifer on Saturday, down at the Digue. They'd escaped the unbearable stuffiness of the flat over iced tea at the Calypso, shaded under the bamboo slats from a scorching noon sun. There was no vestige of breeze. "She's sort of poetic and dreamy," she went on. "A great improvement on Nova. Her make-up's a bit over the top, though. Very beatnik. Very King's Road! Let's hope she'll be tolerable."

Henrietta was into herbs, and medicinal plants. She swore by her remedies. Homeopathy, she called them. She was always concocting weird brews. No one ever knew whether she drank them, spread them on her face, or muttered mantras over them, or maybe all three.

"Strange bird," said Jennifer, sipping her drink. "Very intelligent, though. Seems to have a cure for everything." The ice-cubes rattled as she put the glass down. "Maybe she has a spell she could cast on Pierre and Jean-Claude, to make them disappear for ever." She was subdued, the flippant aside delivered without her customary smile.

"I'll drink to that!" Laura grinned sardonically, raising her glass. Then she became serious. "Talking about strange, we've been getting some more of those weird phone calls recently. Just heavy breathing. Corny, eh?"

Jennifer became concerned, "You didn't tell me. Why didn't you say?"

Laura looked at her friend. Her slender, bikini-clad body was striped tan and gold from rays of sun shining through the slatted canopy above. The hair around her temples was bleached almost white from constant sunbathing. To see Jennifer's glamorous image unassailed – invulnerable to the outside world – when in reality her life was falling apart, was a sad irony.

"With all the troubles you've got," Laura reasoned, "the phone calls seem paltry now. What's a bit of heavy breathing compared to your problem?"

Jennifer was sunk in gloom, her bright hair spilling over her tanned arms as she sat slumped at the metal café table. "What a lot of trouble men cause," she commented miserably. "Wouldn't the world be peaceful without them? I never thought I'd hear myself say that." She sighed heavily. The answer to her question was all too obvious. The girls looked at each other despairingly.

Eventually, Jennifer sat up and squared her shoulders. "Well," she said briskly, "when all's said and done it's a good thing I only ever feel sick in the mornings. Otherwise I'd have to give up work and be skint as well as knocked up!" Her attempt to smile was a failure as tears sprang into the corners of her eyes.

"Oh God!" Laura exclaimed, near to tears herself. "What an utter disaster this is."

Laura was angry at her own helplessness. They were at an impasse. What were they to do? Soon Jennifer would be three months gone, and then it would be too late.

"Shall I get you another iced tea, precious?" she said softly.

"Yes, please." Jennifer's voice was dull. Her spark had gone. She looked defeated; resigned to her fate.

* * *

Over the next few days, Laura barely saw Jennifer, though she worried about her constantly. There was a rush on at work, and she, Fitzgerald and the new secretary, Mary, were all working extra hours. She left the office so late that generally both girls had already gone to the club by the time she returned.

On 20th July, Terry Martin invited Laura, Jennifer, Quintin and a whole crowd of friends to watch the Apollo moon-walk on his television, after the club. A historic occasion – the first man on the moon – Neil Armstrong!

With a lump in the throat and tears in their eyes the friends watched the flickering image of Armstrong in his huge, inflated space-suit bobbing weightlessly out of the lunar module, Eagle. Then he spoke those historic and unforgettable words, "That's one small step for a man, one giant leap for mankind."

It was practically four o'clock in the morning in Europe, but everyone was too elated and moved to feel tired. It was just incredible to witness this extraordinary event, and to realise it was all happening live, straight from the moon! History in the making, and everyone felt they were participating, too.

The celebrations continued for a couple more hours as people were too wound up and excited to leave. So nobody got to bed until dawn. As she had to go to work early, it wasn't worth her turning in at all, so poor Laura went straight from Terry's to the office. The result was, she was absolutely shattered and didn't seem able to catch up on her sleep over the following days.

Soon, Laura was at the end of her rope. The moon-walk night, her studies and extra work had absolutely knocked her for six. It was only four thirty in the afternoon, and she already felt like death. Her head was hollow and she couldn't concentrate. The prospect of three more hours in the office was unbearable. Laura saw Fitz glance across at her. Then he looked at her more intently with his piercing blue eyes.

"Laura, I'm packing you off," he said. "You've worked like a slave, and you look dreadful. I don't want you falling ill on me. Go home and rest. Things are just about straight here now. Mary and I can manage on our own for the rest of the day."

Laura remonstrated, but Fitz pointed to the door. "Out you go!"

She was utterly drained, and beyond protesting. Obediently she left the office and made her way back to the flat. Laura opened the door, and started, as Henrietta appeared, looking whiter than usual, and very distraught. Seeing Laura, Henrietta clapped her hand to her mouth in fright, eyes wild and staring – and promptly disappeared into the lift. What in heaven's name was going on? What could be the matter with her?

With a sense of foreboding, Laura entered the hallway. But the flat was quiet. There was nobody around. Jennifer had obviously gone out. Still bemused at Henrietta's strange behaviour, Laura made her way to her bedroom to change. Suddenly she stopped, frowning with concentration. She thought she'd heard a quiet moan. Her skin prickled. What on earth could it be? Then, nothing. No sound at all. She must have imagined it. She shook her head wonderingly. But there it was again. This time the moan was unmistakable, almost like an animal keening in pain. Full of disquiet, Laura tracked the sound. It was coming from the direction of the shared bedroom.

The moans grew louder as she approached the bathroom. There was steam coming out of the door. Her heart hammered with dread. As she beat away the hot wet clouds that enveloped her as she entered, Laura was aghast at the sight that greeted her. Through the thick blanket of steam she could just make out Jennifer, lying in a scalding bath up to her neck; delirious, her skin a terrifying lobster pink. She was heaving with pain and rolling her eyes, and the steaming water was bright red.

Laura was hit by a sudden wave of nausea and doom-laden fear. What had Jennifer done? Had she slashed her wrists? God help her! What was she to do? Then in a flash, Laura realised what was happening. On the bath edge, by way of explanation was a cup with a peculiar liquid containing bits of a plant, a scattering of pills, and an empty bottle of gin.

Oh, dear God, no! Surely not. What had she taken? Was she haemorrhaging? There was blood everywhere. How long did it take to bleed to death?

"Jennifer, Jennifer! What's going on?" Laura screamed, and started to pull her out of the scalding water.

No. It was the wrong thing to do. She mustn't try to move her. The best course was to leave Jennifer where she was. Panic-stricken, Laura tried to gather her thoughts. What had she learned at first-aid classes, so long ago? Keep the patient warm and dry, and above all – calm. She pulled up the bathplug to let out the blood-stained water. Jennifer was bleeding heavily. How long had she got? Jesus – somebody, please help! Laura was frantic.

"Don't leave me, Laura!" wailed Jennifer, and then lurched as a wave of pain hit her.

She vomited suddenly, and moaned again. Laura felt faint as the rank smell of vomit filled the air over the heavy gin fumes. As she cleaned Jennifer's face with a cold flannel she realised she must keep calm. Jennifer's life depended on her now. She mustn't give in to hysteria. How long would it take to get an ambulance? Did they have enough money for medical costs? Would Jennifer be prosecuted for inducing an abortion? Who could help them? There was no time to lose. This was a battle for life or death.

She racked her brains, fighting off mounting panic, and said, "Jennifer, I must get help. Don't move. Don't try to do anything." She made her way to the door.

"Can't anyway ... I ..." but Jennifer seized up with pain

again. Sweat stood out in glistening beads on her contorted face as she twisted in wracked convulsions.

Laura turned back. Blood was coursing into the bath in pulsing bursts. Heaven help us! First things first. She had to slow the bleeding. Now. Or it would be too late. She flew into the bedroom, seized a couple of pillows, and tucked them under Jennifer's hips, hoping that gravity would help stem the bleeding. Carefully she wrapped a blanket round her friend.

"Jennifer, I have to leave you for a second. I must get help."

"Please, please don't . . . I . . ." Jennifer whimpered feebly, but she was past making any sense, and collapsed weakly in a heap.

Laura had a sudden flash of inspiration. In an instant she knew with certainty who to turn to. Julius. He had the influence, the motive and the wherewithal to sort this out. He'd know what to do!

With shaking, uncontrollable hands, she misdialled twice. Then the number rang engaged. Laura's heart was thudding fit to burst. She tried the number again. Please, please let him answer, and not some minion. Please let him be there! Sweet relief flooded over her as she heard Julius' chirpy voice.

"Laura, duckie! What a pleasure to hear from . . ."

But there was no time for small talk. "Julius," she cried, "we need your help at once. Something terrible's happened to Jennifer, and she'll die if we don't get her to hospital. She's going to need a transfusion."

The chirpy voice became business-like, decisive.

"Where are you, duck?"

"Here, at the Meribel. Oh, please come at once!"

"Laura, it's as good as done. I'll be there in minutes. Got a nurse on board. Wife of one of the crew members. I'll get the jet sorted. We'll fly her to London straight away. Do what you can to keep her comfortable, eh? See you, luvvie."

Laura cried with relief. Thank God, Julius was going to be their saviour. Drying her eyes, she hurried back to the bathroom. Jennifer seemed weaker, even drowsy, but the bleeding had lessened considerably. Perhaps the pains were less intense, too. Or perhaps – and the dread realisation squeezed a tight band round her heart – Jennifer's lassitude signalled the beginning of the end. Maybe there was no strength left in her to fight the pains. Jennifer's skin was now the colour of yellowing parchment, and her closed eyes were hollow. Could she be slipping away? Laura died a thousand deaths.

"Jennifer," she whispered urgently, "don't give up! Please don't. Help's on its way. Any second now. You've got to keep fighting. Please, for yourself; for all of us."

Jennifer took a tremulous breath and her eyelids flickered. Laura prayed silently. If there were a God above, surely he wouldn't take a young life so pointlessly? Jennifer didn't deserve such a fate. God, let her live! She sponged Jennifer's sweating face and brushed wet tendrils of hair off her forehead. Then she held her hand comfortingly and waited with bated breath for what seemed like an eternity.

At last the door bell rang. Thank heaven! Laura sprang to her feet and rushed to the door. Julius strode in briskly, his face grave. With him were the chauffeur, and Laura assumed, the nurse. She ushered them all to the bathroom. The men stood outside the door whilst the nurse quickly checked Jennifer. She called for more blankets and towels. Laura hurriedly complied, and helped wrap up the patient. Then Julius and the chauffeur lifted Jennifer's limp body out of the bath and carried her out of the flat.

"How long will it take to get her to London? I'm not sure she'll even last the journey," wailed Laura. "She's already lost pints, I'm sure of it."

The nurse answered her comfortingly. "It always looks worse than it is, dear."

"Listen, luvvie," Julius added reassuringly, "Mrs Moore's right. I've been through this kind of thing before. Jennifer's young and strong, and she'll survive, honest. She'll be OK. I've already got a doc on tap, and I'm picking him up on the way to Nice. It's all in hand, and my plane's on the runway ready to go. I'll go with her, too, and phone you as soon as I can. Chin up, sweetheart. Juli's in charge, eh?"

Laura wanted to hug him with all her heart. She was speechless with gratitude. Then she remembered practicalities.

"Julius, just to give you some quick details," she explained as she followed the retinue into the lift. "Apart from practically drowning herself in gin, and drinking the oddest-looking infusion, she's obviously taken some pills, too. God knows what they were, or how many she's taken. It must have been that stupid Henrietta who planned this."

A flash of anger, or was it fear, crossed Julius' features. "Find out what it was, love, eh, and let me know when I call you. Get hold of that hippy and threaten her with death if she doesn't spill the beans."

As the nurse and the chauffeur settled Jennifer into the back seat of the Rolls, Julius turned to Laura. He took her hands in his. Quickly he pecked her cheek, and smiled comfortingly. But he could not mask the fear and panic in his eyes.

"Chin up, duckie. She'll be fine, I promise." He squeezed her hands, then turned to the car. Within seconds it sped off towards Nice airport.

Laura was devastated, and in spite of Julius' reassurances, convinced she'd never see Jennifer alive again. And what could he have meant: 'I've been through this kind of thing before'? Was he in the habit of getting his numerous mistresses pregnant and then inducing abortions? It didn't bear thinking about. However, at least he was doing all he could to save Jennifer's life, so this was no time for sour contention. There was no time to lose. Henrietta must be found.

Quickly, Laura telephoned Quintin to tell him the dreadful news, and asked him to find the girl urgently.

"OK, Laura. I'll throttle the truth out of the silly bitch. I think I know where to find her. I'll telephone you as soon as I get word."

Half an hour later he told her.

"Ergot. The silly cow was dosing her up with ergot. Then as a final *coup de grâce* she suggested the scalding bath and the gin, with some weird infusion to boot. Don't ask what it was; I'm so angry I can't remember. Can you imagine? I didn't even know Jen was ... you know ... she didn't say. Poor little thing. Tell me as soon as you have any news. Promise?"

He went on to explain how Henrietta's knowledge of herbs and alternative medicines had enabled her to get hold of the relevant substance by devious means. Jennifer's gut-wrenching spasms and seizures had been caused by repeated doses of ergot contained in a particular migraine remedy.

Quintin sounded really alarmed and upset. "She could have been dead by now, if you hadn't found her. Who knows? She might not survive, even now. I'm absolutely sick with worry! What if we lose her? What a waste of a young life . . ."

"Don't, Quintin, please!" begged Laura. "It's more than I can bear."

"I'm sorry," he said. "I didn't think. You've already been through too much. But I didn't realise how much I've come to depend on Jennifer, not just because she's invaluable at the club, but as a friend. A very special friend. I couldn't be without her."

"I know," Laura said simply. "But let's just keep our fingers crossed and pray she'll be all right."

Laura paced the flat for hours, all thoughts of rest forgotten, waiting for Julius' call from London. She thought it would never come. Perhaps Jennifer was dead, and he didn't have the courage to tell her. It was the longest wait of Laura's life. However, just as she was giving up hope, the telephone rang. She snatched up the receiver, her heart hammering. God, please let her be OK. Please let her be alive.

"Laura? It's Julius. Jennifer's OK. She's out of danger. She's groggy with anaesthetic now and having a transfusion. And, of course, she lost the baby. It'll take a while, but the doctor thinks she'll make a full recovery."

A tidal wave of relief washed over Laura and filled her with a warm glow of happiness and gratitude. There must be a God in heaven after all. Everyone's prayers had been answered. Jennifer was going to survive.

The words poured out in a torrent. "Julius, I can't thank you enough. What would we have done without you? I just don't know what to say. When I think how easily she could have slipped away for ever. Please give her all my love and say I'm thinking of her. And by the way, it was ergot."

"What did you say, luvvie?"

"The pills, Julius, the pills. Apparently they contained ergot. Henrietta conned a doctor into prescribing them for migraine. Then gave Jennifer huge doses."

"Oh, yes, sweetie. We gathered that from bits she was able to tell us on the way to the hospital. Thanks all the same. A dangerous game, that. Too much of it can give you gangrene."

Gangrene? But that could be fatal. Laura's heart was in her mouth with dismay. Did Jennifer have another battle to fight? Surely not. Hadn't she already had all she could take?

Laura's voice was shrill with panic. "What? Oh God! Will she be all right?"

"Of course she will. Don't worry, darlin', she's in very good hands. The best." His voice was low and comforting. "And Laura?"

"Yes, Julius?"

"Thank you. Thank you a thousand times."

Why was Julius thanking her, when it was he who'd been the guardian angel; Julius who'd been their saviour?

"For what?" Laura asked, puzzled.

"Sending for me. Letting me help." Then his voice went husky. "You see, I love the girl. I really do."

Laura finally cracked. Tears of exhaustion, relief and

emotion overwhelmed her, and spilled over in great wracking sobs that shook her small body and soaked her hair. She cried for her own shattered dreams of love, for Jennifer's, for the bitterness of broken affairs that festered on, disrupting and poisoning their existence. For the fragility of life, demonstrated so dramatically by the near-death of her beloved and wayward friend. And for the pathetic, dead unwanted baby, discarded in its metal receiving-dish in an anonymous sluice room, in some anonymous hospital: awaiting disposal amongst countless others. And she cried, because Krep's simple statement of love reminded her of the emptiness of her own life and her fear of the future yawning ahead.

Chapter 14

Jennifer woke in the early hours of the morning to the sound of rain drumming against glass. Through the rain-splashed window she could make out dark rooftops glistening wetly in the grey light of dawn. She had a dragging pain in the small of her back, and the tendons of her left hand felt bruised and heavy. Her hand was strapped palm down on to a cushioned support up to the elbow and there was a needle fastened to the back of it with sticking plaster. Her eyes followed the plastic tube that emerged from it and snaked up to a dimly illuminated bag suspended from a drip-stand beside her. She could hear a faint steady 'plip ... plip ... plip' as it dispensed life-giving blood drop by drop down the tube. A little white plastic ball bobbed up and down with each plip in the drip chamber at the base of the bag, as its precious contents trickled slowly back into her veins. Jennifer watched for a while, hynotised by the barely perceptible sound and movement of life flowing back into her.

Then she turned back to the window where the sky was paling to a dove grey and the rain had stopped. She wondered where she was and guessed it must be London. She had lost consciousness somewhere between the private jet and the ambulance at the other end. Fragments of the journey and snatches of conversation between her, Julius, and the doctor who had attached a saline drip to her arm on the way to Nice, came back to her, but very hazily. She could remember the beginning clearly, though – getting horribly drunk on gin, pressed on her by the low-voiced Henrietta. And a foul-tasting brew. What was it, Ranunculus something-or-other? – from the buttercup family – steeped in boiling water. Then the pills.

And then the pains. Gut-wrenching, convulsive pains that contorted her body and locked her jaw and all her muscles with their intensity. Her tummy was still sore from retching and vomiting. God, the memory of it was horrendous! Still, she seemed to be over the worst now; battered, bruised and fragile, but intact, or at least apparently so.

As her eyes grew accustomed to the half-light she could make out pretty floral curtains at the window, pictures on the walls, and a carpet on the floor. No NHS ward, this. A huge bouquet of flowers adorned her bedside table, the scent wafting over to mask the usual hospital odours.

The door opened, the overhead light snapped on, and a cheerful nurse strode in.

"Well, and how's our patient this morning?" The voice was brisk and cheerful. "You had us all in a flap last night. Just let me take your temperature and blood pressure, and the orderly'll bring tea. I expect you'll be needing that, won't you, dear?"

Jennifer could hear the crisp rustle of her uniform as the nurse reached above the bed for the thermometer, and then felt cool, firm fingers on the inside of her wrist. As she took Jennifer's pulse, her eyes automatically checked the drip's progress just above her. The badge on her white, starched apron read Sister M. Browning. She was middle-aged and plump, with glasses.

"The day nurse will be taking that down soon, when it's finished, and you'll feel more comfortable."

"Good. My hand hurts like mad."

"Yes – but we had to speed up the flow a bit last night. That can cause leakage into the tissues locally with a bit of bruising and discomfort. Oooh, yes," she exclaimed glancing across the bed at Jennifer's hand. Her expression was sympathetic and concerned. "Your poor little hand. It's rather blue and swollen.

Do you want something for pain, dear?"

Jennifer put the thermometer in the corner of her mouth and spoke out of the side of it, which made her lisp. "Yes, please. I don't think there's any little bit of me that doesn't hurt this morning."

"Never mind, dear. We'll soon sort that out. Your first was it?"

"First what?"

"Baby," replied the nurse, looking kindly into her eyes. "Was it your first?"

"Yes. I suppose it was," Jennifer sighed. This was hardly a topic she wanted to discuss. She couldn't face thinking of her terrible experience in human terms: as the loss of a baby. Like Scarlett O'Hara, she would think about it tomorrow, when she'd be stronger.

"Bad luck. Still there's plenty of time for more, isn't there?"

Jennifer closed her eyes and didn't answer. God spare me that, she thought cynically. I think I've gone off men for life.

Sister Browning wound a black cuff round Jennifer's free arm, sitting on the edge of the bed as she pumped up the gauge. Jennifer felt herself slipping into unconsciousness as the cuff tightened, and then came to with a jerk as the nurse slowly let out the air. She compressed her lips slightly as she read the result.

"Better than last night, but still a bit low. You'll have to rest up, dear, till your blood pressure improves."

Taking the thermometer out of Jennifer's mouth, studying it and then shaking it briskly, she said, "Good. No temperature anyway. Now for that tea, eh?"

Jennifer nodded obediently. She was tired, and grateful for the nurse's sympathy and care; thankful that she wasn't being blamed for the termination, and most of all, thankful that the risk she took hadn't killed her. It was good to be alive, even aching from head to foot.

Sister Browning turned to go with another rustle of her

starched dress, then stopped. "Remember what I said, dear. Complete bed rest for you. You lost a lot of blood last night."

Jennifer smiled weakly. "Well, I can't exactly dance around while I'm fixed to the drip-stand, can I?"

The sun was shining brightly as Laura walked to her office, dressed in a cream silk camisole and dark grey straight skirt, her matching high heels clicking briskly on the clean, wet pavement. Ahead of her, a man in blue overalls was hosing down the street as he did every morning, the fine spray taking on all the hues of the rainbow as it arced against the low morning sun and then hit the ground with a satisfying hiss.

He could wash away all the physical detritus of human living so effectively, making the streets sparkling clean for residents who expected no less than pristine perfection. What a pity life's emotional debris couldn't be removed as simply, with the mere turn of a tap and flick of a hose. But all the money in the world could not do that, Laura observed bitterly. Nothing could wash away the pain and fear of last night. Nothing would eradicate the memory of Jennifer's experience.

Laura was furious with Henrietta, whose irresponsible meddling had nearly killed her friend. And even more so with Jean-Claude, who in his determined efforts to be proprietorial, had treated Jennifer as a mere vessel for his ambition. He had tried, and now failed as part of his life's plan to manipulate and engineer his possession of her with no regard for the consequences.

It was infuriating that a man could cold-bloodedly use a woman in such a way, even in this day and age, and walk away scot-free! Jennifer would bear the brunt of his sickening behaviour alone. Jean-Claude would be totally unscathed by any of it, utterly unaware of what he had done. In all likelihood too, if he found out, he would probably just shrug, and say, "Well, she could have married me! *C'est la vie, hein?*"

Bastard! Laura wanted to take hold of his pompous neck and

squeeze, as she thought of Jennifer lying pale, wan and frightened in some strange hospital bed.

Laura's anger was exacerbated by her feeling of impotence at not being able to hit back, because vengeance would achieve nothing. And the last thing Jennifer would want was for Jean-Claude to have the satisfaction of knowing she'd suffered at his hands. Also if he found out that Jennifer had induced the loss of his child, the sanctimonious creature would feel duty-bound to report her. He would pretend his motives were saintly, but they would actually have been prompted by his bitterness at being thwarted. Unfortunately this was one of life's tough lessons they would have to cope with in their own particular way: Jennifer must pick herself up and carry on regardless, and Laura must grin and bear the injustice of it, giving her friend all the support she could.

"Sod's law, and tough titty!" Laura could imagine Jennifer saying, with a courageous and rueful grin on her face. And that would have to be their lot.

At eleven o'clock, Julius arrived. He was dressed in a navy suit and dark tie, weighed down with yet more flowers – a bouquet of white roses and spikes of bright blue delphinium, surrounded by clouds of baby's breath, and carrying a parcel under his arm. He stopped in mid-stride when his eyes caught the drip attachment, and her arm all taped up with pads, sticking plaster and tubes. Jennifer saw him flinch. It was obvious that he was moved by her helplessness.

"Well, precious," he said, making an effort to cheer her, "fat chance of even holding your hand, let alone giving you a hug with all that paraphernalia!" He bravely attempted a wink, but it translated to a nervous tic instead.

"Thanks for the sympathy!" muttered Jennifer with a ghost of a smile. Though the Panadol had dulled her aches and pains, and she'd felt well enough to eat a small breakfast, she was still far from ebullient. She was shocked at the feeble tenor of her voice and wondered if she looked as bad as she sounded.

Julius put the flowers on a side table in the window, and turned back to Jennifer, studying her face more intently. "Hey!" he whispered gently. "How are you feeling – I mean really, sweet girl? Everyone looking after you OK? I told them only the best for that little lady or they'd get it in the neck from me."

Julius sat down on the edge of her bed, and with the tip of his finger gingerly stroked the small part of her hand that wasn't taped up. He looked at her with concern and tenderness, and Jennifer, overcome, suddenly felt near to tears.

"Soldiering on," she replied, her small voice sounding artificially bright. She was mystified at the sudden change in Julius. She could cope with his comical side, even his lechery – but tenderness . . . from Julius Krep? It seemed incongruous somehow – completely at variance with her impression of him so far.

He handed her the parcel, and she took it awkwardly in one hand, turning it over, and wondering how to open it.

"Wait." Julius leant forward, taking it from her. "What a clot I am. You'll never unwrap that one-handed. Let Juli do it."

Out of the wrapping came the most beautiful pale blue silk nightdress with matching negligée, edged with exquisite lace. Jennifer felt hot tears well up, and ineffectually tried to wipe them with the back of her free hand: but Julius was there first, with a soft handkerchief, gently dabbing at the corners of her eyes.

"All right, sweetheart," he murmured gently. "I'm here. Just let it all go, you've had a rough time."

He wanted more than ever to hold her against him but Jennifer looked too vulnerable, too fragile now to take into his arms. She was still so pale, she'd been so near death the previous night, and the drip attachment gave the impression her life still hung in the balance. He was suddenly afraid of his own clumsiness, acutely aware of his lack of allure. Why was it that this girl always made him feel so hopeless?

Julius reached for the negligée to cover his discomfiture, and ran the shimmering fabric between his fingers, showing her the gift as one might demonstrate a toy to a child. His confidence returned as Jennifer smiled gratefully.

"Thank you, Julius," she said. "It's fabulous, and so thoughtful of you. This hospital gown is hideous, and I can't wait to get out of it."

Julius looked down at her. He longed to dress her in silks and couture clothes, to cover her in diamonds. To show her off to the world as his woman. Only the best was good enough for her. Then he smiled fondly. Though pale and tired and dressed in a thick shapeless cotton gown she was still totally bewitching.

"OK, little darling. It shall be done. Nurse? Hey, nursey darlin' – come here, please." Julius hailed a passing figure, and ushered her in. She was small and dark and wearing the uniform of a staff nurse.

"Yes, Mr Krep," she replied equably. "What can I do for you?"

"Nothing for me, luvvie, but can you get Miss Morgan out of this strait-jacket and into a decent nightie with all the gubbins still attached to her?"

The staff nurse smiled at his irreverent description of the life-saving apparatus. "Well, as it happens," she replied briskly, her dark eyes twinkling, "not only could we do that, but it's about time we took the drip down anyway, because the bag's about finished. We'll give the patient a wash and brush up too, and have her looking like new if you can give us twenty minutes."

Golly, reflected Jennifer wryly, the way they go on, you'd think I were a car! Refuelled overnight. Then given a wash and brush up to look like new. How about a quick dust and polish too, whilst they're at it?

Julius' eyes flicked to his Rolex. He turned to the nurse, "I'd love to see her all glammed up," he said in a regretful voice, "but I've got a business meeting, so I d better be off." He stood up decisively. The navy eyes studied Jennifer's with an expression of infinite warmth. "Jenni, love, I'll stop by around seven thirty tonight, OK?" Julius blew her a kiss, and left the room.

It only took a few minutes to detach Jennifer from the drip. The worst part was tearing the sticking plaster off the needle. But the nurse was gentle and considerate and her chatter helped distract Jennifer from the discomfort. What a great relief it was to be freed of the constraining needle and drip-stand. What a luxury to be mobile and have the use of both hands again. She inspected her left hand. It was badly bruised, but not so swollen now. She wiggled her fingers and winced. Still very tender.

The nurse offered her a bed-bath, but Jennifer demurred. Bed-baths were for little old ladies. No way was she that helpless. She couldn't wait to get back on her feet again. She asked if she could have a proper bath instead.

"No, my dear," was the firm reply. "I'm afraid not. You'll get me shot! You're supposed to be on complete bed-rest, Miss Morgan."

Jennifer looked martyred. Then changing the subject deliberately, she asked, "Hey, what's your name, anyway?"

"Staff nurse Baker, dear."

"No. Your first name."

"Ann."

"You can call me Jennifer if I can call you Ann, then."

"OK, Jennifer, but don't let Sister hear you, or I'll get into trouble."

Jennifer sighed and flopped back into her pillows. God, everyone was formal around here. How was she going to adjust to a regime of doing what she was told every second? She pursed her lips and reflected a bit. Then her eyes flashed obstinately. She grinned and pushed the covers off, swung her legs out of bed and stood up, before the nurse could stop her.

"See," Jennifer said triumphantly. "I'm OK. I promise not to faint. If I'm OK to walk, surely I'll be all right in a bath?"

Ann Baker looked very worried.

"I promise I won't tell!" Jennifer whispered conspiratorially.

"Oh, all right then," the staff nurse said reluctantly. "But on your head be it."

She took Jennifer's elbow and led her into the bathroom.

"Honestly, you can leave me now. I'll be all right."

The dark eyes burned adamantly. "No fear!"

Staff nurse Baker insisted on running the bath, and stayed close at hand, testing the temperature with her elbow, as if her patient were a newborn baby. Jennifer would love to have wallowed for hours alone in neck-high bubbles of hot, scented water. Instead she had to make do with a shallow, tepid bath, hospital soap and a watchful nurse.

"I'd love to wash my hair." she groaned, longing to lie back and immerse herself completely.

"No!" came Ann's voice in a desperate crescendo. "Not today. You'll get me the sack if you don't behave. Out you come, now. That's more than enough excitement for the moment. Let's get you dry and into your nightie."

She helped Jennifer out of the bath, wrapped a towel round her, and guided her back to her room, holding on to her arm. What a joy it was to be fresh and clean again. The negligée shone like a jewel in its bed of tissue paper. Jennifer slipped the beautiful gown over her head, relishing the feel as the cool silk slithered down and caressed her skin on its way to her ankles.

"Wow!" exclaimed Ann enviously, admiring the blue silk that shimmered and clung to the contours of her patient's slender body. "Wow! What I'd give for a nightie like that!"

Suddenly Jennifer felt her head spin, and her legs buckle. She reached out for support.

"Oh dear," she whispered tremulously, "I feel a bit light-headed all of a sudden."

Her face went very pale. The nurse shot forward and put her arms firmly under Jennifer's elbows to stop her collapsing.

"Now then, what did I tell you, eh?" she scolded, looking very concerned. "Right, young lady. Back to bed you go, and no getting out without calling me first, understood?"

Ann helped her patient back into bed, plumped up the pillows behind her, found a comb and carefully drew it through the thick golden tangles. "That's better. You look a picture now."

"Thanks," Jennifer whispered gratefully. She felt very drained. "Hey, I mean it. You're a doll!" She grinned feebly and winked at the staff nurse.

Ann smiled at Jennifer, and waved a friendly admonishing finger at her.

"Behave yourself, won't you?" she commanded. Forlorn hope! Obviously this girl was going to charm her way round everyone, and do exactly as she pleased.

Jennifer grinned back wearily, and said, "OK, Annie. You're the boss. I promise."

The bath and the silk negligée had lifted Jennifer's spirits, and though she was weary, she found herself looking forward to Julius' visit later on. There were so many questions she wanted to ask him, and so much she needed to thank him for. At a time like this, it would be so tempting to give in to his kindness and generosity. God, how she needed a shoulder to lean on. If only she could just let go and let him take control from now on. It would be so much easier than struggling on, without money, without a definite future. Yes, tempting indeed. So much for my vow, though, not to be beholden to any man! How are you going to extricate yourself from this, Morgan?

But what could Krep's motive be? Why had he done so much for her? Had she freed herself from the hateful Jean-Claude, only to saddle herself with Julius and his demands? Had she merely swapped one obligation for another? Julius would be entitled to expect, even demand her gratitude. After all, she owed him her life! What would he expect in return? A sex slave, obedient to his every whim? Jennifer shivered. It didn't bear thinking about. She'd have to hope for the best and cross that bridge when she came to it. For now, she was just glad to be alive. She'd had a close brush with death and must be thankful for small mercies.

Jennifer rummaged in her bedside locker for distraction. She saw with great relief that her handbag had arrived with her from France, thanks no doubt to the ever-thoughtful Laura. She applied some mascara and blusher, and a hint of pink lipstick; just enough to leave her pale but not uninteresting. She spent most of the day dozing, or enjoying the sympathetic attention of the medical staff and the orderlies who periodically brought food and cups of tea or coffee on a tray. Just like the Ritz, Jennifer decided, and resolved to make the most of it.

Chapter 15

There was no sign of Henrietta for the next couple of days, and though Laura liaised regularly with Quintin about Jennifer's progress, she didn't mention Henrietta's name to him. She was still too angry. But at least Henrietta had the decency to lie low. Perhaps Quintin was lodging her because she was too ashamed and frightened to face Laura. It seemed disloyal on his part, but, of course, he did have a business to run, and Henrietta was an employee.

It was lonely in the flat at night, and though Laura missed Jennifer intensely, the lack of interruptions afforded her the opportunity to make tremendous headway with her course, which was going well. She had been studying until the early hours, so her assistant at work, Mary, was a godsend. At last, Laura seemed to be in control of her life!

She spread her work out on the kitchen table, and absent-mindedly picked with her fingers at a *salade niçoise* in a patchwork olive-wood bowl. The tuna was succulent, but now Laura had salad dressing all over her hands. She reached for a tissue to prevent her papers getting greasy, when the telephone rang.

"Damn!" she cursed, crossing into the hallway, and picking up the phone with her fingertips. Jamming it between her chin and shoulders, Laura carried on wiping her fingers.

"Whore," growled a muffled voice.

Laura's heart thumped, and then missed a beat. "Whaaat?' she faltered in disbelief, pressing her ear closer to the receiver. This was obviously their anonymous caller, who until

201

now had resorted only to heavy breathing or complete silence. Come what may, she must try to identify the voice, and inform the police.

"All sluts need to learn a lesson," it continued, slowly, menacingly, "And you will... Soon..." The receiver crackled with mirthless laughter, and then went dead.

But, unfortunately, the voice was too muffled to recognise. It was even impossible to tell whether the caller was English or French. The only thing she could be certain of was that the voice was male. Laura was petrified. It would have been bearable if it had only been Nova being bitchy, but this was far worse. Far more threatening. Who could it be? What could have driven someone to say such vicious and untrue things? If only even Henrietta were back. Anything was better than being alone and frightened.

Laura's only place of refuge seemed to be in the office. There, at least, when the phone rang, she didn't jump out of her skin. It was business. The work preoccupied her, and she felt safe in the comforting presence of Fitz, and the ever-dependable Mary.

Despite her antagonism towards Henrietta, she decided it would be wise to ask her to come back. She knew she wouldn't be able to stand another night on her own at the Meribel. She telephoned Quintin, who said he would organise Henrietta's return immediately. He sounded somewhat relieved.

"Is Jennifer OK?" drawled Henrietta when Laura returned to the flat at seven thirty. She was standing in the doorway of Laura's bedroom looking gaunt and spectral. Her long black hair rendered her face completely devoid of colour, and did nothing to flatter her.

Laura felt her hackles rise at Henrietta's cool attitude. In spite of her relief at no longer being alone, she still felt defensive and angry. She was determined that Henrietta

202

should recognise how utterly irresponsible she'd been. Is Jennifer OK, my foot, she thought blackly. How could the creature be so casual after what she'd done?

"Only just, no thanks to you," replied Laura stiffly, pulling off her shoes as she sat on her bed.

"Well, at least she isn't pregnant any more," Henrietta insisted. "That's what she wanted, wasn't it?"

Laura looked up at the impassive face coldly. Henrietta had a ton of white make-up on. Her eyes were heavily blacked, like a panda's. She looked absurd and dated. "I suppose it's the only thing you could say in your defence," she said scathingly, then looked away, massaging her toes. It would be better to control her anger, because she needed Henrietta's presence in the flat. It wouldn't do to drive her away.

Henrietta stood her ground, determined to make her point. "What else could Jennifer have done? It seemed the only solution. Is a back-street abortion any better, or marriage to a man she can't stand? She came to me in desperation, Laura, and begged me to help her. What could I do? I feel terrible that it went so wrong, but she didn't tell me how far gone she was. If she had, I'd never have got involved." She raised her hands in supplication, then dropped them limply by her sides. "What can I say, except sorry to have caused such panic all round?"

Henrietta's plummy drawl was irritating, but Laura had to admit she had a point. Maybe she had been too hard on her. What Laura needed now was a good long soak in the bath to wind down. Then she'd stay at the disco, in spite of the noise, until Henrietta finished. That way she need not be alone. No studying tonight: she was awarding herself a night off. Laura glanced round at the door, but the ghostly Henrietta had drifted away, plainly abandoning the attempt to mollify her.

She threw on a satin peignoir and ran herself a good hot bath. While she was soaking up to her neck in Fenjal, Henrietta's head came round the door.

"A rather strange man on the phone for you."

Laura sighed in disbelief. It must be the anonymous breather again. Bloody hell. Bloody, bloody hell. That's all she needed. Laura closed her eyes wearily and shook her head. But then, suddenly, she was angry instead of worried. To hell with it. She was sick to death of the whole stupid charade.

Laura frowned irritably. "Oh, tell him to fuck off!" she snapped.

Then she smiled. She had never been one for gutter language, but it was immensely satisfying to use it in this context. Her tormentor was a guttersnipe – a low, evil, sick coward. It was the only kind of language people like him understood. It was all he deserved.

"What's fuck off in French?" droned Henrietta, framed in the doorway, her face impassive.

"*Va te faire enculer.* But just say it in English. He'll get the message loud and clear!"

Laura was damned if she was going to be cowed. No longer alone, she felt a resurgence of Dutch courage. She sat up, smiling triumphantly in the bath. Holding her sponge aloft, she squeezed it hard, and gritted her teeth, imagining it were the caller's neck. It released a torrent of water on to her breasts, parting into a shower of silver droplets, splashing and undulating their way down her body, to disappear into the froth of scented bubbles.

Next day, Julius suddenly turned up at the office and surprised Laura.

"Hello, Laura, duck," he smiled, standing in the doorway. "I'm back. How about dinner with me tonight at the Hôtel de Paris? Got a lot of news for you about Jennifer."

Julius was dressed in a revolting dark shiny suit and tie, despite the heat. His round face was gleaming with perspiration.

"Julius, how lovely to see you," smiled Laura, genuinely pleased. "Come on in."

Julius stepped into the office, quickly casting his eyes around, his attention attracted momentarily by the chattering ticker. "I can't stay, luvvie," he said hurriedly. "Got to get back to the phone. Only just got in from the airport. Will you come tonight?"

"Of course, Julius, I'd love to. I finish work around seven, and could be with you at eight. Shall I meet you in the foyer?"

Julius looked away from her and studied the latest US share prices Laura had pinned on the board. "I could pick you up, luvvie," he murmured distractedly.

"No, thanks," she said to his navy-suited back. "I'd enjoy the walk, being stuck in the office all day. Besides I'm more than used to the Hôtel de Paris, as I'm for ever having to leave messages and stock reports at reception, so I won't feel lost there."

Julius turned back and looked at her, chuckling fondly. "You young girls these days, you're so independent!"

Laura smiled to herself. Here was Julius Krep worrying about a five-minute walk, when she'd arrived by train in Monte-Carlo two years ago with a one-way ticket, a hundred pounds in her pocket and not knowing a soul!

"How is Jennifer?" she asked.

But Julius was distracted. Something on the notice-board had grabbed his attention. "Fine," he said vaguely. "Just fine. She'll be coming out soon. I'll tell you all about it tonight."

Laura couldn't wait to hear the latest news. Julius was frowning now and fiddling with his collar.

"Are those the opening prices?" he asked, changing the subject.

"Yes. But I can get you an immediate quote if you want," replied Laura helpfully.

Julius was impressed. His eyes were bright, his voice excited. "Could you, love? Could you get me a quote on Atlantic Richfield? It's down five points from yesterday."

Laura rang John Wilder and got the quote. Atlantic Richfield was down a further four and three-eighths. Julius was in a froth. Laura couldn't tell if he was pleased or angry.

Julius huffed and puffed and made his way to the door. "Got to go, love. Got to cover my short. It'll make me a packet."

"Wait, Julius. Why don't you ring your broker from here?"

Julius looked doubtful. Then the dark blue eyes brightened. "Are you sure, duck? It's a New York number."

"No problem," Laura smiled, and pointed to the phone on Fitz's desk. He was away on yet another business trip.

While Julius talked to his broker, Laura thought about the evening ahead at the Hôtel de Paris. Bang goes another night's studying, but she could maybe catch up on a bit of Margin Regulations after dinner. Her course was going well, in spite of all the interruptions and the frenetic lifestyle. Because of her circumstances and the inevitable delays in airmailing lessons back and forth to the States, the Institute had agreed to send several lessons ahead. She was already halfway through the course, and Fitzgerald was very encouraging, asking her to show him each lesson as it was marked and congratulating her on her grades, which were always in the high nineties.

"What a clever girl you are. Always thought you'd go a long way!" muttered Fitz ruefully, sensing that he would probably lose the best right arm he'd ever had to greener pastures. "And to think I always thought I'd lose you to some stallion who would sweep you off your feet into marriage. Who'd ever have thought it would be the Stock Exchange that'd woo you instead?"

Laura laughed. "You haven't lost me yet. Can't get rid of me that easily!"

Suddenly Laura's thoughts were interrupted by a torrent of anger. Julius was banging the desk and shouting. "I don't care if you sold them long. That's your mistake. I telexed the order and it said as plain as the nose on your face – sell short." Julius' face was a vivid pink. He was bursting with rage. "Well, that's your problem, sonny boy," he snarled nastily. "It's not for me to stand the loss. You'll have to purchase two blocks of ten thou to cover the short and long, and make the short sale, too. As far as I'm concerned, the original execution price still stands." He raised his eyes in exasperation. "Of course it's gonna cost you. That's your bleedin' problem. I knew the price was going to drop. You told me yourself. Why d'you think I sold short, for Christ's sake? I want confirmation of the transaction by close tonight." Then he slammed the phone down.

Laura thought he was going into apoplexy. She wouldn't like to have been the poor broker on the other end. What a disaster for him! He stood to lose a packet on the deal. Julius was obviously a very tough businessman, always exacting his pound of flesh, no matter what it cost the man who crossed him – regardless of whether it was by accident or design.

"Sorry, luvvie," Julius said apologetically. "Thanks for the use of the phone. Damned brokers! I'll have to sack that idiot!" Then he smiled; back to his normal chirpy self, as if the angry conversation had never been. "Must fly, duck. See you tonight, eh?"

It was interesting to see the business side of Julius, the harder side that had obviously made him successful. Intractable, demanding and intolerant of weakness, he would not be an easy man to live with. Maybe Jennifer was right to be suspicious. Would she be another acquisition – to be profited from and then discarded like a block of shares? It was difficult to believe any such thing when Laura remembered the selfless way Julius had dropped everything and whisked Jennifer to hospital, doing everything in his power to save her. Nothing was too good for her, according to him. Perhaps Jennifer brought out a hidden, gentler side of him. And he'd sounded genuine when he told Laura he loved her.

Only time would tell, she reflected. Only time would tell.

Laura swept through the revolving doors of the Hôtel de Paris wearing a long white polka dot dress with a halter neck; into the imposing foyer, flanked on both sides by towering columns of pink marble, and huge, gilt-framed mirrors. In the centre of the hall was an enormous circular seat on which sprawled various guests in evening dress, waiting for their partners, or just watching the never-ending stream of people arriving and departing. This rendezvous was considered *de rigueur*. Whether one was dining at Eze Village, Roquebrune, or dancing at the Maona, one always had to be seen at the bar of the Hôtel de Paris first; it was an unspoken rule!

Julius was standing at Réception, and held out both hands in welcome to Laura. He was dressed less formally than earlier. He had on a sky-blue seersucker suit which made him look like a bright party balloon. It did not flatter him at all. Laura smiled and put her own small hands in his, and he drew them together and kissed the tips of her fingers, prickling them with his moustache. He looked at her intently without saying a word, and then politely gestured towards the bar. Laura walked on ahead of him, and a waiter dashed over and pulled out a chair for her.

There were two flutes, some canapés and a silver cooler with champagne, and little trays with nuts, olives and crackers already laid out on the table. The bar was a hive of activity and every table was occupied with pre-dinner drinkers – bejewelled, coiffed and dressed to kill. They gazed round periodically, with a feigned nonchalance, to hide the fact they were desperate not to be upstaged by the richer or more glamorous.

"I'm so glad you could make it," smiled Julius. "Jennifer sends her love, and she's making good progress. Pity I had to leave her but I had to get back. Business – you know – but she's OK, really doing well."

He then went on to describe the clinic, her medical treatment, the prognosis, and that he'd insisted Jennifer stay a couple of days more than necessary to get a really good rest and set herself back on her feet more firmly.

"If I know Jennifer," said Laura, "she's probably the world's worst patient and getting up to all sorts of mischief."

"Oh, she's practically running the place and has every doctor and nurse twisted round her little finger," laughed Julius, pushing an olive into his mouth, "but at least I know she won't be out drinking and dancing till all hours while she's in there!"

"When will she be discharged, then? Quite soon, by the sound of it."

"Yes. She'll be leaving Wednesday morning. I've got business commitments elsewhere, so I won't be back till mid-August." He reached into his mouth to pull out an olive stone, before helping himself to another olive. Julius seemed to be a compulsive eater; permanently, almost nervously pushing food into his mouth. No wonder he was so fat. "I've arranged for a car to pick her up and get her to the airport, and the flight's all booked to Nice. She insisted on coming straight back to the Meribel and getting back to work, too." He shook his head, smiling ruefully. "I had wanted her under my roof so my staff could look after her. But you know her: little Miss Independent. I just hope she keeps her promise not to go back to work for a long while! In fact, if I had my way she'd never have to work again." The plump fingers reached for a handful of nuts, which he threw into his mouth.

Julius' greed was not attractive to behold. Laura found it off-putting when he talked with his mouth full – sometimes spitting out pieces of nut or olive as he spoke.

"Fat chance of that, Julius. She'll wade straight back into the thick of it. Jennifer doesn't know how to stand still." Then her expression changed. "Honestly, what on earth would we have done without your help? We can never thank you enough."

Julius looked uncomfortable for a moment. Then he grinned broadly, his eyes twinkling wickedly. "Oh, come on! Just make sure she takes iron pills, eh? And there's no need for thanks. I'm just really glad you thought to call me. It gave me the chance to see her in a silk nightie at last!"

Laura was determined that Julius should appreciate her gratitude. That he should understand what his help meant to her.

"Honestly, Julius," she chided gently, "can't you be serious for five minutes?" Then her voice tightened with emotion. "Anyway, I just wanted you to know that we'll never forget what you did."

But Julius waved his hand casually. "It's nothing. Now, how's your glass . . . or are you ready to have some dinner? Shall we go on through?"

Laura nodded her assent as she was unable to speak, her eyes having misted over at Krep's largesse and his light-hearted dismissal of it. Crossing the ornate lobby again, they made their way to the Louis XV restaurant. Inside they were greeted by a deferential *maître d'* and more opulent grandeur than Laura had ever seen. Tremendous mirrors, gilding, and thick, marble pillars swam before her eyes. In the centre of each table was a beautiful flower arrangement from which rose magnificent chandeliers. The table cloths were set with the most elegant gold-plated cutlery, damask napkins and crystal glasses.

When they sat down at their table, Julius noticed that Laura's eyes were bright with unshed tears. He patted her hand comfortingly.

His voice was kindly. "She's going to be all right, you know."

"Only thanks to you. You saved her life!"

Julius looked at Laura quizzically. How much did she know about Jennifer's past history? He hadn't wanted to question Jennifer about the baby because in the circumstances it did not seem right. The last thing she needed was to be reminded of her mistakes when she was drawing on all her resources to help her recover.

"What else could I have done? I'm crazy about her."

Laura didn't reply. She seemed unable to speak, struggling

to regain her composure in the guise of fiddling with the clasp of her evening bag. Julius wondered what she'd be willing to divulge, if anything. He was eager to find out all he could on the seemingly wayward Jennifer, who fascinated, even obsessed him.

"It wasn't relevant whose child it was," he prompted, hoping to elicit information, "I just wanted to save her." Then he jumped in feet first, eyes blazing. "Where was the shiftless bastard who was responsible, anyway?"

Laura looked down and started toying with her napkin. She remained silent for a while, twisting a corner round and round her index finger. Eventually she looked up, and asked quietly, "Didn't Jennifer tell you anything?"

Julius shook his head gravely. "I didn't think it was the right time to cross-examine her whilst she was so low. I didn't want to pressure her."

The *maître d'hotel* handed them an enormous menu, which both of them had difficulty in concentrating on. Eventually they decided to go for a Chateaubriand for the main course, and asparagus to start with. As Julius was keen to pursue the topic of Jennifer, he left the choice of wines to the *sommelier* to save wasting precious time.

Laura in the meantime had decided to confide in Julius. After all, he was her friend's guardian angel, and bearing in mind his generosity of spirit, it seemed churlish to hold back. He deserved better. So, at his prompting she told all. His face became like a thundercloud when she touched on Jean-Claude and his proprietorial and arrogant attitude.

"Has she finished with that sonovabitch?"

"Oh, absolutely," stated Laura with conviction. "She wants nothing more to do with him. I don't think she was ever that crazy about him anyway."

"Crazy enough to have slept with him," Julius retorted, trying to keep the bitterness and jealousy out of his voice.

Laura made a small questioning gesture with her hands,

brushed her hair back from her face, and sat back in her chair, studying Julius quizzically with her large blue eyes.

"How long was this affair?" he continued.

"About a year, I suppose – on and off. I think it was just a relationship of convenience for her really, always a bit one-sided. She used to get fed up with him quite often and refuse to see him for weeks on end."

"Oh, well," muttered Julius ruefully, "I suppose I'll be in for the same sort of treatment then, as I'm mug enough to have fallen for her, too." He leant on one elbow, supporting his chin in his hand, eyes dreamy and distant.

Meanwhile, the waiter arrived with the asparagus, and there was a short silence while he served the couple and laid out fingerbowls for them both.

"May I ask you a personal question?" hedged Laura politely, delicately nibbling at a tender stalk.

Julius leaned back in his chair, looking at her defensively, his eyes darkening slightly.

"If it's whether I'm married – yes, I am. But we live separate lives. My wife doesn't like travelling, and to her great distress we were never able to have children. She lost several babies in the early stages, and suffered a lot."

Suddenly it all clicked in Laura's mind. So that's what Julius had meant that dreadful night, when he said he'd been through it all before.

"Sadly," he continued, "the trauma of it all eventually drove us apart. We never divorced, though, because we're still the best of friends, but we prefer to have separate houses. Capische?"

"I think I understand. But what do you want with Jennifer, then? A sort of mistress?"

Julius smiled and shook his head. His slicked hair gleamed in the light of the chandelier. "No, Laura, love," he murmured softly, "I wouldn't put it that way. Not a bit of it. I want Jennifer as the mainstay of my life. Don't ask me why, but I just want to take care of her, spoil her, provide for her – give her everything she needs. She's not the sort for a second-rate life."

Julius sighed and his eyes grew misty. There was a tenderness about him that touched Laura.

His voice went husky. "She seems to have got right under my skin. I . . . just love and want that girl with me, d'you understand? Maybe it's because I never had any children of my own. Perhaps she's the daughter I never had and now need, to sort of fill the void. Oh, I don't know. That's all there is to it. You know . . . ?"

"Mmmm," Laura murmured thoughtfully, still looking rather doubtful. If he loved Jennifer so much, then why not commit himself properly?

"Old-fashioned little thing, aren't you?"

Laura laughed. "Well, yes, perhaps in certain respects. Maybe traditional more than old-fashioned. I suppose I have traditional views of marriage and a family, but what's wrong with that?"

"Nothing at all. It works for some. And in other cases you need another, less conventional solution. Jennifer needs taking care of. She's not as tough as she thinks she is, and this racketing around in night-clubs is no life for a lady. Honest. What sort of a career d'you call that?"

"I suppose you're right. But it was never really a career – just a stop-gap measure."

"For how long?" Julius interrupted, his eyes blazing. "Stop-gap jobs, here and there, running out of money, men doing the dirty on her, ending up in hospital! It's not good enough, is it?" and he bit furiously into a juicy asparagus tip.

Laura studied his angry face wonderingly. Would Jennifer ever change, though? She was an adventuress. She relished her independence, enjoyed sticking her neck out, even if it got chopped at. Her scrapes were an essential part of her character.

213

"No, it most certainly isn't," Laura answered truthfully. But it was what made Jennifer tick, though perhaps the latest trauma would reform her. "I'll see if I can talk some sense into her, if you want me to."

Julius laughed wryly. "You know, love, it's kind of odd. Here am I, Julius Krep, who can talk the hind legs off a donkey, sell ice to Eskimoes, buy anything I want, make any deal I want, and there's this beautiful wild girl who strikes me dumb, and I can't do a thing about it."

Laura looked at him questioningly. Could she see Jennifer and Julius making a life together? True, Jennifer would have a dream lifestyle – the one she craved. But was Julius her type? Character-wise, maybe yes. He was tough, resolute, funny and led a very interesting life. But physically? Julius had a nice face, except for the horrid moustache, but he was overweight – repulsively so. Swimming in fat. Laura was dubious. Looks were very important to Jennifer.

"Well," she said, "I can't promise results, but the least I can do is have a heart-to-heart with her on your behalf, to see how the land lies."

The Chateaubriands were mouthwateringly tender, the wine mellow, and Laura was pleasantly surprised at how much she was enjoying Krep's company. He told her a bit about his past, how he'd traded up from the beginnings of a small shop left him by his father, to larger concerns which he trimmed and changed, made profitable and then sold on, and had made his first million by the age of twenty-seven.

He described himself as an opportunist entrepreneur, sometimes disparagingly known as an asset stripper – or, for want of a better expression, a multiple-company director! When Laura, fascinated, wanted to know *how* he picked on the right situations so consistently, he smiled and pointed to his nose. "I can scent a bargain," he explained. "Just call it instinct. Mind you, I've picked a few losers, too, but those are the ones I forget about! Pointless, dwelling on failures."

214

As well as being entertaining company, Julius was a good listener, which, in the usual brittle world of the ever-partying cocktail set, made a refreshing change. After a while, his dynamism made one forget his unattractive exterior and see the strength and power of the charisma underneath. Their time together flew by all too quickly, and Laura's admiration and liking for him grew by the minute. All in all, reflected Laura, impressed, Jennifer could do a lot worse!

Laura took her leave at ten, promising Julius in the lobby of the Meribel that she'd take care of Jennifer and try to talk some sense into her. He smiled and kissed Laura on both cheeks.

"Good luck with your studies. You know, Laura – you're a very beautiful and charming young lady. Thank you for a lovely evening. I'll be back in the middle of August. You'll be hearing from me then, both of you. Look after yourselves, eh? Take care, now."

It was visiting time at the hospital, and Jennifer found herself without a visitor. She was surprised to find herself missing Julius' chirpy company. But as he'd explained, he had business commitments in Monaco, and had already taken two days off rushing a certain lady back to London for urgent medical treatment!

"Life goes on, you know. Business doesn't stop, even for Miss Morgan!"

She smiled at the memory, and picked up a *Vogue* which he'd brought her earlier in the day. She switched on the bedside light, and settled herself down to a long evening's reading. She was feeling a lot better today, and wondering if she could handle four more days in bed. Idly she flicked through reams of pages filled with bored-looking models. She yawned and shut her eyes for a moment.

"Hey, are you asleep, flower?"

Jennifer's eyes flew open at the familiar voice. What a

surprise! Her old flatmate, out of the blue! "Caroline! But how did you . . . ? What are you . . . ? Hey! How did you know I was here? How fabulous to see you."

"Laura rang me and told me you were here, so I thought I'd come to pay you a visit."

Jennifer's pale face was radiant. "What a lovely, lovely surprise!"

"Well, babe, how are you," Caroline stood by the bed, smiling down at Jennifer.

"Absolutely great now you're here. Honestly, everything's fine now. How much did Laura tell you?"

"Everything." Her eyes widened as she took in Jennifer's luxurious surroundings and the flowers burgeoning out of every corner and available space. "How amazingly kind of your *white slug* to install you here."

Jennifer giggled. "Oh well, even if I thought he was a white slug, he's a good slug now, and in my good books at the moment. I guess I owe him one!"

Caroline sat down on the bed. "What next then? Millionaire paradise?"

Heavens, Caroline was jumping the gun rather! Jennifer knew she owed Julius her life, but she wasn't ready to commit herself to him for ever. He seemed infatuated at the moment, but all that could change. Julius had a reputation for using women as ornaments, as sweeteners for his business dealings. Jennifer needed to find out more about him, to know whether he was genuine, or whether she was just a passing phase. In any case, she still didn't fancy him.

"God knows," she replied casually. "I've made no plans as yet, and Julius is off till the middle of August on some kind of extended business trip. He's a bit mysterious about where he's going. Me, all I want to do first off is to get my act together and carry on as normal. So it's back to M-C, and lazing on the beach time. I did promise him I wouldn't go straight back to work, so I guess I'll start the weekend after next."

216

"Bad girl," Caroline admonished, waving a finger at her, "It's already Friday now – so the weekend after next is only a week away."

Jennifer grinned at her friend impishly. "So? That gives me Wednesday, Thursday and Friday to recover in the sun, and then I'll start right in again on Friday night. Is that straight away or is it not?"

"Oh, well, be it on your head, then. You always were a twit, but knowing you, you'll be quite fully recovered by tomorrow!"

Jennifer put her thumb to her nose, and wiggled her fingers rudely. "Enough about me," she said. "How's the law degree going?"

"All right. Well, yes, OK actually. I'm quite looking forward to stepping in to the breach left by my brother."

"Why did he leave your father's practice?"

"Oh, a clash of super-large egos. Family businesses are always quite difficult, but I've always got on better with my father than James does, and anyway he says he can make a lot more money in the States, and seems to be proving that point at the moment."

"So it looks as if you won't be coming back to Monaco, then."

"Oh, not entirely. I can take the odd break and spend a month or so over there with you one of these days."

"That would be fun. You must come and see the night-club and get to know Kreppy." Jennifer's eyes gleamed mischievously. "Maybe you can take him off my hands. You might even like him."

The girls chatted on without a break. There was so much to catch up on; so much had happened to all of them. It was strange to see Caroline without her tan, and wearing rather formal London clothes. She looked more grown up and chic than Jennifer remembered, and, she thought wistfully, very much together, in charge of her life, unlike herself. If only she had the application, like Laura and Caroline, to forge a career,

217

some sense of purpose. She sighed. Perhaps her day would come.

"You'll come and see us soon. Promise?" Jennifer extracted that undertaking from her old friend as she was leaving finally, at nearly ten o'clock.

"Of course I will. Just you try to stop me." And Caroline blew her a kiss as she stood framed in the doorway. "Bye, my precious. Look after yourself, hey?"

It had been tremendous to see Caroline again. Jennifer yawned. She felt tired after all the animated chatter. Some of it preyed on her mind. She wondered if people expected her to recompense Krep for his largesse. Caroline had joked in that vein, but it cut a little close to the bone for Jennifer's liking. It was going to be difficult living in the shadow of Krep's generosity. She didn't relish the thought.

Chapter 16

Laura woke up the next morning with a hangover. Julius had given her far too much champagne. Thank God it was Saturday and she could have a lie-in. She climbed out of bed, massaging the nape of her neck and went to find some aspirin, tip-toeing past the sleeping Henrietta to get to the bathroom. She would have to spend the entire weekend studying. So much precious time had been wasted already. She would spend the day finishing lesson eleven – 'Margin Regulation and Practices' – then start the next one, 'The Customer Statement', on Sunday. Not very exciting fare, but nevertheless, important. She could see the finishing line now! Wilder's idea of her going the whole hog and sitting the Stock Exchange exam as well as the diploma was gathering force, but she was still in a dilemma as to how to broach the subject with Fitz.

If he allowed her the time off to attend a stockbrokers' crammer course on Wall Street, it would effectively give Laura the wherewithal to leave him in the lurch and go on to greener pastures. Why should he lash out on improving her status when he'd end up the loser? It was a real poser. All the same, there'd be no harm in taking John Wilder up on his lunch invitation. Then she could find out if Howson May ran in-house crammers for their trainees and would consider letting her attend.

After breakfast Laura telephoned Jennifer, who sounded very cheerful and told her of Caro's visit, that she was dying to come back and getting bored with being a patient! The short chat with Jennifer cheered her. Laura was really looking forward to her return. She hung up, and walked into the sitting-room to her books, ready for a hard day's studying.

Just as she was sitting down, the door opened, framing the gaunt Henrietta. "Morning," she said. "Would you like a coffee? I just brewed some."

Touched by Henrietta's efforts to be conciliatory after she'd frozen her out so many times, Laura softened. It was wrong to bear her a grudge. As Quintin had said, why put the blame entirely on Henrietta for Jennifer's dreadful experience? Jennifer was a consenting adult who must have known what she was doing. The ghastly episode must have scared Henrietta witless and she'd have had no end of a battle with her conscience over it. Her cool exterior probably disguised a great deal of inner conflict. "Thanks, yes," Laura smiled, "that would be super."

Then, as Henrietta turned away, Laura did a double-take. "Good heavens!" she cried, "What on earth's happened to your hair?"

Henrietta gloomily lifted the long black locks. There was a great hole in them at the back. She reminded Laura of a cartoon basset hound with a sombre white face, and long, drooping black ears. She was covered in thick foundation, and her large hazel eyes were all but obscured by a sooty circle of kohl and sticky false lashes. Her brows were plucked nearly bald and then harshly re-pencilled in. Laura wondered why she went to such efforts to spoil her looks.

"Is that a trendy new haircut or what?" she asked, staring with amazement at the extraordinary effect.

"No." The low voice was mournful. "I ironed it last night. It was a disaster."

"You ironed your hair?" Laura said incredulously, fighting a rising mirth. "What on earth for?"

"Well," the deep drone continued, "you see I washed it and couldn't get it dry in time for the club, so I thought I'd iron it dry. Trouble was, the iron was too hot, and burnt a socking great hole in my hair."

Laura spluttered at Henrietta's rueful expression and the thought of her tall, angular frame prostrated over the ironing board. She tried to control herself but finally gave in to a fit of helpless giggling, clutching her stomach, tears running down her face. There was, perhaps, an edge of hysteria to her laughter, but it was a welcome tonic and a release for the pent-up anger inside. Suddenly Henrietta joined in with gales of laughter. It was the first time Laura had ever seen her face show any expression. The almost-white lipstick she wore looked incongruous with her small cream teeth, and made Laura even more hysterical. Then she felt guilty. It was not fair to use Henrietta's mishaps as a palliative. She must pull herself together.

"Sorry," she spluttered, "I shouldn't laugh, but I couldn't help it." Laura wiped away the tears of mirth, but was again overcome by another welter of giggles, though quieter this time. She was behaving like a heel. She should be grateful to Henrietta for lightening her load, albeit unknowingly.

"No offence taken. I'll just go and fetch the coffee," smiled Henrietta sweetly. "Won't be a mo."

When she returned, Laura had an idea. "Henrietta," she suggested brightly, "why don't you let me do something about your hair? You can't leave it like that!"

Henrietta looked defensive. "Like what?"

"Well, couldn't we just even it up a bit? A sort of longish bob. Surely anything's better than great long side pieces and nothing at the back. It makes you look like a hound."

Henrietta was indignant for a moment. "Thanks a lot!" she said, wryly surveying the damage she had wreaked on herself. But then she relented. "OK," she said decisively. "Yah, why not?"

Pleased at the opportunity to do something constructive, Laura fetched a pair of sharp scissors. The long black tresses drifted to the floor as she carefully trimmed round the burnt hair at the back. Then she evened up both sides to just below chin length. When she stepped back to survey her efforts, the transformation was amazing. Like a window with the curtains drawn back. But there was more to be done.

"Wait there!" Laura commanded. "I haven't quite finished yet." She went into her bedroom to fetch some cotton wool, cold cream and her make-up purse.

"What are you doing?" Henrietta protested, as Laura started to wipe away the thick smudged edges of the kohl, carefully leaving only the tiniest outline. As she attacked the layers of Panstick, Henrietta tried to pull away.

"Just hold still," Laura said bossily. "I'm doing a make-over. If you don't like it you can re-do your face again in a minute."

She then cleaned off the white lipstick and replaced it with natural pink, and put some blusher on Henrietta's prominent cheekbones.

"Wow," she said, stepping back a couple of paces. "Nobody would recognise you. Quint will think he's got a new disc-jockey. Gone is the hippy. Now you're all elegant and refined! You might have looked trendy in the King's Road, but in the harsher light of the Med heavy make-up looks garish. Maybe the sun can get to your face now with all that gunge gone and give you a bit of colour. You'll look miles healthier."

Henrietta pushed past Laura impatiently. "Let me see in the mirror."

The girls raced into Laura's bedroom and stood in front of her wardrobe mirror.

"Aaargh!" screeched Hen, "It's amazing!" She turned eyes as wide as saucers on to Laura.

Laura was worried. "What? Don't you like yourself like that?"

"No. I mean, yes." Henrietta stammered. "You're a genius. I feel like a whole new person." She continued to stare at her reflection in disbelief.

Laura was pleased with her efforts. It was good therapy for her to see Henrietta happy, and she was glad that the ice had melted between them. "Do me another favour, will you? No false lashes during the day. And for heaven's sake grow out your eyebrows. Those plucked jobs are awful."

Henrietta grinned foolishly. "Bloody well hurts doing them too. Suppose it seemed the trendy thing to do. You put on the same face just to conform and then get stuck in the habit. Well, it's obviously *passé* now, and time for a change."

The girls smiled at each other. "By the way," Laura said kindly, "Jennifer's doing really well, and she'll be home soon."

Henrietta sighed with relief. "Thank heaven for that! Friends then?"

"Of course," Laura smiled. "Now, I must get on with my studies!"

The Caravelle jet shuddered noisily in mid-air as the pilot applied the air-brakes. The plane seemed to hover motionless over the shimmering peaks of the Alpes Maritimes during its descent to Nice. Within minutes, the sea was below them. Jennifer flinched as the aircraft banked steeply to turn in a wide arc back towards the airport, and the deep blue Mediterranean appeared to rush up to meet her from the ocean bed. It was like a switchback ride. Her ears went dead and she lost her sense of orientation. Jennifer closed her eyes and clenched her fists on the seat rest. She never liked landings.

Then at last the plane straightened up, and almost immediately there was the comforting sight of the runway underneath and the welcome 'thump, thump, thump' of the wheels making contact with the ground. Jennifer made a mental sign of the cross and said a silent prayer of thanks. She followed the other passengers down the metal steps, breathed in the familiar smell of distant mimosas, and crossed the tarmac for the short distance to the low white terminal building.

She had no luggage, so headed straight on through Customs, where the officers idly lounging at the barrier seemed more interested in her legs than her passport. Through the lines of people thronging and jostling at Arrivals, she could distinguish Krep's chauffeur in his dark blue uniform and peaked cap. He took her small bag and ushered her to a red Mercedes parked just outside.

What luxury not to have to queue for the airport shuttle bus, or to jostle for a taxi like the rest of the crowd. There were many advantages to being rich. It was a relief that for the moment she could enjoy the benefits without having to pay. If Julius had been at Nice to meet her, how long would it have been till he exacted the ultimate price from her? The thought of sex with Julius still made her shudder. She conjured up images of whales, walruses and shiny sea-lions, wallowing in blubber, and squirmed inwardly. Was gratitude a strong enough reason for overcoming her revulsion?

How glad she was to see the familiar palm-lined Promenade des Anglais, always chock full of fast-moving traffic; the big hotels on the left and the glittering sea to the right and the endless yellow beaches packed with sunbathers. The chauffeur continued on to Monaco via the tortuous and spectacular Moyenne Corniche which had been carved straight into towering rock. Everything about the Riviera was so bright, so over-the-top and so unreal that even after knowing it for a lifetime, she was still moved by its breathtaking splendour!

She was really pleased to be back! Had she really only been away a week? She'd hovered on the dark edge of death so recently, and now here she was, catapulted back to the brilliance of a golden Riviera afternoon, as if nothing had ever happened.

When she arrived at the Meribel, Jennifer was surprised to be met at the door by a slim, dark mannequin with a chic hairstyle. She laughed when she realised it was Henrietta.

"Wow, Hen," she commented, starstruck, "I didn't

recognise you. You look terrific with that hair! God, you look so different!"

Henrietta smiled, grateful that Jennifer bore her no grudge. She'd been ready with profuse apologies for causing such havoc, but here was Jennifer, smiling radiantly, as if nothing had happened.

Glad to be sidetracked, Hen looked coquettish, turning a circle to allow Jennifer a full view. "Laura did it. Glad you like it. Quite a change of image, isn't it?"

"For the better, I must say. I can't get over how glamorous you are now. Where's Laura?"

"At work still."

"Of course. What a clot I am." Jennifer suddenly felt herself wilting. After several days in bed, the journey had knocked her for six. "God, Hen!" she moaned, "I'm absolutely parched."

"Let's go into the kitchen then," Henrietta said, quickly taking Jennifer's arm and ushering her in. "I'll make you some tea. How thoughtless of me not to realise you must be whacked."

"Mmm, s'pose I am really." Jennifer flopped on to a chair. "Hey, thanks by the way for . . . you know. I do hope Laura didn't give you too much of a rocket."

Henrietta made a wry face. "'Fraid she did, but she's calmed down now and everything's OK. You didn't half give me a scare, though. I didn't know what to do when it all went wrong." She put the kettle on and leaned back against the worktop, her face serious. "I'm sorry, I just freaked, but I wouldn't just have left you. I was actually on my way to get Quint to get you to hospital, but then Laura arrived and I went off in a flat spin. I knew she'd be more help than me, and I was afraid she'd be furious, too. So I hid nearby, and I saw Julius and the nurse and everything and guessed you'd be OK. I was still worried, though. Thank heaven it all turned out all right in the end."

It did all turn out all right, except for the fact that Jennifer was now indebted to Julius Krep. Out of the frying pan, into the fire. Just what she'd dreaded when she first mooted that possibility at the Café de Paris. "Oh, yes. I'm fine now really," she answered vaguely. She must change the subject quickly. "How is he by the way?"

"How's who?" Henrietta asked, puzzled.

"Quint, of course, you idiot!"

"Oh, him." Henrietta smiled fondly. "As lecherous and attractive as ever. He can't leave me alone now with my elegant and classy new image."

"Really?" Jennifer felt a small pang of jealousy despite the fact she had turned him down a million times herself. "And are you screwing him?"

Henrietta giggled and turned her back, spooning tea into the pot. "That's for me to know and others to wonder. Have some home-made carrot cake."

Jennifer laughed. "Spoil-sport. At least you could tell me if he's a good fuck."

"Don't be vulgar, dear!" Hen grinned, filling the pot, "Ask no questions, tell no lies!"

Oh God! That was one of Julius' favourite expressions. There was no getting away from him. Jennifer sighed. "That's what Julius always says, too. Well, how's the club, then? At least you can answer that without being fey!"

"Oh, everything's going fine, though needless to say your presence is sorely missed. Especially by Quintin." Hen's eyes narrowed slightly, though her mouth was smiling.

"Glad to hear he appreciates me. I haven't half missed the club. It's not like work, really. More a way of life. It'll be so good to get down there again."

"Changing the subject, Laura's going to try to get off early tonight, so we can eat soon and you won't turn in too late. We have strict instructions from Mr Krep to look after you and see you get your sleep!" Henrietta handed Jennifer a welcome mug of tea.

"Wonderful! Thanks, just what I need."

Jennifer had already had visions of sloping off down to the Café de Paris later, and then maybe looking in on Quintin at the disco. But it rather looked as if Julius and her flatmates had queered her pitch there. Oh well, maybe it was an over-optimistic thought.

Laura got in at just after six, and gave Jennifer an enormous hug of welcome as she sprang to her feet in delight. They couldn't get much sense out of each other for quite a while, because they were both talking and screaming at the same time. Eventually Henrietta announced the food was ready. Laura quickly shrugged off her office clothes in favour of slacks and tee-shirt, and they all sat down at the kitchen table to enjoy seafood *vol-au-vents* and mixed salad, accompanied by a bottle of ice-cold Kritter Brut de Brut. The girls had so much to catch up on and the conversation was punctuated by much laughter and the odd shriek here and there.

Soon it was nine o'clock, and Henrietta had to go off to work. The other two drifted on to the balcony with mugs of coffee, their elbows on the railings, looking down at the gardens below, where giant cacti and palms threw their mysterious shadows on to the grass.

"Well, what now?" asked Laura.

"What do you mean?" Jennifer replied, her eyes narrowing slightly. She tried not to look defensive.

"I mean, have you made any plans for the future, long-term?"

Absolutely not. She had at least a week of freedom. Time for herself. No constraints and no obligations. She felt she deserved it and was going to make the most of it. She hoped Laura wouldn't start pontificating about Julius' return. The day of reckoning.

Jennifer made her voice deliberately non-committal. "Oh Lord, Laura, you know me. I can't bear to think of the future. I'll take each day as it comes, and carry on as normal."

Laura sipped her coffee pensively. Jennifer knew Laura well enough to be able to read her thoughts, but she didn't want to hear them. She turned away, desperate for any distraction. She looked across at Block C. Good grief! There he was, the voyeur on the hammock, binoculars to the fore.

"Bugger off!" she cried, lifting up her hair and posing provocatively.

Laura turned to her in amazement. "What *are* you doing?" she giggled.

"That twerp Bin Rat is spying on us again. Thought I'd give him something worth looking at!" Jennifer blew him a loud raspberry.

The girls both giggled again, and flopped down on to the chaises-longues, deciding to ignore their resident watcher. Ratti seemed only a minor inconvenience to them now, compared with the traumas of the past. Jennifer had reached rock-bottom. Surely nothing could ever be as bad again?

When Laura set off on the croissant run before breakfast on Sunday, she could see that a large humid cloud had again settled on the peaks of the surrounding mountains. It was like a great thick eiderdown, rendering the air stuffy and hazy with a strange beigey-yellow light. Although it was warm and pleasant outside, there seemed little point in heading for the beaches. Anyway, she'd promised herself she would study the entire weekend. Lesson twelve was a real chore – 'The Customer Statement'! However, it would propel her one good step nearer to her ultimate goal.

She stepped into the dark interior of the Patisserie, the shelves lined with delicious *tartes aux fraises*, gateaux and éclairs. Her mouth watered as the delicious smell of warm croissants and freshly baked French loaves wafted over her. How she loved everything about the Midi!

It jolted her to think that she would probably have to leave all this behind soon. Geneva, Montreux, Munich, or perhaps

Paris were much better bets in the business world than this tiny principality. Even so, it would be tough going for a female. Stockbroking was still a man's domain!

It was slightly better in the States, of course, but then they tended to be more innovative there. They had to be, in a multi-cultural environment, without diehard traditions and centuries of history. But she didn't fancy the States long-term; she wanted to be closer to home.

"*Oui, mademoiselle?*"

Laura started as the small dark-haired *patronne* interrupted her thoughts, the little blackcurrant eyes twinkling beadily and expectantly at her customer.

She left the shop with a sturdy brown-paper bag containing three warm croissants and two baguettes wrapped round the middle with white tissue paper. She walked back to the flat carrying the loaves French-style, tucked under her arm.

Surprisingly Jennifer was already up and about, but then she'd been accustomed to waking early in hospital.

"It won't be long before I'm back to being a sluggard," she said, "when those late nights hit me again. Well? What shall we do today?"

"I'm going to work through another lesson. But we could go down to the Café de P for lunch. What say?"

"Right. And just for once," Jennifer announced grandly, "I'm paying. Julius gave me some *convalescence money!*"

Laura laughed. "You mean money for night-clubbing and champagne! Honestly, you're incorrigible, but I suppose Krep knows that already."

"Yes, but that's why he likes me so much!" Jennifer grinned mischievously.

Sunday passed quietly, with Laura immersed in her studies, Henrietta out with friends, and Jennifer actually reading a book on the balcony. It was the first time Laura had ever seen her quiet and absorbed, but it would doubtless be a very temporary phenomenon!

229

Chapter 17

As July rolled into August, Laura realised that her birthday was coming up. Not just any birthday, but her twenty-first. A landmark. Her age of majority. When she brought up the subject of a party, Jennifer pointed out the advantages of holding it at the club. She was sure Quintin would let Laura have a section of Le Disco, provided it did not interfere with the normal running of the club.

"Just think," Jennifer said, bubbling over with excitement, "you've got music and dancing laid on, waiter service at your disposal, and Quintin will be bound to let you have booze at a discount. What fun we'll have! And it means you'll have no preparation or clearing up. All you'll have to do is send out the invitations!"

It seemed a good idea as Laura had so much on her plate already, and in any case, how else would she get Jennifer, Hen and Quintin to join in the celebrations? She had no choice, really, other than to bring her party to them!

Jennifer tackled Quintin about it. He was more than pleased to accommodate Laura, provided she limit her numbers to no more than twenty.

Once Laura had her birthday party sorted out, she set her sights on Fitz. How was she to break the news that she wanted to go to New York and sit the Stock Exchange and NASD exams in order to start a new career? It was a real poser. First things first, though – the birthday invitations.

When it came to those, Laura was in a quandary. She wanted to invite Fitz and his wife, but somehow couldn't see them enjoying the noisy atmosphere of Le Disco. The problem was solved when upon mentioning her birthday, Fitz suggested taking hèr out to dinner with his wife and a few friends of her choice early on in the evening.

When Laura mentioned the disco party which was due to start at 10 p.m., he laughed, saying, "Oh, discos are not for geriatrics like me. Ten o'clock is my time for a bedtime read in any case. But the dinner invitation still stands. Shall we make it seven thirty for eight at Harry's Bar? That's always a fun place for you young things. Tell me how many you'll be bringing, but don't make it the whole of Monte-Carlo, please!"

"Oh, Fitz, what a fabulous idea," she replied, "but it'll just be me for dinner. Jennifer and Henrietta won't be able to make it, though I'm sure they'd love to come for drinks first."

Laura started making a list, but soon realised it would be difficult to pare it down to twenty. Terry was an obvious invitee and naturally wanted to bring a whole gaggle of amusing people! "My house guests," he'd said. Asking him already put her numbers up by six, and it would have been ten but for putting her foot down! Henrietta had three friends she wanted to invite, too. None of her friends seemed to come in single numbers – they all had a retinue with them! And so it went on.

The week ahead was as usual frantically busy. Laura managed to squeeze in a couple more papers by studying through her lunch-hours as well as the evenings, which meant her social life was non-existent.

"Gawd, I don't know how you can stand it. No booze, no men, no fun!" screeched Jennifer. "All work and no play makes Jack a dull boy."

"Who's Jack when he's at home?" she retorted teasingly, her eyes sparkling with mischief. "Anyway, my theory is all work and no play will make Laura a rich and successful girl, and then I'll have time for fun!"

Jennifer made a sour face. "Huh! You'll have forgotten how. You'll be all dried up, with a pussy like a prune!"

"Well, at least prunes have a nice taste."

"Yeah – for those with constipation!"

"Up yours!" grinned Laura, and stuck her nose back into her books.

Laura was surprised that she had no card from Fitz on the big day. When she tackled him about it, he just winked at her before closeting himself behind the *Wall Street Journal*. Wilder had sent her a dozen beautiful red roses with a note, saying, "Congratulations. Today marks the start of a whole new beginning." It seemed a very dramatic way to mark her twenty-first. How very thoughtful of John Wilder to remember, and how odd for Fitz not to! Very out of character. Laura noticed he seemed very pleased with himself, whistling, drumming his fingers, eyes twinkling at her throughout the day.

At four o'clock Fitz told her to go home early. When she protested that there was too much to do, he laughed and said, "Go on! It's not often I treat you to dinner. Go and get your hair done, or go to the beauty parlour, or whatever you women like to do. You've a really special evening ahead of you!" Then he pushed a couple of hundred francs into her hand and winked.

Two hundred francs would pay for several salon visits! Laura thought she'd better do as she'd been told and have her hair done at one of the smartest salons in the boulevard des Moulins. A rare treat!

The young Italian owner grabbed her the minute she came in. He was as thin as a whippet, had a big nose and a wide, expressive mouth. His eyes were typically Italian. Big, brown and melancholy with a hint of lechery underneath. He smiled at her disarmingly and muttered a few words in Italian, fussing round her, making her feel very welcome.

Laura smiled. The hairdresser probably didn't realise she understood enough Italian to know that he'd just said, "Fresh flesh is best!" No wonder, she thought as she gazed around her and saw the place was packed with spoiled, elderly matrons, their boiling prune faces sagging under the heat of the dryers.

He sat her down, playing with her long, silky locks. "*Ah, bella, bella!*" he cried. Then he paused, deep in thought, before saying. "Signorina, very pretty hair. But too long!" He waved his hands around dramatically. "I can do nothing with such long hair. Except put it on top, maybe?"

They both looked at her reflection as he wound the blonde hank into a long coil and held it on top of her head. He turned her face from side to side, looked unhappy and pouted with indecision.

"No!" Laura decided. It looked too secretarial. A chignon was fine for the office, but not for her big party.

"What do you suggest?" she asked him.

"I cut," he said brutally, stabbing his fingers into the air like scissors.

"Short?" she asked, her eyes round with horror.

"*Ah, non!*" He blanched at the appalling thought. "That would be a crime! I cut six inches only. Then I set it in big, beautiful waves to frame that pretty face." He kissed the air. "*Molto bella!* Yes?"

"OK," she said, trusting his judgment. Her hair had been getting her down lately. It was so long, and so very heavy, and rather limiting stylewise. Time for a change!

She got home early enough to enjoy a long, relaxing soak, carefully looping her newly set hair out of the way. Jennifer and Henrietta had saved their centimes and splashed out on a present of Femme de Rochas which must have cost them a fortune. After her bath she applied her new scent liberally. It was gorgeous – very heady and soignée, and as feminine as the name.

She wore a new dress bought especially for the evening, one of those numbers that clung where it fitted, in lilac silk jersey, halter neck, and almost backless, except where it fastened around the neck with tiny plaited straps. It was not possible to wear anything underneath, because a bra would show, and a panty line would look hideous!

Actually, Laura was a little chary about wearing such a revealing number in front of Fitz and his wife. She hoped to hell there'd be no cooling breezes to make her nipples stand out. She stepped into high-heeled gold sandals, clipped on her amethyst earrings, tossed her wavy, flaxen mane down her back, and studied herself in the mirror. The pale mauve colour contrasted well with her hair, and the slinky dress emphasised her tiny waist, at the same time drawing attention to the firm, high, neatly rounded breasts.

"Behave yourselves, titties!" she implored, and flinging a purple feather boa over her shoulders, she went to join her flatmates.

"Wow!" they chorused enviously. "Get you, glamour-puss!"

"Actually," remarked Hen, "it's amazing how much more alike you and Jennifer look now. Your hair's the same style and nearly the same colour, now Jennifer's is all sun-bleached from her permanent lazing on the beach!"

Jennifer and Henrietta were nearly ready to accompany her to Harry's Bar for pre-dinner drinks, as arranged with Fitz. Henrietta looked very elegant in black evening trousers and a braided jacket. Laura persuaded Jennifer not to wear her white crocheted number which revealed everything in spectacular three-dimensional technicolour underneath, not to say acres of thigh because the skirt was only five inches long. Instead she put on a glittering gold caftan, practically slit down to the waist, and up to it, too. This allowed any onlooker flashes of long, lean, tanned leg, nearly up to her crotch when she took a step.

"I'm *not* changing again!" she grumbled defiantly when Laura raised an eyebrow.

"I'm not asking you to. I think poor old Fitz will be totally overwhelmed, though."

235

"Anyone would think he was a monk, the way you go on. Anyway, look at you. You're bra-less. What's he going to say to that?" Jennifer retorted, grinning.

Henrietta raced to Laura's defence. "If I had tits like hers, I'd show them off, too."

"Come on, Birthday Girl. Let's be having you!" smiled Jennifer good-naturedly and ushered them out of the flat.

The three girls arrived punctually at Harry's Bar. The landlord was Sergio Mantoni, a very handsome and vain Italian renowned for his libido and never-ending streams of women willing to test his prowess, and then regretting their folly when he immediately discarded them for another. There was a pianist playing soft, romantic music in the background, candles on the table and subdued lighting, which together with the comfortable and relaxing seats, lent a seductive and intimate aura to the place. No points for guessing where Sergio brought his women to 'soften them up' prior to bedding them!

Sergio eyed the three girls openly, showing his approval through dark, languid, heavy-lidded eyes.

"*Alore, belle signorine!* What can I do for you?" he asked, rolling his 'r's' in an exaggerated fashion.

Laura smiled politely. "Mr Fitzgerald is expecting us."

"Come," Sergio murmured, eyeing Laura's breasts and then giving her face a deep, lingering look. "Follow me."

The girls smiled at each other with complicity. Sergio was so transparent, so over the top. God, but some women were mugs to fall for his line. He had been known to get through three women a day, and still they rolled up in their droves to be treated like chattels.

Fitz and his wife gave them a friendly welcome and he rose, patting the seat beside him for 'the birthday girl'. He ordered champagne cocktails for them. Fitz was on good form, and his wife, slim, petite and dark-haired, was elegant in black Balenciaga. Her dark eyes took in Laura's mauve dress that

236

fitted like a second skin, but the obvious charms of her husband's secretary and her glamorous friends did not appear to faze her. She charmed everyone with her strong French accent.

Mrs Fitz reminded Laura of a little shimmering blackbird – dainty and sweet – and covered in diamonds. It was difficult not to boggle at the size of the stones whilst making conversation, because their lustre, when catching the light, was of an almost blinding brilliance. She, however, seemed quite unperturbed by their dazzle. Fitz's eyes softened whenever he looked at his wife, which was often, so it was plain to see that they were very close. As they had no children, he doted on her in an almost paternal way, obviously buying her diamonds and couture clothes in the same way an indulgent parent might buy his adored child toys. It was comforting to witness such uxoriousness, and to know that happy relationships did exist. It gave Laura hope. She'd been so disillusioned lately.

Soon it was time for Jennifer and Henrietta to move on, and, as they said their goodbyes, Sergio raced over with the menus. The remaining three chose quickly, as time was short, and so, fortunately was the menu. Laura went for the Parmigiana ham and melon, followed by *lasagne verde*, and Fitz and his wife ordered smoked salmon and then *osso buco*.

"Now, Laura," announced Fitz importantly, "this is for you!"

And he threw a large pink envelope on the table, and pushed it towards her. She opened it, smiling. Inside was a large birthday card which contained another envelope. Hesitantly, she opened it. A return ticket to New York!

"What's this?" she asked, absolutely stunned.

"A plane ticket, young lady, what d'you think it is?"

"Yes, I know. But what for?" she asked, wide-eyed.

"It's your birthday present from me." Fitz smiled mysteriously, and winked at his wife who fluttered her hands excitedly and twinkled at Laura.

"But how absolutely wonderful!" Laura's eyes shone. "Tell me . . . I don't . . ."

Fitz held up his hand and said, "OK, Laura, my dear, let me explain!" He cleared his throat importantly and continued, "Well, now. Many things are afoot, and I've had long conversations with John Wilder, who intimated that you were interested in sitting the Stock Exchange exam."

Laura, blushing furiously at being found out, stammered, "Oh dear, I'm sorry, I hope you don't think me disloyal. I just thought . . ."

But Fitz waved his hand dismissively. "Don't even think about it dear," he continued. "As I said, I've had several discussions with John about your future, and, incidentally, mine. This all ties in very nicely. Now I want you to listen carefully."

Laura leaned forward in anticipation, her heart hammering with suspense, but the waiter appeared with their *hors d'oeuvres*, and there was an impatient pause in the conversation while he served them.

"Pepper, signorina?" Laura waved her assent rather brusquely, and the waiter brandished a huge polished wood pepper-grinder over her plate; very phallic, deliberately taking ages over it.

"Everyone OK?" asked Fitz, sweeping his eyes over his two female companions, and carried on. He was now in full flood. Laura was riveted.

"To get back to what I was saying. All of this ties in very nicely, because I was getting into a cleft-stick situation myself, a kind of impasse. I have been thinking for quite a while that all this travelling was getting too much for me. The funds are doing very well at present, thanks to you and your sterling help and, of course, the stock-market. But now I feel the time is ripe for me to bow out."

There was a pause while Fitzgerald tasted a forkful of salmon, and Laura was dying to know what was coming next.

She waited with bated breath and a pounding heart. Fitz's wife smiled at Laura, absent-mindedly twirling a spectacular marquise-cut diamond ring – probably all of two carats – round a dainty finger.

"Now, the problem was who to hand over the reins to. Managing such a vast portfolio is a huge responsibility. I don't mean this patronisingly," he said, pausing to smile at her kindly, "but you, Laura, are too young for the job. Anyway, the Greeks would never wear that, as they're born chauvinists. What we need is a suitable man with a lot of experience behind him. I've known John Wilder for many years, and he has a first-hand knowledge of the portfolios, having been my main broker. He feels ready to move on in his career, and would like to go into Fund Management. Now this is the plan. I intend to ask John formally to join me at Kulikis, and work with him for six months until he feels happy to take over and run the portfolios by himself."

OK, fine, thought Laura, as Fitz paused again to chew on his food, so that sorts out Fitz and Wilder. Where do I fit into all this? She glanced at his wife to test the barometer, but her eyes were on her husband. Laura wrapped a paper-thin slice of ham round a small wedge of melon, but then put her fork down. She was rapidly losing her appetite.

Fitz finished his mouthful and continued, "In view of the fact that you and I made such a perfect team, I don't think it's fair to expect you to play second fiddle to my replacement. Especially as we've hitherto been a client of John's. Anyway, I don't want to hold you back, you're destined for better things. Mary should be capable of filling your slot, though you'll be a hard act to follow."

Laura was growing somewhat alarmed now. Oh dear, yes, OK! she wondered to herself, What next then? Am I getting the proverbial boot for daring to be so ambitious? She tried to stay calm and took a mouthful of the salty ham and tangy melon, while Fitz took ages over his salmon. This was sheer torment.

"So, obviously," Fitz went on, "John's departure will have left a gap at Howson."

"Yes . . . ?" broke in Laura, beside herself. Her heart was in her mouth, but she pulled out all the stops to remain outwardly composed.

Fitz chuckled, his eyes sparkling with mischief, "Well," he said slowly, knowing full well Laura was nearly falling out of her chair with suspense, "we have, of course, strongly recommended *you* for the vacant slot!"

Laura was speechless.

"That's what your ticket's for," he said, thoroughly amused at her stupefied expression. Her mouth was practically on her collar-bone. "To go to New York and take the big qualification exams! So you can be our stockbroker at Howson. Well? What do you think, eh?"

Fitz sat back, toying with his remaining smoked salmon, amused at Laura's utter incredulity.

Laura put down her fork and stared at her employer. "I'm speechless. I don't know what to say!" She wanted to pinch herself to make sure she wasn't dreaming.

"Well? Are you pleased? Do you like your birthday present or not?" Fitz smiled.

"I absolutely *love* it!" she almost shrieked, "But it's all so sudden. What's the time scale on this?"

"I was thinking in about a week and a half would be a good time, as that's when Howson run their next crammer for the exam in early September."

Laura's heart nearly stopped. New York in less than a fortnight? She'd be sitting the major exams in less than a month! Could she manage them in such a short time? Was this really happening?

Her eyes glowed. "September! So soon? Heavens!" Then she suddenly looked doubtful. Her eyes swept over the

Fitzgeralds uncertainly. "What if I don't make the grade?"

"Laura," Fitz laughed, glancing at his wife, whose black eyes danced as she nodded at Laura encouragingly. "Don't be silly. With the kind of results you're getting at the New York Institute, you'll walk it. Have you nearly finished that course now?"

"Well, two-thirds."

"No problem there. You can plough on with the course and finish it after the NYSE and NASD exams. It'll certainly help you handle the crammer. You'll probably show all the other blighters up. Now, my dear, what's the verdict?"

"I'm absolutely stunned, thrilled." Laura's eyes shone brightly, and her face was flushed with excitement. All her dreams were coming true, and far from letting Fitz down, she'd actually been doing him a favour with her ambition! "Thank you, thank you so much," she said, taking his hands in hers. Then she remembered his wife, and gave her dazzling smile to encompass them both in her gratitude. "I think I never had a nicer birthday. I'm just so bowled over I can't think. New York in less than two weeks!"

Laura's face was a picture, and Fitz's good heart melted at his protégée's joy. He would miss her presence in the office, of course, but at least they would be in touch by telephone every day. She would be his new stockbroker, for six months anyway!

He lifted his glass. "Let's drink to your future!"

Fitz, his wife and Laura clinked glasses.

"Laura, my dear," purred Mrs Fitz, "to you I am eternally grateful. Thanks to you I can at last enjoy some time with my 'usband before he gets too old and crotchety for me."

Laura and Fitz laughed, and beamed at each other delightedly.

The rest of the meal whizzed by in a blur of excitement. Laura didn't think she would ever hoist it all in, it was so unbelievable; too good to be true! This was one evening she could see herself going over the top. Sensing she was getting quite merry already, she thought why the hell not? This is going to be an evening to remember. Just like Wilder had said, "Today marks the start of a whole new beginning."

Chapter 18

As soon as Laura walked into Le Disco, beaming broadly, Hen, on duty at the turntable, played 'Happy Birthday', and all her friends joined in, clustered on the dance floor under the coloured lights.

Quintin grabbed her round the waist and rubbed against her sensuously, murmuring, "There's a birthday present I'd *really* love to give you that we'd both enjoy, but you'll just have to make do with this!" and he flourished a magnum of champagne, decorated with a silver bow.

Laura reached out for it, but Quintin stopped her, drawing the magnum back against his chest teasingly. "Wait," he said, "it's far too heavy for a fragile flower like you to hold." He gave a mock resigned sigh. "Damn. I suppose you'll just have to drink it." He placed it in an ice-bucket on a stand and proceeded to open it.

Laura followed him. "Thank you, Quintin. You are sweet, and thanks for letting us celebrate here."

He smiled, showing off his perfect teeth. "Not at all. I'm the one who should be thanking you for bringing all these lovely people!"

Terry had brought Tab again, looking every inch the film star, just like a blond god. He had the most beautiful woman with him, too, who was trailing a streaky-haired, sullen young man with a pout. Terry rushed forward, wearing a lemon-yellow satin smoking-jacket with silver frogs. He pressed a parcel into Laura's hand.

"Happy birthday, my darling," he breathed. "You remember Tab, of course, and this is Veronique van Doren. She's in films, or *was* anyway, but you'd be far too young to remember those!" he added darting a slightly malicious glance at Veronique.

"Thanks a rock, Terry," the film star drawled in a very husky voice. "Some friend you are!"

Her hair was platinum blonde, and her eyes emerald green to match her dress. From the star's myopic gaze, it was obvious they must be coloured contact lenses. Her dress plunged to the waist at the front, revealing a cleavage as firmly sculpted as the Rock of Gibraltar, and by the looks of her partly revealed melon-sized breasts, as hard, too. The back of her dress plunged to the cleavage of her buttocks, and Laura wondered what feat of engineering was holding the weighty mammaries in place so immovably.

"All silicon, darling!" whispered Terry, in the guise of kissing her ear. Laura laughed, and looked away quickly, realising that her habitual quizzical gaze had betrayed her thoughts.

"Oh, and Laura, this is Carlo," Veronique purred, lifting the sulky young man's hand. "I'm making a film in Rome with him. He's my lover."

Laura wondered if this were in real life, or his role in the film. Probably both. Carlo didn't look a day over eighteen. His artificially streaked hair was worn very long, waving almost to his shoulders. He had smouldering eyes, a short Roman nose and a large sulky mouth, and sported a gold ring in his left ear.

Terry's other guests were dancing. Quintin lost no time in ushering everyone to the long table reserved for Laura's party, where they laid into the champagne.

Laura was getting very light-headed. "I think I'm slightly sozzled," she told an amused Jennifer.

"What the hell," she shrugged, "if you can't get pissed on your birthday, when can you?"

"Come on, Birthday Girl, dance with me!" So saying, Quintin whisked her to the floor, holding her close to his sinewy body. "You are looking exceptionally screwable tonight. That dress is delicious. No underwear again I can feel." His hands roamed over her bare back. He groaned, "I can't stand it, I ache all over for you."

Laura laughed. Quintin could say the most outrageous things with impunity. He had such charm it was impossible to take offence, though he habitually overstepped the mark. She looked up into his bright eyes. "Do you ever give up Quint?"

"Not till I'm one hundred and two and all seized up," he replied. "But seriously, can you think of a nicer way to celebrate your birthday than in bed with me?"

Laura giggled. His lack of modesty was endearing. "Are you really that good, then? You're for ever blowing your own trumpet!"

"Only because you won't do it for me." He pretended to sulk. "Anyway I'm not supple enough to blow my own."

Laura shrieked with laughter. She'd walked into that one! "You're dreadful. You take everything the wrong way!"

Quintin's eyes danced mischievously. "No," he argued, "The right way! Depends how you're looking at it, sweetheart!" His gaze lingered over her mouth.

Then, suddenly he was all over her like a split pack of peas; cupping her face in his hands, giving her a long, expert kiss, his tongue languidly exploring the inside of her mouth. Quintin tasted of champagne. Kissing him was like drinking warm, fizzy wine. Laura was rather tipsy and relaxed enough to enjoy the sensation. He was a far better kisser than Pierre, who had the habit of sucking her tongue so hard that it was painful. Besides, Quintin was devastatingly handsome, and such fun. Laura could feel her saintly intentions melting away. Was celibacy an essential ingredient for a high examination pass mark? God, Laura, what *are* you thinking of! She giggled inwardly, praying silently, "Oh Lord, lead me not into temptation!" Why did Quintin have to be so gorgeous? No wonder he had strings of women falling in love with him.

Jennifer nudged Henrietta with a roguish gleam in her eye. "Hey, do you see what I see? Laura's snogging with Quintin." She studied Hen carefully for her reaction. Maybe this was a good way to find out if she and Quintin were having a fling.

"The bastard," declared Henrietta darkly, and changed the music to a loud, strident beat. She grinned maliciously as the dancing livened up, and Quintin was jostled and distracted from his attempted seduction of Laura by revellers pushing their way on to the floor. It seemed to Jennifer that Hen had expressly chosen a long number, so she could leave the turntable for a while. Then she could entertain her friends while keeping an eye on her wayward lover. Now Jennifer was convinced that the secretive Henrietta was having a discreet affair with everyone's favourite rake.

Hen had introduced her old friends to Jennifer earlier. One of them, Antonia Sampling, was an up-and-coming English actress on TV in a long-running American adventure series. The other was a peer's son and heir, who looked vaguely familiar and owned a park in Sussex or thereabouts, and his current girlfriend, a rather sluttish looking *soi-disant*, model with large breasts and unruly bleached hair with black roots.

They seemed quite fun, especially the actress, Antonia, who was far too attractive for Jennifer's liking. She had a mane of tawny, leonine hair, the wickedest, most seductive, feline eyes set in a beautiful pointed face, and a gloriously lithe body, encased in a white crochet mini-dress that left nothing to the imagination.

"Sick-making!" Jennifer muttered mutinously to Laura, as she stood on the edge of the dance floor. "And you wouldn't let me wear mine!"

"She's probably saying the same about you in that sexy gold number!"

"Speak for yourself, dear heart!"

"I'll second that, for both of you," Quintin added before dashing off to greet new arrivals.

The girls laughed, thanking him for his compliment, though both already knew that they could handle the competition with equanimity. After all, Monte-Carlo was that sort of place. It wasn't for the second-rate and mundane. In a place like this, everyone had to have something to offer. If it wasn't money, or fame, or notoriety, then it had to be looks and personality. Competition just made life more of a challenge, that's all.

"Good party, hey?" said Jennifer.

Laura nodded enthusiastically.

"What were you up to with Quintin?" she teased. "You should have seen Hen's face. She was absolutely livid!"

Laura laughed cagily. "It's all right to window-shop, as long as you don't bring your cheque-book."

Jennifer narrowed her eyes accusingly, chuckling, "Come on, Laura, who are you kidding? Not only did you have your cheque at the ready, but from the looks of you, you'd already signed it!"

Laura gave Jennifer a playful push, giggling bashfully. Then she turned away to hide her blushes. "Oh lor'," she pretended to complain, "here he comes again, with that look on his face."

"Spoil-sport!" whispered Jennifer, as Quintin manoeuvred his way towards them. "He will be disappointed." Jennifer sighed and turned serious. "Talking about window-shopping, I wonder how old Juli-boy's getting on! He'll be back soon."

The thought displeased her. She was becoming restless. Jennifer was quite recovered now, and beginning to regain her high spirits. She had a mischievous look on her face. Idly she wondered whether to nab the earl-in-waiting from under the model's nose, just for the night, to test the water again. He really did look very familiar. Then she remembered where she'd seen him before. At a friend's 'Coming Out' in the early sixties. He was a well-known deb's delight, Alexander someone-or-other with a double barrel. He had been considered a catch by every aspiring and ambitious mother for her emerging daughters. But Jennifer had been very young then. Alexander Double-Barrel had definitely improved with age!

While she was planning her *modus operandi*, Terry distracted her, suddenly grabbing her round the waist from behind.

"Come and dance with me, golden wonder!" he cried, and pulled her on to the dance floor.

"Are you feeling better?" Terry asked. The soft brown eyes were kindly and concerned in his round, friendly face. "I hear you were poorly and had to go to London."

"Yes. Absolutely, completely better," she laughed, her grey eyes sparkling with merriment, "And raring to go. Come on, let's jive!"

Jennifer picked up Laura's discarded feather boa, and draped it round Terry's neck. The fluffy purple was in sharp contrast to his lemon-yellow suit. He beamed with approval, and tossed it over one shoulder artfully.

"Wonderful! Wonderful, darling!" he drawled squeakily, puckering his lips and posing in an outrageously camp fashion to make Jennifer giggle. "Now, how about this bop?"

Terry was an amazing dancer. His heyday must have been the fifties when rock and roll hit the scene. Jennifer who'd been raised on the Twist, was not up to his professional standard, but nevertheless put on a good show. The music speeded up even more, and the dance floor was erupting into a riot of legs, arms and flying hair. The lights suddenly pulsed ultra-violet, and everyone's teeth and shirts glowed neon-purple. The effect was dreamlike and hypnotic, as if the whole scene had been projected on to a flickering three-dimensional screen.

Laura, out of breath on the other side of the dance floor, finally shook off Quintin good-naturedly. "I must have a drink. I'm dying of thirst."

There was no orange juice left on the table, so she swigged some more champagne. The film star's Italian boyfriend started talking to her in disjointed English. She couldn't really understand a word he was saying, nor wanted to, but made a semblance of listening while watching the dance floor. Carlo's large, pouting lips were practically brushing her ear, and she could feel his breath on her neck. She felt uncomfortable and wished he'd go away.

Veronique then appeared and bore down on them. When she grew closer Laura was alarmed to see that her face was contorted with fury. Hell! She'd obviously misunderstood the situation, and thought Laura was after the Italian. Laura quickly moved away a few paces, but the young man followed, as if he were firmly glued to her. Veronique picked up a Coke bottle and brandished it. Suddenly there was a loud crash and a splintering sound as the angry blonde smashed the bottle on to the edge of the table. Laura jumped to her feet as she realised the woman's intentions. The jagged shards of glass were just inches away from her face. God help me, she panicked, backing away from the fearsome apparition.

But Veronique advanced unsteadily, her eyes murderous, threatening Laura's face with the shattered bottle. "Hands off Carlo, you bitch!" she rasped.

"What?" gulped Laura in disbelief, holding her hands out in front of her defensively.

Veronique's face was twisted and sick. The bright green eyes glittered in the china-doll face. What Laura saw frightened her. The eyes were those of a desperate old woman, in an unreal, stretched mask of a face. It was a horrible, discordant sight.

"I said, leave him alone, you bitch, or I'll cut you up!" she rasped again.

The glittering points of glass came menacingly close. Laura averted her face and stepped back. This was ridiculous. She needed to defend herself, but didn't relish the prospect of an undignified female wresting match with a drunk.

Fortunately the Italian boyfriend came to the rescue, squeezing in between the two women. "Veronica!" he cried, remonstrating feebly, *"Basta, basta!"* He pouted and postured, waving his hands around to no effect. Veronique would not be deterred from her intention to wreak vengeance on Laura and tried to struggle past Carlo, her face mottled and purple with hatred, the glass eyes bulging.

Terry, cottoning on at last to what was happening, left Jennifer and raced over to sort things out. He gently took the Coke bottle out of Veronique's hand, speaking quietly and firmly to her. The drunken star's platinum wig had come adrift, shedding its anchoring pins and showing a dark hairline underneath. Her bright red lipstick was smudged in a blurred halo round her mouth – giving her the appearance of a clown. She looked pathetic. The glamorous image was destroyed. All that was left was a fake, tragic wreck, reeking of alcohol and trembling with insecurity.

Terry turned to Laura, mortified. "So sorry, Laura," he whispered. "She's totally out of her head. She doesn't mean it really. She just adores to dramatise."

Dramatise, thought Laura, that's putting it mildly. It seemed more like murder at the time! And what the hell was I supposed to have done, anyway? I was just being polite to the wretched gigolo.

Then Terry turned to the actress, who was now tearful and contrite, taking her firmly by the shoulder. "Veronique, you're a naughty girl," he reprimanded her. "Am I going to have to take you home, or are you going to behave? Go and have a nice dance with Carlo, there's a good girl."

The actress pouted and tossed her head like a sulky child, but complied, yanking Carlo on to the dance floor. There she made a great show of writhing voluptuously against him, his thin chest all but eclipsed by the voluminous, jutting breasts. Her wig was still askew, but clinging on by a wish and a prayer.

She stuck to him like custard on a plate; her hands firmly clenched to his boyish behind. "This boy is my property and no one else's," was the implicit message.

As if anybody cared, thought Laura. Silly woman!

Terry shrugged his shoulders, sighed and looked at Laura apologetically. "Goddamit!" Terry fluttered his hands, somewhat embarrassed. "I'm so sorry. Please don't let this spoil your party. She's a real airhead, very insecure. She's all wigs, false lenses and tits, and everything's so lifted she can't put her arms down. Then, when she sees a gorgeous young thing like you around Carlo she just flips, can't you see? You wouldn't believe she's nearly seventy, would you?"

"Oh, come on," scoffed Laura, "you re joking, Terry!"

"No, my darling, I'm not. Her looks are entirely due to monkey jabs, silicon and cat gut. Her films were thirty and forty years ago, believe it or not. She was quite a big star in those days. Now she ekes out a living singing in night-clubs, making skin flicks and trailing gigolos! Quite sad, really. I'm very fond of her, though. She's an old and very dear friend and I so enjoy her aura of glamour. She's a real trouper. They don't seem to make them like that any more."

Extraordinary. But that's exactly what had so jolted Laura: the eyes hadn't matched the mask face. Obviously they cannot lie. Laura had sensed years of wear and tear, decades of tired experience in those glassy, emerald eyes. For all Veronique's attempts to keep the years at bay, her eyes betrayed her – revealing all and giving the game away. The windows of the soul. It was sad, and Laura suddenly felt sorry for the drunken old broad.

"Oh well, then, let's not make an issue of it," Laura smiled sportingly, "if she's not seriously going to kill me! I'll keep well away from her gigolo. He's far too thick to be my type in any case! Hey," she added, glad to change the subject, "talking of glamour, what happened to your other friends? Weren't you due to be six?"

"Ah, they're over there, dancing." Terry gestured, his eyes twinkling again.

"But that's Yul Brynner, isn't it?" Laura exclaimed, picking out an exotically handsome man with no hair, entwined on the dance floor with an elegant, dark-haired woman.

"Yes, that's Yul and his wife. I'm entertaining them tonight for Sam Spiegel. They're staying on his boat, but he had a prior engagement, so I've brought them to your party."

"Golly, it's like a miniature film set here: anyone would think we were in Hollywood!"

"Oh, but, precious, Monte-Carlo's so much better in every way! Hollywood's so fake!" Terry replied.

Laura was really enjoying her party, in spite of the drama. She was in great demand on the dance floor, whilst all the time she was like a kettle simmering on the boil of her excitement at Fitz's proposals for her. She was on the threshold of realising everything she'd dreamed of for so long! It was all too incredible for words. Her dreams all made possible, in one fell swoop! Her excitement was palpable.

"I've never seen you sparkling like this before," Quintin said, bumping into her again. "Are you sure you wouldn't like to sleep with me tonight? I want to lick your every crevice . . ."

"And climb every mountain," she sang artlessly. "I'll think about it, handsome. But the night is young, this is my twenty-first, and I want to enjoy my party."

Suddenly there was a commotion on the dance floor. Jennifer was wheeling in the most gigantic cake with twenty-one candles on it. Holding it aloft was the model, sitting in the lotus position on a food trolley. She was stark naked except for a G-string, and covered from head to toe in fluorescent paint, whose psychedelic hues and patterns were picked out by the flickering strobe lights. The effect was surreal.

"Who's going to take this fucking cake off me? It's bloody heavy!" The low, slurred voice broke the spell.

"Good heavens! It speaks," exclaimed Quintin, grinning, as

he relieved the sulking Venus of the cake and put it on the table, to a loud round of applause and cheering.

Laura blew out the candles in one go. This brought more applause, and a drunken rendition of 'She's Twenty-one Today' and 'Happy Birthday'. Laughing at the dreadful racket, she cut the cake into pieces and distributed it amongst her friends.

The model stayed on the trolley, which was casually being pushed this way and that as everyone milled about the night-club. She seemed rather spaced out, and would probably have been incapable of standing anyway. The party-goers were unperturbed by the naked figure in their midst, as if she were a multi-coloured statue, and just part of the decor. In any case, the champagne had gone to everyone's heads and they were all way beyond caring about anything except having a good time.

"D'you ride?" asked the peer of Laura.

Before she could answer, Quintin had sighed, "No. But I wish she would!"

"Do shut up," Quintin," giggled Laura, and turning to Henrietta's friend added, "And he's wrong. I do ride. Horses, I mean. Fat chance of that here, though!"

She gathered his name was Alexander Fortescue-Tempest, he owned strings of polo ponies, and had a stately home. Alexander was in his late twenties, with light brown hair, hazel eyes and an open face, attractive in an understated sort of way. He was of medium height, and looked very fit – quite muscular and athletic-looking, probably from riding horses regularly.

Like so many young Englishmen, with the exception of Quintin, who never drew breath, he wasn't much good at small-talk, and the conversation didn't drift beyond horses, hunting and polo. Still, as Laura had spent all her childhood romping around country fields and stables with her four brothers and younger sister, this was not alien to her. In fact, it was refreshing to be reminded of a way of life now so far removed from her present one.

Even if he were an earl's son from exalted circles, she decided, she still had far more in common with Alexander than she'd ever had with Pierre! Yes, she reflected, relationships were funny things. Anyway, all that was in the past now, and the future was beckoning in a big way! So much could be hers. It was all there for the asking. All it required was a bit of hard work and application on her part.

The birthday party eventually broke up at four in the morning. Henrietta had disappeared, probably with her friends. Laura and Jennifer walked home accompanied by Quintin, who'd doubtless been left in the lurch for misbehaving. All three had their arms wound round each other and were giggling with merriment.

As the threesome approached the Casino square, Jennifer, not to be outdone by the earlier psychedelic floor show, hitched up her gold dress and did an impromptu ballet dance all the way up the Casino gardens. She weaved gracefully in and out of the palm trees, and leapt over the flower-beds like a gazelle. This was much to the amusement and approbation of three policemen on night duty patrolling the Casino, who stood watching with their arms folded, absolutely spellbound.

"Careful, you might get arrested!" laughed Laura, drawing Jennifer's attention to the audience.

"If they're handsome enough, I might accompany them willingly to the station," Jennifer replied, completely unconcerned.

"It's almost breakfast time, d'you think they'd make us coffee?"

"It was not coffee I was thinking of!" she replied airily, vaulting over a shrub, and performing a perfect arabesque. Her hair had gone completely wild, standing out in a golden cloud, and she looked like one of those romantic wood nymphs from Greek mythology. She floated gracefully this way and that, momentarily disappearing and reappearing behind bushes and trees, her gold dress and hair catching the thin morning light in muted flashes.

"To hell with it!" Laura cried as she threw down her bag, kicked off her shoes and hoisted up her dress. She soared over a hedge as lightly as a bird and joined Jennifer for a wild *pas-de-deux* finale, which culminated in climbing up a very tall palm tree. This left a bemused and amazed Quintin gazing up the trunk, trying to coax the dancing Naiades back down, holding two evening bags and four dainty gold slingbacks.

"Why are you doing this to me?" he groaned, as he tried in vain to ignore the fact that neither girl had any knickers on.

Laura knew that this extraordinary tableau would be fixed in her memory for always: this evening was a watershed in her life. So much had happened, and nothing would ever be quite the same again.

All this time, Quintin and the girls had been totally unaware of Ratti lurking in the shadows, watching their every move, with his pale, suspicious eyes.

"*Et merde!*" he whispered to himself.

Why did those girls have to look so alike? He really couldn't tell one from the other. They even had the same hair-style now. Damn! And it was such a job to keep up with them. They were all over the place, always gallivanting: never at home! They made things very difficult for him these days. But now, at last, he would have something to report to Lejeune. A threesome, no less, with that playboy night-club owner. It wouldn't hurt to add a few juicy bits. He didn't want Lejeune to think he was shirking in his duty.

"*Alors, mes belles,*" he muttered darkly, "you'll live to regret this! Just you wait . . ."

With a sinister expression in his eyes, he watched their retreating backs as they followed the narrow road between the straight line of palms edging the Casino gardens.

"And then . . ." He sliced the tip of his index finger across his

255

throat with a murderous sneer, *"Allez! Toc!"*

Ratti sniggered menacingly, adding, "No more than the sluts deserve!"

Chapter 19

Jennifer's restlessness since Laura's birthday party was getting worse, and she seemed unable to settle down. Maybe it was a depression caused by a sudden drop in hormone levels due to the abortion. Or maybe she needed someone or something exciting to help recharge her batteries and stimulate her back into action. It was as if she had cleared the decks for no useful purpose: where was her particular ship going to sail? Suddenly she'd been handed back the helm, had forgotten how to steer and had lost her bearings.

Julius was no longer around to spoil her, though she was not sure she'd want him around anyway. Neither was there the daily routine of hospital life to fall back on. She felt physically better now, so there was no excuse for her to expect sympathy and attention. But this did not prevent her from missing it.

She had gone through all this drama, solved an overriding problem, been the centre of attention, and now suddenly she was cast back into ordinariness. Everything was empty and anti-climactic. She wasn't given to introspection as a rule. She lacked the expertise to be objective and to be able to pinpoint any reason for her malaise and lack of direction. It was most annoying and frustrating to be in this state of limbo. She fidgeted around the flat, smoking too much and drinking endless coffees, which, of course, made her jumpier than ever, like a long-tailed cat in a room full of rocking-horses.

Laura, who was usually a sympathetic listener, seemed too distracted and over-excited about her future these days to spend time with Jennifer analysing her problems. She didn't mean to be unsympathetic, it was just that she was up to her eyes at the moment. There were so many things to arrange, including a visa, accommodation in New York, interviews with Howson, applications for her exam, plus the continuing diploma course – which all needed to be crammed around her daily work routine. She barely had time to eat, she was so busy. Jennifer envied her sense of purpose. Laura never had time to be bored or mooch around. What an asset that must be, she thought wistfully.

"Trouble is with me," she told Hen, over a late breakfast in the kitchen, "I should have been born in the last century when women had bevies of servants, and expected no more from their daily life than to drink tea, gossip, have the vapours and do their needlepoint. Still, knowing me, I suppose I'd have been too bone idle even to sew!"

Henrietta laughed. "I expect you'd have had men in breeches fawning all over you and been banging them senseless to while away the time!"

Jennifer laughed listlessly. "I'm bored, Hen. What shall we do?"

Henrietta had already arranged to meet Antonia and Alexander at the Café de Paris for after-lunch drinks. She asked Jennifer along, an invitation which was accepted with alacrity. The two girls made an interesting contrast as they wended their way along the narrow streets to the Casino gardens in the town centre: Jennifer, the epitome of the golden girl, blonde and coltish, and Henrietta, darkly chic with her sharply sculpted hair, cream skin, and patrician profile.

It was a pleasant, sunny afternoon and as the two arrived, they could see Antonia and Alexander sprawled back comfortably in their white chairs, a carafe of wine on the table, under a large coloured parasol. Alexander got up as they approached, and pulled out a couple of chairs for them. In the daylight he looked much more English. He had the fresh complexion of a healthy, outdoor type, none of the sallow, lounge-lizard look of the Continental studs draped around the principality. Alexander summoned a waiter for another carafe of chilled white wine and a couple of glasses.

Antonia was very entertaining company, telling them all about the film she was in. The cat eyes danced provocatively when she recounted the shenanigans on set, and the tantrums and the foibles of some of the well-known actors she'd worked with. The next scene was to take place in the Casino, and after that, her double had to drive a car off a cliff. Antonia's part in the filming would then be over. "I'm to have a spectacular death!" she grinned wryly. Alexander didn't say much, except to mention that the painted lady had pushed off to St Tropez, which didn't appear to bother him.

Jennifer studied him discreetly. She liked his open face and regular features. He wasn't overwhelmingly handsome, but everything about him was pleasing in an understated way. She liked his quiet voice and his build. He had a slow smile that she found sexy. His clear, hazel eyes occasionally engaged hers in a mildly flirtatious, but never overt fashion. Nothing about him jarred.

"Definitely fancyable!" she told Hen later, and thought she might work on him that night if he came to the disco, just to lift her spirits and get her hand back in. She'd never tried a viscount before.

If Jennifer had been waiting impatiently for some action to liven up her life, she got more than she bargained for on this particular evening!

She and Henrietta left the Meribel at eight thirty – leaving Laura as usual poring over her books – all set for a busy night at Le Disco, Jennifer in charge of greeting, seating and feeding, Henrietta of choosing and playing the right music to suit the mood of the punters, thus keeping the dance floor full.

They were very busy to start with, and the place was

packed with celebrities. There were David Niven, ever the quintessential English gentleman and his dark-haired, Swedish wife Hjordis, and Gregory Peck. Then later on Peter Sellers came in with a beautiful blonde. One always expected Peter Sellers to do a Clouseau – to trip up, or do something foolish, but he was quietly attentive to the glamorous star and unobtrusive. She was wearing a scarlet mini-dress and her wavy blonde hair was held back with a pair of huge, psychedelic sunglasses worn on top of her head. She was breathtakingly pretty and unselfconscious – completely wrapped up in her partner.

Shortly afterwards, in trooped Terry and his companions. This time Veronique had on a purple plunging dress with purple lenses to match, plus, of course, the petulant Italian lover who was sporting a purple silk jacket. Jennifer couldn't help but be amused at the notion of matching lovers to one's eyes and wardrobe.

Then there was the enormously rich Italian motor heir, Agnelli, and his beautiful young wife, Atalanta, dressed in a stunning Pucci print dress and Rufo, the Prince's enigmatic equerry who had an enormous aquiline nose and enough charm to sink three battleships. He had a sprinkling of Italian counts in tow. And last but not least, Alexander with the gorgeous and lethal Antonia, dressed to kill in a long white slipper-satin dress with a keyhole-cutout round her smooth, tanned navel.

"Blast!" thought Jennifer. "She would have to be with Alexander, and here I am, rushed off my feet with no time to work on him."

She approached them, but was pipped at the post by Quintin, who made a great show of dancing attendance on the emergent star and her titled companion, seating them next to the Sellers.

"Blast again and sod you, Quint!" muttered Jennifer under her breath. Fixing a flashing rictus grin to her face, she dashed off to look after Terry and his friends. Time passed quickly and the girls and Quintin were kept absolutely rushed off their feet, though Quintin was still to be glimpsed from time to time laying the charm on Antonia.

But then, as suddenly as everyone had piled into the club, they nearly all left *en masse*, apparently to go on to the Maona at the Summer Sporting, on the water's edge, leaving a mere sprinkling of people dotted around the tables. Amongst them was Alexander, cradling a beer, but oddly enough – no Antonia.

"Where the bloody hell's that sod Quintin?" asked Henrietta as Jennifer was clearing one of the tables.

Jennifer, busy stacking glasses on a tray, was unperturbed. "Search me," she answered, "He was here a minute ago. I saw him talking to Antonia, but wasn't she with Alexander?"

"Not now she isn't," thundered Henrietta. "I'll bet she's sloped off with Quintin. I'll kill her!"

Jennifer stopped stacking for a moment a gave Henrietta her full attention. Now was the moment of truth. "Hey! You *are* having a thing with Quintin, then!" she said triumphantly.

"So?" Henrietta replied defensively.

"What's he like? Is he as good as he says he is?" asked Jennifer avidly.

Henrietta folded her arms and fumed. "He's bloody fucking magnificent, if you must know, as that randy bitch is about to find out."

"But I thought she was a friend of yours. I must say it's a bit off going with your man."

"Oh, but so typical of Antonia," Henrietta stormed. "I've known her since we were toddlers: even then she always took my favourite toys!" Henrietta was near to tears.

"But, Hen," remonstrated Jennifer, "surely you already knew that Quintin's a complete swine, gorgeous or not!"

Henrietta looked dreamy. "Oh, I know," she said, "but he's not really a pig through and through: he can be adorable. It's just that he has a low boredom threshold, and Antonia is just about as lethal as a woman can be for someone as easily tempted as Quint."

"And I thought she was going to work on Alexander, just as *I'd* set my sights on him. Tell you what, Henny," said Jennifer, suddenly brightening, "let's shut up the club and take Alex to the Tip Top. We'll all get pissed. It's much better than your going back home with your tail between your legs."

"I'll bet his is already between hers, the bastard!" Hen commented sourly.

Jennifer smiled, though sympathetically. Henrietta was genuinely upset, and despite all the warning lights, had obviously fallen hook, line and sinker.

Jennifer approached her target. "Alexander," she cajoled, "How about taking Hen and me to the Tip Top?"

Alexander looked pleased and surprised. "OK," he replied, in his light baritone. "Why not? Sounds fun." He had not hesitated. "Come on, then. I'll help you shut up shop."

The three made a production out of stacking chairs on tables, clicking lights on and off and clattering bottles around. Henrietta put on a monotonous and discordant LP, and it wasn't long before the remaining punters took the hint and their leave.

The Tip Top as usual was packed, and there were also customers spilling on to the pavement outside, to take advantage of the only slightly cooler air. The Tip Top was a ramshackle Italian-run bar, next door to the disco, very popular with the younger set and open till dawn. There was a long bar, festooned with bottles hanging from the ceiling and the barmen were generally in pandemonium trying to keep up with the never-ending orders for beer and cheap wine.

Hot snacks were also available, cooked fresh in the tiny kitchen in the rear section by a huge, fat Italian momma who toiled over bubbling pans of pasta. There was a table free in the upper section at the back, next door to the kitchen. The juke-box was playing an oldish Beach Boys number, 'We Had Fun,

Fun, Fun Till Daddy Took the T-Bird Away'. Their songs were currently the rage in Monaco. The waiter was finding it difficult to squeeze through the milling and noisy crowd who always frequented this popular bar in the small hours.

"Yummee," murmured Jennifer, as the smell of fresh garlic and onions assailed her. "Couldn't I just happily put away a spag bol! They make them fresh here, in about twenty minutes, but it's well worth the wait. Tip Top spag is unsurpassed."

"OK," said Alexander gamely. "Count me in. How about you, Hen?"

"Great, and oodles of red wine. I'm going to need it."

"Never mind, Hen. We'll help you commiserate," laughed Jennifer.

The three of them laid into a giant carafe of house red. It wasn't long before their order of spaghetti arrived, by which time they were all merry enough not to mind about the mess the tomato sauce made of their faces as they fooled about. They sucked in the trailing lengths of pasta, one occasionally grabbing the end of another's and giggling stupidly as they sucked together until the spaghetti broke, or their lips collided.

This silly horseplay, combined with the fact that the three of them were squashed into a banquette designed for two, made for immediate and exaggerated intimacy, but nobody minded at all, least of all Alexander. Because of the racket made by the other customers and the juke-box, they had to put their heads close together in order to make themselves heard, so in spite of the bright lights, the noise and being very much in public, the three were nevertheless in an intimate world of their own that shut out all else. The continuing eye contact, cheeks that occasionally brushed together, coupled with body contact and liberal helpings of wine, heightened their physical awareness of each other in a very sensual way.

Jennifer was acutely aware of Alexander's muscular leg pressed against hers, and every time she leant across him to address Hen, her left breast brushed the top of his arm, and he responded instinctively, caressing it with a slight movement of his shoulder, which she did not resist.

Henrietta, by the same token, who'd known Alexander all her life, felt in need of his warmth and friendship, and relished the idea of spending the night wrapped in his arms. She found herself wanting to touch him, to run her hands lightly over his hard, rippling chest and feel his silent strength, to help take the pain of Quintin away. Alexander didn't know which way to turn. He was overcome with desire but didn't want to break the mood by making the wrong move, or saying the wrong thing.

Then Henrietta's slurred tones broke into his reverie. "We've finished the wine. Shall we order more, or what?" And she gazed mistily into his eyes. Alexander instantly saw a window of opportunity, and seized on it.

"Tell you what," he suggested casually, "I've got a beautiful Cognac at home. Let's lay into that."

"You're on!" chorused the girls, and the attractive threesome left the bar, clinging on to each other – though not for warmth – as they emerged into the sultry night air. They found a taxi at the rank near the Winter Sporting, woke up the driver, and piled into the back seat, Alexander putting his arms round both girls as they snuggled into his chest, making outrageous comments and flirting shamelessly.

Alexander's villa was tucked into the lower slopes of the surrounding mountains overlooking the Beach Club and the sweeping bay beyond. Umbrella pines and slender columns of juniper dotted here and there on the rolling hillside framed a view that was utterly breathtaking. The moon cast a glittering path of myriads of shimmering flecks that sparkled and danced on a sea that faded into navy nothingness where the horizon met the star-studded sky above. Beyond the pale stone terrace outside the enormous french windows was a swimming-pool, surrounded with huge stone tubs, housing small palms and masses of burgeoning pink ivy-leaved geraniums.

"What a gorgeous place!" sighed Jennifer, as he led them into the sitting-room overlooking the pool. "Is it yours?"

"Well, sort of. It belongs to my family actually, but I'm on my own here at the moment. How about this famous brandy now?"

Alexander came back almost immediately with three balloon glasses and a bottle of Courvoisier and poured huge slugs into each. They all sprawled into a long, squashy beige sofa, kicking off their shoes.

"Christ!" exclaimed Hen, examining her glass. "We'll be paralytic."

"That's the idea," murmured Alexander mischievously.

"Mmmm, I just adore the smell of this stuff," said Jennifer swilling the mellow amber liquid around in the enormous snifter. "It's so, well, well . . . so . . . wanton and heady!"

"You can be as wanton as you like," whispered Alexander, caressing her neck. She leaned over, and nibbled the lobe of his ear, running a hand over his muscular chest, between his shirt buttons, which gradually came undone.

"If the pair of you are going to get engrossed in a cosy two-some," declared Hen coolly, "I'm going for a swim!"

And she set down her glass. She threw off her dress; her slender boy's body gleaming pale in the moonlight as she made her way to the french doors.

"Wait, I'll open them for you," said Alexander, jumping to his feet. As he approached the tall, dark girl he ran a hand approvingly down the curve of her waist, pulling her gently towards him, adding seductively, "And who said anything about a *two*-some?"

Henrietta paused, contemplating him challengingly.

"Why don't you take your knickers off, Henny?" giggled Jennifer. "You'll get them wet!"

"Knowing you, yours already are!" retorted Henrietta, but she had a wicked smile on her face as she stepped out of her brief panties and casually tossed them across the room.

"I'll buy that!" laughed Jennifer as in a trice, she, too, stripped naked and ran towards the moonlit terrace, the stone flags still warm from the day's sun. Jennifer and Henrietta plunged into the tepid pool, shrieking with delight. Alexander watched for a moment as the girls fooled and frolicked around, periodically floating on their backs and kicking their legs, Jennifer enticing him with her rounded breasts and neat gold triangle, and Henrietta, her black mound in sharp relief against a body as smooth and white as a marble statue. He slowly took off his clothes, his eyes never leaving the frolics in the pool, until he was down to his silk boxer shorts, when he seemed to hesitate.

"Come on, you coward, take those knickers off or I'll do it for you!" shrieked Jennifer.

He complied with a grin on his face, throwing them off with a flourish, before flexing his biceps and executing a perfect dive into the water.

"Christ Almighty!" giggled Jennifer nervously. "He's hung like a horse!"

"Well, you know what they say about men with short legs!" Henrietta spluttered, with a mixture of laughter and excitement.

"Bull! It's just that a cock looks much longer on a short-ass!"

The girls were quite breathless with mirth and anticipation as Alexander finally reached them.

"What are you two laughing at?" he asked mock indignantly.

"Nothing at all. We're just enjoying ourselves!" they countered.

"Rubbish!" he retorted. "We haven't even started yet!"

The horseplay started up in earnest now as Alex grabbed each girl in turn and threw them up in the air repeatedly. They crash-landed back into the warm water, shrieking and spluttering, with flying limbs and hair, causing great frothing waves to swish and lap over the sides of the pool, and kept coming back for more. Jennifer then decided he needed some of his own medicine, so quietly she approached the young viscount from behind, to try to duck him whilst he tussled with Hen, but finding this impossible because he vastly outmatched her in strength, she climbed on to his shoulders, swaying wildly back and forth, in an attempt to make him fall over. But he was too sturdy and strong for her, until Hen leapt up to join in, and pulling Jennifer over from behind, all three over-balanced in a great welter of foaming splashes and screams of laughter, blowing out mouthfuls of water.

"Enough! Enough!" spluttered Jennifer, and swam towards the shallower water, where she lay floating on her back, lazily contemplating her toes, with her arms outspread on the barre that ran along the pool edge. Alex swam towards her with an athletic crawl, then dived down under her legs, his head emerging between them as he surfaced, and stood armpit deep in the water.

"Bullseye!" he murmured, and putting his hands under her buttocks he hooked her legs over his shoulders.

Jennifer felt herself go weak as she gave in to the exquisite sensation of his warm tongue exploring and caressing her lips with small flicking, darting movements, up and down, up and down, and up again, where he found the most sensitive bit of her and concentrated on that, which drove her wild. The water gently massaged her partly submerged body with a soft sucking sound as her hips took on a slow insistent rhythm of their own in response to his expert touch. She could feel that tickling, almost unbearable sensation of heat building up inside her to a fire, when Alex suddenly took his mouth away to whisper to Henrietta, "I've got something for you under the water!"

"But I might drown!" she replied indignantly.

"Well, sit on it, then!" he grinned, and swivelled his lower half towards her invitingly, before burying his mouth into Jennifer again. Henrietta plunged her arm under the water to feel him, closing a hand around the long, hard round weapon, and pushed it slowly inside her. Relishing its smooth, slippery, warm invasion, she straddled him diagonally, her legs wrapped firmly round him, gripping his upper arm and the pool edge for support. The rippling wavelets caused by the rhythmic movements of the three soon built into larger waves that gently swished and soughed around the pool, suspending them in a surreal world of liquid sensations inside and around their bodies.

The three remained oblivious to everything but their own pleasure as the warm water took on a life of its own, sighing and slopping against the pool edges, occasionally cascading over the sides, the moonlight silvering the spray as it rose and fell, with a gentle hiss and whisper on to sun-warmed stone.

Suddenly Jennifer's cries rent the air and her body arched and quivered as her senses caught fire and sent ripples of ecstasy radiating through her lower body, the cries turning to soft sighing moans as the intensity of her orgasm flickered and gradually faded to a satisfying glow of well-being that permeated her.

Eventually she unhooked herself from Alex's shoulders and swam away lazily, turning round and round in the water contentedly like a dolphin at play, enjoying the feel of the water washing over and around her body, before hoisting herself out of the pool, where she sat on the edge, watching as the other two continued to churn up waves with a gradually accelerating rhythm.

It was not long before Alex bucked, cried out and threw his head back, as Henrietta felt the pleasurable pulsing sensation of his heat shooting wetly inside her, which made her want to come, too. "I want you to make me come, but I can't do it this way. I want to lie down," she whispered into his neck.

"Well, get out of the pool then before I fade away entirely!"

he answered, and hoisting her out of the water, he laid her down on the pool edge before heaving himself nimbly out. Jennifer watched the continuing erotic scene through half-closed eyes, hugging her knees, as the bodies interlocked again, looking almost spectral as the moonlight lit up and silvered the wet sheen of their skin. After a few moments, Henrietta came with a long, quiet shuddering sigh, and the pair lay still for a while, oblivious to anything or anyone around them.

Jennifer suddenly shivered as a light breeze wafted up the sweet scent of jasmine, cooling her wet skin and disturbing her tranquil reflections. She got up and gracefully dived back into the warm pool, and swam across to the other side.

"Hey, Alexander! You're not falling asleep, are you?" she asked. "How about some towels to dry your water nymphs?" She climbed out of the pool again and wrung out her long hair.

"Why don't you two just lick each other dry and let me watch?" he murmured lazily, without moving a muscle.

"Darling Alexander, what a swine you are," Hen complained. "This stone terrace is very hard and you're getting very heavy." She tried to wriggle out from under him without success.

"If you two would kindly comply with my request, it wouldn't only be the stone that's hard around here!" commented Alex, grinning wickedly as he rolled off Hen on to his back, and contemplated the stars above.

Chapter 20

About mid-morning, on her return from a shopping trip, Laura discovered her two very bleary-eyed flatmates sitting in the kitchen drinking coffee. Jennifer and Hen were unusually quiet, and had dark shadows under their eyes. Laura put down her shopping on the table and looked at the weary pair quizzically, but not without amusement.

"I went on the croissant run at nine this morning," she said accusingly, "but you weren't in your beds when I looked in to see if you wanted breakfast."

"We went for a swim," replied Jennifer quickly, looking down to avoid Hen's eyes. Her explanation, too swiftly delivered, bore a faint vestige of truth. But then, as Oscar Wilde once said, "Truth is rarely pure and never simple."

Laura smiled slowly and wisely, shaking her head. "It must have been a mighty long swim and a very early one!"

Her eyes twinkled perceptively as her gaze swivelled from one girl to the other.

"Oh, believe us, it was!" countered Hen, looking totally impassive but fighting a rising mirth. "Coffee?"

Laura demurred. "You two can put these things away," she said, indicating the few provisions on the table.

She was off for a swim and quick sunbathe at the Digue and then back for an afternoon of studying. The door clicked shut behind her.

"Golly, doesn't she ever let up?" wondered Hen.

"Of course," said Jennifer, jumping quickly to Laura's defence. "She's not like this all the time. It's just that she's

271

bitten off rather more than most people could chew. And don't forget she's off to New York in a few days. That's enough to make anyone preoccupied. I don't envy her doing those exams. Yuk!!"

"Changing the subject," Henrietta said mournfully, "I wonder what sort of a night Quintin had with my so-called friend and rising star?"

"Oh, Hen, for heaven's sake!" Jennifer snapped impatiently. "Don't give Farmiloe the satisfaction of thinking you care." Then she grinned wickedly. "Tell him about our interesting threesome: that's bound to make him livid with rage and jealousy. I'll wind him up for you, if you like, especially if I tell him we took Alex up on his last suggestion. That'll really get him going!"

"Which one was that?" queried Hen innocently.

"You know, tongues instead of towels!"

Hen sniggered. "Don't you dare! Quint'll accuse us both of being dykes."

"Hardly. He'd go a real bundle on it!'

Henrietta chuckled, "D'you reckon?" Then a cloud passed over her face. "I'm still really pissed off with him, but it doesn't stop me wanting him back."

"You're silly. You should let drop the odd, tantalising hint about our wild night, to infuriate him. It's much better than a tearful scene. If you exaggerate our antics, embellish them all you like, he'll come rushing back to you like the bullet out of a gun, hoping we'll do the same for him, – the greedy, opportunist little sod!"

Henrietta sighed heavily. "I suppose you're right. I still wish it all didn't hurt so much, though. It upsets me so much to think of him with Antonia."

'Oh, for heaven's sake, don't be so soppy; you've given him back a dose of his own medicine in far bigger measure. Don't tell me you didn't enjoy last night!"

Henrietta giggled wickedly. "Bit of a riot, wasn't it?"

After breakfast, which was late enough to double for lunch, the two girls put away the shopping, and washed up. Then they went in search of Laura at the Calypso, and spent the whole afternoon sleeping off their excesses in the hot sun, on the baking concrete blocks of the Digue.

That same evening, Quintin, as Jennifer had predicted, was livid that he'd missed out on the *partouse*, as he insisted on calling it. He followed Jennifer around the club like a dog on heat, demanding to know all the variations of play, which she thoroughly enjoyed recounting – much exaggerated.

Antonia had disappeared altogether with the film crew, and left no word. This added insult to injury for Quintin as Henrietta was ignoring him, too. She was playing it very cool, letting Jennifer wind him up, loving and hating her teasing, really rising to the bait.

Jennifer quietly sidled up to the turntable where Hen drooped, playing a moody, sad number by Jacques Brel, '*Ne Me Quitte Pas*', which always brought tears to her eyes.

"He's really pissed off, Hen," she giggled, trying to cheer her. "Hopping with rage, creaming and slavering with thwarted lust, just like I said! He'll be ready to take you back now at the drop of a hat, or rather your knickers. If I were you, though, I'd leave him to stew in his own juice and ignore him for a while. It'll serve him right!"

Hen brightened up. A wicked grin came to her face as Jacques Brel faded out. She reached back to her disc store with gleaming eyes, and followed it with Serge Gainsbourg/Jane Birkin's '*Et Toi Non Plus*'. This sexy number was full of suggestive sighs and moans, had been banned by the BBC, and left nothing to the imagination.

Jennifer's eyes danced. "That's more like it!" she commented approvingly. "By the way, where's our inventive and well-endowed aristo lover tonight?"

There was no sign of Alexander. Jennifer was disappointed,

as she'd been looking forward to enjoying him again – this time on her own, and maybe less drunk!

Laura stretched and yawned. She was thoroughly bored with the National Association of Securities Dealers' rules and regulations. She pressed her fists to her eyes hard, creating black swirling patterns in front of her, and then blinked several times to clear her brain. She yawned again, and went through the french doors to get some air. Her eye was drawn to the block opposite, out of habit.

Ratti was on the balcony, without his binoculars. He seemed to spend his life there! She decided to go out and get some light relief from studying and worrying. Then she did a double take. There was another man with Ratti and they were deep in conversation. There was something uncomfortably familiar about the set of the stranger's shoulders, even at a distance and in the fading light. From his gestures, he appeared very angry. If she didn't think it were so utterly improbable, she could have sworn it was Pierre Lejeune.

"Fresh air and a change of scene is what I need," she said to herself, dismissing the notion as fanciful and ridiculous. She decided to walk down to the port: maybe take a capuccino at one of the adjacent cafés and then stroll around looking at the yachts.

It was a lovely night – a soft twilight, the time the French rather quaintly described as *entre chien et loup* (the short period of time between when the dog goes to sleep, and the wolf awakens for his nightly forays). The lights twinkled in the harbour, casting their shimmering reflection into the water which was faintly ruffled by the tiniest of breezes. Laura slowly walked down the winding hill that led to the port, passing a noisy bar that was the favourite haunt of all the crewmen from the yachts that lined the Port de Monaco in stately rows. She ignored the loud chorus of wolf-whistles that greeted her as she passed, emanating from its sweaty interior where, no doubt, the crews were getting thoroughly tanked up on endless beer. There wasn't very much else for them to do in a place like Monte-Carlo. All the attractive French girls seemed to disappear into their homes after dusk, though their fiancés were normally out on the make. The very few ex-patriate girls that were around, had come to this playground of the *richissime* in order to seek their fortune, (or already had one in the bank). So what chance had a mere deckhand?

Laura walked down the stone steps that led to the quay-side Café-Bar tucked into the nearest corner of the harbour. She sat outside in the twilight and ordered a large capuccino. Stirring it slowly, she found it hard to imagine that in less than a week she would be working in New York. She listened to the quiet lapping of the water, the French voices all around her and the muted clanging of the rigging on the smaller yachts nearest to her. It seemed unbelievable that she would soon be in a totally different world, a bustling, frantic world of grey skyscrapers and grey suits.

At the far end of the harbour, all along the Digue where the water was deep, the enormous and fabulously expensive motor-yachts were moored stern-to, allowing easier access for guests and owners. Standing out noticeably amongst them by dint of its three gigantic masts which towered above everything, was the *Xerina*.

Julius would be back soon. It was odd, but every time Laura brought him up these days, Jennifer clammed up. She seemed non-committal and discontented, fidgety and nervous. Perhaps it was a reaction to the trauma she'd suffered. Or was she still uncertain about his motives? Certainly Julius had appeared sincere to Laura, but could she have been taken in by an astute scoundrel?

She paid for her coffee, and strolled to the far end of the harbour. The further she walked towards the Digue, the larger the yachts and the bigger the crews. Several of the boats had parties in progress and were lit up gaily and dressed overall to mark the occasion. Others had deck-hands quietly working away, hosing down the decks, or polishing the brass and woodwork. There was little sign of activity on *Xerina*, but the deck lamps were lit. The saloon was in darkness.

Laura breathed in the salty night air and walked up the steps of the massive harbour wall to the top, where the light sea breeze caught her hair, lifting it and softly feathering her face. She looked down over the outer, sea-facing side, which was reinforced by huge, flat concrete blocks. These were haphazardly laid, as a deflecting barrier to the sometimes cruel, surging seas of the winter, that hissed, roared and crashed their defiance against those man-made defences. But now, on this balmy evening, that same sea only quietly grumbled and swished tamely around the Digue.

All summer long, the younger element sunbathed and swam there, and the pale grey blocks would be draped all day with bright towels and browning bodies stretched out in the sun. An enterprising local had set up a bar here, with a shady roof of bamboo slats over its long counter, and a juke-box playing early-sixties hits, or the odd French number. There was a large, raised sun terrace with tables and chairs, where one could get a snack and ice-cold drinks, too. The Calypso was a very handy and relaxing lunch-time spot for those who worked nearby, especially for Laura, whose office was just up the hill.

She could hear strains of 'Hey, Mr Tambourine Man' drifting up the high harbour wall from that same juke-box, to a background chorus of young and happy voices, punctuated by bursts of laughter. Usually the Calypso was closed at night. It must have been a private celebration.

Laura suddenly felt rather sad, and very alone – almost afraid of the future she had mapped out. Would she ever see the likes of the Calypso again? Or would her life become too sophisticated and far removed from this ramshackle and simple bar, with its noisy juke-box and casual, rather infantile banter?

Laura breathed in heavily, gazing beyond all the noise and lights, far out to the horizon, where the sea met the sky with a faint, misty deep-blue line, and all was serene and peaceful. Who was to know what could be lying ahead? Life could be so uncertain. So full of problems and pitfalls. Then she tossed her hair back decisively, straightened her shoulders, and set off to return at a brisk, steady pace to the Meribel.

Soon she reached a part of the coast road pierced into solid rock, tunnelled out, and left open on its outer side, supported by a series of massive arches. Laura paused to listen to the hollow swishing of the sea as it surged energetically amongst the rocks below, soughing, hissing, sending jets of silvery spray several feet into the air, the staccato rattle of the myriad droplets like machine-gun fire on stone, as they rained fiercely back down. The sound was intensified tenfold by the acoustic properties of the tunnel, reminiscent of the chancel of some vast cathedral, created and hewn from nature. The constant movement of the water was mesmeric, and Laura would have lingered longer, had she not suddenly been aware of a leaping shadow. Alarmed, her mouth went dry as she turned to look at the arches behind her, sure she'd heard the echo of sudden retreating footsteps, too. But all she could see were the massive, shadowy arches, and all she could hear now was the sea churning and rumbling below her. This was the worst place she could think of to be caught by an assailant. Lonely, isolated – the only witness the sea and the rocks. She shivered with fear, and bolted as if her life depended on it.

Behind her, she could hear heavy footsteps pounding and pounding inexorably, echoing hollowly around the rocky walls of her prison. Her heart hammering fit to burst, she ran on, her breath coming in gulping gasps. In all her life, she had never been this frightened. On and on she raced, down the dark, endless tunnel, desperate to flee her relentless pursuer. At last, her lungs burning with exertion, she was out in the open air again. She didn't know how long she could keep up the pace, but panic put wings on her feet, and still she sped on, despite the cramping pains, until, at last, to her relief, she saw the headlights of an oncoming car. Its driver slowed down, probably with curiosity at the sight of a distraught and bedraggled blonde running like a gazelle in the middle of the night. Laura looked quickly back over her shoulder, and saw to her great relief that her assailant had ducked back into the tunnel. Thank heaven! Now she could make a break for it, and head straight for the club, where she'd be safe with Quintin and the girls. Thank God it was not long now till New York, where she'd be oceans away from this inexplicable terror.

Next day, Jennifer had a phone call from Alex. Her heart leapt. He told her his parents had arrived earlier than expected the previous evening, and they'd had a family dinner at the villa, which he'd obviously had to attend.

"A lucky thing they didn't turn up the night before, wasn't it?" he'd added, chuckling.

"I'll say," replied Jennifer. "How long will they be staying?"

"Oh, they're off again tomorrow to Paris and then Deauville. Shall we meet up tomorrow evening?"

His voice sounded very husky and appealing over the phone. It made her weak at the knees.

"Brilliant," she replied, "I'll see you at the club, and try to get off early."

Her bright and casual tone belied her thumping heart and wet palms. She felt her spirits soar, but wondered if he were expecting Henrietta, too. She would have to use strategy here and encourage Hen to go back to Quintin, without arousing any suspicion that she had a vested interest in so doing.

As it happened, of course, the lady needed no such persuasion. Quintin couldn't stand to be ignored. He brought all his charm and experience to bear on Henrietta, who immediately succumbed, like a toddler to an icecream, that very same night.

Jennifer was all pent up with excitement, like a girl on her first date, and couldn't wait to see her new lover the next day. Julius, and all her promises to him went by the board. In fact she didn't even give him a second's thought, she was so taken with Alex.

Laura had stacks of things to do before she set off for New York. It was good to be busy, as the excitement took her mind off her nasty experience of the previous night. She had to see the head of Howson to sort out her papers and finalise a few details that would allow her to take the Stock Exchange exam without having been a long-term employee of a member firm. This, she had been assured, would not be a problem because of her present job and her coursework with the New York Institute of Finance.

Hal Petersen, the managing director of Howson May International, her prospective boss, was very charming and helpful. Laura instantly knew that she'd be happy stepping into Wilder's shoes, especially as she would be taking over one of Howson's biggest accounts, and would not need to scratch around for new business, like most newly qualified brokers. It was a job on a plate, too good to be true, unheard of for a twenty-one-year-old, and a female to boot!

She then had to go to pick up her passport with the visa stamped in at the American Consulate in Nice. Then off to her bank to order some dollars for her four-week stay in New York. Then she would have to start thinking about packing. How much easier it was to be a man, she thought: he'd only take a couple of suits and some changes of shirts and underwear. A woman needed far more variety; a total change of image between day and evening wear. Then all the associated bits and pieces – belts, bags, scarves, earrings, shoes. How on earth could she fit everything into two cases?

Laura got back to the flat before Jennifer had left. She noticed she was taking more care than usual with her appearance – not that it made much difference. Jennifer always looked stunning.

"What's up tonight, then?" she asked.

Jennifer was in the bathroom, doing her face, the basin surrounded with all her clutter, towels draped soggily over the edge of the bath. What a mess! But she would as always emerge the picture of elegance.

"Who's this in aid of?" she tried again.

Jennifer grinned at her friend. "Mind your own beeswax, nosey. Anyway," she lied, "I'm not making any more effort than I usually do."

Carefully she applied yet another coat of mascara to her lashes, her little pink tongue delicately clenched between her teeth. She had drenched herself in Chanel No.5. Her hair, newly washed, shone in silken rivulets that cascaded everywhere.

"Not that you'd notice, no!" said Laura, laughing. "What goes on that you can't tell your best friend and confidante?"

"If you absolutely must know," Jennifer said, studying her lipstick in the mirror and pouting her full lips, "I'm seeing Alexander later."

"Oh, really? Pretty fancyable, when all's said and done," Laura commented approvingly. "Is he the one you and Henny had the long swim with the other night? Swim, my foot!" she grinned knowingly.

Jennifer inspected her nails evasively. "Could have been," she muttered.

"You behave yourself," Laura reminded her. "You're practically betrothed to another."

Jennifer whipped round, as if stung. Her eyes were wide and defensive. She looked about to remonstrate, then thought the better of it, murmuring wickedly, "What the eye doesn't see . . ." She winked at Laura and made for the door. "Well, I'm off now, OK? Don't wait up!"

"Unlikely. I'm off myself to have a goodbye dinner with Fitz and his wife and some friends. Smart do. Black tie and long dress, don't you know."

"Oh," said Jennifer, impressed. "Well, come and show us your glam self at the club later, so we can defend you from all perils and dangers of the night. Can't have your being terrorised again now, can we?"

Laura shivered at the memory. "God spare us! Might see you later. But I expect Fitz will see me home. He's such a gent! I'll be OK."

"As you wish! *Ciao, bella!*" Jennifer drawled. "Be good!"

Laura watched her departing flatmate with a wistful smile. How marvellous to be so unfazed, so unbound by any strictures, and yet still appear so vulnerable and innocent. In the eyes of those who didn't love her, Jennifer often seemed selfish, yet she wasn't really, nor uncaring. She was a paradox – lovable and kind, but at the same time thoughtless and wayward – impossible to pin down. Julius would have his work cut out. But then millionaires who had everything probably strove constantly for new challenges. He'd certainly found one in Jennifer!

Jennifer rushed around all evening with only half a mind on her work. She smiled and took orders mechanically, but it was easy to see she was several sacks short of a full load tonight, as she asked for "three coffee-on-the-rocks and two white scotches please," and delivered a mink stole into the kitchen.

"Hey, Jennifer, wake up, will you? Are you in love or something?" asked Quintin, as he removed the mink from the cooker, luckily switched off. Jennifer apologised, and skipped out of the kitchen laughing.

She was beginning to think Alex would never come. She couldn't bear the suspense. It was driving her mad. But then, suddenly there he was, walking in to the strains of Procol Harum's 'A Whiter Shade of Pale': *"We skipped the light fandango, turned cartwheels 'cross the floor . . ."* And it was

Jennifer's heart that turned cartwheels, and her knees to jelly. She was annoyed with herself. It was ages since she'd felt like this, and she didn't like being so out of control.

"Hold on to your hat, girl!" she chided herself. "This won't do at all."

Alex was even more tanned than before, and his light brown hair had gold streaks in it from the sun. He was wearing a beautifully cut blazer in dark green twill that accentuated his broad shoulders, a paler green lawn shirt and black cords which emphasised his narrow hips. Despite not being tall, he exuded a masculinity and strength that was overpowering, and Jennifer loved his confident and graceful stride. He smiled at her, showing even, white teeth, and his hazel eyes lit up with warmth.

"Hello, beautiful," he said, kissing her on the cheek.

"Hello, yourself," said Jennifer quietly, smiling back and hoping she looked calmer than she felt. "What would you like to order?"

"What I'd like to order is certainly not on the menu," he grinned devilishly. "What time d'you finish?"

"Oh, not long now. It's quiet so I expect I can get away in half an hour."

"Good. I'll have a small scotch then, please. No ice."

It wasn't long before Jennifer managed to sneak off. Alexander had brought his car, a dark blue Alfa Romeo, and it only took a few minutes to get to his villa. He parked just inside the wrought iron entrance gates, and as Jennifer climbed out of the car, jasmine and the scent of pines and juniper filled the air. The rocky walls were smothered in rich, purple bougainvillea.

"What a fabulous place this is!" she remarked.

"You said that last time," he replied, putting his arm round her shoulder and lightly kissing her cheek. She turned towards him, put her arms around his neck, and kissed him properly. His lips were full and soft, and she loved the taste and smell of him, the strength and feel of his body, the texture of his skin.

She had never wanted anyone more, and the intensity of her longing frightened yet excited her. The *frisson* that overcame her transmitted itself to him because he suddenly drew away and looked at her almost savagely. Then he took her face between his hands and kissed her very gently on her forehead.

"You're a beautiful, wild thing," he murmured wistfully. "I don't think I could ever get enough of you."

"Well, you had two of us the other night," Jennifer replied with a lightness she didn't feel.

"It was you I wanted though, really. I'm not normally that greedy."

He took her hand and led her inside. "Do you want to swim?" he asked.

"Afterwards," she whispered, her grey eyes smiling up at him mischievously through her long lashes.

"Nobody's ever made me feel that way before," murmured Jennifer later, as she caressed the soft brown curls on Alexander's chest with her finger tips, and laid her head contentedly on his shoulder.

"Nor me," he replied, lighting a cigarette. "Have you had many men?"

"A few," she answered, not wanting to elaborate. She took the cigarette from his lips and drew on it herself.

"I'm sorry," he said apologetically. "I should have offered you one."

"No. We'll share this one. It's more romantic."

He smiled. "Didn't know you were the romantic type."

Jennifer smiled tenderly. Her feelings for Alexander were overwhelming. For the first time in her life, she felt totally lost and out of control. It was frightening. She must be in love.

"Neither did I," she answered, "but you live and learn."

"Why do you feel so good when I make love to you?"

"You tell me! Maybe it's because you feel so good to me at the same time. Maybe you were specially invented for me. I

283

can't feel that way all by myself. It must be your special magic."

Alexander looked at Jennifer. She was extraordinarily beautiful and sensuous. The most feminine creature he'd ever met. She was so different from the many brittle debs he'd bedded. He always got the feeling they were doing him a favour and wanted it over as soon as possible. Not so Jennifer, who had no reservations about her desire for his body. And an uninhibited way of showing it. It made him feel intensely masculine.

He reached for her, murmuring, "Shall I put another spell on you then to see if it works every time?"

But Jennifer had stubbed out the cigarette, and was working her way down his body with her lips, until she found her target. She loved the round, silky smoothness of him in her mouth, the slightly salty taste on her tongue as she ran it around the tip, to feel him growing and stiffening with excitement. She worked her way back up his body, covering him in kisses and caresses, feeling she could devour him and drown in him at the same time. It was as if she could never hold him tightly enough or have him inside her long enough, to feel him, taste him, smell him, all her senses overpowered by his very being. She clung to him as if he were a mirage that could float away – wanting him all over around and inside her, tonight and for ever.

It was eleven o'clock when Fitz saw Laura to the lift of the Meribel.

"Long past my bedtime," he'd remarked smiling, as he tugged open the lift gates, and ushered her through. It had been a thoroughly pleasant and relaxing evening. Everyone had wished Laura luck, and drunk toasts to her success. She'd been fêted, admired and fed champagne until her head swam. How she'd miss Fitz! Yawning, she pushed the button for the sixth floor, and the lift slowly edged upwards.

Laura stood outside the doorway of No.613 and sighed

heavily as she wondered whether she could muster up the enthusiasm to mug up on another lesson tonight. It was already so late. She reached for the cold, heavy key in the evening bag, and was just putting it into the lock when she felt a large hand gripping her shoulder. She reeled and almost fainted as the blood suddenly drained from her head with fright.

"Alors, ma chère," whispered the familiar voice hoarsely.

Laura's heart went cold and her skin crawled at the dread realisation that here, at last, was her nemesis. It was Pierre, obviously, who had been her pursuer all along. She should have known, she told herself dully. Somehow, she must escape. *"Pierre, je t'en prie . . ."* she remonstrated, a pulse thudding thickly in her ears.

"Je t'en prie!" he mimicked nastily, his mouth twisting in a snarl. "Pretending to be so pure and virginal. Little English slut – with your disgusting, promiscuous friends. I know what you've been up to with that playboy Farmiloe. Threesomes, orgies, dope! God knows what else. I've been keeping an eye on you. Don't even try to deny it. Nobody lies to Pierre Lejeune."

"For God's sake, I don't know what you're talking about. Don't make a scene here." Laura's voice was quiet and firm, belying her steadily growing panic. "I think you should leave."

"I'll leave when I'm ready." His hand was still gripping her shoulder.

"You're hurting me. Let go."

He pulled her round to face him, and looked her up and down, a lewd expression on his face. "You look thin and tired. And you're drunk."

"When I need your opinion I'll ask for it."

"Don't push me too far, you bitch."

She looked at him coldly. Around the hard black pupils, small yellow flecks burned angrily in his brown eyes, and she noticed that his thick, dark brows were joined in the middle, which, added to the vulgar cast of his sneeringly loose mouth, made her wonder why she had ever thought him handsome.

'Will you please go away," she said quietly, "or I'll call the police."

"The police!" he scoffed. "And what do you think they'll do? They're all friends and colleagues. I'd just tell them my fiancée and I were having a tiff. In any case," he added, looking smug, "what on earth makes you believe they'd accept your word against mine? You don't stand a chance, and your name will be mud, your stupid slut."

"We have nothing more to say to each other," answered Laura, and, turning her back on him, she opened the door, stepped in and prepared to slam it shut in his face.

But Pierre was too quick for her, and had already wedged his foot in the way. Panicking, Laura threw her weight against the door. Pierre, who had the strength of an ox, easily pushed it open and followed her in, kicking it shut with a crash behind him. He stood facing her, his chest heaving with anger, as Laura tried to back away.

He wrenched her bag from her hand and threw it on the floor. Then he slapped her face sharply, seized her and pushed her up against the wall so that her head cracked hard against it. Grabbing the long hank of hair at the nape of her neck, he twisted it so hard that she was immobilised, pinned against the wall. He lifted up her long dress with his foot, until he could grasp the hem of her skirt with his free hand, then drew the silky material up to the level of her briefs. Laura struggled violently to free herself, kicking at his ankles with the sharp heel of her shoe.

'Stop that, you bitch," he snarled, "or I'll really hurt you."

He twisted her hair so hard that every root in her scalp screamed with agony and she thought her neck would break. There seemed to be nothing Laura could do to defend herself. She was paralysed by pain. Pierre pressed himself hard against her body, unzipped himself, and forcing her legs apart with his knee, hooked the flimsy lace briefs to one side with his fingers, and roughly pushed himself inside her. His breath came in hoarse gasps that stank of stale wine as he brutally lunged at her, making her head thump against the hard plaster with each savage thrust. Laura gritted her teeth, and squeezed her eyelids hard together to hold the tears at bay. He'd never have the satisfaction of seeing her broken in spirit or defeated by his attempt to humiliate her.

Pierre's frantic lunging seemed to last an eternity, and she lost all sense of time. At last, came a long shuddering groan, and he slumped heavily against her, his whole body trembling and growing weak as his hot wetness pulsated inside her. Then she felt instant relief as he relinquished his grip on her hair, and eased out of her. The pain slowly ebbed away, and Laura tried to break free. But Pierre gripped her tightly, almost squeezing the breath out of her body, whispering, "Laura, you bitch. You destroyed me. You drove me to this!"

She struggled out of his grasp, and looked at him with disgust. His eyes were dilated with spent lust and his lips were drawn back in an animal snarl. How she hated him! How pathetic and ludicrous he looked with his trousers hanging down! Lejeune caught her look of disdain, and irritated by her dignified contempt, he bent to pull his trousers up, finally zipping the fly as his hair flopped over his flushed face.

"Bitch," he hissed, angrily shrugging it back from his sweaty temples. "I haven't finished with you yet. This is just the beginning. Believe me, you'll have good reason to wipe that arrogant look off your face before long."

But Laura realised that indifference was the most effective weapon. She ignored his threats, and remained unmoved, outstaring him with an icy blue gaze. Pierre had wanted to see her fear; to witness her cowed and humiliated, whereas all he'd gained from this latest sordid outrage was her total contempt. One day, she vowed, she'd make him pay.

"Just go," Laura said coldly. She watched him walk away

curiously defeated: still the victim of his sick, overwhelming obsession for her.

Jennifer didn't get back to the Meribel till ten in the morning. She was floating on a cloud. There was no sign of Henrietta, and Laura was at work. There was a note pinned on her bedroom door. "Julius rang to say he'll be back early next week. I told him you were out with friends. Please ring him soonest, Moxton Leap 843. L & K, Hen."

Jennifer's heart went cold, as reality intruded. What on earth was she going to do now? She was completely besotted with Alexander – had never felt such an overwhelming passion for anyone. It was frightening how much she still wanted him, even now, though aching, chafed, her legs weak and trembling after their vigorous, passionate all-night love-making. The very sound of his voice, his scent, the feel of him permeated all her senses, his body and soul indelibly imprinted on hers. Everything she saw, smelt, touched, heard, was imbued with Alex.

"Oh, help," she groaned out loud.

She owed Julius so much. Her life, no less! In a moment of weakness when she so needed him in the London clinic she'd more or less promised herself to him. What was she to do now? From everyone's point of view, but especially Krep's, her latest behaviour would be morally inexcusable. How would he react to her falling hopelessly in love with another man so soon?

But how could someone like Julius understand the meaning of love anyway? Surely his knight-in-shining-armour act had been underlaid with strong ulterior motives? He'd swayed her when she was weak, which was dishonest. She was a slave of obligation, for ever indebted by her gratitude to him. It was a classic catch twenty-two.

He wanted her, all of her, entirely at his disposal. And then what? Would he grow bored with her and pass her on to his business friends as a trinket, an inducement for yet another deal? If Krep was so used to being motivated by money, lust and greed, why should he ever change? Jennifer shivered. What was she to do?

Chapter 21

At last the great day dawned for Laura, and now here she was, on a Jumbo jet bound for New York. It was an evening flight, luckily not too packed, so she had three seats all to herself near the back of the aeroplane. Her accommodation had been arranged by Howson May, and she was to be met at Kennedy Airport by an employee of the company.

A smiling stewardess was walking down the aisle handing out earphones for the in-flight movie. Laura took a pair, although she was doubtful if she'd be able to concentrate on a film when she had so many things to think about. She studied her armrest controls, flipped her seat back to a reclining position, selected the classical music programme, and shut her eyes, reflecting on recent events.

The ghastly episode with Pierre had caused her great pain and left her scarred with a tremendous sense of betrayal. How could he have reduced the love they had shared to nothing more than a sordid weapon with which to insult her? She'd never wanted the memory of it to turn to poison. What kind of a person was he to twist and warp something so special into such bitterness and hatred? When Laura recalled the viciousness of his attack, it made her skin crawl. Instinctively her hand went to the painful bump on the back of her head, where he had repeatedly banged it against the wall. She shivered at the memory. Pierre had been terrifying.

It didn't seem possible that he could be so warped and cruel: a violent thug, fuelled by revenge and the determination to hold on to her by foul means rather than fair. He obviously felt that he had taken what was rightfully his – the end justifying the means. Nothing she could say, nothing she could do would make him see reason. There was no logic to his behaviour. She could spend the rest of her life brooding over it and still not come up with an answer. It was pointless to speculate; pointless to waste time on anger and recrimination, or to dwell on the rights and wrongs of it.

She must put this whole vicious episode into context. It had happened before, so many times, when she was living with Pierre. It was just a repeat of a past she thought she'd managed to tuck away for ever, and unfortunately, a part of it had escaped into the present. That was, perhaps, a convenient philosophy, but for the moment the only way to look at the situation. Life must go on. She must not lose sight of her goals. If she gave up now, it would be conceding defeat. Pierre would have won by violent, cowardly means. Laura was determined not to let that happen. Thank God she was flying away from it all. Her sense of purpose, her determination to succeed would see her through.

The day after the attack, the girls had been horrified and very protective, never leaving her side. Quintin had demanded she report Lejeune to the police, but Laura refused. There was nothing to gain by it, and she had no wish to relive the experience in front of a certainly hostile audience. It would be too degrading to bear. Besides, she had too much to do, and only two days before her impending trip.

They'd thrown an impromptu leaving-party for her at the disco, but unfortunately it had been spoiled by a blazing row with Jennifer over Julius, who had sent an anxious telex to Laura at Kulikis asking Jennifer to telephone.

Jennifer was not at all pleased. "Oh, Laura, please help me out. Please talk to him for me," she pleaded, when Laura passed on the message. "I really can't face Julius at the moment. I'm hopelessly in love and I don't know what to do. Just give me some breathing space."

"Oh, honestly, Jen," Laura had retorted crossly. "Hopelessly in love, my foot! That's no excuse. I can't believe you've been ignoring Julius all this time. He's obviously worried sick about you. All he wants is to hear your voice, know you're OK. God, after all he's done for you, you're being awfully selfish and ill-mannered!"

"Oh Lord," complained Jennifer, pouring foaming Coke into her glass, which spilled over the top. "Damnation." Irritably she mopped it with a paper napkin. "Why does everyone always hassle me? Jean-bloody-Claude tries to trap me into marriage. Then Julius gets me out of the trap, only to put me into another one called gratitude. What am I supposed to do, spend the rest of my life on my knees to him, saying thank you?"

Laura flopped back into the leather banquette, angrily running her hand through her hair. "I think you're a spoiled and ungrateful brat. The man saved your life, for heaven's sake! The least you could do is thank him. Why snub him when he's been such an angel? It's obvious to me that he's desperately fond of you. He thinks the world of you, and all you can do in return is cavort with that polo-playing poodlefaker."

"Alex is *not* a poodlefaker!" she shouted, her eyes blazing. "Don't you dare call him that! He's absolutely the most adorable man I've ever met."

"Oh, really," Laura said scathingly, "you've been with him for a few hours here and there, mainly horizontal. All you've got is a severe case of the hots. You can't call that true love! Honestly, you don't even know him."

"Well, then, maybe it's time I did," replied Jennifer, jumping to her feet. She was white with rage, and her eyes were cold. "And it's about time you stopped playing the sanctimonious nun from the safety of your self-imposed chastity belt. I'm sick of your sermonising! You're no fun these days. Come to think of it," she added spitefully, "you're probably frustrated, which is why you're so bloody sour."

Laura bridled. She couldn't believe her ears. Jennifer's behaviour was outrageous.

"In that case," she commented coldly, "all I can say is thank heaven I'm not a slut like you. I've got better ways to pass my time than lying flat on my back admiring different ceilings."

"You bitch!" cried Jennifer, jumping to her feet in a rage.

"And what am I supposed to say to Julius?"

"As far as I'm concerned," Jennifer hissed, stalking away, "you can both rot in hell!"

The stewardess interrupted Laura's thoughts with a proffered tray of cold meats, bread roll and salad. She wasn't really hungry, but took it all the same. It would break the monotony of the flight which was due to last another five hours.

As Laura idly fiddled with her food, she brooded on her row with Jennifer. Jennifer's behaviour *had* been intolerable, but then the poor girl had been through the mill that summer. Maybe it had all got on top of her and she'd been temporarily knocked off balance. Was the viscount just a passing escape from reality? Perhaps Laura had been unnecessarily harsh with her.

If only they'd had time to make up their differences before she left for New York, but Jennifer had been so angry that she'd flounced off with Alexander and hadn't returned before Laura's departure, not even for a change of clothes. Not that she'd need any really, given the circumstances, Laura reflected with a wry smile.

Laura resolved that as soon as she had time, she would write to Jennifer and apologise. It was just a silly row. She had been overwrought and should not have been so condemnatory. Pushing her food tray away, she closed her eyes, clamped on her earphones and listened to classical music again to help her relax. It would be her last chance for a while. She had a hard slog ahead of her, but it would be worth it. Success was beckoning. It was exciting to be so near to her goal.

* * *

After the interminable flight, Laura walked into Arrivals at Kennedy Airport, New York, pushing her trolley of luggage. There was a young man at the barrier, holding up a notice with 'Howson May for Miss L. Forsythe' printed on it in large letters. She waved at him, relieved to see a friendly face amongst this enormous, bustling crowd of overweight bodies and unfamiliar accents.

"Good evening, Miss Forsythe," the young man said formally, "I'm here to meet you and take you to your accommodation."

He took her trolley and ushered her outside, where he deposited her and her luggage into a gleaming dark-grey limousine. Although it was the middle of the night for her body-clock, here in New York it was early evening and not yet dark. Laura leaned back into the comfortable seats as the limousine left the airport behind. She took in her surroundings which were as different as they could possibly be from the small, winding, tortuous roads and rocky, colourful scenery of the Riviera.

Laura had often seen pictures or films of the Manhattan skyline, but nothing prepared her for reality of it when it eventually came in to view; the sensation of actually being there. The size and scale of the buildings looming up around her was utterly awe-inspiring. Laura was wide eyed and open-mouthed at the towering immensity of the skyscrapers, sheer columns of glass, steel and concrete rising up on either side of her, making the traffic and people scurrying about seem Lilliputian and unreal.

"Have you been to the States before, ma'am?" the chauffeur asked, noting her amazement in his rear mirror with some amusement.

"No. This is my first time, and I'm quite staggered," she replied.

"Quite a city, this. Seein' is believin'. Let me give you some advice, though." The rapid-fire delivery of speech was like bullets out of a machine-gun. "Don't walk around alone after dark, OK?" he continued, "Always call for a cab in the evenings if you need to go out, and when you go shopping, keep your eyes in front of you, and walk on the outside edge of the kerb, not near the buildings, just in case someone jumps you from a doorway."

A far cry from Monaco, where one could stroll around anywhere and at any time without a care in the world. Or maybe not, on second thoughts. At home she'd had to beware of the lurking Pierre, instead of strangers in dark doorways!

"I don't think I'll be going out in the evenings," she said, daunted. "I'll be studying."

"It won't be so bad where I'm taking you. It's a nice area you'll be staying in, Miss Forsythe. The company apartments are on Fifth and Seventy-fourth. Easy trip downtown to Wall Street on the Subway, 'bout twenty minutes, no problem."

"Which one's mine, Fifth or Seventy-fourth?"

The chauffeur laughed. "No, miss. The building is at the corner of Seventy-fourth Street on Fifth Avenue, geddit?"

Laura was not sure she did, but supposed she would soon get familiar with New York's geography, its transport system, and to the quick, staccato way of talking, the paucity of words when being given directions – the assumption that everything was 'quick and easy, no problem'.

She had never seen so much traffic. So many people, almost wedged together in one mass, but nevertheless moving, a constantly changing kaleidoscope of large, unfamiliar vehicles, constantly hooting their horns. Hundreds of yellow cabs, steam emanating from manholes in the road, pedestrian lights commanding 'WALK' and 'DON'T WALK' alternately, a milling mass of people and sights that made her head spin. The shop fronts were enormous, too; huge expanses of plate glass, shimmering and crammed with luxury and glamour that caught the eye and turned the head. Was anything insignificant or immobile over here? Even the gigantic skyscrapers had a life of their own, catching the light and reflecting the sky as they stretched impossibly towards the roof of the world. This was the most unbelievably exciting town. Maybe the danger would add an edge to it.

Yes, Laura thought, I think I can handle this all right.

Next morning, if it had not been so full of panic, Laura would have laughed at the chauffeur's bland, "Subway's easy – no problem." She got up very early as she'd been fitfully awake from 2 a.m. New York time. Until she adjusted to the five hour difference, the middle of the night was early morning back in Monaco and dawn her old lunch-time.

It was strange not being able to open windows for fresh air, and difficult to ignore the hum of the air-conditioning which replaced that option. Neither could she get the room temperature right. It was pre-set too cold, but when she fiddled with the thermostat, she got too hot and nearly died of suffocation. Consequently, she hadn't had much sleep. It didn't matter, as she was so pent up with excitement that she wasn't tired when she rose at 7 a.m.

The shower was a revelation. A torrent coming out of a huge, wide showerhead, fingertip adjustable and very efficient. In fact, rather too efficient! She had learned very quickly to cover her nipples with her hands to stop them being beaten to death by the powerful jets – a very painful experience for the unwary. And the rapping of the water on the top of her head nearly deafened her: it was like being caught in a scalding hail storm. Laura was beginning to cotton on that the Americans do nothing in half measures!

Laura arrived at the nearest subway station very early, but when she asked the man in the ticket kiosk for Wall Street, he ignored her. Then she was practically lifted off her feet by the flood of people following her, and jostled towards the barrier. People were streaming all around her in droves. She felt like a piece of jetsam, wedged against a rock in fast-moving rapids, which could be dislodged and submerged any moment by the forceful current round her and carried away to an unknown fate.

Nobody acknowledged her requests for information. No-one answered her pleas for advice. Eventually and with all the force she could muster, she pushed her way back through the fast-moving and anonymous stream of humanity. She found a small space between the kiosk and the wall, where she could observe, unencumbered by jostling commuters, exactly what one had to do to get through the magic barrier. Eventually the penny dropped. Everyone was holding a round chip which they slotted into the barrier to release the turnstile and allow them through. Obviously what she needed was one of these tokens which one obtained at the kiosk. Why hadn't the ticket man told her it was that simple, instead of ignoring her so rudely? Now she had wasted ten precious minutes fighting the crowds.

Laura pushed back to the kiosk, dodging commuters hellbent on fighting their way to work, then dashed in between two hurrying grey suits, and asked for a token, tendering a dollar bill. The curt attendant slapped down a slotted coin and gave her the change. She allowed herself to be carried in the surging, human current this time, popped in her token and followed the crowd down to the trains, hoping every train would stop at Wall Street. After all, wasn't Wall Street the hub of everything?

Laura hopped on to the next train, hoping for the best. The train ran very fast. Terrifyingly so; shaking and screaming, rattling from side to side; it was amazing it didn't de-rail itself or self-destruct! She wanted to ask someone for instructions, but everyone was too preoccupied, staring into space or reading papers, leg-watching, straphanging and jolting with the train's movement, anything to avoid eye-contact. She felt surrounded by anonymous robots who had been pre-programmed to follow a certain path without deviation or interruption. It was like being on an alien planet. She had never felt more isolated.

A quarter of an hour later, Laura was still sitting on the train, which had screamed into several stations, swallowing and regurgitating passengers like so many busy ants. Then, all of a sudden she realised she was quite alone. She felt uneasy. Something was obviously wrong. The carriage was completely empty; all the seats were bare. Where on earth was she now? Where would the train end up? There was no one to ask, not a soul around – no way of finding out where she was. What's more, now the train had emerged into daylight and some vast, sprawling suburb of mind-numbing ugliness.

Suddenly the adjoining door burst open while the train was screeching round a bend that went on for ever. A huge black man in dark clothes stood in the doorway, looking menacing, and Laura jumped with fear, her heart pounding.

"What are you doing, lady?" rasped the voice. It was unfriendly, threatening.

"I don't know," said Laura, petrified. "I want Wall Street."

The huge black face scowled. "You won't find it here, lady. We're going round the loop. You're not supposed to be on the train."

He sounded very aggressive and irritated. Laura was relieved at least to see he was some kind of official, most likely a guard, from his uniform.

"I'm sorry," she stammered, "I'm completely lost and I don't know my way around. What's the loop?"

"The loop, lady, is what we go round in order to come back again, and start over."

"Oh dear!" she replied, flummoxed and running her hand through her hair distractedly. "What shall I do then?"

The guard, touched by her flustered innocence and unfamiliar accent, suddenly relented and broke into a friendly grin.

"Ain't much you can do, lady, 'cept stay put now," he said,

taking off his hat and scratching his wiry curls. "Tell you what, if it's Wall Street you want, all you have to do is get out at Fourteenth and then change. Easy as that! We're going back the way we came, back uptown, so you can't miss it. But you still shouldn't be on the loop!"

He shook his head, clapped his hat back on and grinned, his huge white teeth contrasting with the blackness of his face.

"Did you ever hear the like of it?" he muttered to himself, chuckling, "Only ever find drunks and stiffs on the loop, 'cos they's past knowin' or carin'." He added, "Get off at Fourteenth Street, and change for Wall, OK?" He passed down the carriage and disappeared, still chuckling, into the next carriage.

Laura wondered if she'd be late now. It was already twenty to nine and she was due in at nine to start the course. Damn. And she'd left Seventy-fourth Street just after eight o'clock to leave a wide margin of time. If only she'd left sooner. But she had been told that the journey was only twenty minutes downtown, and a cinch. A cinch to New Yorkers, that is, she thought ruefully, not to a girl totally unused to the big city.

When she finally arrived at her destination, Laura was late, but only by a few minutes. She apologised profusely, and thought the course tutor was unnecessarily harsh with her in the circumstances. He could have made some allowances, some concession, given the fact that she was a stranger abroad, and a very young one at that. Instead, he gave her a stern lecture on time-wasting, which she bore gracefully, though she couldn't help noting the smug looks on the faces of her co-students. Fourteen of them, all male, who obviously already knew the ropes. They had doubtless arrived well before nine, their pencils sharpened and their clipboards ready.

Ruffled, Laura found an empty chair, and sank into it, wishing it were oblivion. Nobody smiled or looked her way. Nobody looked sympathetic. The instructor looked an absolute beast: he had a huge nose and bulbous eyes, and his mouth was mean. He looked like a grey vulture, ready for the kill, ready to peck at the vulnerable and defenceless. He made no attempt to help Laura settle in as a new student, but just continued with the lesson in a somewhat irritated manner. He gave no hint of what she'd missed, what page they were on, or what topic they were covering that day. Laura didn't dare ask, having too obviously blotted her copybook already, so she surreptitiously glanced at her neighbour's textbook. Quietly and with a sinking heart at having made such a bad first impression, she turned to the corresponding page of the book in front of her.

All the men around her looked so confident, smart and attentive, taking notes assiduously, their eyes shining with endeavour, every so often nodding meaningfully, with a male complicity that excluded her. She wondered if she'd be able to compete in such a negative environment. Were they university graduates? Were they the rich and privileged sons of successful fathers with firms of their own to inherit eventually? Laura would have to work very hard to prove her worth in this chauvinistic atmosphere. It was bad enough to be the only female in a thoroughly male preserve, but her accent set her aside too as a complete oddity, making her feel even more alienated.

It was an ignominious start and Laura was afraid she would soon be bitterly regretting the ambitious streak that had brought her to New York.

Chapter 22

Jennifer delayed her return to the Meribel until the day after Laura's departure. She, too, was desperately sorry they'd had such a row, but even though she wanted to make up, she had been unable to face another disapproving lecture from Laura. Especially as she didn't have a leg to stand on. Jennifer had been hoping all along that everything would come right in the end. She'd been putting off her problems till tomorrow as always, knowing that tomorrow always turns into today ultimately.

The concierge of the Meribel looked up in surprise, blinking his small, beady eyes. At last the other demoiselle had returned, looking unusually preoccupied. It was already midday. He had important news for her. He raced out from behind his desk, gesticulating wildly, the moment she came in through the large entrance doors.

"*Mademoiselle!*" he cried. "*Mademoiselle! Regardez dehors là, dans la rue. Elle est pour vous. Là! Regardez!*"

He grabbed her wrist and pointed outside. Jennifer didn't have a clue what he meant, and looked totally blank. In a frenzy, he pushed her out into the road and steered her towards a beautiful silver sports car, parked right outside the block, which she hadn't even noticed on her way in. She'd been too wrapped up in her thoughts.

"*Une belle Mercedès, mademoiselle! Regardez!*" He was beside himself with excitement.

"Yes, I'm looking at it!" she replied impatiently. "So?"

The concierge's eyes were like organ stops. He gabbled

away at full pelt, mentioning Krep's name several times. At last it dawned on an incredulous Jennifer that the silver Mercedes convertible was a present for her from Julius.

"Wow!" she whistled. "Unbelievable!"

Then the concierge pushed into her hand a set of ignition keys, which she was fingering with stunned disbelief. The concierge, always ready for business, was already asking her if she wanted to rent a parking slot in the underground car park across the way. It was true one couldn't leave such a beautiful car parked in a busy avenue.

"*Attendez, attendez un peu!*" Jennifer reprimanded.

This was just too much to take in. She'd have to return a present like this. I mean flowers, bikinis and negligées, OK – but a sports car costing several thousands? Anyway, she'd forgotten how to drive! She walked round and round the beautiful vehicle, her mouth watering. Wouldn't she just love to swan around in something like that? Her friends would drop dead with envy. Then, somewhere from the dim and not-so-distant past, a little message flashed in her brain, reminding her of her resolve never to swap true love for unadulterated luxury and riches. Could she live up to it now?

"Oh God!" she whispered despondently, lovingly stroking the gleaming silver bodywork, and taking in the rich patina and expensive smell of the leather upholstery. "Hell . . . What now, Morgan?"

Her hands caressed the squashy cream leather seats longingly. This was a real dilemma.

"You'll have to give it back," she whispered to herself. "You know you really must!"

Was the tone of her present resolve a little half-hearted? She looked at the keys, and wondered what it would feel like to sit in the driving seat. It was all too much to take in. Suddenly, Alexander appeared at her side. She'd temporarily forgotten him as she'd been so knocked sideways by Krep's present.

He'd just driven her back to the Meribel for a quick change of clothes, having parked his Alfa further down the avenue.

"Oh hell!" she exclaimed under her breath. This was not something she could share with Alex. Far too complicated to explain, it would surely jeopardise their burgeoning relationship. Quickly she stuffed the leather fob into her bag.

"Hi!" she smiled disarmingly, and turned towards the Meribel's entrance door.

"Golly!" he exclaimed, taking in the Mercedes. "What a beauty! Some lucky owner there!"

Jennifer tried to distract him from it. "Come on, darling. Let's get moving." But Alex stopped to inspect the car more closely. Damn! She turned back impatiently.

"Why were you running your hands longingly all over it just now?" he asked, smiling teasingly into her eyes. "Have you just stolen it?"

"Not in so many words," whispered Jennifer, non-plussed, then fibbed. "It belongs to a friend of mine."

"Who to?" Alex's voice registered surprise.

"Oh, no one you know," she blustered quickly. "It's not important. I'm just looking after it for a while."

"Well, lucky old you, that's all I can say!" he remarked admiringly.

But Jennifer had started to walk away, hoping he'd follow, and drop the subject. It was all getting too complicated. At last Alex tore himself away from the car, and followed her into the Meribel. Phew, what a close one! Jennifer's heart was in her mouth, and she was sure her face was crimson with embarrassment. Perhaps she could blame it on the heat.

As soon as they entered the flat, though, things went from bad to worse. Henrietta had left her a note pinned to the bedroom door, which Alex saw before Jennifer could hide it:

"Dearest J, Kept meaning to tell you Julius came back a couple of days ago. Sorry I forgot. Too busy with Q! Can you ring him at yacht soonest? xxxxxx Hen. PS Miss you!"

Damn and double damn, swore Jennifer silently. What now? Alex was looking livid.

"Julius, eh?" he said scathingly. "Surely not the fat little millionaire on the *Xerina*! What the hell does he want with you?"

"He's just a friend," Jennifer replied, bridling.

"A friend? Of that common, jumped-up little toad? Oh, nice one, Jennifer." Alex's eyes were cold and critical.

God, she thought, he's beginning to sound like the odious Jean-Claude.

"Oh, don't be such a snob," she shouted angrily. "And mind your own business. My friends are my concern. You're not my keeper."

Alex was dumbstruck, and stared at her with disbelief. Eventually he said quietly, "I don't like your tone of voice, and there's definitely more to this than meets the eye. Is there something you haven't told me?"

Jennifer's heart sank. How could she even begin to explain? "It's more than a little complicated," she began hesitantly.

Alex gazed at her scathingly, running his fingers through his hair, then flicked the thick hazel mop back decisively. "Well, as you obviously don't want to tell me," he said, his hazel eyes dead and lifeless, "I might as well push off right now. I don't like bad temper, or dishonesty."

"Suit yourself," she said sulkily, though inside her heart was breaking.

She felt her whole world collapsing, but was too proud to plead with Alexander. She wanted to call him back, but somehow she couldn't. Devastated and tearful she stood and watched as he walked out of the flat, head bent and shoulders slumped, and slammed the door. It was too late now to explain.

Jennifer was very heated and after pacing around in agitation for a while, took a cold shower to calm herself down. She spent ages letting the water cascade all over her. She needed to keep busy doing little things, mundane things, anything to numb the dull pain inside. She took a long time drying herself, re-doing her face carefully. She studied her wardrobe before finally getting dressed; all in slow-motion and all to stave off the eventual self-appraisal she felt she couldn't face. She poured herself a stiff brandy, and winced as the strong liquid burned down her throat.

Eventually she told herself that she simply had to face up to the fact that her selfishness was alienating everyone. Not just Alex, but perhaps more undeservedly still, Laura and Julius. Who would be next in line? It was time to take her head out of the sand. Julius was back. She could no longer ignore him. It wasn't fair to him. Whatever his motives were, he had been good to her. He had saved her life. The car had added a new dimension to her dilemma, an expensive reality that made her sit up. Overcome with remorse, she decided at last to phone him. But first she had to arm herself with a good reason for her reluctance to contact him these past few days, a viable excuse.

"Damn it, I wish Laura were here!" she grumbled. "She'd know what to do in a situation like this."

Gradually it filtered through to her that she couldn't think up any excuse, because there was none. Not even if she dredged the murkiest depths of subterfuge. She'd been floating around in a romantic dream and enjoying it so much that she'd neglected the people who really mattered; the ones who'd rallied round without any hesitation and with total selflessness when she needed them.

Laura was so right. How could Jennifer ever explain or justify her thoughtlessness? It was impossible. With any luck, maybe Julius wouldn't ask what had been going on. He'd surely be so pleased to hear from her that she could be suitably vague about the last few days. Perhaps pretend she'd gone away alone to think things over? He certainly didn't want or need to know the truth. Who was to know whether Alex would ever come back? The very thought was like a kick in the gut, but why burn all her boats on a romantic dream that had possibly ended? If that were the case, Julius could be her sheet anchor. Anyway, she owed him. He'd pulled out all the stops for her, without a moment's hesitation when she needed him.

At last she steeled herself, and composed his number. The telephone rang and rang. No reply. Maybe he was out at lunch. She was rattled because she'd finally plucked up the courage to face her responsibilities and had been thwarted, her resolution nipped in the bud.

She took herself off into the kitchen to make a cup of tea. The flat was hot, so she opened the windows, unsuccessfully trying to wedge them to stop them swinging about. Stupid country! Had they never heard of window-stays? And the French *would* have windows that opened inwards, just to be annoying.

Jennifer prowled around the flat like a bored cat, jumping out of her skin each time the windows banged, and wishing she hadn't quarrelled with Alexander. It would have been so much better to have levelled with him in the first place, then none of this would have happened. She had only herself to blame. Why on earth, though, she thought, did he have to be so unutterably gorgeous? Alex had so totally turned her head that she'd been in the clouds. She hadn't been able to resist floating in his aura at the expense of everyone else. And now her dream was shattered, and she felt utterly miserable.

When the phone rang, she dashed across to it, hoping it would be Alexander. Perhaps he was regretting his anger.

"Hello?" Jennifer said, her heart skipping a beat.

"Is that you at last, duckie?" came the familiar voice.

Her face fell.

"Julius!" she said, carefully masking her disappointment. "Where've you been? Why didn't you come to the club to see me?"

"Come now, precious," Julius chided, "don't kid me. You were like a broken phone: permanently unobtainable. You're the one that's been avoiding me!"

"I haven't!" Jennifer fibbed. "I've tried to ring you several times. Anyway Julius, I've got a mammoth bone to pick with you. Why in heaven's name did you send me that beautiful car?"

"I haven't sent it. I'm giving it to you," he replied. "As you haven't the energy to pay me a visit or pick up a phone, I thought a nice pair of wheels would get your moving!"

"Whaaat?" Jennifer exaggerated the word. "Julius, you know I couldn't possibly accept a present like that! It's too unbelievably fabulous for words."

"Well, then," he persuaded her, "how's about getting into the driving seat and seeing just how fabulous it is to drive, on your way down to me? Then we can discuss ethics and things."

Ethics and things. What things? Like when would she go to bed with him? How long could she go on stalling him, before he became angry, insistent on his reward? But now was the time to confront him head on. She would have to tell him the truth, that she was infinitessimally grateful to him and would be for ever more, but she couldn't bring herself to sleep with him. What would be his reaction? Resentment? Fury? Would he force himself on her? Look what happened to poor Laura, and she owed the wretched Pierre nothing, had not been indebted to him in any way.

"All right, then," she agreed slowly. "What time? But I'll walk, I'm too petrified to drive a brand new Merc."

"Sweetheart," he laughed, "just start the engine, point her in the right direction and she'll cruise along without any help from you. She's all automatic. Easiest thing in the world to drive."

"Well, I don't know . . ." said Jennifer hesitantly. She would have to return the car, but she didn't fancy crashing it on the way down to him. She would already be in enough trouble when she levelled with him, let alone pranging his brand new Merc!

"Tell you what," he suggested, "I'll come up at four o'clock to show you the ropes, and then we can go for a short spin. I'll put a white carnation in my buttonhole so's you'll recognise me. How about that?"

She had to smile wryly as she put down the phone. In the space of five minutes that cunning Julius had manoeuvred her into a corner; Jennifer the arch-manipulator of all time! No wonder he'd become a millionaire so early in life, with persuasive techniques like that. What company, what business could resist a golden touch like his?

Perhaps seeing Julius, going for a drive would take her mind off the hurt inside. Anything was better than being alone, waiting for a silent phone to ring. That was agony.

Jennifer lit a cigarette, and went out to the balcony. It was only a little cooler than inside, and she had a couple of hours to kill. She stretched out on the chaise-longue and suddenly felt rather sleepy. She'd had a long night, or rather a series of long nights. Yawning languorously, she put the cigarette down, and allowed herself to drift off into somnolence.

Images of Alex – smiling, carefree – of sun-filled days of laughter and soft nights, their bodies entwined, his tenderness and passion, crowded into her dreams, and imbued her with regret. Life was so unfair. If only she had met him a year ago, before everything got so complicated and out of hand.

Why did Alex have to be such an unforgettable and unbearably sexy lover? Why did Julius have to be so rich, tempting her with all his power and luxury? Why couldn't she have them both? Would she ever see Alex again?

As the day progressed, Laura recovered from her initial dressing-down and concentrated on absorbing the facts and tips being crammed into them all. She began to feel herself rising to the challenge she had undertaken. At first, she found the tutor's accent very hard to understand, as he spoke very fast, in a grating voice. Then she gradually acclimatised and was able to follow him with the visual prompt of the textbook provided. She was relieved to discover that the technical points he was covering were all familiar, thanks to her broking course and her prior knowledge of the business.

At eleven o'clock they had a break, and the young man who'd been next to her during the lesson offered to get her a coffee. He had very short, brush-cut hair, brown eyes and looked to be in his late twenties. Thank heaven someone was at last being friendly.

"Oh, thanks. I'll come with you," she said, relieved, "I don't know my way around at all. My name's Laura, by the way. Laura Forsythe."

He shook her proffered hand formally. "Pretty name," he said. "Mine's Andrew Packard. Are you from England?"

Laura smiled. "You guessed right."

"Pretty dumb question, really," he grinned, setting a beaker under the spout marked 'Coffee'. "It's obvious from your voice. But say, aren't you kind of young to be doing this?"

The coffee hissed and spluttered into the white beaker. He put it to one side, and repeated the process for himself.

"Yes," she answered, "probably the youngest in the class. I had my twenty-first two weeks ago!"

"Wow," he said, impressed. Then his brow furrowed. "But why's an English girl doing American exams? Don't you have your own famous Stock Exchange in London?"

"Yes, we do, but it's an all-male bastion at present. Inherited partnerships, the old-boy network; that sort of thing. You have to start as a blue-button on the Stock Exchange Floor, and as women are not yet allowed to tread that hallowed ground it's a non-starter for the female sex!"

Laura grinned wryly at Andrew's surprised face. The Americans appeared to have a more lenient and modern attitude towards women in business than the British, but it didn't alter the fact that she was still the only female candidate

311

out of a total of fifteen! "That'll all change one day," she continued, "but not soon enough for me. That's why I'm over here taking your exams!"

"You going to be a dealer then, the first to break with tradition?"

Laura laughed. "Heavens, no, I'm going be a broker with Howson in Monaco. In the South of France," she prompted, at his blank expression. "Anyway, they're called jobbers in the UK, and it's too complicated and boring to explain the differences between the London system and here."

"White with sugar?" he asked. "And you can call me Andy. Everyone does. I'm with Howson in Boston. Flunked my exams twice, and this is my last chance!"

"Thanks. Milk, no sugar." Laura accepted the paper cup from him. What a relief to hear that her co-students weren't all smart Alecs!

She smiled at Andrew, "Well, here's to success this time, then! Third time lucky."

Laura felt considerably more confident when she rejoined the class after the break. Andrew introduced her to a couple of colleagues, and they all seemed much more friendly than she'd first dared to hope. Now she felt far less an outsider. The vulture still rasped on in his unsympathetic way, the class took notes, scratching away on their clipboards, and Laura absorbed as much as she could, determined to give the exams her very best shot. Her face fell when the vulture, whose name was Vass, handed out NASD manuals to them all. The books weighed a ton, and were at least three inches thick.

"Now," he hectored, "I expect each and every one of you to know this manual inside out and back to front, or you'll never make it through. This is your Bible!"

An audible sigh went round the room, and hearts collectively sank at the prospect of having to wade through such a book, let alone learn its contents by rote.

The rest of the morning was uneventful, except for the

titters Laura provoked when she pronounced 'leverage' to rhyme with 'beaver', whereas the Americans rhyme it with 'clever'. Her answer to Vass' question on the advantages of margin trading then turned out to be spot-on and very comprehensive. The tittering subsided quickly, to be replaced by an envious unease and the realisation that this young blonde was by no means a dumb one.

Lunch was extraordinary. They all crammed into a fast-food Burger place, which had no tables. Instead there were narrow circular shelves around columns, where people put their drinks, and ate their hamburgers standing up. Everyone was in a rush. No leisurely lunches over glasses of wine in Wall Street. It was a snatch-and-grab affair. Sandwiches at your desk, or burgers standing up, with diners packed shoulder to shoulder as far as the eye could see, and shouted, frantic dialogue. A far cry from the sunny Digue, or the Metropole and long, lazy lunches by the pool. If Fitz could see me now, Laura thought, smiling in amazement at the strangeness of it all.

After lunch, the trainees were taken on a tour of brokerage, the division that was relevant to them in the Howson building. There were countless other floors as well, containing analysts, settlement clerks, accounts offices, the International Department, Personnel, the Chief Executives, and many, many more. Other parts of the vast Howson building were leased out to different companies.

The trainees were given a very brief welcome speech and an introduction to Howson May, New York, and a resumé of the company's make-up, including the vast network of branches throughout the States. Then followed a guided tour by the Chief of Personnel, whose name was Bob Dawson. He was a very tall, gangly man with a freckled face and pale, thinning hair. Bob was to be the one who would deliver the exam results in a couple of weeks' time to all the students in turn, summoning them separately into his office for the bad or glad tidings.

The brokerage department, which was endless, was separated by partitions into various divisions. There was a private clients division, mainly manned by younger brokers, and an institutional section manned by greyer heads. There were also areas given over to bonds and other specialised securities. On the electronic tape, which had superseded the noisy Reuters' ticker of their less sophisticated European cousins, were share prices and large-volume transactions. They flashed by second by second, all round the edge of the room at ceiling height, an endless green snaking ribbon of news that could make or break fortunes. Nobody took their eyes off the flickering green neon for long. It was the whole meaning of life here, and an eighth of a dollar either way, however trite it might seem, made one hell of a difference in any transaction.

Laura had never seen such an enormous company in all her life, and was amazed that this was only a fraction of the Howson empire. The place was a hive of activity, and the business generated must have been incalculable. So many phones, such a cacophony of voices, each conversation leading to transactions worth thousands of dollars! Secretaries and young men dashed from desk to desk, snatching up bits of paper, frantically staring at the prices flashing by, consulting each other then snatching up the phone again to make another deal. It was a very exciting yet daunting atmosphere to be in. Laura longed to be part of it.

She could see her dreams enacted in front of her, see with her own eyes that the reality was even more exciting than she could possibly have imagined. Why couldn't she stay on here in New York? It seemed so enthralling to her. Laura gazed around her, spellbound with awe and envy, and wondered if she could handle the pace, day in, day out. Perhaps she was luckier to have only one big client to cope with. Fewer orders, but bigger. Blocks of shares worth a fortune every time. It had to be easier than coping with numerous small transactions from hundreds of different clients! Oh, but Howson May, New York, was so exciting!

Then Laura was suddenly brought back to reality and ushered away, though reluctantly, to the humdrum business of cramming. The rest of the day flew by, interspersed with coffee breaks. Everyone's head was bursting with rules and regulations. Upticks and downticks, settlements, dealing in odd-lots, short and long sales, put and call options, and all the minutiae of the brokerage trade. It seemed absolutely endless, and Laura's brain felt like a conveyor belt.

At last the first day was over. She set off for her temporary home, wondering if her head could accommodate anything more, the dreaded manual tucked under her arm. She'd have to learn a section per evening until she'd covered the entire contents over the coming two weeks.

Then she'd have to face the moment of truth, the culmination of all her hard work. She had to pass the two major examinations that would change her life and lead on to success and fortune! Everything she'd dreamed of, strived for, sacrificed her summer for, hinged on the outcome of those four fateful hours.

The telephone rang shrilly and broke Jennifer's reverie. Good heavens, four o'clock! Had she really been dreaming for two hours? Sleepily, she walked across to the phone and picked it up.

"Jen, love, I'm down in the lobby. Get your skates on, I can't wait to see you."

She picked up her bag, ran a comb through her hair, and made her way to the lobby. As she came out of the lift, she started. Facing her was a small, elegant man, impeccably dressed, who resembled Julius and could have been his younger brother. Her face must have been quite a picture, because suddenly the stranger erupted into laughter.

"Well," he said, "how about a kiss for old Juli, then?"

"Julius?" Jennifer faltered. She couldn't believe her eyes.

Gone was the moustache and the greased-back hair. Gone also was at least two stone. This man looked fifteen years younger. His face was tanned and she could see the line of his jaw instead of double chins. His hair was a wavy dark brown, and stylishly cut.

"Well," he asked feigning innocence, "are you going to keep me waiting for ever for this kiss?"

He held out his arms, smiling. Jennifer felt herself responding with affection as he enveloped her in a bearhug. She was surprised at how pleased she was to see him again. How strange it was not to feel her usual revulsion at such close physical contact with him. She took his arm as he steered her out into the street. Jennifer was speechless and couldn't get over the change in his appearance. It was a complete metamorphosis. In less than a month he had become another person, a new Julius.

He looked at her with amusement. "Lost our tongue then, have we?" he teased, his eyes twinkling.

This new Julius was a revelation. It was going to take some time to adjust to the fact that he was by no stretch of the imagination repulsive now. He was even attractive. Debonair, well-dressed and eminently respectable. Gone was the vulgar wide-boy, the flash dresser with his appalling seersucker suits and loud two-tone shoes. Now he was dressed in a dark, well-cut blazer and immaculate dark grey trousers. His shoes were a plain, classic black, and polished to a mirror finish.

What was she to make of this? She had forgotten in the rush of infatuation for Alex how much she'd liked Julius' chirpy personality even when he was fat and vulgarly dressed. She'd forgotten that for all her suspicions of his motives, she still couldn't help enjoying his company.

She was flummoxed, her large grey eyes as round as a kitten's. "Yes, I think I have," she said. "I'm totally flabbergasted. You're practically unrecognisable."

But Julius just smiled disarmingly, deliberately playing down his change of image. "Have you got the keys to the jalopy, sweetness?"

"Yes, in my bag. Just a sec."

As she rummaged for the key, she shot him another glance, shaking her head incredulously. She noticed he was making his way to the passenger seat.

"No, please!" she pleaded. "You drive first, and I'll watch. I don't want to have a prang in front of the beastly concierge."

"Coward," he laughed.

They set off seconds later, with Julius at the wheel. The silver car purred expensively past the Casino gardens, down the avenue des Spelugues, *en route* for the quiet and abandoned site of Monte-Carlo's demolished railway station.

"Right," commanded Julius. "Out you get, madam. Let's swap places."

He switched off the ignition and applied the handbrake. Obediently she slid into the driver's seat. With Julius' patient and thorough instructions, from starting the car and taking off the handbrake, through to putting her into gear, Jennifer was soon driving the Mercedes as if she'd done so for years.

"OK, sweetness," declared Julius, when he was fully satisfied with her expertise, "where are you going to take me?" His eyes swivelled across to her artfully. "I'm your willing passenger for now and always."

He put his hand over hers possessively, and smiled into her eyes.

Jennifer's thoughts were a mass of contradictions. She felt less inclined to come clean with Julius now. She should maybe think twice about burning her boats with him. It was true she was still besotted with Alex, but it would be wiser to continue seeing Julius, keeping the relationship platonic. Then she could cover all her options. If Alex came back she could edge away tactfully, and if not, Julius would be there to console her. Who knows? She might even become fond of him. Julius was so good to her, and it was wonderful to be spoiled and cosseted.

"I think I'll just point the car in the right direction and let her cruise along and surprise us!" she teased, deciding to play it by ear.

Jennifer drove the silver sports car to Beaulieu. She'd enjoyed the drive and being at the wheel of such an enviable car. It made her feel very glamorous and privileged. It was exciting to have a millionaire lifestyle. Julius told her to park at La Reserve, and they made their way to the terrace by the pool, to sit under one of the yellow umbrellas, overlooking the sprawling coast in both directions. Visiting La Reserve was the height of luxury.

The sea was a glittering aquamarine. Behind them the mountain-face loomed sheer, menacing and pockmarked, bare of life or greenery, reaching palely into the sky like a giant cliff in a moonscape. Beaulieu nestled narrowly between the towering mountain and the sea. Adjacent to the luxury Reserve Hotel were the beginnings of an ambitious marina that would eventually breathe new life into the sleepy, olde-worlde town. To their right, the bay of Cap Ferrat curled lazily into the sea, its slopes clothed in pine trees and dotted with luxurious and grandiose villas, stucco-fronted, pillared and balustraded. The rocky outcrops that jutted into the sea were moonscape white, the terracotta soil in their crevices sprouting wild fig trees, agaves and plumbago.

Although they were only twenty minutes from Monaco the scenery was already very different – somehow wild and unspoiled. This was the charm of the Côte d'Azur. The settings were all breathtaking, but each headland, each bay, had features peculiar to itself, which made the area so full of magical surprises.

"Well?" Jennifer demanded over a glass of ice-cold white wine in the late afternoon sun. "I'm dying of curiosity. How on earth did you do it?"

"Do what?" asked Julius, playing dumb. He took a languid sip from his glass, and smiled at her. His teeth looked very white against his dark tan, and his slate blue eyes danced, lighting up his face appealingly. She couldn't stop staring at him. The change was so extraordinary. As if he'd gone back to how he must have been in his early forties. He'd already told her he was fifty-three. Before, he looked all of that . . . and then some!

She replied, "You know perfectly well what. How did the fat frog turn into a prince?"

"OK," he relented, "since you're bursting to know, I decided to take myself in hand, as I'd let myself go a bit, you know. So I went to a health farm, did the whole works, diet, workouts, massage, mud-baths – even facials. Good as gold I was, nibbling lettuce, pumping iron, swimming up and down the pool all day! Never do anything in half-measures, me. Then I booked a day with this 'image consultant', who revamped the old Krep from hairstyle down to clothes. Everything. Everything that is, except the voice, but a bit too late for that, eh?"

He laughed, and winked at her. She grinned. She couldn't possibly imagine him 'talking posh'. It would have been too much!

"Tell you what, though;" he continued, "I was so impressed with the joint, I bought it. Lock, stock and barrel of mud!"

"You didn't!" said Jennifer, impressed. "You actually bought a health farm? But who's going to run it?"

"No problem. I took on the whole shebang, staff, manager and all. Your fault, you know; you shouldn't have complained about my pot-belly. Anyway, I'm never one for letting a good thing get away. I had some residue left after bidding successfully for a group of supermarkets. Can't let money lie idle, can I? It was too obviously a goldmine, that place!"

"Well, you shouldn't complain, then. You look fabulous. Are you going to keep it up?"

"With you around, darling, it's up all the time!" he chuckled.

Typical, she thought. He's back to his old perky ways in no time at all! She was going to have a job keeping him at bay.

"Julius, you've got a one-track mind," Jennifer chided. "You know perfectly well what I mean. Are you going to keep up this routine of diet and exercise?"

She noticed he'd only drunk half a glass of wine. Then he ordered Perrier with a slice of lemon. He was obviously taking his new regime very seriously. Jennifer preferred to stick to wine. She needed to relax because she had so many things on her mind.

"Yup, not half. I like myself this way; clothes hang better and feel comfortable round the middle! Makes me a lot more on the ball businesswise. Bags of energy now. You're going to have to watch out!"

Oh, damn! How much longer could she fend him off?

His eyes took on a lustful glitter. He took her hand and kissed the tips of her fingers. Jennifer didn't flinch from his touch, but she needed time to think. She was still cautious of his motives. Still unsure of Alex. She needed time to sort herself out. The last thing she wanted now was an uncomfortable tussle with a randy and demanding Julius, albeit a somewhat more desirable one.

"Watch out for what?" she asked evasively.

"Hah!" he barked, smiling. "No excuse, now; you said you'd quite fancy me without my paunch. Anyway," he added, "if I'm a prince now, shouldn't you already be kissing my hand?"

Then Julius turned serious. He looked at her with concern. "You OK now, love?" His voice was quieter. "Everything settled down, eh?"

"Well," she lied, "I think I'm nearly there. Just shell-shocked, if you know what I mean." She put on a convincingly delicate air. Julius would be more patient and understanding if she played on her fragility.

Julius put his hand over hers gently. "Sweetie, I'm not going to rush at you like a bull in a china shop, so relax, all right?"

Jennifer looked at Julius quizzically. Was he calling her bluff? Was he being a clever strategist, putting her at ease, softening her up prior to the kill? He was too clever by half. Jennifer was used to being the wily one, but she'd met her match with Julius. This was like a complicated chess game, with him as the more experienced player.

"About the car, sweetie," he went on, "it's yours to keep, with no strings attached. I want you to have it. You've had a bad time and I want to spoil you rotten. Believe me, nothing would please me more . . ."

"But . . ." Jennifer interrupted, shaking her head.

Julius held up his hand. "No buts. You keep the car, and you let me look after you until you're back on your feet again. Come to the yacht and sunbathe, use my cabana at the beach. I want to make sure you eat properly, get your strength back. You need taking care of. The car's yours, duckie. I mean it."

Jennifer looked very dubious, but she was deeply touched.

"A beautiful girl like you needs beautiful trappings," he went on earnestly. "You should be draped in beautiful clothes and jewels and furs. Precious, all I want is to care for you and take you out. I'm proud to be seen with you on my arm. Believe me, it's all I want for now. Nothing more. Would you let me do that for you?"

She didn't know what to think. "Julius," she replied, "this all very touching, but I need time to think. I can't accept the car. I just can't."

Julius leaned forward and grasped her hand firmly. "Yes, you can, and you will!" he said, his dark blue eyes insistent. "Or I'll be extremely offended."

Jennifer smiled resignedly. "All right. But I'll feel more comfortable if I think of it as a loan."

"All right, duckie," he said tenderly. "If you prefer to think of it that way, then that's OK by me. But as far as I'm concerned, she's yours. Finish your drink and then we'll be off.

321

You can deliver me to the *Xerina*. I'll enjoy being dropped off by a stunning blonde. It'll give me no end of a kick. All my cronies will be green with envy."

She enjoyed the drive home. The car went like a dream, running smoothly along the Corniche, with no engine noise at all. Only the tyres could be heard murmuring quietly on the hard road. She loved the feel of the light evening breeze in her hair, the low, slanting sun sparkling on the sea. The rocky, sheer mountain loomed up on the other side, with villas carved into it, and high up in the distance, Eze Village perched precariously on a peak, like something out of a fairytale.

Could anything possibly be more beautiful and enchanted? Julius thought so, as he glanced at Jennifer's profile, the breeze whisking clouds of pale gold silk into her lightly freckled, beautiful face. Come what may, he determined, he was going to have her. One of these days, she would be his, and his alone.

Chapter 23

Although Laura had been preoccupied with her studies over the last few days, she still had time to marvel at the pace of life out of the office; the blatant stares of the executives as they mentally undressed her, the frantic speed and rush of city life. Then there was the incredible sensation of the express lifts, which by-passed whole sections of the building – whooshing up like space-rockets through eighteen floors in seconds, to deposit her more slowly on the twentieth. And all in the interests of saving valuable time in this frenetic and pacey world. The downward trip almost left her hair standing on end and her tummy on the twentieth floor.

She had to smile when she thought of the archaic lift in her block at the Meribel. It would be considered a museum piece over here. These New Yorkers would have a fit if they had to travel in a lift like that every day, thought Laura. Still smiling, she made her way across the Howson building's huge marble lobby towards the exit.

"Are your thoughts always happy ones?" came a voice from her right-hand side, as she crossed the lobby.

Laura stopped to see who had addressed her. The voice belonged to an absolute dish. He was about six feet, and the owner of the most beautiful eyes Laura had ever seen. They were green with gold flecks, and had enormously long black lashes. His face was tanned and his mouth, under a short, straight nose, was generous but not too full. It turned up at the corners, as if always ready to break into a smile. His hair was the dull gold of burnished copper. It was very thick and straight, brushed off his face in a floppy quiff, and short over the ears, giving him a boyish look, belied by his immaculate and well-cut suit. He had the kind of face and personality one instantly took to, and Laura did, with a vengeance that practically bowled her over.

"Hey! What happened to that gorgeous smile?" he continued. "You suddenly look like you've seen a ghost!" and smiled into her eyes.

"Oh, I'm sorry," replied Laura, discomfited. "You just startled me, that's all. I was miles away."

"I see you've got your homework for tonight," he grinned, taking in her bulky files. "Here, let me carry them for you. Then I'll give you a lift home in my car. They're too heavy for a dainty girl like you."

So saying, he took her books and marched her towards the exit.

"Wait," she said. "Wait. It's very kind of you, but I don't know you . . ."

Laura faltered, taken aback by his confident and proprietorial manner, and she tried rather unconvincingly to take her books back from him.

"Ah, but I know you though," he said, "so that's OK, isn't it?"

He took her arm and steered her out of the building. There was a dark grey limousine drawn up just outside the main door, into which he ushered Laura, protesting feebly.

"Ssshh," he chided, putting a finger to his lips. "Not everyone gets to be privileged like you. You're much too pretty to travel on the subway alone, and I don't want you to be kidnapped."

He sat down beside Laura and tapped on the glass partition. "Take the young lady home before you drop me off, OK, Henry?"

"Yessir," came the answer, and before Laura could gather

her wits, the car drew away from the Howson building, and out of Wall Street.

"Now," said Laura, "I insist you tell me what's going on. Here I am, with a complete stranger I've never met before, and a chauffeur who's supposed to be driving me home, before I've even given my address. I should be cross with you, or even uneasy, but you haven't given me time to draw breath!"

Her companion grinned hugely. "Oh, wow!" he cried. "That voice! I could listen to it for ever. Do me a favour, will you? Just talk. Your accent is so adorable it drives me wild."

Laura smiled, in spite of the cheek of this total stranger. He had such irresistible charm that it was impossible to feel uncomfortable with him – even though he had practically kidnapped her.

"Now look," she remonstrated, "this is ridiculous. I don't even know your name, and I really think you should drop me off right now at the nearest subway so that I can get home."

She did her best to sound insistent, even commanding. But he just looked at her with those melting eyes that twinkled with fun, and ignored her protests.

"You might not know mine, Miss Laura Forsythe," the young man chuckled, "but I sure know yours, and where you're headed, and so does my chauffeur, so just quit worrying, and enjoy the ride!"

Laura was dumbfounded, and stared at him with huge, round eyes. "What is this? I just don't understand. How on earth do you know my name and address?" Then her tone changed. Laura was getting angry now, and the indignation showed in her voice and manner. "Now look here," she demanded, "will you please tell me what's going on or I shall be forced to get really cross! So why don't you let me out of the car right now, or there'll be trouble!"

"OK, OK, I give up!" he exclaimed, laughing and throwing

his hands in the air in a gesture of truce. "Let me introduce myself. Thomas Howson II, and if I'd known the trainee from Monaco was so beautiful, I'd have met you personally at the airport, and not sent my chauffeur instead. How I wish somebody had told me. What a wasted opportunity!"

Thomas Howson studied her unselfconsciously, the expressive eyes registering their approval as his gaze roamed over her face and body.

Laura was irritated to feel herself blushing at his appraisal. She also felt a fool for not having realised who he was, or recognising the chauffeur. She fervently hoped she hadn't been too rude to Howson. She was at a loss for words now. It would be better to try to regain her composure before she said anything to make her look even more foolish. She sat still, her hands in her lap, looking back at him quizzically, wishing he weren't so disturbingly attractive and likeable.

"Are you still angry with me now?" he asked, trying to look contrite, and not succeeding.

"No... Of course not," she smiled, "but I wish you'd introduced yourself earlier, before letting me make a complete fool of myself."

"How can I make amends, then? May I take you out to dinner tonight?"

"No, you can't," she smiled. "I've got far too much studying to do, thanks all the same."

"Pity," he sighed. "Are you absolutely sure?"

"Yes, absolutely," she laughed. "I didn't fly all the way over here just to be wined and dined. I want to pass my exams. I've got to. I've got a job waiting for me in Monaco and can't let people down."

Tom Howson II's face took on a pained and petulant expression. Then he suddenly grinned. "Ah well, you can't win 'em all. You're right. Studying comes first. But how about Saturday?"

"I'm afraid not. I've really got to keep at it. I must spend every second revising and memorising my notes and studying the beastly manual." Laura ran her fingers through her silky hair distractedly, tossing the white-blonde mass behind her shoulders – her eyes huge blue pools of earnestness. "I've really got to get through these exams!"

He regarded her with amusement for her Englishness, and admiration for her dedication. However, just as Laura was absolutely determined to attain her goal, so was Thomas Howson II, who was used to getting his own way. Ever since birth he'd been doted on by his mother who'd indulged his every whim. So had his many girlfriends. He knew how to turn on the charm to get whatever he wanted. It was second nature to him. Anyway, he held the trump card. He was after all, head of the International Division and her direct boss!

"No," he countered, "I absolutely insist you can't study all weekend. And here's an order from me. Henry will pick you up on Saturday night at seven thirty and I'm taking you to '21' for a study break. It's a new company policy I've just drafted for our European subsidiaries. There is no way you can refuse, because you have to obey or be fired!"

Laura laughed. Thomas Howson II was very persistent, and very charming. Maybe one evening's break would do her no harm. And it was true, Laura reasoned humorously; he had her over a barrel. How on earth could she refuse an order from her boss without jeopardising her career?

Jennifer woke up feeling depressed. Still no word from Alex. She seemed to have lived an eternity since those last angry words between them. And that was only yesterday morning. She sighed heavily and lit a cigarette. It tasted foul on top of her hangover. What should she do today? It was nearly midday. One thing was certain, she was not going to hang around brooding and waiting for Alexander to contact her. There was nothing worse than waiting for the phone to ring, because invariably it didn't! Why not take Julius up on his invitation to sunbathe on the *Xerina*? That would be most of the day taken care of, and a good way to take her mind off her hurt feelings.

Jennifer yawned and got out of bed. It was a stifling day. She had a terrible head on her. It was Quint and Henny's fault. She, Quintin and Henny had stayed till four at the Tip Top drinking red wine. It had seemed a good idea at the time, but not now. She groaned and went to search for some Alka-Seltzer.

After a shower she made her way to the kitchen for some coffee to perk herself up. As she passed the telephone she glared at it. She wanted to smash it for sitting there so useless, and grey, and silent. She must get out of this stuffy flat. It would cheer her up to give the car an airing. She loved being seen in the Merc and watching heads turn enviously. It made her feel like a film star.

The drive down to the port was only three minutes, but Jennifer followed a longer route, doing a circuit of the Casino square first. She cruised past the Café de Paris slowly, flaunting her beautiful new toy.

"Eat your hearts out, you stuck-up frog bastards," Jennifer mouthed to the assembled drinkers lounging in the sun. She grinned cockily, tossing her hair arrogantly behind her shoulders. The course of true love might not be running smoothly right now, but life still had its compensations!

She accelerated past the Hôtel de Paris, round the bend and down the hill to the harbour where the *Xerina* gleamed in its stately whiteness under the strong midday sun. She drove slowly along the marina edge towards the Digue. At first the *Xerina* appeared to be deserted, but as soon as Jennifer set foot on the gang-way, a crew member in pale blue uniform accosted her. Jennifer smiled sweetly and asked for Monsieur Krep. He let her pass without another word.

She found Julius down below, talking on two telephones at once. One receiver was tucked under his chin and another clamped to his ear, with the mouthpiece averted.

"No, the bid still stands at two and a half million," he was saying into the chin phone, "yes, two and a half." Then he swivelled round the other phone and shouted, "You heard. No. You can tell them to take a running jump. Two two five mill ain't enough. Yep . . . Well, tell them however you like, but that's the score. OK?" He banged down both receivers, and almost instantaneously one of them rang again and he snatched at it. "Krep," he said curtly. "Yes?" He looked across at Jennifer and acknowledged her with a small wave. He listened for a few seconds impatiently. "Look, I'm in a meeting at the moment." he snapped, "I'll call you back, all right?" Then he hung up.

Jennifer was impressed that Julius was so adept at lying on her behalf. Meeting, indeed!

"Hello, duckie. What a lovely surprise!" he said walking across to her and kissed her warmly. He glanced at his Rolex. "You timed it well. Let's have a spot of lunch and some sun on deck. Have you got your bikini, love?"

The navy eyes glinted approvingly as his gaze swept over Jennifer's body and long tanned legs. She was dressed in a minimal pink jersey mini. It was strapless, and revealed much more than it covered.

Jennifer smiled. "Of course. I've brought the Pucci number especially."

Julius looked pleased. "I can't wait to see you in it. Come on then, beautiful. Let's be having you. You can change in my stateroom."

Jennifer followed him hesitantly. Was this to be the moment of truth? Julius held open the cabin door for her, and gestured for her to enter.

The memories of that stateroom were very clear in her mind still. The circular bed, the black satin sheets and his voracious tongue. How could she ever forget? She shivered involuntarily and reluctantly crossed the threshold. But to her relief, Julius left her alone to undress, politely closing the door behind him. Jennifer was surprised. He was very restrained and circumspect these days. And the bed was respectably and tastefully draped in cream padded silk, with matching cushions neatly arranged against the bedhead. No sign of the vulgar black satin! Had he refurbished his bedroom as well as his appearance?

She made her way back to the deck, where she found Julius sprawled on a luxuriously upholstered sun-lounger, wearing black swimming trunks. Undressed, his recent weight loss was impressive. He looked powerful and solid now: muscular rather than fat. He had the kind of skin that tanned easily and had darkened to a very smooth, mahogany brown. There was a piratical, almost sinister look about him, that added to, rather than detracted from his new allure. Not at all bad, thought Jennifer. She couldn't see what he was thinking because he wore dark, gangster sunglasses, but his mouth was smiling. He was doubtless admiring his taste in couture bikinis and women.

"Well, duckie," he commented approvingly, "I was right about your size, wasn't I? You look beautiful. I knew that Pucci number would suit you. Come and lie here, by me." Julius patted the sun-bed close to his invitingly, and handed her a flute of champagne.

Hair of the dog. Just what she needed to cure her hangover! She lay back on the comfortable lounger enjoying the warmth of the sun on her skin, and admiring the elegant surroundings. Julius had a telephone beside him. He dialled a long number, no doubt another international business call. His voice subsided into the background as Jennifer sipped her ice-cold champagne and let her thoughts drift. This was the life! Sun, champagne and luxury. She was in clover. But what a shame he wasn't Alex. And what a shame Alex couldn't offer her this luxury.

She sighed as she recalled one of her longer and more serious conversations with Alex.

"Stately homes cost a bomb to run," he'd said, 'and my father doesn't and can't provide the means to support my estate as well as his own. Anyway, why should he? Everyone, no matter what his origins, should work to make his living. Running a polo team is bloody hard work – a lot of travelling to matches, at home and abroad. Then there's constant exercising and practising to be the best, ponies to be mucked out, fed and watered, vet's bills, sundries, plus all the other admin. Honestly, there never seem to be enough hours in the day with everything that needs to be done. And all that on top of keeping the sponsors happy. However much I earn, it's gone before I've spent it!"

Jennifer had never thought of the practicalities of inherited privilege. It was automatic to assume that a viscount with a stately home would have money to burn. She found it difficult to imagine Alexander's struggle to make ends meet. Seeing him in the South of France, racing around in an Alfa, he was the epitome of the carefree playboy. What a contrast to the life he'd just described. She couldn't help but admire Alexander's quiet resilience. Life with him would be anything but easy, but given the choice, she thought she'd go with him to the ends of the earth, broke or not.

They were lying in bed at his villa, having made love for hours; in the pool, under the shower, then on the bathroom floor, and finally in his bedroom. Thoroughly sated, they were now talking quietly, exploring each other's worlds, learning about each other's lives, in the way that lovers do after exploring each other's bodies.

He'd taken Jennifer's slim, manicured hands between his and laughed as he drew his strong fingers down her long, tapering ones, pink tipped and delicate.

"I could never see these mucking out horses!" he said, kissing a painted nail.

"Are you implying that I'm lazy?" asked Jennifer indignantly.

"No," he grinned, "just pampered. I just can't envisage you in tatty jeans and a Husky, down in the stables mucking out at six o'clock sharp every morning come frost, rain or storm!"

"Huh. I wouldn't wear a Husky if it came up and bit me.

They're hideous, and only suitable for mature and sexless county ladies with labradors!" Jennifer's mouth turned down disdainfully.

Alexander smiled teasingly. "My grooms wear Huskies, and they're definitely not sexless."

Jennifer suddenly looked mutinous. "Oh, yes . . . I'll bet you can vouch for that, you swine. And I really don't want to know, thank you."

She flopped back into the pillows crossly, with her elbows behind her head.

"And you're digressing, sulky," he said. Then his expression grew more serious, and he continued quietly, "The point I'm trying to make is that my life isn't for you."

Her heart grew heavy. This discussion was suddenly becoming very negative.

"We both know it isn't," he went on, his tone gentle and soothing, as if he were comforting a tearful child. "Believe me. There's nothing I'd like more than to share it with you, but I know it just wouldn't work. I'm really not ready yet. I've got too much on to be able to give you the attention you'd need, much as the thought tempts me."

Alex stroked her cheek with the back of his finger, and looked at her with a tender wistfulness.

"There are still too many hills to climb, too many targets to go for, too much struggling before I get things properly up and running. Trouble is, I need a rich wife with enough loot to keep the whole show on the road whilst I work towards my goal. She'd need to have an all-consuming love of horses and be totally undemanding of my time. There's no way I could support a beauty like you who'd distract me, get bored and prevent me working as I must, to make ends meet."

"Sorry I'm not rich, then!" quipped Jennifer with a lightness she did not feel.

She gently nibbled an earlobe so that Alexander would not see the pain in her eyes. She felt rejected out of hand; heavy

332

inside, cheated, when she remembered the rich and privileged childhood that had been so suddenly nipped in the bud by her father's downfall. Things could have been so different but for cruel fate! All the same, she'd decided to keep quiet about her family's sudden plunge into misfortune. Alex didn't have to know, and, she reasoned, witholding information was not tantamount to lying.

And now, not a word from Alex; nothing. For all she knew, he could have left the Côte d'Azur, and gone back to his precious horses. They were all he seemed to care about. Never had she felt more frustrated or thwarted; she, who was so used to men falling at her feet.

She simply couldn't believe that their small tiff could have affected Alex so adversely, turned him right against her. Surely he'd be back soon, with his wonderful smile and glorious body. God, how she missed him!

But how could she even begin to explain to Alex what a debt of gratitude she owed Julius? There was no way she could spill the beans about Jean-Claude, about the abortion, about Krep's help, or he'd have been even more turned off. As Alex had said, there was more to all of this than met the eye; and the more he knew, the less he'd like it. But he had a nerve to make allusions about her dubious lifestyle, when he'd, albeit jokingly, referred to his need for a rich wife to bank-roll his polo team! Talk about one law for him and another for her! Jennifer felt very depressed; it all seemed hopeless.

She sighed and took another sip of champagne. Still, for the moment there was always Julius, good old Juli to fall back on. He would give her the silk shirt off his back and everything else she could possibly wish for. The thought comforted her. All the same, it wouldn't do to push her luck. He wouldn't wait around for ever. And after taking off all that flab and changing his image he was far more presentable now, and could easily be snapped up by a rival. Monte-Carlo was crawling with beauties in search of millionaires!

The telephone pinged as Julius put the receiver down, and cut into her thoughts.

"Did I hear you sigh, duckie?" Julius voice was concerned. "Is it too hot for you out here?"

"No, I'm fine thanks, really," she answered quickly.

"You're very thoughtful today."

Jennifer grinned. "I'm sorry. It's just that I've got an ace hangover! You can blame Quintin and Henrietta for that. They kept me up until dawn at the Tip Top!"

Julius threw back his dark head and laughed. "You're supposed to be convalescing! What am I going to do with you, you bad girl?"

A white-clad steward arrived with a tray. Jennifer wasn't hungry, but when she noticed there was cold lobster and mayonnaise she changed her mind. Lobster she could never resist! Lunch was delicious. Afterwards Julius suggested she should go to Monte-Carlo Beach. He was ensconced in several important deals that were near completion, and needed to get back to work as soon as possible.

"I'll be up to my ears until at least seven thirty, duck," he explained apologetically. "I'd ask you to join me for an evening drink, but I expect you'll be getting ready for the club, eh?" He tried to keep the irony out of his voice without success.

Jennifer knew he disapproved of her job, but it was the key to her independence. It was all she had, and she was determined to hold on to it. "Thank you for a lovely lunch," she smiled.

"Thanks for coming, precious. Stop by tomorrow, same time, will you?"

Julius waved a fond farewell as Jennifer got into the silver Mercedes and negotiated her way carefully along the harbour edge. She was too engrossed in avoiding bollards, cleats and fishing nets, to notice a young man with hazel curls staring at her wide-eyed and open-mouthed in disbelief.

It was Jean-Claude, going out for an afternoon's sailing with his cousins. He was standing on the foredeck of a small yacht as it backed slowly out of its mooring. He coiled a warp neatly and methodically for stowage, and turned away from Jennifer to gaze at the magnificent *Xerina*, in envious disgust.

So the bitch who'd dumped him was screwing a millionaire as well as a viscount now, was she? News travelled fast in Monaco and friends had lost no time in telling him about the titled polo player and his randy ex, the cow! And now Krep too, eh? Well, he'd soon see about that! Revenge could be sweet. A bitter smile crossed his handsome but sour face.

As soon as he'd finished his sail, he would pay the millionaire a visit. Monsieur Krep would no doubt be greatly indebted to Jean-Claude for warning him that he was wasting his time and resources on a money-grubbing, cheating little slut!

Chapter 24

Thomas Howson II was true to his word. At 7.30 p.m. exactly, the door bell rang, and Henry was there to pick her up. For a moment, perhaps uncharitably, Laura wondered why Tom hadn't come to the door himself. Maybe, she decided, he was just being discreet.

Tom was waiting for her in the comfortable depths of the limousine, and as their eyes met, Laura was again struck by his good looks and charm. In fact, it was his boyish charm that was his most dangerous weapon: it put any but the most cynical woman immediately at ease. His disarming manner dispelled any doubts Laura might have about the well-worn cliché of getting involved with the boss's son. Tom and Laura chatted easily as the comfortable limousine purred through New York on its way to '21'.

The '21' lived up to all her glamorous expectations of it. It was well known as the place to be. Full of sophisticated couples in couture clothes, with smart waiters dancing attendance on them, the atmosphere reeked of old money and privilege.

Laura noticed that heads turned as they came in. She was pleased to be seen in the company of such an attractive and eligible man. They must have made a handsome couple. They were the ideal height for each other. Tom's shining head of copper-coloured hair was half a head above hers. Laura stood five feet seven in her three-inch heels. She was of medium height only, but her upright and graceful bearing and slender frame lent the mistaken impression that she was tall and willowy.

She was wearing her favourite cocktail dress. It was in black *crêpe de Chine*, discreetly plunging, and had tiny straps trimmed with rhinestones. Around the skirt, which was in two layers, and three inches above the knee was the same trim of sparkles. Understated chic.

The evening turned out to be a delight. Laura found herself spellbound by Tom Howson. She couldn't believe her luck. At last she had met a man who seemed perfect in every way. He was attentive, good-mannered and interested in everything she had to say: the anthithesis of the surly Pierre. Tom was intelligent, perceptive and understanding. The first man she'd ever met who truly liked and appreciated women. Most of them, in her limited experience, had been either intimidated by her intelligence and ambition, belittling her at every opportunity, or had ignored it, preferring to leap on her straight away with their tackle pointing north. She found this tiresome and predictable. The fight that invariably ensued was undignified and annoying. But Tom was different. He actually listened to her, respected her opinions, was fascinated by her.

Laura was hypnotised by Tom's face. He had the most beautiful eyes she'd ever seen. They were the most unusual shade of green, and had a brilliance about them that was enhanced by a thick fringing of long black lashes. He had a way of looking at her that made her feel special, ultra-desirable and very feminine, as if she were the only person in the world that mattered. She was riveted by his words, the timbre of his voice, his accent. It was very sexy. She found herself watching his lips as he talked, and wondering what they'd feel like to kiss. She forgot all her promises to herself as she blithely strayed unaware into dangerous territory. All her carefully nurtured reserve crumbled under the weight of Tom Howson's practised charm. Laura found herself wanting him, but not chiding herself for her wantonness. Everything about the evening so far had been perfect. So right, so romantic.

How could she upbraid herself for falling for him? Tom Howson was the man of her dreams.

Later they went on to a night-club. She couldn't remember the name. All she remembered was the feeling of Tom's body against hers as they danced. With his arms around her, his lips against her cheek, the music, the whole outside world melted away and left her entranced. How she'd missed that all-encompassing feeling of warmth and intimacy lately. Her life had been empty for so long. Laura wanted to stay cocooned in this enchantment for ever. She was hardly aware of his soft words.

"Hey, pretty girl," he murmured into her dreams, "you weren't even listening to me! I asked whether you wanted a coffee?"

Tom smiled down at her teasingly. There were tiny creases of mirth at the corners of his eyes which lent him a vulnerable air, and made her ache with desire for him.

"I'm sorry," she replied, suddenly aware of what he'd said. "I must have been in a world of my own."

"What do you say?" he continued, stroking her cheek, a gentle expression in his eyes. "How about we drive uptown and I show you the view from my place? It's the best view in New York. You can see the whole of Manhattan, all lit up from my terrace."

Laura was uncertain. In her present mood she knew she wouldn't be able to resist him. He held her face in both hands and kissed her lightly on the mouth. All her instincts cried out to let go. She wanted to kiss him back with total abandon and float into oblivion with him. But suddenly she was distracted by a sharp pain, as a stiletto heel ground into her foot.

"Ouch!" she exclaimed. The pain made her eyes water.

"Gee, pardon me. I'm so sorry!" drawled a young brunette in a silver catsuit. Her face was contrite.

"Did I ladder your pantyhose?" the girl asked apologetically, as she left her partner to examine the damage.

Laura rubbed the top of her foot. There was only a small snag and no broken skin.

"Don't worry. No harm done!" she replied pleasantly.

The silver-clad dancer smiled, apologised again, and went back to her companion.

"Are you sure you're OK?" asked Tom solicitously.

Laura nodded. "Of course."

But the incident had intruded. The dangerous intimacy had evaporated, and now Laura's common sense prevailed.

"It's getting late, Tom," she said, looking at her watch. "I think if you don't mind, I should be heading back."

He looked disappointed for a moment; then brightened. "Why don't you come back home with me first? I could get some ice for your foot!"

A good try! Laura smiled wisely, looking at him quizzically, but didn't answer.

"I could get lost in those gorgeous bright blue pools of yours," he said quietly. "You have the most beautiful eyes I've ever seen."

Tom assumed a pleading expression. It was very appealing. "Come on, Laura. What do you say? Do you take your coffee black or white?"

He was certainly very persistent. She shook her head, but with polite amusement.

"No coffee, thanks. And no ice. My foot is fine."

"Well, tea, then! Isn't that what you English prefer?"

"No thanks!" she said, kissing him lightly on the cheek. "Come on, Prince Charming. It's well past midnight!"

Tom sighed, then smiled. "OK, Cinderella, but just make sure you leave your glass slipper, so I can return it to you another day! Let's go find Henry outside."

Tom held her hand on the drive back to her apartment, and, as the limo came to a gentle halt at the yellow canopied walkway to the building, Henry jumped out and held open the door for Laura. Laura made a move to get out of the car, but

Tom pulled her back towards him. Then he cupped her face in his hands, and gently kissed her full on the mouth. She felt all her senses come alive and that dangerous element of abandon overwhelming her again. She was excited and yet frightened by the passion and helplessness enveloping her. She was not used to being so out of control.

The chauffeur, who was still holding the door open, coughed discreetly. Laura recovered her composure instantly. She detached herself reluctantly and gave Tom a friendly peck on the cheek.

"I'm heartbroken you're leaving me this way," he chided, smiling at her with great tenderness. "Thank you for an almost perfect evening."

Laura smiled. "Thank you, too, for a lovely evening; I've loved every minute of it."

"Me, too. It was a great pleasure." He sighed, "But over too soon!"

Then the handsome face split into another of his irresistible smiles. She felt herself melting again at his proximity as he leaned across her and addressed his chauffeur.

"Henry, will you accompany Miss Forsythe to her door, please?"

Henry complied. Once inside her small apartment, the starstruck Laura collapsed back into the door, her knees trembling with excitement.

"Wow!" she sighed. "Careful, Laura. I think you're falling in love!"

Laura found it hard to concentrate on her studies the following morning. Memories of Tom kept flooding her mind whilst she was grappling with the technical facts and figures she needed to digest and memorise. Every so often she had to screw her eyes up and shake her head in an effort to clear her brain. She lost count of the number of cups of tea she brewed.

Eventually, after struggling fruitlessly, she took herself off on a walk down Fifth Avenue. Gazing into shop windows and stopping off at Schrafts for a snack, all she could do was daydream about being with Tom again. Had she been hasty in dismissing him last night? Would he call her again? Could he have taken offence at her refusal to go home with him?

"Oh, come on, Laura! Since when have you ever considered sleeping with a man on your first date?" she told herself crossly.

Of course she'd done the right thing! Now she had to get a hold of herself and remind herself of why she was in New York at all. It was to pass her exams for the start of a brilliant new career. That was her *raison d'être*, not a reckless love-affair. The exams were just one week away. One week's work, which would open a whole new door to untold rewards and success. Was she going to throw it all away for a romantic dream?

It was with a fresh sense of purpose that Laura strode briskly back to her studies, the staccato clicking of her heels on the hard pavement echoing the firmness of her renewed intent.

New York was engulfed by a blanketing cloud of stuffy heat as Laura worked with a vengeance in the final few days leading up to her big exams. There was no word from Tom, and though this upset her, she did not let it distract her from the task in hand. Come what may, she had to succeed. She needed to have all the facts at her fingertips, needed to know them by rote, without hesitation.

She spent most of the week on tenterhooks, with her nose firmly in her study books. She found it difficult to eat. There were times she was almost dropping with exhaustion. All she wanted to do was to sleep and sleep and then find it was all behind her. Unaccountably she became very homesick for her friends, her office, Fitz, and the parochial atmosphere of home. Laura wondered how Jennifer and Henrietta were, and

Quintin and Julius – even poodlefaker Alex! Not long now. Just a few days' hard slog, and she'd be home and back in familiar surroundings. Oh, would that it were all over!

The vulture had softened a bit; at times she even drew a grudging smile from him or a gruff word of encouragement. Her co-students seemed fairly relaxed, and sometimes invited her for a drink in the evenings, but she always declined. Not for her the hangovers and late nights. If that's what they wanted to do, fine. Laura didn't fancy returning to Monaco having let herself and everyone else down. No. Far too much hung on the outcome of her months of hard work. She wasn't going to throw it all away on buddy-buddy evenings with her young colleagues!

The day before the exam, there was an official lunch with the powers-that-be at Howson May. Laura's heart beat faster at the possibility that Tom might be there, but he wasn't, though his father was. She recognised him instantly. The same thick hair, now greying, and the same green eyes, though kindlier. She wondered if he'd been a lady-killer too, like his son. She sighed and wondered if she'd ever see Tom again.

Bob Dawson made a short rallying speech, wishing them all luck. Laura was wistful that Tom hadn't sent a good luck message via his father, or the personnel chief. Still, she thought, that obviously wouldn't do – it would have been favouritism. Tom Howson I shook each of them by the hand. Laura fancied he held on to her hand rather longer than anyone else's, reserving an especially warm smile and a twinkle for her.

"The very best of luck, young lady, though I'm sure you won't need it" he praised her. "I hear you're a star pupil. Well done! Go on out there and show them that women have brains too!"

Laura smiled and thanked Mr Howson warmly. It was cheering to hear some encouraging words. But it was a daunting thought that she would have already sat one two-hour exam by this time tomorrow. And then after that, a second paper. She'd be in a strange and anonymous exam hall, with masses of other candidates from different firms. She shivered at the thought.

The afternoon was mostly revision, a question-and-answer session with Vass, to help them all with their own particular problems or any points that needed last-minute clarification. At the end of the day, Vass told them all they weren't such a bad class – he'd seen a lot worse.

"Give it your best shot," he said, "and most of all, don't rush it. A lot of the questions look simple, but they're traps for the ill-informed."

His students listened to his words carefully. You could have heard a pin drop.

"Read the questions," he continued, his hawk eyes studying the earnest, upturned faces, "and then re-read them, OK? Make sure you understand before you rush into the answer. Now get an early night, and good luck to you all!"

For the first time, he actually smiled at them, broadly. "Don't let me down now, or I'll be out of a job!"

The telephone woke Jennifer with a start. She jumped out of bed and dashed into the hallway to snatch up the receiver. It could be Alex at long last! Her heart lifted in anticipation, and then sank with a thump as she heard the familiar, low female voice.

"Hello, is that you, Jennie?" Henrietta said. "Quintin and I are throwing a party on Monday night. It's club night off, so we thought we'd have a small bash at the flat. Will you come? Also, if you and Alexander are speaking, why don't you bring him?"

"Hi, Hen," she responded, trying to sound casual and cheerful, "that's just it, though; I still haven't heard from him. I haven't a clue whether he's playing hard to get or if he's really livid with me." Then a thought struck her. Henrietta had known Alex all her life. Maybe she could persuade him to come to her party? Jennifer sighed heavily. "Do me a big favour, Hen. Can't you ask him for me?"

"Oh God, you poor old thing, I know just what you're going through," sympathised Henrietta, "it wasn't so long ago things were like that with Quint and me. OK, I'll see if I can get hold of him; I'm sure I've got his number somewhere."

"Thanks. You're an angel."

Jennifer's heartache and frustration was exacerbated by the mental picture she had of Henrietta and Quintin's sudden and recent flush of domestic bliss.

"I'm sure he'd much rather hear from you, though," Henrietta said doubtfully.

"No, Hen." Jennifer's face set obstinately. "I can't face a rebuff. Anyway, I've never chased a man in my life. Wouldn't know how to go about it. And I'm not going to start now!"

Henrietta laughed. "You are a card, Jennie. Still, you never know, things might buck up. See you at work tonight!"

Henrietta's cheery manner made Jennifer's gloom worse, but at least there was a chink in the clouds. There was just a possibility that Alexander would come to the party. That forlorn hope was all she had to cling to for now.

Meanwhile she might as well console herself with Julius on the *Xerina* again, and then spend the afternoon at the Beach Club. It was becoming quite a familiar routine. She looked at her watch. No, it was too early yet. It was only nine thirty. Julius would be wheeling and dealing no doubt. Besides, they'd arranged to meet for lunch. She decided to go straight to the beach instead and to join Julius on the yacht later on.

Jennifer made her way to the Vigie. At this time of the morning, the air was fresh with the scent of pines that threw their shadows at her feet as she followed the winding path to her favourite spot. There was hardly anyone there, but an obliging waiter took her order promptly. She asked for a large *café au lait* and sipped it slowly, wondering why she didn't get up this early more often. It was the best part of the day, before it got too hot and hazy. When she'd finished her coffee she descended the stone steps to a semi-circular sun terrace, and stretched out on a striped mattress to sunbathe.

She hoped Alexander would come to the party. She was desperate to see him again. Missing him left her with a dull ache, a feeling of emptiness and despair that permeated her body and invaded her every thought. It was sheer agony. Thank heaven for Julius. Being spoiled by him made her aching heart less heavy. He was her life-line; her port in a storm. It was a comfort to think he'd be there to pick up the pieces if the worst happened and she never saw Alex again.

Jennifer got up and stretched. The water looked clear and inviting. She started towards the metal steps that led into the sea. Then she changed her mind. She positioned herself on the edge of the sun terrace and dived in gracefully. The cool, salty water rushed past her ears as she plunged in, to surface a few seconds later, about ten yards out. That was one way to sweep away a hangover, if not her sadness.

Her eyes took in the view as she did a lazy backstroke towards the raft. Beyond the Vigie, with its white tables and multi-coloured parasols, was the curved, coral-pink Beach Club Hotel, nestling against a backdrop of pine trees, and mountains in the distance. Further to the left was the pool fringed by tall, straight palms. Their trunks were like telegraph poles, crowned with giant green mopheads, tired and dusty from the long, hot summer. Then came the serried ranks of striped cabanas, prepared for their rich and glamorous occupants to spend endless sunfilled days of idle luxury. Bevies of waiters and minions were on hand, ready to attend to their every whim.

What paradise! Jennifer turned over and made for the raft by means of an energetic crawl. There she lay in the sun for the rest of the morning, with the sparkling azure water lapping around her. When all was said and done, she reflected ruefully, it was better to suffer a broken heart in idyllic surroundings than in a cold garret. Life could be worse! It was small consolation, but a thought nevertheless worth appreciating.

The warmth of the sun on her skin, the hypnotic rhythm of the wavelets and the gentle bobbing of the raft soon combined to relax her. She drifted off into a dream world of Alexander, of requited love, and of happier days.

Laura had a snack at Schrafts on her way back to the apartment, prior to settling in for one final night with the revolting manual and her NY Institute Study Course. How glad she'd be to see the back of all of this. As she entered the lobby and asked for her key from the receptionist, she noticed there was a small envelope in her pigeon-hole.

"Good evening, Miss Forsythe. Some flowers came for you," she said, "Oh, and three telegrams. I have them here behind the desk."

The receptionist ducked down and struggled up with a lovely flower arrangement in a mixture of peach and white which she placed on the counter, before reaching back for a tiny pink envelope and the telegrams. Laura was thrilled. So Tom had thought of her after all! The receptionist held open the lift door whilst Laura loaded the flowers, her books, telegrams and her bag, and then made her way to her apartment. The coffee table was only just large enough to accommodate the magnificent display! Laura smiled, and opened the envelope with a beating heart: "Best of luck, duckie! Thinking of you. Ever – JK."

Disappointment was her first reaction, an overwhelming disappointment that it wasn't Tom after all. But she was ashamed to be so unappreciative of Julius' kindness. What a sweet and thoughtful gesture! It was the most beautiful bouquet she'd ever seen, of peach roses, lilies, exotic orchids, sweet-smelling freesias and frothy white gypsophila. She studied the flowers in detail, fingering the soft petals tenderly. Even if Tom hadn't thought of her, Julius had, and there were

347

the telegrams, too. Quickly she slit them open, and smiled. One was from Jennifer, Quintin and Hen, wishing her luck and love. The second was from Fitz, and the other from her family. Everyone was cheering for her and it lifted her spirits.

It wouldn't do to let them down. She must do everything she could to prepare for the heavy day ahead. Tomorrow was to be the culmination of all her efforts: her whole future depended on the outcome!

Jennifer must have fallen asleep on the raft, because when she eventually swam back to the Vigie, she found it full of people finishing lunch. She wondered whether Julius would be cross with her for missing their rendezvous on the *Xerina*. Too late to worry about it now! She decided to order a *salade niçoise* straight away, and to drop by and surprise Julius later on, in time for drinks.

Then she walked back to the beach, and spent a blissful afternoon relaxing and sunbathing at the cabana. At about five, she dressed, brushed her hair and put on some lipstick. She checked her reflection and was pleased with what she saw. Surely Julius would forgive her for missing lunch if she made up for it by seeing him now.

Using the long, straight coast road, she sped back to the town of Monte-Carlo. It was ironic, but the world-renowned Monte-Carlo Beach was not part of the principality. It was all of a ten-minute drive into France! The only way to get there was by a shuttle bus run by the SBM, the syndicate who owned the Casino and Hôtel de Paris, or by car.

Fifteen minutes later, Jennifer parked her car under the towering harbour wall, and boarded the *Xerina*. A worried blue-uniformed steward tried to tell her something, but she smiled and walked past him into the luxurious saloon. She'd imagined Julius would either be on the telephone, or out on deck enjoying the late evening sun, with the inevitable glass of champagne by his side. But there was no sign of him. How odd!

She glanced further into the interior, towards his stateroom. Maybe he was taking a quick nap. Perhaps she should make his day and disturb him! The thought brought a wry smile to her face. She shook her head knowingly. It would be better not to risk it. He'd doubtless pounce on her, thinking his luck was in at long last!

As Julius was obviously not around, Jennifer decided to return to the Meribel. She'd write him a short note apologising for missing lunch. She found a pad and a pen, and sat down on one of the silk sofas to compose it. As she wrote, she thought she heard faint giggling from the direction of the stateroom. She paused for a moment, listening, but it was nothing. She must have imagined it. She looked around her. There was a vast bowl of flowers on the low table placed between the two plump silk sofas. There were exotic orchids, scented lilies, ferns and tea roses. Their heady perfume filled the air. Did he have them flown in from Pulbrook and Gould every day? What a lifestyle! It took some beating. Then she continued with the note.

All of a sudden Jennifer started, as the door to Julius' cabin burst open. To her amazement, a brunette teetered out on five-inch red stilettos, wearing nothing more than a matching G-string and a pair of handcuffs. The girl was tall, exquisitely proportioned, beautiful and had a tousled mane of dark brown curls. She had very full, rounded breasts with dark brown, jutting nipples. There was no hint of sag. In fact, the breasts were so firm they looked as if they'd been pumped full of air. Her almond-shape eyes were highlighted with green shadow, and her big, pouting lips were painted bright, glossy red, like her ultra-long fingernails. She looked like a younger, tarty version of Sophia Loren. The perfect body glistened with oil, and was deeply tanned.

What on earth was going on? What was the brunette doing in his cabin? Jennifer's mouth dropped open in puzzlement.

"You arrr bad boy!" the naked girl screeched in a loud Italian accent, giggling drunkenly. "I need bathrrroom. Wherrre I find eet?" She looked back into the cabin, and giggled again. "I need it now. Undo me pliss!" She waved her manacled arms and pouted fetchingly.

The girl did not notice Jennifer, as she was looking away from her. Almost immediately a male hand came out of the open doorway and strong fingers hooked her handcuffs, pulling the girl back into the stateroom. Then the door closed to louder, husky shrieks of laughter and muffled Italian expletives.

Jennifer had seen enough. She was leaving. Why was Julius doing this to her? It was as if he'd set her up on purpose. Wanted her to discover him *in flagrante* with the brunette. His deliberate lack of discretion sickened her. And all because she'd stood him up for lunch? Surely not! It seemed incredibly spiteful and bitchy.

She was surprised to feel hurt, too. Disillusioned, because Julius had seemed such a rock. A haven in the middle of her turmoil; someone she could trust implicitly. Now he was thumbing his nose at her. She'd obviously been well and truly taken in by him and his so-called sincere concern for her well-being. Well, to hell with him. He'd made a fool of her. Obviously all the stories about him were true. He was no more than a cheap pimp and a bastard, using women as playthings, and dumping them callously if they didn't do exactly as he wanted.

Jennifer slowly tore the note into tiny pieces and strewed them all over the carpet like white confetti. Goodbye, Julius. If he wanted the Mercedes back, he could bloody well come and fetch it himself!

Chapter 25

Laura had such butterflies on the morning of the exams that she almost forgot to pay the taxi driver. She hardly noticed that it was a glorious, sunny day. Her brain was full of facts that she kept recalling like clockwork – all the different facets of stockbroking: settlements, mutual funds, stock-market history, options, bonds, over the counter markets, margin regulations. Her mind felt fit to burst. The building where the exams were to be sat was very imposing, with huge stone steps leading up to a sort of atrium. Hundreds of people seemed to be filing into the examination hall.

It must be huge in there, she thought, suddenly awestruck and almost paralysed by fear. Her legs felt like lead, and she had a ridiculous urge to bolt. But hemmed in as she was by a steadily moving column of candidates, doubtless as petrified as she was, it wouldn't have been possible.

The hall was bigger than several gymnasiums put together. Rows and rows of small wooden tables and chairs stretched almost as far as the eye could see. These were gradually being occupied by the advancing line of candidates. A clattering and scraping of furniture and feet filled the air.

Oh Lord, thought Laura, this is far worse than I'd imagined.

A man with a megaphone sat at a large desk on a raised dais at the end of the vast hall. He seemed miles away.

"Hurry, please," was all Laura could make out of the distorted and disjointed voice coming from the loudspeaker.

She pulled out a chair and sat down about halfway down the

enormous hall, the sixth row across. She seemed to be right in the middle of it, and felt very small and isolated in the endless sea of candidates. The invigilator's accent was Bronx, and Laura couldn't follow a word he said, but he mentioned special pencils and what sounded like computer markings. Laura's heart thumped and her throat went dry as she looked at the folder in front of her. This one was the New York Stock Exchange exam. She was unnerved and worried that she seemed to have missed a crucial part of the instructions.

The next words were clearer. "Please don't turn the page yet. Write your name and company on the front cover, where it says 'Name and Company', OK?"

There was a pause, and then the voice droned on. "In a few minutes, when I tell you to start, you can turn the page, and you have two hours to complete your NYSE exam. I will be patrolling the aisles, but don't let that distract you. Please do not confer, please do not leave the hall or your papers will be void. If there is any problem, kindly raise your hand, and wait till I come to you. Please do *not* call out. OK?"

There was a general quiet shuffling while each candidate filled in the necessary details, and then an interminable silence as the nervous examinees awaited the signal to start. The pencil was a strange shape – sort of triangular, with a very thick lead to it. It looked clumsy and awkward to use. Supposing she didn't understand any of the questions? There was a knack to multiple selection; it was a very American way of doing things. She had no experience of it, unlike all of the others. There must be hundreds and hundreds of candidates around her. A surreptitious glance round showed her she was the only woman, the only girl, marooned in a sea of dark suits and ties. How terrifying! Now she felt even less sure of herself: completely lost. What on earth was she doing here?

The raucous voice burst into her terror.

"OK, everyone. You can start . . . *now!*"

Laura's heart hammered hard in her chest. A sudden rustling of paper filled the echoing hall, then a clatter of pencils being picked up. Laura turned the page with shaking hands. Each question was followed by four little boxes, one of which had to be ticked opposite the appropriate answer. She felt rising panic. The first questions seemed awfully easy . . . but then, were they the trick ones? Which were the trick ones Vass had warned them of? Oh, come on, Laura. Pull yourself together, and get on with it!

She picked up the strange pencil and started filling in the relevant boxes, first hesitantly, and gradually more confidently. Any questions she was unsure of, she left, and went on to the ones she knew. She could always come back to the difficult ones later in a calmer frame of mind, rather than waste time racking her brains and getting into a state. Vass had given them a few hints and tips like that. Maybe he hadn't been such a ghastly old stick after all! This exam wasn't so bad, was it? Quite straightforward, really. Laura put her head down and forgot her surroundings completely, as she got into the swing of things. She must have been over halfway through the two-hour paper when a voice suddenly hissed in her ear.

"Miss! What do you think you're doing?"

She jumped a mile as the invigilator put a hand on her shoulder.

"What? What do you mean, sir?" Laura whispered, her heart in her throat.

The man angrily jabbed a large, square-tipped finger at the boxes.

"You have to make the marks thaddaway, or the computer won't register them. Your answers right now will register a blank. You'll have to go back over them all and re-mark the boxes like so!"

Laura's heart sank like a stone. This was devastating.

She stuttered, "But then it'll come out like an 'X', won't it?"

"Sure it will, but no matter. The new stroke will register over the old one which is void anyway. So go ahead and fill in the boxes the right way, across what you've done, or you'll get no marks at all."

Laura was mortified. She couldn't believe it! Surely she'd never finish in time now. She went back to the beginning in a panic, and was horrified to find that she'd made several mistakes as well, on re-reading her answers. She'd fallen straight into several obvious traps.

God, her paper was going to look such a mess, with two boxes differently marked in some of the groups, and others splodged with 'X's'. She hoped the invigilator was right that the computer would ignore the strokes to the left, or she was sunk. What a nightmare! This was worse than the worst, the kind of thing that only ever happened in bad dreams.

Oh God, help me, she thought in dismay. I come all this way just to foul things up and make an idiot of myself.

Laura completed the rest of her paper in abject misery, feeling totally wretched and hopeless. What a fool she was!

When the invigilator eventually called out, "Would you all stop now, please," Laura felt an overwhelming sense of relief that her ordeal was at last over.

She didn't even care how she'd done, all she wanted to do was get out of the place and curl up alone in a corner. Dejectedly she walked out, her head bent.

Outside, she bumped into some of her colleagues who compounded her misery by chattering excitedly and comparing notes. She didn't want to hear any of it. Wan-faced, she wondered how she could ever dredge up enough courage to go through a repeat performance that same afternoon with the NASD exam. Still, she'd know how to mark the boxes this time. That was at least something!

Andrew smiled at her sympathetically, his brown eyes concerned and kindly. "Not too much fun, eh?" he said. "You'll do OK, Laura, don't worry. Just you see! Me now, ah well, it's my last chance. I've got to pass this time, or try something different. Come on. Chin up, let's join the others for a beer and a sandwich."

The afternoon went a lot more smoothly than the morning. Laura finished the NASD exam well before the two-hour deadline, and felt much more confident of her performance this time. She ran through her paper again, but didn't feel the need to alter anything. The rest of the time she sat quietly, her arms folded, and let her thoughts drift to Tom. Would she ever see him again? Why had he seemed so riveted with her, and then just summarily dropped her without a word? Maybe he was unused to not getting the girl on the first date.

Now she'd never know. She would be returning to Monaco towards the end of the week, after the results, which should be through next Monday morning. How she dreaded the prospect of a weekend alone, brooding and regretting her stupidity in the NYSE exam. Fitz would be so disappointed and probably surprised, too. Ah, well, too late now; no use crying over spilt milk.

At last came the monitor's voice, and everyone filed out. There were so many hundreds leaving, that Laura didn't get a chance to see Andrew or any of her co-students. A pity, because it was the one time she would have liked their company for consolation. Now Laura would have to face up to a lonely and disappointing weekend rueing the events of the morning, with no one to provide sympathy or distraction!

As she walked forlornly down the steps to the street, she heard a voice, calling, "Oh, Miss Forsythe! Miss Forsythe, please!"

She looked round, surprised to hear her name, and there was Henry, the chauffeur, smiling broadly and waving to her. "Would you follow me please, Miss Forsythe?"

She hardly dared believe what was happening, but there, a

few yards or so away, was the familiar limousine.

"Well, beautiful, are you going to stand there all day, or are you going to get in?" came the husky voice.

Her heart leapt with joy; he hadn't forgotten her after all! She got into the back, smiling broadly. Tom leaned forward. "Hey, don't I get a kiss?" Happily, she obliged.

"May I ask what's going on?" she asked, her eyes sparkling.

"No, you may not. Surprise is the order of the day. This is your reward for being such a hardworking and serious girl."

Tom was not dressed in his office clothes, but wore a pale blue short-sleeved shirt and navy slacks. Dressed like that he looked more boyish than ever. The car took an unfamiliar direction.

"Where are we going?" she laughed.

Tom put his finger to his lips in a gesture of secrecy, and then leaned forward to take out a bottle of champagne, and proceeded to fill two flutes.

"I'm not sure there's anything to celebrate," Laura whispered as he handed her a fizzing glass. "This could be a little premature. I don't think I did that well!"

Tom laughed. The clear green eyes lit up his boyish face. "Ah, well, let's celebrate our being together, then. Isn't that enough?"

His voice was gentle, almost a whisper. How adorable he was! Suddenly the examinations didn't matter. It was marvellous just to be in his company. Laura sat back and enjoyed the champagne. Oh, how she needed it! Nothing mattered any more except Tom.

"Where are we going?" she asked again, a few minutes later.

"Wait and see," he answered mysteriously.

She couldn't get anything out of him except compliments and tendernesses. He held her hand, stroked her fingers gently, brushed her hair back from her face, kissed her cheek, told her how much he'd missed her, and had thought of no one else all week. Laura melted under all his ministrations. She couldn't believe what was happening. Her nightmare had turned into a beautiful dream. But wait: wasn't this the airport? What were they doing at the airport?

Tom smiled, and again said, "Wait and see!"

Two hours later, they were in Bermuda. The warm, humid air hit Laura like a soft filigree blanket, as she stepped from the plane, hand in hand with Tom. A car was waiting for them outside the small airport, chauffeured by a very good-looking black Bermudian with a lovely sing-song accent. He greeted Tom with familiarity, and treated Laura with friendly politeness. What a beautiful, beautiful place it was.

The narrow lanes were banked high with blossoms, hibiscus, and pink, cream and dark red poinsettias. Everywhere freesias grew wild, and filled the air with their sweet scent. The roofs of the pastel low-built houses were sparkling white and ridged.

"To catch the rain," Tom explained, "which then goes into underground tanks for the water supply. It rains mostly at night, not often during the day, and then it only pours for a short while. Just enough to keep everything fresh and green. It's a lovely climate, never too hot, never too cold. I've always loved Bermuda, and I wanted you to see it." Tom smiled at her lovingly. "I wanted to share it with you. It's very special to me. I've been coming here since I was a child."

The sea was absolutely beautiful. Laura had never seen a multi-coloured ocean before. The beaches were of palest pink sand, and the water at the shoreline started a pale bluey-green, darkening to a deep teal. Then it appeared almost navy blue further out, where the ocean was bisected with an undulating strip of snaking, brilliant white that marked the outer reef. Closer to the shore was the inner reef, where Tom explained they could go snorkelling and see fish of all colours and sizes, swimming up really close.

"You can reach out and touch them, and the water is so

warm you need a shower to cool down afterwards!"

Laura was so excited she was like a child, chattering and pointing around her with amazement. Tom smiled indulgently. He was pleased to see her so happy.

"All I want to do is to spoil you," he said. "I love to see you smile. You're so pretty, but especially beautiful when you smile and laugh. I could watch you for ever."

Laura's eyes misted over. Nobody had ever said such sweet things to her before. Nobody had ever spoiled her like this before! To think, she was in Bermuda, an absolute paradise, with this glorious man! She simply couldn't believe her luck.

Tom's house was right on the beach. Like all the other buildings, it was low, with the same white ridged roof. But it was immense and sprawling, and reached by its own long driveway lined with unfamiliar trees, which were draped with a kind of blue-grey hanging moss. The entrance door was flanked by enormous banana trees, hung with great yellow bunches of fruit. The whole place had a magical quality about it.

The rooms inside were light and airy, with enormous windows overlooking the sea. The couple walked out to the verandah that ran all along the beach side of the house. There were huge stone pots of exotic and scented plants, spilling out in a confusion of riotous colours, and rattan furniture, including a huge and comfortable swing hammock with fat, striped cushions.

"What a wonderful, wonderful place!" Laura breathed, spellbound.

"Shall I make you a Bermuda rum punch?" Tom asked.

Laura shook her head, "Later, maybe. I think the champagne is still having an effect, or maybe it's just this paradise! I still can't believe I'm here. But wait—" she said, suddenly panicking, "I've got no luggage, no change of clothes, nothing. You kidnapped me, do you realise that?"

Tom laughed. "Do you blame me?"

Laura was dressed in a linen suit of royal blue, with a pale

358

blue silk blouse that had a pussycat bow at the neck. Her flaxen hair was piled on top of her head in an elegant chignon. She looked chic and beautiful, but totally incongruous and over-dressed in this lush, tropical setting.

"There are closets full of clothes you can borrow if you like, but who needs clothes anyway?" he continued, "We've got our own private beach right on the doorstep. We can swim, and relax, eat and drink. There's not a soul around except us. There was never any need for clothes in the Garden of Eden! I'm not concerned with practicalities, are you? We can be creatures of impulse."

Laura sighed. "How romantic it all sounds."

She untied the bow at her neck, loosened the collar, and threw off her jacket. She undid the pins in her hair, and the long, white-blonde mass tumbled in silken disarray over her shoulders. Then she shrugged off her high-heeled shoes, and curled up on the hammock.

"Believe me, it is romantic," he smiled, "Just you and me, and all the time in the world . . ."

Tom sat down beside her, stroking her hair and nuzzling her neck. Gently he pulled her to him. He kissed her long and hard. Laura felt herself melting in his arms, and knew it would be hopeless to resist. She wanted him with all her heart. She'd never felt this way before about a man: reckless, with not a care in the world, wildly shrugging off all her conventions. All she was aware of was the fierce need to feel him against her, inside her right now, this very second, and not a moment later.

"I want you," she whispered, surprising herself. "I want you so much . . ."

He did not reply, but picked her up, cradling her in his arms. Carrying her to the bedroom, he laid her down tenderly on a huge carved four-poster bed with a white goatskin bedspread. Laura threw her clothes off with careless abandon, and lay back on the bed, relishing the sensuous caress of the cool, soft fur on her naked skin. Kneeling above her, Tom looked down at her, and sensing her urgent hunger for him he tore at his clothes, discarding them with a speed bordering on panic. Laura ran her hands down his bare chest, admiring the beauty of him. Then impatiently, wanting to feel every last inch of his body against hers, she drew him down to her. Burying her fingers in his hair as they kissed, she clung to him as if she were drowning.

All the emptiness of the last few months made her need for him more acute, the taste of his lips, the feel of his body on hers. She was on fire, every part of her tingling, wanting him. Running her fingertips gently over his bare skin she felt a current that surged and coursed through her body down to the very melting depths of her, as if her entire existence were centred there, until, unable to wait any longer, she locked her legs round his and pushed him inside her. She could feel him invading all her senses, and she absorbed him with every particle of her being as the tide rushing on to a deserted shore consumes and soaks every grain of dry, parched sand in its flow. Then she arched her back so he could take her hips, pulling them closer to his own, to go deeper into her, where, flesh on flesh, curve matching hollow, light playing on the sheen of their skin, they were transported beyond time and space as wave upon wave of primeval ecstasy flowed through their bodies. Then, as the intensity of feeling gradually ebbed away, the lovers stayed clinging to each other; shuddering, breathless . . . and ready for more . . .

The magical weekend flew by all too soon. Laura had never spent time with anybody so perfect in every way as Tom. He was loving and tender, patient and humorous. He was also tremendously athletic, and swam like a fish. They splashed about in the warm, clear water like children, laughing and playing, until, suddenly tiring of their games, they'd look into each other's eyes with hunger, and kiss passionately; then spend hour upon hour making love: never seeming to get enough of each other without wanting more. And more still.

And all the time Tom was so tender and affectionate, whispering the most beautiful words, always more concerned with pleasing Laura, taking a real pleasure in her body's responses rather than his own. He was a true lover in every sense of the word. Tactile, romantic, affectionate, sensuous; loving the feel of her skin, "as fine and delicate as a butterfly's wing," he said, and her hair like spun silk; loving her scent, the taste of her, telling her she was the most beautiful and exciting woman he'd ever known. He made her feel like a goddess, insuperable, vibrant, womanly and wonderful in every way.

Laura drifted in a cloud of love, a kind of heaven that transcended anything she'd ever known. The adrenalin of her joy pushed away all her cares, as her face took on that glow of a woman deeply, hopelessly in love.

In the evenings, the young lovers would take long, moonlit walks along the shore, strolling hand in hand; the fine, soft sand still warm under their feet, the sea murmuring softly. Or they'd spend ages just quietly talking, swinging gently on the hammock under the verandah, her head on his shoulder, taking occasional sips of white wine from a shared glass.

He taught her the art of snorkelling and deep-sea fishing. Laura had never seen such brightly coloured varieties of fish, or so many of them. It was true that they could reach out and touch the many-hued creatures that swam lazily and weaved confidently amongst them. Laura's favourites were the blue and yellow angel fish, which seemed to be the tamest of all. It was paradise under the water as well as out of it.

Tom had a Boston Whaler moored close by, which he loved to race at top speed, showing her other bays and amazing rock formations further along the coast, or zipping amongst the small islands peculiar to Bermuda. He took Laura to the outer reef, too, where they spent an idyllic afternoon fishing. Laura's first attempts were most inept, and she lost a couple of lead weights in the rough coral bottom of the reef, so that the line had to be cut, to free the rod. Tom, however, was very good-humoured and patient about it all. He enjoyed showing her the ropes, proving himself to be an expert instructor, because, later on when the sun was lower in the sky, Laura surprised them both by catching an enormous grouper, which she insisted on landing by herself, despite its great weight.

That evening, after sundown, Tom barbecued the grouper, having expertly gutted it with a fisherman's knife. He was an excellent cook, and obviously an expert at *al fresco* feasts. There were not many Bermudian homes, he explained, without a barbecue outside. Besides, there was not much to beat the taste of fish or steaks cooked over charcoal. Tom had prepared the table out on the verandah, with candles, and a vase of hibiscus. Amongst them was one enormous white trumpet-shaped flower like a lily, with the sweetest, most heavenly scent.

Laura was enchanted, the setting was so pretty. To start with they had cantaloupe melon, and with the wonderful, wood-smoked fish they ate a mixed salad he'd prepared. Then he picked a couple of bananas off one of the trees and placed them, still in their peel, on the charcoal, while they finished their main course. A few minutes later he brought them to the table, the hot golden crescents frizzling and splitting out of their skins. The peeled, melted, syrupy fruit was wonderful with a generous helping of thick yellow cream.

Laura thought she'd never had a more delicious meal in all her life. Was there anything this man couldn't do? She sat and watched him, her eyes full of love and tenderness, but underneath, there was just a hint of melancholy that Tom couldn't help noticing. Concerned, he reached across the table and took one of her small hands in his. Her eyes were strangely bright, though their expression was subdued.

"What is this flower?" Laura asked him, lightly fingering the white, scented trumpet. "I've never seen anything like it before."

"A night-blooming cereus," he said. "Sometimes known as Queen of the Night. Very special and very beautiful. It only ever comes out for one night, then it dies at dawn."

"For ever?" whispered Laura, her eyes wistful.

"'Fraid so. But I guess because it's so short-lived, it's all the more precious."

"I've never seen anything more pure and beautiful, or smelt a sweeter fragrance."

His green eyes were filled with tenderness as she spoke and there was a touch of sadness in his expression, too.

"I think," Tom murmured gently, "that whenever I see one again, I'll always be reminded of you."

A cricket chirruped from amongst the trees, and a soft breeze momentarily chased the leaves into silent whispers. The candles flickered, throwing shadows across Laura's face as she fiddled with the stem of her wine glass and fought to keep her eyes from brimming.

"Penny for them," he said quietly, taking the cereus out of the vase and twining the flower into her hair "There. Now you're a princess."

He tilted her face up to kiss her and noticed an escaping tear. "What is it, precious?" he asked with concern.

"Oh, nothing," she murmured. "Just that I wish this could go on for ever."

Tom got up from his chair, and knelt by her feet, taking her hands in his.

"My sweetest, beautiful girl, the future is decided by fate. What matters is here and now, and us. What matters is that we're happy right now, at this moment of our lives. Nothing else counts. Please believe me, and remember it always."

Tom's words touched Laura, but didn't dispel her underlying feeling of sadness. If anything, they made her sadder still. He leaned towards her and gently brushed a tendril of hair back from her forehead, kissing her softly on the lips, and holding her close.

"Let's go inside. We can clear up later."

Laura looked at the sleeping figure with a heart full of love, and a heavy sadness because it was already Sunday morning. The beautiful white flower lay withered and fragile amongst the rumpled bedclothes. Laura picked up the night-blooming cereus, and held it to her face, but nearly all its fragrance had gone. Carefully, she placed the delicate flower on the bedside table.

She turned back to look at her lover. In repose Tom had the sculpted face of a god. The burnished copper hair fell back from his forehead in a widow's peak, and she lightly traced its outline with a butterfly touch of her little finger. Tom's straight nose twitched slightly at her caress, and he sighed contentedly, but did not wake. His finely chiselled mouth turned up slightly at the corners, even whilst he slept, and Laura thought she'd never seen longer, thicker lashes, or more perfect features. Oh, but he was beautiful!

She propped herself up on one elbow, and at that moment believed she would be happy to spend the rest of her life just looking at this man who meant the world to her. Laura didn't know how long she spent gazing at Tom, absorbing his every precious feature, marvelling at her love for him, wishing upon wish that he would stay with her always, and love her in the same way, too, for ever, and without end.

"Is that you, Lejeune?" came a drunken, barely coherent voice over the telephone.

"What do you want, Ratti?" Lejeune replied irritably. He had been away on a course for a fortnight, and had had a long, hot day catching up on paperwork. Now it was time to go home.

"I finally did it."

"Did what?" snapped Lejeune. "Speak up, man. I can hardly hear you."

"I . . . cut . . . them . . . up," slurred the voice disjointedly.

Lejeune suddenly sat up, squeezing the receiver tightly. "What are you talking about?"

"The sluts. I cut them with my knife."

"What?" Lejeune's voice rose an octave, and his heart thumped in his ears. What had that fool Ratti done?

"Cut them into ribbons. I enjoyed it. They deserved the punishment, the sluts."

Lejeune was horrorstruck. This was unbelievable. It was true he had wanted to get even with Laura all summer: even more so since she'd rebuffed him so coldly after he'd made love to her at the Meribel. Christ, how she'd been contemptuous! But murder, mutilation? God in heaven! Lejeune put his head in his hands and groaned. Christ, what had Ratti done? What now? What if it were ever found out that Lejeune had been in collusion with him? He'd be an accessory to the crime. What a mess! He must get up there straight away to check on the *status quo*.

Pierre Lejeune flew to his car and raced off to the Meribel. Hammering on the door, he was answered by a very drunken Ratti, dishevelled, his hair and clothes awry – but there was no sign of blood on him.

"Where are they?" he screamed at the drunk.

Ratti shook his finger at him. "Temper, temper," he slurred.

Lejeune grabbed him by the throat. "Show me, you stupid little bastard, or I'll throttle you."

Ratti took him down a dark corridor into a small bedroom.

"Look!" he said triumphantly, swaying unsteadily, and pointing through the door.

Lejeune pushed past him. "Where's the light switch?"

"No bulb. My darkroom," volunteered Ratti.

Pierre peered inside. Through the gloom he could see the floor was littered with long, pale, patchy strips. What on earth were they?

365

"What is this?" he shouted. "Clothes? What have you done, you bloody little idiot?"

"My cuttings! I did it with my knife," Ratti said triumphantly, reaching down to the floor. "Look!"

Lejeune snatched the strip from his damp, scrawny hand, and inspected it. Then his face cleared and his pulses stopped racing. For heaven's sake! He didn't know whether to punch Ratti's stupid great nose, or whoop with relief. There was nothing to panic about. Ratti had only cut what were obviously photos of the girls into thousands of strips, and strewn the floor, the bed and the furniture with them.

"You crazy, pathetic fool," sneered Lejeune at his accomplice. "Is that all you can do for your kicks? You abysmal little toad! You dismal pervert! You scared the living daylights out of me. Don't ever do that again! But you could at least have saved some pictures for me for evidence. Now you've destroyed them. Were any of them compromising?"

Ratti waved his skinny arms around dramatically. "Naked sluts, cavorting. Orgies. Dope smoking." He was in full flood now. He might as well exaggerate the girls' activities to keep Lejeune sweet. He looked longingly at Lejeune's fly and stretched out his hand. "Be nice to me and I might let you have the negatives."

Lejeune slapped his hand away. "Stop that, you leery perv, or I'll have you for importuning a police officer."

"Ooooh! So masculine and authoritative. Have a drink, darling. Louis is loaded tonight and feeling very horny."

"Go fuck your nose. Just keep reporting back to me, especially on the blonder one, Mademoiselle Forsythe."

Ratti didn't think he'd seen her for a while, but wasn't about to admit it to Lejeune. *Quelle différence?* Blonde, brunette. They were all tarts who used men up and made their lives a misery.

"Yessir!" he said, making a drunken attempt to salute, and

poking himself in the eye instead. Wincing, *"Et merde,"* he cursed and blinked rapidly, still swaying.

Lejeune shook his head slowly. "Stupid bastard,' he commented coldly and took his leave.

Laura stood in Tom Howson's office on Monday morning in a state of shock. She simply could not believe her ears. Tom would be 'out of town' for at least three weeks, according to his secretary, and had left no message. Tom had given her no indication at all last night that he was going away. Surely his office was mistaken! How could it be possible to be so tender and loving when he dropped her off at the apartment; so tearful and apparently regretful, and then just . . . nothing? No word.

Surely he must have left some message or a note for her? Especially as he knew full well that Laura had to return to France by the end of this week. And he'd promised to join her for a few days, too. How could he just disappear without any explanation at all? None of it made any sense. This just couldn't be true!

Laura's eyes brimmed, and a lump came to her throat when she thought of their wonderful weekend. His sweetness, his soft words, the caresses, the caring, his magical love-making, the sheer beauty of the time they'd spent together. How could this all die in such a meaningless fashion? There was surely some mistake!

Laura made an effort to pull herself together, and her voice took on a businesslike tone. "Please could I leave a message for Mr Howson if he calls in?"

'Sure thing. But he's unlikely to bother to phone the office in the circumstances!" the pert brunette answered with a friendly giggle.

"Oh?"

"Well, with the wedding and everything, he's gonna be pretty busy."

"Wedding?" Laura frowned in puzzlement.

"Yeah. I mean, who bothers to ring the office on honeymoon?"

The words felled Laura like a bullet. All the colour and strength drained from her as her mouth dropped open in disbelief. She swayed slightly, suddenly feeling faint.

"Are you OK?" said the young girl, alarmed. "I mean, can I get you anything? A coffee or something?"

Laura fought valiantly to regain her composure, her face as white as a sheet. Then, with mammoth self-control, she calmly handed over a small piece of paper.

"No." Her voice was flat. "Thanks all the same. Here are my exam results. He said he wanted to know them."

"OK, I'll make sure he gets them," said the secretary , putting the note, unread, with a stack of other papers on her desk.

Absolutely devastated, Laura was unable to voice her thanks. She quickly turned away to hide her tears of heartbreak, and hurried out.

When the truth had dawned about Tom, all Laura wanted to do was crawl away from the humiliation. She couldn't bear to spend another moment in New York. She could not face the celebration-cum-consolation party for the examinees, most of whom had passed. Bravely she had congratulated Andrew, who had just scraped through on his third attempt. She was pleased for him. He deserved the success after his long struggle to make it.

Then Laura turned tail and fled. Crying her heart out, she made her way straight to the airport to catch the next flight home.

Chapter 26

Quintin's flat, overlooking the harbour and Prince Rainier's floodlit palace, was absolutely crammed with party guests, most of whom Jennifer knew. Henrietta was wearing the most amazing chiffon trouser-suit in bright swirls of orange, pink and purple, with wide-legged trousers that floated like flimsy veils around her slender limbs. Her face was lightly tanned, and her expression animated, yet serene. Jennifer had never seen her look more fetching.

"It must be love!" she thought darkly, enviously wishing herself a week back in time, when things had been so idyllic for her, too.

Jennifer was still fuming over the humiliating scene on the *Xerina*. It exacerbated her misery and heartache for Alexander. But there was no sign of him yet, and she'd not had the opportunity to find out from Hen if he'd be at the party. Anyway, there was such a crush of people to get through, and Jennifer was damned if she was going to let people know how she felt.

"Damn and double-damn him!" she muttered under her breath. "So what if I never see Alex again? What do I care? It's not the end of the world."

Now even Krep, her life-line, her sheet-anchor, had royally and blatantly snubbed her. She'd heard no word from him, and certainly had no intention of contacting him for an explanation. She wouldn't give him that satisfaction.

As usual she had had a devil of a job deciding what to wear, and in the end settled for a raspberry-pink *crêpe* ensemble with a top that knotted just above the waist. The matching, tight hipster trousers showed off her navel, flaring out at the ankles to hide her very high-heeled silver sandals, making her look taller and leggier than ever. The dark pink, flowing material was a wonderful foil for her hair, which cascaded in pale titian flames over her arms and back. She was a knock-out from the beholder's point of view. Inside, she felt anything but.

"Penny for 'em, you gorgeous thing," purred Quintin in familiar dulcet tones. "If Hen would let me, I'd have you both tonight!"

He grinned at Jennifer lasciviously, having emanated from nowhere and handed her a glass of champagne which she was desperate for. Quintin was dressed entirely in white. His flimsy lawn shirt was unbuttoned to the waist, and his bright flaxen hair waved over his ears in wings from a centre parting. But somehow, though outrageously foppish, he managed to carry off the look with casual masculine panache.

"Quintin, you handsome bastard!" she laughed. "Some people never change, thank God. Give your old friend Jennifer a kiss, I need cheering up."

She instantly flirted back, pouting her lips, consummate actress that she was. Quintin responded with a French kiss, having briefly checked that Hen wasn't looking. He followed on by nuzzling her ear with his tongue.

"Hey," he murmured into her hair, "How about a quick knee-trembler, divine sex-goddess?"

"But, Quintin," Jennifer protested mock-seriously, "you must know I'm worth far more than a paltry quickie!"

"Too right, my darling; that you are!" he agreed, his eyes dancing. "Some other time, then. But now, alas, I must move on and attend to my numerous guests!"

Jennifer smiled. He was such a tonic. At least Quintin and Hen were happy, even if she wasn't. She couldn't begrudge them that, and it was better for her to be partying than sulking alone at the Meribel. She bolted down her champagne, wishing she had a whole jeroboam to hand to drown her sorrows. Agitatedly she twirled the stem of her glass. Now she had a genuine excuse to seek out her hostess for a refill.

Jennifer pushed her way through the noisy and happy crowd until she found herself beside Henrietta. She'd gone out on to the balcony for a breath of fresh air and was idly fingering the scented oleander blooms growing in large ornate pots.

"Sweetie!" she cried, her face lighting up. "Do you need another of those?"

"Do I ever!" replied Jennifer, holding out her glass. "Super party. Nice crowd, and heavens, what a lovely view!"

Henrietta bent down and pulled a bottle out from among the several stashed in coolers on the cold mosaic floor outside. The ice-cold champagne hissed into the glass very satisfyingly, and Jennifer contemplated the bubbles racing up to the rim before looking appraisingly at her friend.

"You look tremendous tonight. So does Quintin. I must say, being in love suits you both."

"Thanks," said Henrietta, blushing faintly, "but honestly, it's such a struggle keeping up with Quint. The rotten louse always looks gorgeous. I mean, have you ever seen him look ghastly, even after the most frightful hangover? It's really not fair!"

Jennifer's face was rueful. "No, I suppose you're right. Women look haggard when they're hungover and tired, whereas men just look interestingly raffish. Life's a bugger."

"Hey! Talking of love, Alex said he might stop by later, but I haven't seen him yet."

Jennifer's heart lurched. "Did he ask whether I'd be coming?"

"No, but he was in a dreadful rush, and just going out as the phone rang. What news of Julius, is he still on the war path?"

Why did Hen have to ask about Julius, when all Jennifer wanted was news of Alex? She swigged back her champagne too quickly.

"Oh, very much so," she lied dully, "but being quite low-key about it. I don't think he was any too thrilled at my refusing to go out with him tonight. He'd been making plans to take me to the Chêvre d'Or."

"Phew!" whistled Hen, impressed. "Well I'm jolly flattered you chose our party instead, then! Actually, I think Julius is rather a good egg, and Laura is most impressed with him."

"So everyone tells me," said Jennifer moodily, "But..."

"You fancy Alex better. I know. Life's never easy, especially when you're as spoilt for choice as you've been."

Being spoilt for choice was hardly the case now, thought Jennifer miserably. Everything was going wrong. "Don't be sarky Hen," she protested mildly, "It's not like that anyway."

"I wasn't being sarcastic, actually," Henrietta replied. "Just stating a fact! You know that men seem to cling to you like pollen to a bee. I ask you!" Hen snorted wryly, "You're grumbling, and you've got a millionaire nuts about you as well as an aristo lover on the side! Nice work if you can get it, as the old song goes."

Nice work if it were true. If only it were! Jennifer looked moodily into her glass, and drained it angrily.

Henrietta smiled tolerantly at her friend and then looked towards the harbour where the tiniest breath of wind was stirring the reflection of the yachts at anchor in the water.

"I don't think I could ever get tired of this view, you know," she commented dreamily, leaning out with her elbows on the balcony rail. Then her tone changed. "Hey, wait a minute. What's going on here? Isn't that the *Xerina?*"

"Oh, Hen, surely you must know by now Krep's yacht's been there all summer, so what's new?" said Jennifer irritably, fiddling with her empty glass.

"No, listen, silly, she's on the move, I tell you." Henrietta's tone was adamant. "The gang-plank's up and she's not on her mooring. One thing's for sure, Mr Krep most certainly ain't going to the Chêvre d'Or tonight!"

"What?" said Jennifer, suddenly alarmed. She looked down at the harbour, then started, her eyes widening with amazement. "Hey, you're right!" she shouted incredulously. "What on earth can be going on?"

"Don't say your millionaire's running out on you! He wouldn't do that, would he?" asked Hen disbelievingly.

"To tell you the truth, Hen," sighed Jennifer, "I'm not so sure he wouldn't. Maybe he finally got fed up with not getting his oats."

Jennifer simply couldn't believe her eyes, but there it was. The *Xerina* was gracefully slipping out of le Port de Monaco without so much as a by-your-leave; right under her nose, and there wasn't a thing she could do about it! Never had she felt more impotent as she watched the yacht slowly, inexorably sliding out of her life, with agonising grace and stateliness.

Julius must have been much angrier than Jennifer thought. But why? Why had he suddenly changed from one day to the next? When she left him after lunch that last time he'd been fine; loving and attentive. None of it made sense. Bloody men! Damn. And damn again. This was unbelievable! Absolutely intolerable! Jennifer was so hopping mad she was grinding her teeth in rage at being made to look a complete fool. What a rotten party this was turning out to be. Alex not bothering to turn up, and now Julius had the neck to jilt her.

"Quick, Jen, here's a pair of bins Quint keeps for talent-spotting. Take a look through those."

Jennifer snatched the binoculars from Hen's outstretched hand, and hastily adjusted the view-finder. She focused on the yacht's enormous cockpit, sweeping the lenses over its occupants. There were several. And there was Julius, looking very elegant in a pale blue shirt and dark blazer. His mouth was set. He was gazing straight out towards the harbour mouth and the open sea beyond . . . with his arm casually draped around a familiar, lissom, pouting brunette. The only difference was, she was wearing a sparkling bracelet instead of manacles, and a scanty and plunging cocktail dress instead of a G-string. Italian tart! Krep was welcome to her.

Jennifer needed no further confirmation that Julius had cold-bloodedly discarded her now. She'd been right all along. He was an unprincipled bastard!

"Shit!" she said dully, "I don't believe this. I don't bloody believe it!"

"What? What is it, Jen?" cried Henrietta, looking at her friend with concern. "Oh, do tell me what's happening!"

All the colour had drained out of Jennifer's face, and she silently handed over the binoculars by way of reply, taking an enormous slug from her glass before topping it up again to the brim.

"Golly Moses," said Henrietta, stumped for a better expression, as she took in the situation. She shook her head and then turned back to Jennifer. "I wouldn't worry if I were you. I think the old fart's trying to make you jealous!"

"See if I care!" said Jennifer arrogantly. She stuck her tongue out and blew a raspberry at the departing yacht. "I think I'll get wonderfully pissed and enjoy the party, and I hope his bloody boat sinks."

Jennifer was sick with frustrated rage, but no way was she going to show it to the world. She pushed her way back into the room, less crowded now that some of the guests had drifted off to other gatherings. Stitching a grin on to her face, she affected to be the life and soul of the party. She might as well make the best of a bad situation. Quintin had cleared part of the floor and turned up the music for dancing.

Jennifer grabbed a shocking-pink carnation out of a vase, and rolled down the waist of her trousers as far as possible without exposing herself. She hitched up her top still further, and did an impromptu belly dance in the middle of the room. She stroked the flower up and down her smooth, tanned tummy, writhing sensuously to Mick Jagger's 'I Can't Get No

Satisfaction'. Rather appropriate, in the circumstances, she thought.

She allowed herself to be carried away on a cloud of male approbation that temporarily took her mind off the unsatisfactory state of her affairs. Closing her eyes she danced on, throwing herself into the song, mouthing the words and deliberately grinding her pelvis provocatively to cheers and applause, and ribald cries of "Geddemoff! Geddemoff!"

Jennifer, enjoying being the centre of attention, did not notice Alex's recent arrival. He was quietly scowling in the background, unimpressed by her showing-off.

She was obviously completely unmoved by his deliberate strategy of coolness over the last few days and didn't seem to be missing him at all. What a heartless creature she was! Alex had been miserable and dejected since the quarrel. Eaten up with rage and jealousy; perhaps unjustifiably, in the circumstances, but nevertheless suffering pain and grief at the loss of her. And here she was, laughing, dancing, and flaunting her body provocatively at hordes of slavering men. She didn't seem to have a care in the world!

Thoroughly irked and hurt by her apparent nonchalance, Alex would have discreetly left the party there and then. But Henrietta suddenly collared him and steered him towards a tray of drinks and canapés.

"Alex, darling," she greeted him warmly, "how lovely you were able to make it. Here's a drink, and help yourself to some eats. There's plenty to go round. I'll go and tell Jennifer you're here."

"No," said Alex, gripping her arm rather tightly, "please don't bother. She's obviously enjoying herself far too much to be disturbed."

Henrietta could see he was tight-lipped with fury. What a pity Alex had to have turned up just as Jennifer had gone totally over the top. If only he had arrived earlier. Jennifer would have been too occupied with Alex to have seen the yacht slip away, and probably wouldn't have cared much anyway. Now he was resenting her wildness and he'd quite naturally misconstrued the whole situation.

"She's had a few too many," said Hen, in mitigation for her friend.

"Quite," replied Alexander still scowling.

He took the proffered drink and went out on to the balcony away from the merriment, away from Jennifer's uncaring bravado, where it was quieter and cooler. He could look at the harbour lights and forget what was happening, forget that his stomach was churning. He didn't feel like being sociable at the moment, so he just leaned on the wrought-iron railings, silently drinking in his surroundings.

Although he had a lovely sea view from his parents' villa, Quintin's was better still. There was nothing to beat the sight of yachts in a harbour, lined up in all their majestic splendour, their hulls and masts reflected in the water, anchor-lights making tiny stars twinkling and winking in the barely perceptible ripples. There was always something going on; fishing boats quietly chugging out and back in with their catch, at the unfashionable end of the port. New arrivals and departures. Endless partying on the luxury yachts lined up along the inside of the sea-wall, the expensive end. There was always something to watch.

But wait a minute! Where was the familiar three-master? There was a gap where the *Xerina* was usually moored. Could it be that Krep had left the principality? Could it be that he'd totally misjudged Jennifer, that Krep was not, and never had been, her sugar-daddy?

"Anyway," he thought angrily, "why on earth should I care?"

The sounds of merriment and laughter from the party, drifting out into the soft twilight air seemed to mock at him and heighten his feeling of melancholy and restless anger. Suddenly, he knew it was a mistake to have come. It was

him all along: she did have another man. Since when? And several more according to Ratti. He would kill her. How dare she humiliate him by professing undying love for another man? The duplicitous slut. It was untenable. No way would he let her show her lying, cheating bitch-face in the principality again. He was going to teach her a lesson. Yes, he'd fix her car . . . Fix her . . . and her wretched lover, for good!

Deranged with grief, Lejeune left the Meribel for Nice airport. He had revenge in his soul and murder in his heart.

Alexander and Jennifer, speechless with desire for each other, made straight for Quintin's king-size bed. There he practically ripped her clothes off and exploded into her with a passion that took their breath away. Moments later they made love again with a tenderness that brought tears to Jennifer's eyes. Her dearest wish had come true: Alex had come back to her. He had a way of lighting up all her senses at once. There was an explosive chemistry between them, the touch of his skin on hers, the sound of his voice, the taste of his lips, the merest sight of him evoked a helplessness that enslaved her.

No one had ever inspired such depths of feeling in her before. It was like drifting into a strange and wonderful paradise of conflicting sensations, uncontrollable and stronger than she was. She felt herself veering from intense happiness to a wistful fear of the unknown; the terrible fear that anything so beautiful couldn't possibly last for ever. The inner turmoil was agonising, blissful, frightening, all-encompassing and terrifyingly fragile. She'd never been so hopelessly in love.

"God, you're wonderful. I've missed you so much," whispered Alex, stroking her hair tenderly.

"I'm sorry I shouted at you last week. It all seems such an age away now. Forgive me?" said Jennifer.

Alex kissed her in reply, and murmured, "Let's go home. I just want to sleep in your arms for ever."

Quietly, the lovers stole out of the party. They could thank

Hen and Quintin later. All they wanted now was to be together, to make up for lost time.

Outside, unfortunately, Jennifer's Mercedes, which had been lost in a sea of other cars earlier, now stood out like a beacon, parked crookedly on the pavement on its own.

"Oh dear," she said, not thinking. "I'd better not leave it like that."

"Give me the keys. I'll re-park it for you."

Jennifer waited admiringly on the pavement while Alex expertly manoeuvred the car into a proper parking space. God, how gorgeous he was!

She made her way towards him as he switched off the ignition and got out of the car. Glancing at the key fob, he made to hand it back to her, and suddenly started, looking at it again in disbelief. Jennifer's mouth went dry.

"What's the matter, Alex?" she said, with a sinking heart.

His voice was cold and flat. "Well, I never did. The keys are initialled 'J.K.' The number plate says 'J.M.' How very cosy! You lied to me, Jennifer. What do you think I am, a fool? The Mercedes is yours, from none other than your sugar-daddy, Julius Krep. Just as I suspected all along."

Jennifer was dumbstruck. Slowly she shook her head, her grey eyes wide with dismay.

"Don't try to deny it," he said furiously. "It's as obvious as the nose on your face. You haven't levelled with me, Jennifer. You used me as your bit of fun on the side while that toad Krep funded your extravagant lifestyle. You're no more than a greedy, two-timing slut." His eyes burned with contempt and his voice shook with emotion.

"Alex, please," she pleaded, as tears poured down her face. "You just don't understand. I swear I've never loved anyone as much as I love you. Please believe me." She made to put her arms round him, but he shrugged her off. She felt her chest turn to ice as her whole world collapsed around her. Now she was sobbing uncontrollably. She couldn't believe what she'd just heard Alex say. She couldn't understand what was happening. Nothing made sense any more.

Then her face twisted in bitterness as anger rushed in as her defence for her anguish and heartbreak. "Anyway, how dare you call me a slut! I'm not by any stretch of the imagination. You're no better. You told me yourself you were after a rich wife to bankroll your polo team. If that's not hypocrisy, then what is?"

For a moment Alex was stumped for words. Then quietly and in measured tones he said, "No, I'm not a hypocrite. At least I was honest about it. Perhaps we're one as bad as the other; two of a kind, living beyond our means and using others to attain our goals. There never was any future in this relationship, so we might as well be realistic and say goodbye now."

Jennifer was too stunned and heartbroken to speak. All she wanted was to take him in her arms and wish all the hurtful words away. Just to let things be the way they were only minutes before. But the distance between them might as well have been from the North to the South Pole. The chasm that had opened up was uncrossable. Heavy despair hung in the air like a wet cloud on a dreary weekend. It was hopeless, and both of them knew it.

The tension was palpable, unbearable. Everything around her seemed unfamiliar, hostile, the shadowy buildings and street corners closing in on her accusingly, imprisoning her in a new world of abject misery. Jennifer felt trapped in a helpless spiral of anguish and pain, plunging inexorably into a black world of despair. Her feelings of self-worth were shattered, destroyed. She believed she'd never be the same again. Nothing mattered any more, except her feeling of utter wretchedness, heartache and disillusion.

She could bear it no more. She snatched back her key from Alex and rushed to her car without saying goodbye. Almost as soon as she'd slammed her car door shut, she could hear the angry scream of his exhaust as Alex jumped into his car and roared out of her life for the last time.

Jennifer couldn't even remember taking the lift, or opening her door. Everything was a blur of misery. Once she found herself alone in the flat, she realised that she couldn't bear her own company. She found herself composing Julius' number. Then she remembered with dull exasperation and despair that he, too, had jilted her. He would be at sea, or already at his port of call with the Italian starlet and his coterie of jet-set friends. The thought of him enjoying himself in glamorous company made her feel doubly rejected. Had she ever had a worse evening in her life? Nothing had ever been this bad before. This really was the end of the line.

She had lost two men in one week. Julius had not broken her heart, but he'd insulted her pride. It was still a jolt to her vanity to be so callously and suddenly discarded for an Italian plaything in five-inch heels! The thought of Alexander returning home alone gave her such intense pain that she had to put it out of her mind, or go mad. She must do something. Anything to distract from the issue of her broken heart.

Maybe she should return to Quintin's party. Or would it be over now? She must pull herself together. She took herself to the bathroom and splashed her face with cold water to help her get rid of her tear-stained puffy look. The cold water cleared her brain, and made her feel slightly better. A couple of Alka-Seltzers and a large brandy later, she felt nearly human, and certainly drunker.

She picked up the telephone, glanced out of the kitchen window and saw that the idiot Ratti was staring across at her as usual. She put down the receiver and gave him two fingers, but that didn't deter him.

"Stupid bastard. He's all I need right now."

Jennifer staggered to the light switch and clicked the light off. In the semi-darkness she was still able to dial Quintin's number, and felt great relief as she heard his shouted reply over a thump of background music.

"Jennifer, my little darling! What can we do for you? Why have you deserted the party? Come back and brighten up our lives again! Nearly everyone's gone. Even Hen's deserted me. She's gone to bed, and I'm still in a party mood."

"I really don't know whether I'd be in a fit state to drive, Quint. My head's full of brandy, and I certainly couldn't walk a straight line."

"OK, then, darling. We'll bring the party to you. Won't be a tick. We've got plenty of booze left still."

"Who's 'we'?"

"My cousin Hugo. You'll like Hugo – he's almost as much of a raver as I am, but not half so good-looking, though the girls still seem to flock round him!"

Thank heaven for Quintin, she thought.

It wasn't long before they arrived, clutching a brace each of champagne and wearing expectant expressions. Quintin introduced Hugo, who was a darker, younger version of himself. He was tall, in his early twenties, blue-eyed and had long, dark, curling hair, brushed back from his face, which was classically handsome. He had Quintin's perfect teeth and strong chin, but a longer, more aquiline nose. Through her alcoholic haze, Jennifer was impressed.

"Told you she was divine, Hughboy. I was right, wasn't I?"

Hugo eyed Jennifer up and down unselfconsciously, just grinned appreciatively and said nothing.

"Come on you two, let's go into the sitting-room," said Jennifer, ushering them both in front of her. "I've got glasses in there."

"Hugo, you be barman," Quintin ordered as he plonked himself down on to the sofa. "I'm going to sit next to my dream girl."

Quintin pulled Jennifer down on to the cushions with him, and gently caressed the nape of her neck. She felt herself succumbing to his touch, and relaxed, letting her head drop forward as his expert fingers massaged her neck, and gently pressed out towards her shoulders with the ball of his thumbs.

"Aaah," his voice said soothingly, "but you really needed that. Heavens, you were tense."

Quintin's turquoise eyes looked into hers persuasively as he turned her face towards him. "I do a really good back massage. You should let me try it on you. I'll bet your back is a mass of knots." He trailed his fingers down the bare skin under her halter top into the curve of her waist. She liked the feeling of his hands on her body. It was very consoling, and distracted her from the black depression.

Hugo interrupted them with a glass of champagne each. He was wearing a pale, embroidered caftan over his tight slacks, and looked like a young Roman gladiator. What a joy it was to have such good and attractive company for drowning her sorrows. Perhaps there was life after death after all!

"Good old Bollinger! This is really hitting the spot!" exclaimed Quintin. "Come on, Jen, knock it back – that's the spirit." His white teeth lit up the tanned face, and his eyes sparkled mischievously. He looked back at Hugo, who was hovering uncertainly near the sofa, wondering whether to sit down. "Go on, Hughboy," ordered Quintin, grinning and lifting his glass to him. "Fill us up again."

Jennifer tendered hers, too. The champagne hissed satisfyingly into their glasses. Quintin got up and placed the lamp on the floor behind one of the armchairs. It gave off a dim and relaxing glow, and the three sat in the half-light, gradually growing more and more mellow, the conversation more and more trite and giggly.

"Got'ny grass left?" Quintin asked Hugo, languidly stroking Jennifer's arm. Little gold hairs glinted in the dim light against the satin sheen of her forearm.

"Enough, probably," he murmured lazily.

Now what were they up to? She'd thought Quintin had a

thing about dope. He'd made enough fuss about it earlier on in the summer. "Quintin! I thought you were dead against dope!" laughed Jennifer incredulously.

"Only for my employees. Anyhow, this is different, and it's only hash," Quintin grinned.

He took a long drag at Hugo's joint, and inhaled languorously, with his eyes shut.

"Hypocrite!" she chided lightly. "Anyway, I'm an employee . . . of sorts."

"Nope. You're a special friend." He passed her the roll-up. "You can do no wrong."

She took a long puff, passed it back to Hugo, and relaxed back against Quintin, her head in the clouds.

"Flattery will get you everywhere," she drawled.

"That's what I was hoping," Quintin whispered under his breath, then continued, "hey, where did you dispose of the viscount? Didn't you leave the party together?"

Bugger Alex. He was a bastard. He could take a running jump. She had to exorcise him from her life.

"Alex is hishtory," she slurred. "He loves horses more than women. I exshpect he'll marry one soon and they'll have lots of foals together." She giggled at her wit.

Quintin winked at Hugo, and they both grinned. "Ah, well. Plenty more fish in the sea," Quintin pronounced. "There's always Hugo and me – we love you far more than horses."

"I thought you loved Hen," remonstrated Jennifer mildly. Her thoughts were getting jumbled and distorted. Every so often Hugo became Alex. They had very similar voices.

"Cluck cluck!" said Hugo, flapping his elbows like wings. He had a childish sense of humour, too, like Alex.

"Shut up Hugh, you twit," said his cousin, smiling at his impersonation of a hen.

Quintin turned his attention to Jennifer and stroked her hair, his voice seductive and caressing. "Henrietta's not here now though, is she?"

There was nothing Jennifer liked more than having her hair stroked. It was so soothing. She could feel Quintin's breath on her neck, like a caress, a whisper of breeze. Gently he nibbled her ear. Jennifer felt herself melt. "No, I s'pose that's right," replied Jennifer, closing her eyes and taking another long puff. She didn't notice Hugo quietly getting up and extinguishing the light.

Jennifer was floating. All her senses were tingling with a sweet feeling of anticipation, flooding her body with desire. She was transported to a world where nothing mattered except physical sensation and instant gratification. Nothing mattered any more. There was no heartache, no despair. Just a desire to be pleasured and cosseted and soothed.

Quintin's lips were at her throat, his breath gently feathering the soft and sensitive skin of her neck. Jennifer rubbed her face against his chin, like a cat reaching for affection.

"Let me sort your back out," Quintin whispered soothingly, gently nibbling her earlobe. "It's going all knotted again; I knew I shouldn't have mentioned that prick Alex. Lie down now. I'm an ace *masseur*."

Jennifer obeyed without protest and lay face down on the sofa, and Quintin undid the halter neck of her top, massaging the back of her neck and the tops of her shoulders. It was pure heaven. Jennifer gave in to his wonderfully manipulative fingers, and drifted off into quasi-somnolence. She hardly noticed when Quintin skilfully removed her whole top and worked further down her back. He walked his thumbs up and down her spine, stroked her back muscles with circular movements, massaging her with strong and expert hands, then loosened her trousers and worked her lower back.

"Mmmmm, what paradise!" sighed Jennifer. "This is wonderful..."

"Let me do your whole body," Quintin murmured. "Come

on, off with the lot. Here, Hugo, give me a hand."

The pair of them gently removed all her clothes, as well as their own. Jennifer was so relaxed she was past caring – all she was aware of was the sensuous feeling of her body being massaged.

"Hughboy," whispered his cousin, "get some baby oil, almond oil, anything like that from the bathroom."

A few moments later Jennifer groaned with pleasure as warm oil was poured on to her skin and she felt hands slithering all over her body, then down her legs, and up again, then down and in between her legs – more oil, more caresses, then, oh heaven, his slippery fingers in the cleft of her buttocks – she could feel her hips start to move rhythmically, her senses taking control. Then Quintin gently slid himself inside her. But this felt totally different, a feeling she hadn't experienced before, nobody had ever done that to her. But, oh . . . oh, yes, so pleasurable. Sliding in, and out, and in, and out, again and again, slowly, teasingly, between the firm cheeks – oh, what a glorious, unbelievable sensation – then hands came round underneath her, arching up her hips, caressing her vulva, fingers sliding into her wetness, and she could feel other hands on her breasts, gently twirling her nipples, until she was on the point of orgasm.

"Hugh," whispered Quintin silkily, "squeeze in underneath her."

Quintin took his own weight on his arms and Jennifer felt herself being lifted up, while the younger man's naked, taut body positioned itself under hers. Hugo's athletic body arched up towards Jennifer's as he grasped her slender hips, searching greedily for the slippery warmth and wetness inside her as the heavy globes of her breasts lightly grazed his chest.

"Now, goddess, this is the *apotheosis*," came Quintin's voice in a soft murmur, as Hugo found his target and slipped his stiff weapon in between her wet, silky lips.

Jennifer squirmed with surprise. But, no, surely it was not

possible. She now had both men inside her. "Please," she murmured, "you feel too tight."

"Alternate thrusts," murmured Quintin, as he pulled back slightly, "she's only a little thing: we don't want to ruin her for life."

Jennifer felt suspended in the most unbelievable liquid world of writhing bodies, soft skin, the sweet smell of almond oil, and the incredible sensation of being caressed and stroked all over, as well as everywhere inside, her body. There wasn't a single part of her being neglected. Quintin was gently biting and sucking the nape of her neck, Hugo was running his tongue all round the inside of her mouth, his hands playing with her nipples, whilst they were both alternately, slowly thrusting into her. As Quintin partially drew out, she could feel Hugo slowly sliding in, an extraordinary and exquisite sensation. Time stood still. She didn't have one sense that wasn't replete, sated. All three bodies were as one, all in pursuit of pleasure, of pure unadulterated hedonism. The stroking, sucking, rhythmically thrusting bodies seemed to take on a life of their own, floating away from reality, floating away into a world of dark, hot, fluid sensation that rippled and flowed into eternity.

"God, I'm going to come!" she shrieked. "Oh, yes!" and her body shuddered and shook in spasms of sheer ecstasy that burned through her with the intensity of fire. Jennifer screamed with uncontrollable delight, her cries gradually tapering off into soft, animal moans of satisfied contentment.

Quintin slowly eased himself out, and sat aside from them, while Hugo continued, raising Jennifer's shoulders so that they both could watch and admire her breasts as they bobbed gently with his rhythmic thrusts. Then with a sudden unbearable agony of longing he lost control, quietly sighing as he came. Jennifer was on the edge of orgasm as she felt Hugo's throbbing wetness emptying inside her. Her hips involuntarily took over the rhythm he had lost; then she groaned and collapsed on to his chest as he waned and slipped out of her.

Seconds later, she felt Quintin's hands on her waist. Gently he lifted her off his now inert cousin and stood her up. Propelling her to the arm of the sofa, he bent her over it. Standing behind her, he spread her legs, and thrust into her again, with long, firm strokes, his supple fingertips feathering her clitoris, until Jennifer felt the familiar hot surge that heralded another climax. As she wildly writhed and moaned again with pleasure, Quintin thrust harder and faster, his body making slapping sounds against hers, until he, too, came, roaring and buckling at the knees.

Afterwards, nobody spoke for quite a while as, exhausted and sated, the threesome lay around the foot of the sofa, in varying positions of collapse. Then the younger man fumbled around for his tobacco tin, and rolled another joint. Quietly, he passed it round, and all three, still sprawled naked on the floor, enjoyed its sweet, heady sensation.

Jennifer closed her eyes, and suddenly shivered, feeling the heat ebbing from her body. She reached for Alex in a dream. But no, of course it wasn't Alex. It was Quintin ... or maybe it wasn't. Maybe it was Hugo. She shivered again, and the champagne and tobacco suddenly tasted sour in her mouth. Quintin felt her tremor and threw his shirt round her shoulders.

"Got another one of those, Hughie?" asked Quintin, his eyes sleepy and shadowed with satisfied lust, as he passed the joint back to him for one last puff.

"Nope – last one, I'm afraid," Hugo replied, leaning back contentedly as he blew smoke back through his nostrils and inhaled again. The dark curls flowing on to his naked shoulders and his aquiline profile gave him a dangerously decadent and Byronic air.

"Ah, well, anyone for more champagne?" Quintin invited. Through the dark gloom his blond hair shone as he ran his fingers through it and flicked the thick waves behind his ears. The dark and the fair. Quintin and his cousin were a dangerous and attractive pair, an irresistible and heady mix of disarming charm and sex-appeal.

"Jesus, I couldn't," groaned Jennifer.

"Hughboy?"

"Don't mind if I do," he answered lazily, stubbing out the roll-up into a small ashtray.

"I'm for a coffee," said Jennifer, stumbling to her feet with trembling legs, "or I'll keel over."

Ratti smiled triumphantly. He lifted the receiver and composed the familiar number. He waited impatiently for a reply.

"*Enfin!*" he said. "Is Lejeune there, please?

"Nope."

"But he told me he was on night duty at the moment."

"Yep, but he's gone to Nice to attend to some business there. Who is it?"

"Oh, never mind. It's just that I had something to report to Lejeune."

"*Et alors?* Why can't you tell me? I'm his superior, Madoc."

Ratti paused. Why not? There was no reason why he shouldn't curry favour with the higher ranks. It would stand him in better stead than running around that bully, Lejeune. Ratti cleared his throat, "Monsieur Madoc," he said importantly, "I have reason to believe that there are drugs on the premises of No. 613 Le Meribel. Pierre Lejeune asked me to keep a watch on them. My name is Louis Ratti, and I live in the block opposite. There are several English people there behaving atrociously; drunk, disorderly and doped up. You should go up and take a look."

He paused and listened to the raised, excited voice at the other end. "Of course," he replied. "The evidence is bound to be there. But you'll have to hurry to be in at the kill. I'll wait for you in the lobby if you like. I'll be your principal witness."

The line clicked as Ratti put the phone down with a sigh of satisfaction. The cold, pale eyes were glassy with triumph. He walked back to the balcony and retrieved his binoculars from the hammock.

Pity the glasses weren't equipped with night vision, because one of them had switched the damn light off after a while. But then, he'd seen all he had to, before then. That was definitely a joint they were passing round. The trap was set, and the glory would be his, not Lejeune's! Those sluts would get their come-uppance at last, after a long summer's wait.

Jennifer padded to the kitchen in her bare feet and filled the kettle. Whilst waiting for the water to boil, she became aware of how stickily wet she was, and went into the bathroom for a wash. As she dried herself, she caught her reflection in the mirror. She didn't like what she saw. Her eyes looked as empty as her heart now was. Crossing back through the bedroom, she angrily shrugged off Quintin's shirt, climbed into some jeans, and threw on a tee-shirt.

The kettle was hissing furiously in the kitchen. Numbly she spooned coffee into a mug, poured on the steaming water, and as she approached the sitting-room she could hear the mumble of male voices.

Then Quintin's, "No, but now you know what I meant by the *apotheosis*," a quiet snigger and more mumbling, then Quintin again, "No, you idiot... But she obviously likes it that way too, though not all of them do. A spot of sodomy makes a change every now and then.".... Another bout of sniggering. "Inventiveness is the name of the game, or it can get boring... Well, you live and learn ... try it yourself some time..." ... and more muffled laughter from both of them.

Jennifer froze in her tracks. She felt disgusted and humiliated by the men's casual and clinical dissection of their evening's entertainment. Another notch on the belt, another successful lay for the trophy wall. Oh, boy, had she performed well for them!

All her earlier pain came back in great floods, the reason for this hollow charade. Her heart constricted as waves of anguish overwhelmed her. She thought she'd burst with misery. Oh, Alex, why did you drive me to this? Why did you throw me out of your life? Why couldn't she have been with him now instead of providing cheap thrills for Quintin and his cousin? Her eyes filled with tears as she remembered how different it had been with Alex. Tender and meaningful. He'd meant everything in the world to her. Now he'd left her. Now it was all gone.

Everyone had used her and then abandoned her, like jetsam flung broken on to the beach by the surging sea. She was all alone at the mercy of the elements. Nobody cared about her any more. A tidal wave of nausea and tears welled up into her throat, all but stifling her. Jennifer ran back into the kitchen, poured the coffee down the sink and reached for the Courvoisier Alex had given her in happier days.

"Damn them all to hell! To hell with the whole greedy male sex!" she cried aloud in anguish and drank straight from the bottle.

The next thing Jennifer knew she was staggering out of the Meribel on her bare feet, clutching the bottle of Cognac, her hair in a wild cloud, her expression crazed and vacant. She lurched around the streets as the first grey fingers of dawn crept up the sky. She would never remember how she got to her car, but suddenly she found herself in the driving seat of her beautiful silver Mercedes, swigging great gulps of Courvoisier like anaesthetic, longing for sweet oblivion and an end to all her pain.

Laura rubbed her red-rimmed eyes as she disembarked from her long flight with all the other weary passengers. The journey had been purgatory. Sleep would have been a blessed relief for her shattered, aching heart, but such was her agitation and grief, she hadn't been able to close her eyes all night. The sight of the palm trees and the mountains in the misty Riviera pre-dawn only added to her anguish. It brought back memories of Tom and her Bermuda paradise and brought on floods of tears again. She didn't remember going through Customs, or even how she got to her car, but suddenly, there she was, sitting in the driving seat. Her small hands were clenched and a livid white, as she gripped the driving wheel and blinked hard to clear the tears from her vision. How could she face life again? Nothing seemed worthwhile any more. There was nothing to look forward to in a world without Tom. There seemed no point in living.

Eventually, she wiped the tears from her eyes, and as she wrenched her key into the ignition, the engine roared into life. The open-topped car hurtled through the deserted streets, the screech of its tyres reverberating hollowly against the tall, flaking buildings, echoing the pain in her heart. Soon she reached the switchback mountain road, the highest Corniche, with its hairpin bends and dizzying drops into infinity and death.

The cool air felt like balm as it whipped pale blonde tendrils of hair from her face, and she pressed down harder on the accelerator. Blinded by tears, oblivious to danger, she put her foot flat down. The speed excited her. Now she was invincible, in control of her destiny. Nothing mattered any more. Faster she drove, and faster, into the ghostly grey fingers of dawn: until, at last, she was lighter than air.

She didn't hear the crunch of metal, the sickening thump and crash of the tree exploding into a million shards; she just soared peacefully like a spectral bird on silent wings – on and on, above it all, into ever-darkening, ever-quietening blackness.

Chapter 27

Quintin jumped violently and Hugo leapt to his feet as the two men were suddenly jolted out of their post-coital stupor by a tremendous banging on the door.

"What the hell?" exclaimed Quintin, staggering to his feet and looking for his trousers in the dim light of dawn. "Hugo? Jennifer? Where the hell is she? Christ, what is that racket?"

"Shit!" said Hugo. "Where are my clothes? Quint, get dressed, you silly bastard. Maybe she's locked herself out."

"Oh, come on, Hugo. As if Jennifer could possibly make a din like that. Where the hell is she, anyway? Jennifer?"

But there was no sign of her anywhere.

Quintin hurriedly pulled on his trousers. "Where the fuck's my shirt?"

"Holy Christ!" groaned Hugo. "It sounds like an army out there. Hurry up, Quint, or the whole bloody building'll be round here."

The two men lurched around ineffectually in the gloom, tripping over their own feet and each other, struggling to get dressed with mounting panic as the din increased, this time accompanied by loud voices.

"*Allez. Police! Ouvrez la porte, ou on va la forcer.*"

"Jeez – the police! Hugo, you're more dressed than me, you go," hissed Quintin, trying to focus his mind. "Hurry up, before they break down the door. Christ almighty, this is all we need! Quick. I'll throw open the french windows to freshen the air. Oh holy shit, I don't bloody believe this!"

Hugo staggered to the door, tucking in his shirt with shaking fingers, leaving his panic-stricken friend tussling with the sliding balcony doors. There was an almighty crash and expletive as the police continued their efforts to force the entrance door, but it only groaned and didn't yield.

"Yes?" queried Hugo, as he opened it, feigning calm. There were three men confronting him; but only one of them in uniform. All wore threatening expressions.

"*Alors, enfin!*" exclaimed the shortest one.

"I'm sorry, I don't speak French," lied Hugo, his heart thumping with dread. What the hell was this all about?

"We are looking for Mademoiselle Forsythe. Miss Laura Forsythe."

Hugo felt instant relief. Thank God they weren't after him, or Quintin.

The shortest man, who appeared to be the spokesman, had hard, grey staring eyes and a jutting nose. Standing next to him was a tall, muscular man in uniform, with a glowering expression in his dark, hooded eyes. His brows were thick and furrowed, and met in the middle. Hugo didn't like the look of them. The short, beak-nosed man pushed his way into the flat, followed by his sinister, uniformed companion, and a thin, scrawny pale-eyed man.

"Never heard of her," replied Hugo, keeping up a front.

How long could he keep it up though? Hurry up, Quintin, you bastard. Come and get me out of this.

The chief conferred briefly with the scrawny man, whose name appeared to be Ratti.

"*Alors, ne nous racontez pas d'histoires, hein?*" sneered the dark henchman.

At last, Quintin emerged from the sitting-room, swaying slightly.

"He's not making up stories," he said. "Miss Forsythe is not here. She's abroad."

"Do not be absurd. We saw her earlier. Where is *la blonde*

... er, the young lady I saw you both with earlier?" demanded the pale-eyed Ratti, who up till now had not addressed them.

"Well, it quite obviously appears she's not here," answered Quintin.

This made no sense at all. First they ask for Laura, and now it was Jennifer. What the hell would the police want with either of them, anyway? Quintin didn't see why he should fall over himself to give these idiots information. The visitors eyed him with cold suspicion, but Quintin didn't bat an eyelid.

"And you, monsieur," said the inspector, "are quite obviously lying. You give us no alternative but to search the premises for evidence, and for the young lady."

"Search away," replied Quintin with a cocky grin. "You won't find anything."

"In that case," the officer went on sneeringly, "you will not object, *alors*, if we search both of you for certain ... er ... substances you were seen passing around, as well as searching the premises?"

"Nope, search away!" grinned Quintin, hiccuping volubly.

"You are drunk!" declared the man, gesturing to his colleagues to start searching.

What an observant clever-dick. Anyone could see he was legless. Paralytic.

"Yep! And shirtless, too!"

"There is no need for foul language, monsieur."

Quintin giggled. "I said s.h.i.r.t.l.e.s.s., you halfwit! Is there a law against being drunk and shirtless indoors?"

And he hiccuped again. What twerps these frogs were! The steely grey eyes hardened, but the man did not reply.

"*Tiens, tiens, Madoc! Voici son chemisier!*" said the uniformed officer, emerging from the main bedroom with a malevolent sneer on his face.

Big deal, thought Quintin. What's so brilliant about finding my shirt for chrissakes?

"Merci, Noireau," replied Madoc. Taking the shirt from his sneering cohort with a flourish, he searched the pockets to no avail. Undeterred, Madoc turned back to address Quintin and Hugo. "Just so, *hein*? In the bedroom. May I ask what your shirt is doing on the young lady's bed? Although, of course, the answer is obvious in a household of drugs and orgies!"

Quintin felt uneasy now. Maybe the police had something on them after all! But he decided to brazen it out. He folded his arms over his bare chest and faced his aggressors cockily.

"So how come you know this place inside out? Have you been spying on us or something? In England we have a law against peeping Toms."

The hard, grey eyes flared for an instant. "Shut up, or I'll arrest you for insulting behaviour."

Madoc conferred with the scrawny Ratti, and left the latter in charge of the drunken Englishmen before disappearing off into the sitting-room with the uniformed officer. There were sounds of furniture being moved, drawers being roughly opened, boxes being slid across the floor. They sounded as if they were making a real mess of the place.

"Alors, où est Mademoiselle Forsythe?" asked Ratti with open hostility.

"What's it to you?" said Quintin, "Don't you speak English?"

"Non," he answered, discomfited. *"Où est-elle?"*

"Mademoiselle Forsythe est à New York. That's in the USA. *Aux Etats-Unis* to you, thicko."

"Hein?" Ratti's mouth dropped open with surprise. Lejeune had stressed all along that Laura was his target. It was her blood he was after, and now she wasn't even here! But how was he to know which blonde was which? Christ, they were so alike, the bitches! Now Lejeune would be down on him like a ton of bricks for sending his boss on a wild goose chase and making a fool of him. There was going to be hell to pay!

"She's been in New York for three weeks, you twerp,"

Quintin crowed. "But you should have known that, being policemen. Christ, what an incompetent lot!"

Hugo gave his cousin a worried look. "Quint, watch it . . . Go easy," he said quietly.

"Don't worry, Hughboy," Quintin reassured him. "This halfwit doesn't speak our lingo. What's more, I don't even think he's a policeman. And we're obviously in the clear. They can't prove anything."

"What about the . . . you know . . . the . . ." Hugo whispered in Quintin's ear.

"No sweat, Hughie. I hoinked the old ashtray into space, with the baccy tin which was empty anyway. Into everlasting oblivion. I think they're sitting in a palm tree, six floors down."

The two men sniggered conspiratorially. Then Quintin turned back to their glowering guard. The turquoise eyes were triumphant. "Well, you seem to have made a complete bog of this, you and your frog detectives. An utter shambles, wouldn't you say, old fruit?"

Stone-faced and uncomprehending, Ratti stood his ground, square against the exit door, his slack lips twisted into a snarl, hating the two smug Englishmen who were ostensibly making a mockery of this long-planned operation. Hating them for their expensive clothes, their fashionable haircuts, their arrogant air of affluence and superiority.

Dieu merci! He'd like to see the grins wiped off the faces of these *filthy anglais!* When Madoc threw the book at them, the boot would be on the other foot! They'd probably be thrown out of Monaco for good.

Five minutes later, in a filthy temper, Madoc and his cohort came storming out of the bedroom. Ratti quailed at the sight and his heart sank.

"You're an idiot, Ratti," shouted Madoc, his voice trembling with rage. "This place is in the clear. I'm going to have you for wasting police time."

"It wasn't my doing, Inspector, I swear," he whined, cringing and rubbing his sweaty white hands together nervously. "Pierre Lejeune put me up to it. He was the one who made me keep a watch on the flat. He told me there were drugs hidden in the bathroom. It was Lejeune ... I promise you."

There was not much activity in the small white hospital room. Submerged under a whole battery of equipment was the figure of a young woman. She was as pale as death, but the hair spilling all over the pillow shone like a pale gold beacon. All that could be heard was the constant 'blip, blip, blip' of the monitor. Her breathing was imperceptible. No change, noted the doctor. Sitting beside her, watching constantly over her, was a dark-haired man, who had not left her side.

"Well?" the man whipped round, suddenly aware of the doctor's presence. His face was gaunt with grief and lack of sleep. "How long has she got now, would you say?"

"It's always hard to tell in these cases. I wouldn't like to say." The doctor's voice was soothing, but non-committal.

"I don't understand. You're the doctor. You're supposed to know these things!" he cried in anguish. "Surely we can do something?"

"We have limited facilities here, sir, but I'm afraid it would still be of no use to transfer her to Paris or London. It's too late. We can do nothing but wait. It is out of our hands now."

The doctor turned on his heel and walked out of the room, leaving the man utterly defeated: alone with his guilt and sorrow.

Pierre Lejeune crept into the hospital room with bated breath. He'd just heard about the accident. It was a glamorous young blonde in a sports car, he'd been told. She was near death – unlikely to survive – and the car a complete write-off. He had rushed straight away to the Princess Grace Hospital, suddenly consumed with terrible guilt.

The first sight that greeted his eyes in the small side room was a man with his back to him, wracked with grief, his head in his hands. Beyond him, her life hanging on a fragile thread, her face obscured by a respirator and tubes, he could see the familiar cloud of silky blonde hair. His heart lurched as heavy guilt rose in his throat like sour bile and stifled him. God, what have I done? he asked himself. Pierre wanted to die. Shame and remorse overcame him in great choking sobs. This was all his fault. His bitterness had caused this desperate scene: this utter, wretched grief. It was all his doing.

Pierre was devastated. Wiping the tears away to clear his vision, he moved forward very quietly, not wishing to disturb her companion. He needed to see her face more clearly, even afraid as he was to be confronted by the tragedy he had caused. Then, in an instant of blessed relief, he realised that the pale, translucent face on the white pillow was not Laura's.

"Dieu merci," he prayed now, as the tears flowed down his cheeks with no restraint. "Laura is safe." Thank God in heaven above, who in his mercy had spared Laura, and spared him the burden of carrying a death on his conscience for the rest of his days. His bitterness had driven him over the edge. He had behaved like a mad man, vindictive, jealous, beyond reason, and he fully deserved to pay the price. But somehow, fate had intervened to absolve him from the most terrible sin of all. This accident, though desperately tragic, was not of his doing.

He must see Laura again, just to convince himself that she was all right. He must confess everything – throw himself on her mercy, and hope that she would have it in her heart to forgive him, or he would be unable to live with himself. It was likely she would hate him more than ever, just as he now hated himself, but it was only what he deserved, for wanting her dead and disgraced. Just before he tip-toed out of the room, he looked at the frail blonde again, his heart now full of compassion. "May God bless you, too," he prayed, "and make you well again."

Laura turned the key to No. 613 and stepped inside. It was already mid-morning, and she was dropping with fatigue. She'd taken ages to get to Monte-Carlo because almost as soon as she left the airport for the Promenade des Anglais, she'd discovered to her horror that her brakes were not working. So she had to get the car to a garage and then take a taxi home. The mechanic looked totally mystified when he examined the cables, which appeared to have been severed, and said it would take a while to fix them. "The car is undriveable like this, mademoiselle," he'd said apologetically, "an absolute death-trap." Thank God she had noticed before reaching the mountain road!

At last she was safely home. Now she could rest and hide from reality for as long as she needed. She put her bags down in the hallway, and went into the kitchen to make a cup of tea. Heavens, it was a mess! Why was everything pulled out of the cupboards? She filled the kettle and looked round amongst the clutter for the tea caddy and a mug. While the kettle was boiling, she decided, she'd put some of her bags in her room.

She crossed the hallway to her bedroom, and stood aghast. Her room had been ransacked. The mattress was pulled off the bed, the sheets and covers rumpled and thrown on the floor, and all the drawers and contents pulled out and strewn around. She wanted to scream. This was a nightmare!

Laura ran to the other rooms, and found everything strewn around in the same way. She collapsed on to the floor, sobbing hysterically. God, this couldn't be happening, not on top of her broken heart and shattered life! Didn't she have enough to contend with already without finding her one refuge wrecked? What on earth had she ever done to deserve this? What more could go wrong? This had to be rock bottom. She couldn't take any more. Laura banged her fists on the cold floor as she cried her heart out, shaking and convulsed with grief. She'd never felt suicidal in her life, but if she'd had a gun in her hand now, she'd have ended it all.

Laura was making so much noise that she didn't hear the door open quietly behind her.

"Laura. Laura, love," came the anguished voice, "what are you doing here? We weren't expecting you until the end of the week."

It was Henrietta. She ran towards Laura, knelt on the floor beside her and cradled the weeping girl's head in her arms.

"Oh God, this is so awful for you!" she said, rocking Laura gently against her. "But believe me, it wasn't meant to happen this way. We were going to clear up before you returned, but you're home earlier than we expected. You told us you wouldn't be back till the weekend at the earliest. Oh dear, I'm so sorry. Here, take my hanky and blow your nose. Then I'll give you a shot of brandy and explain it all to you. There now. Everything's OK, honestly. Come into the kitchen. Come on."

Henrietta took Laura's arm, and helped her to her feet. She led her to the kitchen and sat her down. Laura mopped her tears and blew her nose volubly. The kettle was boiling furiously. Hen turned off the gas. A few moments later, she handed Laura a brandy and sat down beside her.

"Here, drink up. You need this much more than tea. I really don't know where to begin, so much has happened."

Laura looked at the brandy with distaste, but obediently sipped it while Henrietta told her very briefly about the abortive raid (or anyway, only as much as Quintin had wanted to recount to her, from his drunken recollection of the evening): that the police had stormed in, searched him and Hugo, and the flat, and then stormed out again, leaving the whole place like a tip.

"Since then we've heard nothing," concluded Henrietta.

"But it's a long story, Laura. You can ask Quint the details later. Now, as a first priority I think you need some sleep. You've had a dreadful shock; but you simply can't stay here in this mess, all alone."

"Hen, please. I'll be all right. I just need to be by myself," replied Laura obstinately.

"Don't be silly," Hen reasoned. "You look whacked and you're obviously very distressed. I've got the car downstairs. Come and rest at Quintin's place. I've got some marvellous sedatives for trauma, and you'll sleep like a baby. Then tomorrow you can put your feet up while Quint and I get your flat spruced up. Believe me, it's probably not as bad as it looks, it's just that everything's a bit jumbled."

Laura looked hesitant, and then, realising this was the only sensible option, her expression changed to relief. "Thanks, Hen, you're an angel. I don't know what I'd have done if you hadn't turned up just now."

Laura meekly allowed herself to be led away by Henrietta. The story seemed incredible, and she was curious to hear it in more detail. But for now, it could wait. She was all cried out, flattened with exhaustion and heartache, and oblivion for a few hours with a sedative seemed like the answer to her prayers. Maybe things would seem better in the morning.

The next day, Quintin and Henrietta sat on the balcony, lounging on their chaises-longues, enjoying the bright morning sun and a leisurely breakfast of coffee and croissants. The couple chatted amiably. From time to time Quintin glanced vaguely down at the copy of the *Nice Matin* across his knees.

"How's Laura this morning?" he asked, smoothing down the newspaper.

"I looked in on her, but she's still sleeping, so I thought it best to leave her."

"She seemed in an awful state last night. Why was she so upset about the mess? After all, it's only rented, that place, and she's got nothing of value there. It's a dump anyway and the furniture's horrible."

Henrietta's green eyes blazed. "Oh, honestly, Quint, you are unsympathetic. That sort of thing's pretty bloody to come home to, isn't it?"

"I suppose so," he agreed, "but she's usually so calm and ordered. Not the hysterical kind."

"Perhaps the tears were a bit excessive," Henrietta mused, "a bit over the top. I didn't dare ask, but do you think maybe she failed her exams?"

Quintin's face cleared. "You could have a point there. That could explain it."

He pondered for a while, crumbling a croissant and putting the melting slivers of pastry in his mouth. He took a sip of coffee and looked at Henrietta reflectively.

"Still," he continued, "she's awfully young. She can sit them again. It's not the end of the world, is it?"

Henrietta shook her head slowly, and raised her eyebrows. "Pragmatic old fart. Where's your milk of human kindness?"

"In there," he laughed seductively, sliding his hand up her slender thigh, "But I'll give you some more if you play your cards right."

God, what a one-track mind Quintin had! Why could be never be serious for more than five minutes at a time?

Henrietta smiled wryly. "I can imagine, you insatiable sexpot," she said, "And anyway, what's so kind about that? I thought kindness came from the heart, not from below the waist. For heaven's sake!" she squealed, squirming impatiently as she pushed his insistent hand away. "Do be serious, Quint. We're digressing as usual. Stop changing the subject, and let's be practical. We must get Laura sorted out. It's already nearly midday!"

Quintin sighed. "You women are all the same!" he said good-naturedly, and resigned himself to reading the *Nice Matin*.

Henrietta sipped her coffee and looked down at the harbour. The stately *Xerina* was back at her mooring, she noticed. She wondered whether Julius was still partying with the starlet. Heavens, but hadn't Jennifer been hopping mad and upset when Krep had sailed out of the port as cool as cucumber, right under her nose! Come to think of it now, where was Jennifer? Nobody had heard from her since she went off with Alexander at the party. Ah well, doubtless they were still together; celebrating their reunion in time-honoured fashion.

Maybe it would all work out, and Jennifer would be a countess one day. Henrietta smiled at the thought of her crazy friend filing in solemn procession with dozens of others into the House of Lords, wearing a tiara and an expression of dignity. Just imagine it! Jennifer was so anarchic and irreverent!

Rather like Quintin, really. She looked at him with affection. The bright hair flopped over his eyebrows as he squinted at the local paper in the sun, lounging back languidly in his chaise-longue. His favourite Herbie Frogg shirt, a riotous peacock-blue number, was unbuttoned to the waist, showing his deeply-tanned chest; tucked into tight, white trousers that barely allowed him to sit. What a gorgeous creature he was! Come to think of it, that's what he reminded her of: a peacock, for ever strutting around, showing off his colours – and, she smiled, his tail – to all who attracted him.

What a pity she'd grown so fond of him, because it couldn't last. Henrietta had better things to do than be a disco-dolly in a night-club and swan around the Riviera getting a suntan with a playboy, however lovable! She would always adore Quintin and treasure the memory of her idyllic summer with him, but now she seemed to have grown up and left him behind. All of a sudden she felt restless and dissatisfied.

So much had happened in these few months. The simmering undercurrent of bitterness, revenge and near-tragedy in the lives of Laura and Jennifer had touched her deeply. On the face of it, those two had everything. Beautiful, popular, successful

. . . and yet. Pierre had done his utmost to wreck Laura's summer, and Jennifer had lurched from one dire catastrophe to another.

In all truth, though, realised Henrietta guiltily, it was she herself who had almost killed Jennifer with those pills and potions. It was clearly not enough to dispense cure-alls. In fact, it had been damn dangerous and irresponsible. 'A little knowledge is a dangerous thing,' as the saying went. Henrietta had to stop dabbling in medicine. Either that, or go the whole hog and do it properly. It was time now to make amends, both for Jennifer's sake, and for Henrietta's own self-respect.

Henrietta decided she would have to tear herself away from this seductive and sybaritic existence, and make something of her life, as Laura was doing. Why shouldn't women do something worthwhile and have proper careers and qualifications? Then, if all else failed, at least one had a sense of purpose, as well as respect from others.

Henrietta got up from the table, and started to clear away the breakfast things when Laura suddenly appeared in a white dressing-gown, looking pale but calm.

"Good morning, Laura, did you sleep well?" asked Hen kindly.

Quintin put his paper down and smiled at her. "You certainly look better than you did yesterday."

"I do feel a lot better," she replied without enthusiasm, "And yes, I did sleep well. Very well, thanks, Hen. Those sedatives did the trick very efficiently."

"I'll go and make us a fresh pot of coffee," Hen said, picking up the tray. "Are you hungry? Because that gannet Quintin's finished all the croissants. But there's yoghourt or fruit, if you'd like."

"No, I'm not at all hungry, but coffee would be lovely, thanks."

"Come and sit down. I'll pull up another chair," said Quintin, getting up from his, and motioning her into it. Laura did as he bade, and gazed at the view of the Rocher de Monaco towering over the idyllic harbour.

"You must have the best view in Monaco," she said. "Honestly, one forgets just how beautiful this place is."

"No, I don't – because I'm reminded of it every day, but of course you've been away, so it's bound to hit you like a ton of bricks."

Laura smiled wanly at the inaptness of the expression. "How are things?"

"Oh, everything's the same. The club's fine. Nothing much happens here really."

"Except for the raid," Laura corrected him.

"Oh, that! Yes," he admitted. "The raid was definitely a happening."

"Henrietta only told me about it very briefly, but I'm puzzled as to why they were looking for *me* in particular, especially in relation to drugs. I mean, what could possibly have induced them to follow that line? It makes no sense at all."

"Well, the chap in charge was shouting his head of at this scrawny little weed, when they found nothing. Ratti, I think his name was."

Laura jumped with surprise at the mention of his name.

"Ratti?" she exclaimed, her eyes widening in disbelief. "Ratti? But that was the name of our Bin Rat, the peeping Tom on the hammock."

This was absolutely incredible. Quite extraordinary!

"I don't believe it!" she continued, her voice rising in amazement. "It simply doesn't add up. I mean, we've never even spoken to him and don't know him from Adam, though he has been watching our flat all summer. We dismissed him as a nuisance, a minor inconvenience, thinking he was just a *voyeur*. But a policeman? . . . Never!"

"Well, I'm doubtful he was a policeman; more like a grass, really. Definitely in collusion with them. They seemed to know all your movements this whole summer, except the major fact that you were out of the country. I suppose with all the comings and goings, he got you confused with Jennifer. After all, you're both blonde and beautiful."

"Yes," she went on, not noticing the compliment, her brow furrowed and perplexed, "but I still don't understand why he should waste the whole summer on such a ridiculous notion."

"Somebody must have tipped them off, albeit mistakenly. They couldn't just draw your name out of thin air, could they?"

Laura looked sceptical. "A tip-off? But who? Who could possibly do such a thing?"

Quintin went on. "My mind's a bit of a blank I'm afraid, but right at the very end the Ratti chap was whining about someone with an odd name. Said he put him up to it. Sounded like *le déjeuner*, or something like that. Well, not exactly. God, I wish I could remember. I'm sorry, Laura!"

Suddenly it hit her. Who was it had been threatening her all summer? Who'd been making her life a misery and had sworn to get even? Laura's face cleared. Of course!

"The name wouldn't have been Lejeune, would it?" she asked, trying to stay calm.

"Yes!" he exclaimed, his voice registering surprise. "I'm fairly sure that's the name I heard. Why? Do you know him?"

Laura's mouth was compressed into a thin line of contempt. The blue eyes were ice-cold.

Pierre. The bastard! The vengeful, spiteful bastard! As if he hadn't already done enough to ruin her summer!

"Oh, absolutely!" Laura replied, her voice quiet, but shaking with anger. "He's the ex-boyfriend. You must remember, Quintin, the one who attacked and threatened me just before my trip. Oh, yes, it all makes sense now."

"What all makes sense?" asked Henrietta, returning with a tray of coffee.

"Would you believe it, my darling," Quintin said, "but that whole bodged raid was initiated through a tip-off by the peeping Tom of the Meribel! And just guess who put him up to it? None other than that bastard, Laura's embittered ex-lover, who wanted revenge!"

Henrietta's jaw dropped in disbelief. Then she recovered her composure.

"The Bin Rat, eh? Oh God, yes. It's all coming together now. So it was you he was spying on all the time! Well, they didn't find anything to stick you with, did they? Honestly! You'd think it was a French farce, the way they all behaved," she exclaimed scathingly. "They fell flat on their faces, looking complete fools."

"And how!" smiled Quintin. "I've never seen anyone so spitting angry as Madoc was with Ratti when nothing was found. What a shambles it was! The air was positively blue, or should I say, *bleu*, when they all finally stormed off. I wouldn't like to be in Lejeune's shoes. He'll obviously have to lie low for a while, maybe even lose his job!"

"And jolly well serve him right, too, the utter bastard!" said Hen in great indignation.

When Laura imagined what the outcome could have been, she shivered. Thank heaven the operation had been so amateurish. A more professional outfit could have framed her by planting drugs or other incriminating evidence in the flat. The consequences didn't bear thinking about.

Quintin looked across at the pensive Laura. She still looked rather wan and miserable, in spite of a good night's sleep. Maybe it was just jet lag. Idly he picked up the *Nice Matin*, which he resumed reading whilst the girls chatted softly in the background. Suddenly, he shouted, his eyes great saucers of horror. "God, but that's awful. Look at this!"

Quintin brandished the newspaper in front of the girls' noses and pointed to a blurred photograph with a shaking finger.

"But that's Jennifer!" cried the girls, alarmed.

"Yes. It says she's been seriously injured in a car crash," Quintin translated, absolutely mortified. "Wait just a sec, let me read the rest." And his eyes scoured the page, which shook from his trembling hands, while the girls agitated in an agony of suspense.

Distraught, Laura begged, "Let me see. Oh God, Quintin, give me the paper!"

"Wait. Wait," said Quintin miserably, scanning the column. "It seems she's critical. In a coma at the Princess Grace."

"Then let's go to her immediately!" cried Laura.

"No, wait," he suggested, his face grey with strain. "Rather than flying off there in a complete panic, shouldn't we telephone? I mean, if she's in a coma there's not much we can do, is there? In any case, it's a moot point they'll even let us in to see her if she's critical."

He was right, of course. There was nothing they could do except telephone the hospital for news.

Quintin pushed past the table blindly, clumsily, and made his way inside. He was utterly devastated. In every way, he was responsible for this. He'd greedily taken advantage of Jennifer's drunken unhappiness that night, and made everything worse for her. He'd driven her over the limit of humiliation. What a shit he was! A heartless, selfish, irresponsible bastard.

God! Quintin thought in dread, Jesus, what if she dies? What if she's already dead? Oh, God forgive me!

His legs shook and his heart felt like lead. He could hear a pulse in his head as his mouth went dry. He wanted to throw up.

Laura made to follow him, but Henrietta signalled her not to.

"No, Laura, wait. Leave Quint for the moment. Drink your coffee and calm down."

The girls waited impatiently, straining to hear what Quintin was saying. At last he came back, his face grave. Laura's heart sank. Her own problems seemed minimal now.

"Well?" they chorused.

"Apparently she's just regained consciousness, but is not up to seeing visitors yet. They tell me her *husband* has been at her bedside day and night, and will remain with her every day."

The concerned expressions briefly changed to amazement at the mention of a husband.

Chapter 28

"I've left my number for her husband to contact us, whoever he is," Quintin said. "I presume they mean Alex, although I really don't know. Anyway, she's in good hands and he obviously cares, so she's not alone."

"Thank heaven for that," sighed Laura, tears of relief welling up, "and thank God she's alive!"

"I'll second that!" added Henrietta. "Gosh, I do hope and pray she survives."

"I think I need a stiff brandy," said Quintin, looking very distressed, not far from tears.

Henrietta had been observing his mortification, with, it appeared to her, an element of guilt thrown in. Why this should be, was a mystery. But this was no time for dwelling on nuances.

"Have some coffee instead," she soothed. "It's far too early for alcohol. And anyway, we've got work to do. Let's leave Laura here to listen for any messages and to rest up. We'd better sort out the mess at the Meribel."

Both Laura and Quintin started to protest, but Henrietta was adamant. It would serve no purpose for everyone to wait around the telephone with bated breath. Far better to keep busy. In any case, the moment Laura received any further news from the hospital, she could telephone them at the Meribel straight away.

"Yes," agreed Quintin, after hesitating for a few moments. "She's right, of course. All right then, let's get cracking. Laura, we'll leave you with the coffee-pot and the telephone.

Call us the moment you have any news. But we won't be far away."

Jennifer opened her eyes. Her head felt as if it had been run over by a tractor and then beaten with sledge-hammers. He was still there, quietly dozing with a book on his knee, in the small armchair by her side. This was the second day he hadn't moved from her bedside. He flatly refused to leave her until she was completely out of danger.

What a warm and secure feeling it was to be cherished and cared for. "To love and to cherish for better for worse, for richer for poorer, in sickness and in health." Now, what on earth had brought those words into her head? Yes, of course. She felt cherished. Maybe for the first time in her life! How wonderful those words were, and how wonderful the feeling to be truly loved and cared for. It was a new experience for her. Jennifer smiled in spite of her throbbing head.

"Why are you smiling, precious?" asked her companion.

"You're supposed to be asleep," she murmured, with half-closed eyes.

"Well, I'm not now. Do you need anything?" he asked tenderly, taking her hand.

"A new head, please. This one hurts."

"Let me kiss it better."

And he leaned forward and took her in his arms, kissing her gently on her hair, holding her as if she were a delicate rose that could be crushed. Jennifer leaned against him, relishing the feeling of warmth and security his embrace instilled in her. She wondered if she could ever feel safe again without him.

"I'll call the nurse for some more pain-killers. Please let's not change your head. It's too pretty," he whispered into her hair.

He got up and left the room, and a few seconds later, came back with a nurse, who brought her a small tumbler and two capsules. Jennifer took the pills obediently.

"Et voilà, madame," she chirped brightly. Then she turned to the man. *"Votre femme va mieux ce matin, n'est-ce pas, monsieur?"*

The woman smiled at Jennifer encouragingly, and tip-toed out again.

"Why did she call me your wife?" Jennifer asked, her grey eyes puzzled.

"Because I said you were."

"But I'm not. In any case, you said marriage was not on the cards."

"I know, but I have to take care of you: you're absolutely hopeless. Anyway, I love you. Will you marry me?"

Jennifer started in surprise, and then clutched her throbbing head. "This is rather sudden, isn't it? I don't think in my present state I am fit to hoist it in, let alone answer you."

"Well, what do you say?" he asked impatiently.

She smiled at him. "I'll let you know later."

Jennifer put her finger to her lips as he remonstrated. "Later," she said, "I promise."

Laura lay in the sun, unable to chase away the misery that weighed so heavily on her shoulders. She felt utterly used. She'd been naïve and unrealistic, wrapped up in a dream world that had no substance. And all the time Tom must have been laughing up his sleeve at her innocence. How could he have been so cruel and dishonest? What had she done to deserve such cavalier treatment from him? When she thought back on all the wonderful things he'd said and done to her, knowing full well that the next week he was off to marry another, her heart lurched and she had to choke back her tears. It just didn't seem possible for love and deception to hurt so much.

Now what? she thought. She didn't feel like going back to live at the Meribel, ever. It would remind her of the whole rotten and wasted summer. In fact, she didn't even feel inclined to go on living in Monaco now. She wanted to run away from it all, and go back to her loving and close-knit family in the country. Just forget her career and ambition, and the whole damn mess she'd made of her life.

There was a tentative knock at the door. Wearily Laura went to answer it, and was stunned to find Pierre standing there.

"What on earth . . . ?" she started to say, absolutely furious that he should have the gall to turn up out of the blue, on Quintin's doorstep. She made as if to slam the door in his face, but he'd blocked it with his foot.

"Laura, please listen to me. It's very important. I have to talk to you." Pierre's voice was contrite, his expression pleading, even humble.

"After all you've done to me? I really think you're the last person in the world I want to see."

"I know, Laura, but I've come to beg your forgiveness. Please hear me out, or I shan't be able to live with myself, and then I promise I'll never bother you again. It's desperately important. Please let me explain."

Something in Pierre's expression told Laura he was sincere, and that she could trust him. Perhaps she should hear him out for her own peace of mind, too.

"You'd better come in," she said coolly. "Quintin's already told me about the drugs raid. Honestly, Pierre, how could you?"

Pierre hung his head. "I was crazed with grief at losing you. I just wanted to get even. And I even wanted you dead. You and your lover."

Laura flinched at the reminder of Tom, and bit her lip to stop herself crying. She too knew the pain of unrequited love.

"But as you know," he went on, "nothing was found at the Meribel. It was because I'd taken away the packet of dope to plant in your car."

"What dope? And the brakes . . ." Laura asked incredulously, her voice almost a whisper. "Did you fix them, too?"

Pierre nodded mutely, near to tears.

"God! I might have been killed!" Laura exclaimed. "How could you?"

Pierre shook his head slowly, his eyes full of pain and contrition. "I just don't know what got into me. I read the telegram about the other man, and went mad with grief and jealousy. Please forgive me. It was a terrible thing to do."

"And where are the drugs now?"

"In your car, still taped under the dashboard. That's mainly why I came, to find out where your car was, so that I could get rid of them. They were Nova's, quite obviously. She rang me from England to say they were yours. Of course, I knew they weren't. But I thought it was the perfect opportunity to get even with you. Dead and disgraced. And your lover, especially him, too. I'm sorry. Believe me, I really am. It was unspeakable of me." His dark eyes were now brimming with tears. He went on in a choking voice, "I won't be surprised or resentful if you report me to the authorities for what I did. I mean everything..." Pierre's wet eyes met Laura's pleadingly. "I know I deserve it."

Laura remembered how she'd vowed to make Pierre pay for his violent attack on her at the Meribel. She had been bitter and angry then, hellbent on revenge. But now her expression softened to one of infinite sadness, her blue eyes glistening with unshed tears. Suddenly, she felt no anger; only a deep, dull compassion. Now she had experienced the agony of a broken heart herself, with its searing, all-encompassing pain, she could understand and even forgive the irrational madness that had driven Pierre to thoughts of murder.

"I believe," said Laura quietly, "that there have been enough tears and more than enough bitterness between us. Any more would be pointless. I think it would be better to forgive and forget, don't you?"

Then she quickly wrote down the name of the garage in Nice, and handed it to him. Pierre, now even more chastened at Laura's instant forgiveness, shook his head with grateful disbelief. Silently he marvelled at her magnanimity. Though tired and worn, her gentleness shone through her pallor and she looked more beautiful now than he ever remembered. The pain of losing her was unbearable, but it was too late; Laura had gone from his life for always.

"I promised you when I arrived that I'd leave you alone now," he said quietly, "and I will. I swear I'll never bother you again. I just want to wish you success and happiness, and to say I'll miss you every day of my life. I'll never love anyone again the way I loved you."

Laura went back to her sun-bed, still shaken at Pierre's confession. His love for her had been obsessive, frightening in its intensity. How sad, too, that love had to be so often unrequited. Why couldn't Tom have loved her the way she did him? Or why couldn't she have loved Pierre instead and been happy? She sighed. Hell! 'The course of true love never did run smooth.' Shakespeare was right; there was never a truer saying. Laura jumped as the telephone rang shrilly into her thoughts. She ran into the hallway and picked up the receiver.

Her heart beat faster with relief, and her expression lightened.

"Jennifer!" she cried, tucking away her cares. "How are you? We read about the accident in the paper . . . No, of course it's me . . . Yes, but I decided to come back early . . . Yes, yes, everything's OK, but it's you we're all worried about . . . Yes, precious. Of course, Hen and I will visit . . . When . . . Today? . . . Are you sure they'll allow it? . . . Are you sure you're going to be well enough? . . . You've got something to tell me . . . Will it? . . . OK, it'll have to wait, then . . . Love and kisses to you, too. Bye!"

Laura smiled with weary gratitude. Thank heaven Jennifer was out of danger! She sounded exhausted but cheerful. Quickly Laura picked up the receiver again and dialled the

Meribel. Henrietta would be coming straight over, Quintin said.

"Jennifer, please let me take care of you. You can't go on like this," he pleaded, stroking her head to make it better. "You know, when I first met you, I thought you were so tough and resilient and independent: a wild thing that didn't want to be tamed, a real challenge, spunky, fearless and sexy; but really all you are is a vulnerable kitten who needs looking after."

He took her pale and lovely face in his hands. His eyes were infinitely tender, his voice gentle and persuasive. "I want to be the one to do it, with all my heart. Anyway, you're fast notching up your nine lives, and you'll soon run out if someone doesn't take you in hand."

Jennifer looked back at him disbelievingly. She didn't know what to think. It was all too much. Everything was happening so quickly.

"But you're already married, Julius, and you'll never ask your wife for a divorce. You said so."

"True, I did, but now I've changed my mind. It seems my wife would be quite happy to accept a settlement. After all, we've lived apart for years." Julius took Jennifer's hands between his, and kissed her fingertips. "You need me, Jennifer," he continued, "You know you do. Anyhow, we can't go on meeting like this, I'm blooming sick of hospitals!"

Jennifer laughed and winced as her head throbbed again. "In the remotest eventuality that I ever said yes, would you still go on handcuffing Italian tarts to your bed?"

Julius laughed and waved a remonstrating finger at her. "Is the pot calling the kettle black, by any chance?" His navy-blue eyes twinkled wickedly in the dark, pirate face. "Anyway, I was just getting my own back for the polo player."

Jennifer pouted and blushed. "You didn't have to believe that bastard Jean-Claude!" she argued feebly. He'd got her over a barrel now.

Julius grinned back at her, teeth flashing rakishly against his tan, but he didn't pursue the point. Then his expression changed and his eyes became serious.

He leaned forward and looked into Jennifer's face earnestly. "Clean slate, eh?" he said, taking her hands in his. "Perhaps I am a rogue, but you're no angel either, Jen. We're two of a kind, us two. Believe me, I love you. Of that you can be sure. And I know I can make you happy. You need me, love."

"Give me a kiss, then," she said, "and I might be persuaded to give you a reply!"

As soon as Henrietta arrived, the girls set off for the hospital in Quintin's car, stopping off on the way to buy a bunch of flowers. The Princess Grace was so small, it didn't take them long to find Jennifer's room. She was sitting up in bed, luxuriating in a plethora of plump pillows, looking pale but otherwise unscathed.

Julius got up as they came in. Laura was open-mouthed at the change in him. He looked almost dashing now. What had happened to all that excess weight? And what was he doing with Jennifer in the hospital? Where was Alexander?

"Welcome, girls," he said, smiling and coming forward to kiss them both. "I can take a break now you're here. I know Jennifer's safe in your hands. Do you mind if I go and stretch my legs, lovey?"

"Of course not." Jennifer smiled up at him. "Why don't you get some proper sleep? I promise I'll be all right."

"Precious," he said, with a teasing look of resignation in his eyes, "I've heard that one before. I'll be back in an hour or so."

He smiled at Laura and Henrietta, adding, "Don't tire her, will you?"

Then Julius blew them all a kiss and left.

Laura and Henrietta exchanged a glance of discreet puzzlement. They couldn't wait to find out what was going on. Once they'd assured themselves that the patient was comfortable, and arranged her flowers, they bombarded her with questions.

"Remember what Julius said," Jennifer teased. "You're not to tire me."

"Oh, all right, then. First things first," said Laura patiently. "Most importantly, how are you now? What's the prognosis?"

"Are you sure you're going to be OK?" Henrietta added, her green eyes filled with concern.

"Yes. A bit of concussion that's all. No lasting damage to the brain. Apart from my normal brainlessness, that is."

Jennifer grinned. The joke was an attempt to cheer her friends, but they still looked worried.

"Once I've rested up, everything'll be fine. Honestly."

Her expression grew more earnest as she looked at the concerned faces.

"Really, you two," she soothed. "I'm OK." Then she chipped in with her usual bravado. "You should know it'd take more than a slight prang to bump me off!"

"Slight prang!" scoffed Laura. "We read in the paper the car was smashed to pieces. You must have the luck of the devil, Jen!"

"Tell us about it," said Henrietta.

Jennifer had no recollection of the accident. It was a complete blank. She was told that she was lucky to be alive, with the car a total write-off, and the offending tree in splinters. It seemed she'd been thrown well clear of the car, then had rolled down a grassy slope, hitting her head on a tussock, and been found unconscious by a motorist. All she could recall was waking up in the hospital with a mammoth headache and Julius bending over her. Apparently, he hadn't moved from her side the whole time she was unconscious.

"Yes, but how did he find out about the accident?" Hen puzzled. "If you remember, we both saw the *Xerina* sailing out of the harbour that very same night, at the party.

"Ship's radio out at sea. The Mercedes was still registered

in his name of course, so the police put out a call to alert him about the crash. He left his crew in charge of the guests, had the Riva launched straight away and motored all the way back in the dark. He didn't give a single thought for his own safety, just wanted to get back and make sure I was all right."

"It's lovely to be so loved and cared for," mused Laura, her thoughts far away and her eyes misting over.

"What's got into you, then?" said Jennifer. "That's what love's all about, isn't it; caring, commitment and constancy? I mean, when I started raving on about sex in the old days, you'd say it wasn't the be all and end all of life and go all romantic and slushy on me."

Henrietta laughed. "I can't believe I'm hearing this. Our resident nympho lecturing Laura about love."

"Perhaps it's a case of this leopard changing her spots at last," replied Jennifer enigmatically. Then she looked at Laura. "Anyway, talking of you, Laura, you haven't told us a thing yet about New York. How was it?"

"OK," replied Laura evasively. She studied her hands in the guise of inspecting her nail varnish.

"Come on, Laura. Don't hedge. We're dying to know all about your trip," Henrietta implored.

"All right," she sighed reluctantly. "Actually, it wasn't OK, really. You see, I fell in love and it all went wrong."

Then she told them, making a sterling effort not to break down in tears. Her friends listened patiently, making the odd encouraging noises, while Laura poured her heart out.

"Golly!" exclaimed Henrietta. "It all sounds terribly romantic. Bermuda with the boss's son, no less. Well, you can't win them all, can you?"

"I'll second that!" whispered Jennifer softly, her face slightly wistful for a moment.

Laura looked hurt and indignant. Her friends weren't being at all sympathetic.

"Honestly, you two! I've got a broken heart, and all you can say is you can't win 'em all," she said accusingly.

"Look," reasoned Jennifer, her expression unusually introspective. "You had a beautiful, romantic weekend, with a gorgeous man. Two days in paradise with him in the most idyllic islands. You had enthralling sex, which I'm sure you enjoyed every bit as much as he did. You can both have blissful memories of each other for ever more now. Nobody can take that away from you, ever."

Laura's eyes started to brim, and Jennifer passed her a tissue from the box by her bedside, continuing in a gentler voice, "Nobody can take that away. Except you, if you insist on adulterating those wonderful memories with bitterness and rancour. Keep them in your heart, and be reminded of them when you're old and grey."

Laura still said nothing, but wondered why Jennifer suddenly seemed so grown-up, so very wise. What she said was making a lot of sense.

"Life's for living, Laura. It doesn't all stop because of one weekend in the thousands more you've lived and will live yet, in the years to come!"

Jennifer's face shone with conviction and sincerity. She had a radiance about her, tinged with overtones of wistfulness. She took Laura's hand and squeezed it.

"We didn't mean to be unfeeling or unkind, but for heaven's sake, sweetheart, do please keep things in perspective."

Henrietta joined in thoughtfully. Her voice was compassionate. "Jennifer's right, you know. Most people go through the whole of their lives without any sort of beauty or romance. It's actually a privilege to have had an experience like yours. In a funny sort of way, you're lucky. I don't see how that sort of idyll could have lasted, not at those heights of romantic passion. So the affair's all the more poignant and wondrous because of its ephemeral quality."

"Like a sunset," added Jennifer mistily, in a world of her own.

423

"Yes, exactly. Beautiful and sort of sad, because you know you'll never see that particular sunset again. A sunset always makes one wistful because it's over so soon. But at the same time it lifts the heart, because you know there'll be others. Never the same, but always beautiful in their own, unique way."

"What a lovely way to put it," sighed Laura, feeling the burden of her sadness lifting. There was a ghost of a smile on her face as she added, "Like the flower he gave me. He said it would always remind him of me."

"And I'm sure he meant it, every word of it," said the girls with conviction.

"It was the most exquisitely pure and wonderful flower I've ever seen," she breathed. "It only ever comes out for one night, and then it dies at dawn. Like you said, ephemeral, and all the more beautiful and precious for it. Just like the memory."

Laura's eyes still glistened with tears, but her face was wrapt and serene. She could hear Tom's voice again.

What else was it he had said?

"What matters is here and now, and us. What matters is us, and that we're happy right now, at this moment in our lives. Nothing else counts. Please believe me, and remember it always."

Yes. Remember it always. It would be their own precious legacy to each other; belonging to Tom and Laura and no one else. She was infinitely glad now she'd kept the cereus flower and pressed it. The only tangible symbol of their love-affair. She would treasure it always, with the memory of Tom.

The sound of gentle laughter woke Laura out of her reverie, and she smiled at her friends with warmth and affection, though there was still a hint of wistfulness in the large blue eyes.

"If you could see your soppy expression!" Jennifer smiled fondly. "She's a lost cause, our little Laura. A romantic baby who'll never change. And thank heaven for that!"

There was much to be said for sweetness and romance, Jennifer reflected. Her brief, idyllic love-affair with Alex had exposed her own vulnerability when it had ended so sadly. It had opened her eyes and made her appreciate other qualities which hadn't seemed important before. True friendship; loyalty, constancy and affection. Laura and she had learned much from each other in the last few month, and they were doubtless both the better for it.

Laura's soft laughter broke into her thoughts. "OK, I admit it. Guilty as charged. Come to think of it, Jennifer, what was it you wanted to tell me on the phone?"

But she didn't feel ready to tell them yet. In a while, maybe.

"Oh, that," she said casually. "It can wait for a while. Now, what about you, Hen? What's your news?"

"I," Henrietta began portentously, "have decided to go into medicine. I mean, I adore Quint, but Quintin is Quintin and he'll never be anything else. He's sexy, utterly charming, devastatingly handsome, but he's the ultimate playboy who'll never be faithful and never be serious."

Too true, thought Jennifer wryly. It wouldn't do to bear him any grudge, though. She'd led him on that fateful night in order to kill the pain of Alex. As a temporary palliative. She'd used Quintin just as much as he'd used her.

"So," went on Henrietta, "I'm taking a leaf out of Laura's book and I'm going to concentrate on a career now – in homeopathy. It'll take a few years, but I'm convinced there's a future in it. Anyway, it's exciting and I just get this feeling I'm doing something really worthwhile."

"That's fantastic news, Hen! What a brilliant idea," her friends enthused.

The girls were so engrossed with each other they didn't notice Julius had been standing in the doorway for some time.

"Talking about worthwhile careers, Laura," Hen went on, "with all the shenanigans you got up to in Bermuda, we still haven't heard how you got on with your exams. And I didn't dare ask, because you've been looking so wretched ever since you arrived that I assumed the worst!"

But Julius interrupted them, striding across the room, champagne in one hand, flowers in the other.

He handed the bouquet to Laura, announcing, "The clever girl passed, of course, with two 'A' grades! Beat all the men hollow. I just wired Howson May in New York to get the results. She's a fully qualified stockbroker now. The Kulikis empire isn't going to be her only client. Laura, say hello to number two!"

The girls all shrieked with joy, and Laura's face lit up with undisguised delight. Her two friends rounded on her accusingly.

Henrietta first. "Why didn't you say, you idiot?"

Then Jennifer. "Honestly. Fancy keeping us all on tenterhooks like this!"

Laura's happy smile spoke volumes. She was too choked with emotion to elaborate.

"Congratulations, kiddo!" they laughed.

"Well, my little beauties," smiled Julius, brimming over with happiness as he flourished the champagne bottle. "This is an appropriate time for celebration. Let's drink to all three of you clever girls."

He peeled the gold paper off the neck of the bottle, beaming at them with pride.

"What a summer's tally! A stockbroker, a fledgling doctor, and . . ." he paused, undoing the wires round the cork, "a millionaire's wife! Well, nearly, anyhow!"

"What?" shrieked Laura and Henrietta in unison. They stared incredulously at Jennifer, who looked like the cat who had just got the cream. "Say that again!"

The staccato sound of the champagne cork popping was all but drowned in the cacophony of happy voices emanating from the small white room.